DEDICATION

This book is dedicated to all of you who are not afraid to go beyond ... to the other side of life ... the side where dreams come from ... the side that makes the difference ... the side that allows us to care about what's happening here.

This book is being dedicated to all of you who have a dream and are not afraid to go after it ... to all of you who can afford the luxury of love and are not afraid to show it ... to all of you who can laugh and are not afraid to do it ... to all of you who have a dream ... this book is dedicated to you because this book is my dream, and I'm sharing it with you ...

TABLE OF CONTENTS

In her many books on spirituality and candle lighting, Tina Ketch has opened to us the realm of all things being possible. She is an expert in the field of candle lighting and the new and extraordinary field of Feng Shui Candle Lighting, which incorporates aspects of the ancient Chinese art of Feng Shui with the ancient art of Candle Lighting, to assist us in achieving that which we so desire, and that which is ours to have.

Most of us are looking for answers to our questions about happiness, success, love and peace of mind. Many of us are looking for the answers to many other questions, as well. As we move more and more into a spiritual age - an age of inward understanding and outward manifestations - we have become more aware of how these questions are answered, and the desires that go with them are manifested.

Unbeknownst to our conscious mind, there is a guiding, directing force behind us all. We will refer to this force as an inner wisdom, that we allow to make decisions for us. These decisions, which are made on a subconscious level, aid and guide us to the next level of our growth and development. We might not know why we light a white, or even a yellow candle during our meditations, and we might not give it a second thought when we light pink or purple candles at the dinner table, or a blue candle to read by before we drift off to sleep, but all of these spontaneous and intuitive decisions to light candles set up the energy for manifestations.

Our subconscious knows to what we are aspiring, and what we need to do in order for our desires to manifest. When we become inspired to light candles, it is because of this psychological response within ourselves that imparts the power of manifestation in our lives. Most of us think we are lighting candles because we like them, and we do, but there is a much deeper, subconscious "need" to light, or be drawn to, certain colors, and a definitive subconscious response to the candles' energy once they have been lit. As you begin to discover the power of candle lighting, as well as this subconscious energy within yourself, you might ask, "How does this all happen?"

This happened because the subconscious mind knows much more about what we need than does the subconscious mind. This quiet mind knows where our fears and blocks lie, and what it will take to rid us of them. When we consciously say, or feel, that we want something, this inner wisdom will kick into action, guiding us to that which will fulfill those desires, that which has to happen, as well as to put us in the direction that we need to go in order for our desires to manifest. It's the underlying phenomenon of human behavior.

It is psychology, by today's terms, but in its purest form.

The power of candle lighting, the psychology of human behavior, and the dynamics of relationships, all fall into one category when you begin to discover the cycles of your life through the power of candle lighting. This category is referred to as being "bio-cosmic."

The motivating energy of candle lighting is based on your relationship to this bio-cosmic universe. The effectiveness of candle lighting is determined by the power of light through its spectrum and how the eyes translate that color. This color, as it is being emitted from above in conjunction with the light emanating from within you, reacts with each other bringing about a concentrated amount of activity for manifestation to occur. The time in which you light the candle will dictate the successfulness of this manifestation. All of this, I might add, is done primarily on a subconscious level, oftentimes unbeknownst to the conscious mind.

We all know that everything vibrates, and that all things have form, color and odor, according to its unique vibrational level. When you look at something, you are seeing it on a physical level, which is what you "see," on a vibrational level, which is what you "feel," and on a spiritual level, which is what you "perceive." All of these levels and experiences function simultaneously.

The correlation between what you are seeing, feeling and perceiving is the same correlation that you maintain between yourself (man), the heavens (cosmos) and the earth (physical). The relationship between you, the heavens and the earth is what we will call the *balance of nature*. Man is the resonating energy between the heavens and the earth, as he takes the psychic energy from above, and through intent, manifests it below.

In order for your candle lighting to be successful, there must be balance. When you try to control your environment, by taking the free will of others, you are giving up your own free will, thus creating an imbalance in nature, and disrupting the balance within your own universe. You should not manipulate the free will of others by lighting candles for your own selfish gain. Always maintain your disnity when lighting candles. If there is something that you want, you must first ascertain whether or not it is yours to have. Before you light a candle to get "something," you must first confer with your conscience. Your conscience will always be truthful to you. If your conscience tells you that it is not yours to have, and you light candles to obtain "it" anyway, you will get what you desire, but the energy that you create in doing so, will come with karmic strings attached. These strings will have long lasting and far-reaching ramifications, thus creating issues and problems in other areas of your life.

Your universe is round, and the karmic issues that you have created are round, and will continue to come back to visit you, thus lending to the common saying, "What goes around comes around." The cycles of the seasons are round, your time is round and so are your eyes, which are the center of your universe. You see and perceive with your eyes. Your eyes allow the light from within you to resonate with the light from above, which for this bio-cosmic universe, is your sun. Without this cycle of exchange, you would not exist. Without your eyes and your ability to see and perceive, you would, as you know it, not exist. Thus, your eyes and your ability to emit and emanate light, create the center of your universe. Your eyes are emanating the light, which is vibrating within your being. By doing so, it is showing you the gateway to your soul.

Your intent, desires, hopes and dreams are viewed through your eyes. The light from above, when joined with the light from within, as viewed through your eyes, allows you the energy of manifestation. Your eyes perceive color. Thus, color as it vibrates, dictates what you will be manifesting. Your intent is the time in which you activate the color candle with fire, as fire is yet another form of intense light. The combination of the sun, the light from within yourself, and the light of the fire, will stimulate the light of your soul for the purpose of manifestation.

When lighting candles, we allow our eyes to view vibrational levels, as color. There are six basic colors: red, orange, yellow, green, blue and violet. White and black are not viewed as colors, but rather the absence of all color, as in black, or the combination of all colors, which appears as white. There are three primary colors: red, yellow and blue, and there are three secondary colors: orange, violet and green.

Each secondary color is comprised of two primary colors. Red and yellow make orange, blue and red make violet, and yellow and blue make green. When you light two candles, one being red and the other being green, you are lighting one primary color and one secondary color. So, in a sense, you are lighting four color vibrations. This is because the secondary candle is emanating three colors at the same time. The three colors are: first, yellow; second, blue, and the third color vibration is green.

In this case, you are lighting one red, one yellow, one blue and one green candle. Your conscious mind is only seeing two candles, which are red and green. During this time, the subconscious mind is seeing all four vibrational energies. This is called the "Law of Simultaneous Contact."

Each color vibration emanates not only the color, but also an emotional response. When you close your eyes to visualize a color, that color will stimulate an emotional response within your psyche. Blue is a color that we often associate with warmth. With the color green, you may feel a nurturing sensation, as we associate the color green with grass, trees and other living plants, which are green when they are thriving and basking in the summer sunlight. As each color triggers this emotional response, these responses will dictate what you will manifest when lighting the different colored candles.

When lighting candles, you will need to determine the exact window of opportunity to manifest your hopes and desires. There are several methods you can use in order to insure your success.

The first cycle of opportunity is that of the lunar cycle that we all follow each month. There are 13 lunar cycles within each year. The time of the new moon until the time of the full moon will be the operative time for you to light your candles to incite something new in your life. This cycle will last for approximately two weeks.

The second cycle of opportunity is from the time of the full moon until the time of the new moon. Again, this cycle will last approximately two weeks. This will be the time that you would light a candle to release something, or somebody from your life.

The second method may be a bit more difficult for some. In this method, you would first determine where within the lunar cycle you were born. Let's say that, at the time of your birth, the moon was in its crescent stage. In this case, your personal "new moon phase" would be every month when the moon returned to that same position. Thus, you would light your candles to bring something into your life during the crescent moon phase.

The full moon phase, for you personally, would be when the moon was in the opposite point of your natal crescent mooning, which is called the *gibbous* moon. An example of this would be if you were born when the moon was in Gemini, your new moon phase would be every month when the moon is in Gemini. The opposite sign from Gemini is Sagittarius. Thus, your full moon will be every month when the moon goes into the sign of Sagittarius.

The third cycle of opportunity will be one that may appear to be the simplest to follow. Just as the month has a cycle that is attuned to the larger cycle of the year, the month has a lesser cycle that is attuned to itself. This cycle is referred to as "the day."

Within each day, there are even lesser cycles that are attuned to all of that of which it is a part, such as the bio-cosmic universe itself. With this in mind, we are going to take our lunar cycle and divide it one more time, into a daily cycle.

In using the new and full moon cycle, we are going to divide it into twenty-four hour cycles. There will be eight cycles, each will have a corresponding color, and each will last for three hours.

We will start at 12:00 a.m. The color associated with this time is white. White is the encompassing vibration of all colors, and will exemplify the same effects as the new moon. This will be the time of new beginnings. If you have the desire for change, and the courage to accept it, you may light a white candle anytime between 12:00 a.m. and 3:00 a.m. This cycle represents the three hour time frame that will be vibrating on the same vibrational level as the color white, and will hold all of the same promise that comes with the new moon.

The next cycle is from 3:00 a.m. until 6:00 a.m., and is represented by the color red. This is a time of renewed strength and enthusiasm. This is the perfect time to light a red candle for strength, focus and the energy to begin your day with the enthusiasm needed to conquer your objectives.

The next cycle is from 6:00 a..m. until 9:00 a.m. The color which is vibrating at this time is orange. Orange is the color of consistency. If there is anything in your life that has been inconsistent, or anything that you are having trouble completing, this would be the operative time to light an orange candle, so that the energy vibrating at this time might be enhanced, thus giving you the opportunity to focus on that project or desire in order to bring it to fruition.

The last cycle before your "full moon" for this day will be vibrating at the same vibrational level as the color yellow, and between the hours of 9:00 a..m. and 12:00 p.m. This is the color that represents intellect, and your ability to align yourself with those things important to you, so that the success you have been working on, whether it is personal, emotional, financial or spiritual, will be successful.

From the time of 12:00 p.m. to 3:00 p.m., the cycle is the same as the lunar full moon. This is the time that is absent of color, which is represented by the color black. During this time, you will be releasing those things in your life that have been causing you discomfort or disease.

The next cycle is from 3:00 p.m. until 6:00 p.m. This is the cycle that you require in order to reflect on your day, your life and our ability to cultivate your relationships. The color which is vibrating at this time is green. If you feel any anxiety during this time, the universe is telling you that you have too many irons in the fire. Thus, it is time to let go of what does not work, so that you might pay more attention to those things in your life that you have been avoiding, out of your fear of commitment.

The next time cycle is from 6:00 p.m. until 9:00 p.m. The color which is vibrating during this time is the color blue. Mentioned previously, blue is a color of warmth and balance. This color emanates peace of mind and serenity. When you light this candle, you are letting go of issues and problems from your day that have denied you the peace of mind that is so desperately needed in maintaining balance within your universe.

The last cycle of our day is from 9:00 p.m until 12:00 a.m. This cycle is one of the most important. It is vibrating at the same vibrational level as the color violet, which is a spiritual color. Although the color is spiritual, the time is indicating a need to release, or to let go. During this time, you will be lighting a violet candle to let go of conflicting belief patterns. Oftentimes, society dictates our beliefs, where our hearts may be saying something else. Let go of the conflict, sleep easy and awake in the morning refreshed and renewed.

When you use the lunar cycle as it stands, you will be lighting your candles to bring your desires to yourself. You will light your candles between the time of the new moon and the time of the full moon. If you are lighting your candles according to the lunar cycle, and are in need of releasing yourself from dysfunction or problems, you will be lighting your candles between the time of the full moon and the new moon.

The proficiency of lighting candles corresponding with the lunar cycle has been matter-of-fact and accepted for decades. It is hard to beat the tried-and-true methods of candle lighting when implementing the consistency of the lunar cycle, as well as the time of the day, which has, up until January 1, 2000, been consistent to the second.

For the purpose of the information in this book, we will rely heavily on both of these methods of time, the lunar cycle and our daily time.

New Moon	*Full Moon*
Aries	Libra
Taurus	Scorpio
Gemini	Sagittarius
Cancer	Capricorn
Leo	Aquarius
Virgo	Pisces
Libra	Aries
Scorpio	Taurus
Sagittarius	Gemini
Capricorn	Cancer
Aquarius	Leo
Pisces	Virgo

THE HISTORY OF CANDLES

During primitive times, people used fire to ensure a feeling of security and comfort. The first candle implemented was made of animal fat. The fat was lit to provide light and heat, as well as to ward off evil spirits that seemed to haunt the natives in the night.

In 5 A.D., candles were viewed as a holy presence. The Catholic Church viewed the white flame of the candle as a symbol of the purity of Christ, as well as the infinite power and wisdom of God. The flame also represented the power of God to help individuals in times of need.

During the Middle Ages, color was added to candles. These colors were derived from bark, berries, and vegetable skins.

During the Italian Renaissance in the late 1500s to the early 1600s, Michelangelo used ores to add a blue hue to his paints, and later into candles. The metals were later found to have a cobalt base.

At the same time, the Catholic Church started to light red candles during High Mass, noticing by doing so, the energy and enthusiasm of the parishioners seemed to rise.

The black candle developed a bad reputation. As black is the absence of all color and the opposite of white, people equated this as good against evil.

In later years, Saint Candles came into existence. These candles were golden in color to symbolize not only spiritual wealth, but also material wealth, as the saints symbolized by the candles came to them in prayer.

At the time of the early settlers in the United States, couples exchanging wedding vows received a white candle to symbolize prosperity and fertility.

When candles were first designed to bring in money, hemp was added to the wax to ensure wealth. Aloe was added to candles, as it is said that aloe can relieve financial, as well as physical distress.

Throughout history, our actions have been dictated by religion and culture. Human behavior and social mores have been at the forefront of our minds.

Where to go and what to do have been two baffling questions of our time.

PSYCHOLOGICAL EFFECTS OF COLOR

In recent years, studies have been performed to determine the psychological effects the various colors may have on human behavior. These results of these studies proved conclusive.

In studied conducted in universities around the United States, it was determined that a profound behavioral difference occurs within an individual when he is introduced to various colors. Test results show that a violent person will become calm when placed in a pink room for a short time, and if a child's room is painted blue, the child will sleep through the night without interruption.

Yellow is a color that has been found to stimulate the intellect.

Red invokes impatience and a high anxiety level, coupled with a tremendous amount of energy. Is it any wonder that waiting at a red light inevitably seems to take hours?

Purple has always been viewed as a regal color, and rightfully so. Purple is a color of confidence that seems to emit a sense of high esteem from within.

Green is a refreshing color and will instill a feeling of vitality.

Orange is a festive color and seems to heal and soothe the body and mind.

Black is a color that causes fear. The psychological effects of black invokes suppression, with obvious signs of withdrawal.

Brown is an earthen color, stabilizing and consistent.

White is the color of purity, with intent. Surrounding oneself with white makes one feel fresh and renewed.

In this book, we will incorporate the psychological aspects of color - in conjunction with human behavior, ancient wisdom and religion - to light candles.

While there are as many different sizes, shapes, and colors of candles as there are people to light them, we will only be using the pure colored candles. Muted colors are aesthetically beautiful; however, they have not been proven to have any noticeable effects on human behavior.

The premise of lighting candles is to incite something new into your life, or to rid yourself of someone or something that may be causing you distress or concern. Timing is essential. Lighting a colored candle at the wrong time may be detrimental to your desires and intentions.

A colored candle should always be lit with a small white candle. This will enable your colored candle to be pure with its intent.

After you light your colored candle, you may snuff out the flame on the white lighting candle. You should **never** blow out the flame on a candle. Blowing out the flame on a candle has always been viewed as the ending of intent for the candle. You should always allow the candle to give you all that it is capable of giving.

The longer your colored candle stays lit, the more assurance you will have that your wish or desire will come to pass. Once you light your colored candle, you must allow it to burn itself out.

With this, as well as safety in mind, candles have been designed to stay lit for five to seven days. These seven day candles are made in tempered glass cylinders to ensure the longevity of the flame, as well as your safety.

Candles need not be placed in a prominent place in your home. Every time you see your candles, you should envision your wish, reiterating your desire, thus enabling your wish to come true. This does not mean an altar, simply, somewhere visible, so that you may reiterate your wish.

Use the timing guide in the back of this book to receive your wish in a timely manner.

The candle lighting dictionary will help you choose the color that is the most advantageous for your wish.

14

The art of lighting candles has been comprised with both positive and negative connotations. Only the individual will dictate the amount of success or failure that he will obtain in lighting candles.

When the temporal person becomes involved with candle lighting for a specific intent and purpose, this action will incite opportunities for even more people to benefit. With this in mind, know that your results will be consequential to your intent and faith.

Being centered, focused, and not losing sight of your objectives is essential. Psychologically speaking, if you light a candle with little faith or intent, you will sabotage your desire. The candle will bring to you your desired wish; however, your desire may change before your wish has had a chance to manifest.

Candles should always be lit with the good of yourself and others in mind. Knowledge of candle lighting is essential. Before you begin lighting candles, consult the timing guide, making sure that what you want can be obtained. Lighting a candle at the wrong time can bring you the opposite of what you may be asking for.

EXAMPLES OF CANDLE LIGHTING

Larry needed money in the worst way. He had no job and no money, with alimony and child support payments in arrears.

One of Larry's friends told hm that if he lit a green candle, money would come his way. Given no other explanation, Larry was left with the candle and his thoughts. Alone with his adversity, he lit the green candle.

Andy is hyperactive and has a talent for attracting trouble at school. He has a big heart and lives to help people, but his intentions seem to be misunderstood by teachers and staff.

The county's only solution for Andy seemed to be the disciplinary alternative school, instead of permanent expulsion. Rumor had it, the children in this new school were the most infamous children in the county. Their crimes ranged from stabbing other children to setting teachers'' cars on fire.

Andy was afraid and so were his parents. Andy's mother, being accomplished in the field of psychology, chromotherapy, and candles, lit a purple candle to ensure Andy's stay in the alternative school would be as short as possible. The purple candle would also ensure that due process would be just that - due process.

The meeting was held. Andy's mother was to call the new school to set up an appointment for enrollment.

The school's telephone lines were terminally busy. By the time the appointment was set up, records were transferred from one school to another, and county transportation was arranged, Andy's attendance in the "bad school" was a total of fourteen days.

Time has passed since this story was written. Andy got sick and only spent six days in the school that could have psychologically caused great hardship. The candle worked.

Karen lit three red candles, setting up the perfect seduction scene; however, the candles lasted longer than one evening. The next day, she was back to the redundancy of daily life, yet the candles continued to burn, emanating energy.

Karen's anxiety level began to climb. Giving no thought to the candls lit in her bedroom, Karen was in a frenzy - living with more energy than God or the law legally allowed. Two days of hell passed, and Karen left a war-torn battlefield wherever she went.

Realizing that there was a problem, Karen's friend questioned her about recent events in her life. Confiding in her friend, they discussed Karen's affair being the onset of her anxiety.

The solution was easy. "Snuff out the red candles and light a white candle for peace," Karen's friend said. Karen did and felt relief instantly.

Some say that a candle lit for intent and purpose has a mind of its own. How can this be?

Christine grew up in a large Catholic family. Lighting candles and saying prayers were a part of her life.

One night the phone rang. "Christine," said the voice on the other end, "Your sister is sick and the doctors don't expect her to make it." Christine hung up the phone, lit a white candle, and made arrangements to go to her sister's side.

To make a long story short, Christine spent as much time with her sister as she could, keeping a white candle lit at home at all times.

One morning while at her sister's side, Christine called home. The phone was answered by her son. "Honey, it's all over," she said. "Aunt Kathy passed away in the middle of the night."

"Was it around three-thirty?" her son asked.

"Yes, it was. Why did you ask?"

Her son replied, "I stayed up late last night watching T.V. At three-thirty the candle went out. There was wax left. I didn't know what to do, so I left it alone."

What can you say?

John was nine years old when doctors told his mother that he tested positive on his T.B. time test. He spent two weeks in the hospital, enduring one test after the other. John was a sick child.

After returning home, John's mother lit an orange candle. The candle was designed to stay lit for a week (it was made in a glass jar). She felt confident and safe.

Before the candle went out, John's mother lit another orange candle to ensure that there was a candle lit at all times. One morning, she noticed that the candle had put itself out.

John had an appointment with his doctor that morning. A miracle had happened. The T.B. germ that had plagued John's little body during the past few weeks had seemed to disappear.

When the candle's work was over, it had put itself out.

Mary's life seemed to be a financial disaster. She lost her job and, with the present recession, there appeared to be no job prospects in sight.

She had two children, rent to pay, and food to buy. For Mary, life seemed bleak.

Mary passed by a candle store and felt compelled to go in. She wandered aimlessly, looking at all the candles, colors, shapes, and sizes. She seemed almost mesmerized by the green candles.

When approached by the sales clerk, Mary told the clerk about all of her woes. The clerk gave Mary the green candle, instructing her to go home and light it. The clerk explained that the candle could help bring in money, and perhaps another job.

Two days after lighting her candle, Mary received her first child support payment in five years from her previous husband. With the money, she paid her rent and bought food.

18

She was so excited about her experience, Mary went back to the candle store to tell the clerk of her good fortune. When she got there, the store manager was so pleased with Mary's news, she gave her a job.

Karen divorced when her son, Mark, was ten years old.

Karen and Mark had a number of various roles in each other's lives. They were mother and son, as well as best friends. Mark, growing into his early teens, adopted the role as Karen's father, or protector.

So as not to disrupt their home life, Karen would invite her friends to her home at night only after Mark had fallen asleep. She began to notice that her friends were having trouble getting to her house. Some would have flat tires. Some had the flu over and over again.

Karen could have developed a complex had she not noticed a white candle in front of Mark's outside entrance to the house. When Karen questioned Mark about the candle, he explained a friend had told him that if he would light a white candle outside of his home at night when he went to bed, no one would be able to enter the property.

Karen, expressing her gratitude for his concern, asked Mark not to light candles outside his door again.

CANDLE LIGHTING DICTIONARY GUIDE

The candle lighting dictionary will enable you to improve the quality of your life. Anxiety, confusion, and distress will become a part of the past.

When using the candle lighting dictionary, you must first define your intentions. What is it you want? When do you want it? These are two questions that you must have answered before you begin.

Let's use some examples:

1. I need more money, even though my regular job pays me well. I just have an unexpected bill.

A) First, look up money in the candle dictionary. There are two listings for money. The first denotes to have money, you should light a green candle. The second shows to keep money, you should light a green candle and a yellow candle.

B) Second, determine when to light the candle by using the ephemeral timing guide.

This will give you a list of days to light candles, in order to bring something to you, and a list of days to light candles in order to release something from you.

To obtain your wish - in this case, it is to have more money - light your green candle as close to the first day listed under the bring time frame as you can, enabling your wish to be granted as soon as possible.

Let's say today's date is June 1, 1991, and you want to light a candle to bring you more money. The ephemeral timing guide indicates that the first day to light a candle to bring something to you is not until June 12th. If you light a candle to bring money before the dates indicated, you will lose money, not bring it to you. **Always** light your candles using the dictionary and the ephemeral timing guide.

After lighting your green candle to get more money, you decide you want money to keep. You would light another green candle, and then a yellow candle. This will enable your money to flow, allowing you to keep more of it.

In the candle lighting dictionary, you will see words listed, such as: "attractions," "austerity," and "awkward." To the right of these listings, you will see an "R" in parentheses. This is to indicate that the situation will be released by lighting the appropriate candle.

Remember: always light the candle that is listed first. You must light all of the candles listed in the order that they appear.

Second example:

1. My relationship has been causing me copious amounts of frustration. How can I find relief?

A) Using the candle lighting dictionary, look up the word "frustration" - frustration (R) the ability to release. The candle to light will be red and then the second candle will be yellow.

B) The timing guide for releasing is indicated from June 1st through June 11th. Light your red candle and then your yellow candle between June 1st and June 11th.

THE VIBRATIONAL RATES OF COLOR

The vibrational rates of color is one principle that can be disputed by no one.

In 1666, Sir Isaac Newton was credited with the first valuable theory of color through his use of a prism. Newton, who also formulated the law of gravity, may have been looking for universal principles - principles not to be understood during his time - such as the correlation of his seven primary colors with the seven chakras of the body.

The colors viewed by Newton were the same colors and, in the same sequential order, as the colors of the seven chakras recognized by many spiritualists and new thought trend people throughout the world. The order in which these colors appeared were: red, orange, yellow, green, blue, indigo, and violet.

Following the premise that the body is a four-pole magnet with seven mini batteries, referred to as chakras. These batteries (chakras) emanate energy. Each chakra emanates a different vibration, thus projecting a corresponding vibratory color of its own. This lends much to the effectiveness of color therapy - and rightly so.

If one of your chakras has shut down, or is not functioning to its maximal potential, you may need a strong dose of that particular color to get yourself going. This may be the basis to the saying, "I feel blue." Since blue is one of the colors for balance in and around the body, if you are in need of blue, you, in turn, <u>feel</u> blue.

One method of measuring vibrational rates is called the Angstrom method. One Angstrom unit is 100 millionth of a centimeter. The vibrational rates of each color by Angstrom units are listed below:

Angstrom Vibrational Chart

Red	6000 - 6700 Angstrom units
Orange	5900 - 6000 Angstrom units
Yellow	5800 - 5900 Angstrom units
Green	5000 - 5500 Angstrom units
Blue	4700 - 5000 Angstrom units
Indigo	Exact vibrational rate inconclusive.
Violet	4300 - 4600 Angstrom units

6700 Angstrom units is a lower vibrational rate than 4300 Angstrom units. This method of measurement will help you determine your daily needs, as well as your growth and development.

If you wake up feeling the need to wear something red, you will know that your vibrational rate is somewhere between 6000 and 6700 Angstrom units. Correlate this with your mood and the different listings recorded in this book under the color red, you will see where your energy is being directed.

When your mood is vibrating in a direction that is atypical of your character is not congruent with what you want, light the colored candle that will give you what you are aspiring toward. You will only be able to use this method during the bring time frame. If you are under a release time frame, you may light a red candle upside down, this will free you from any anxiety that you may be feeling; however, it will not give you what you want. It will only get you comfortably through the existing time frame.

To raise your vibration rate, light the colored candle representing what you want <u>right side up</u>. To lower your vibration rate, light the colored candle that represents where you are presently <u>upside down</u>.

- A -

ABANDON	(TO)	RED		
ABDICATE	(TO)	YELLOW	BLUE	ORANGE
ABDUCTIONS	(R)	WHITE		
ABILITIES	(TO HAVE)	YELLOW	ORANGE	
ABILITIES	(TO USE)	YELLOW		
ABNORMAL BEHAVIOR	(R)	BLUE	YELLOW	
ABNORMALITIES	(R)	BLUE	WHITE	
ABORTIONS	(SAFE)	ORANGE	YELLOW	
ABRASIONS	((R) PAIN)	BLUE		
ABRUPTNESS	(RELEASE)	WHITE		
ABRUPT	(TO BE)	RED		
ABSENT	(TO BE)	BROWN		
ABSENT-MINDED	(R)	YELLOW		
ABSTRACT	(TO BE)	YELLOW RED		
ABSURD	(TO BE)	RED		
ABSURD	(NOT TO BE)	WHITE	PINK	
ABUNDANCE	(TO HAVE AN)	GREEN	YELLOW	
ABUSE	(R)	WHITE		
ABUSE	(R) CHILD)	PINK	WHITE	
ACADEMIC	(TO BE)	YELLOW		
ACADEMIC	(FREEDOM)	BLUE	YELLOW	
ACCEDE	(TO)	BLUE		
ACCELERATE	(TO)	YELLOW		
ACCELERATION	(MENTAL)	YELLOW	ORANGE	
ACCELERATION	(PHYSICAL)	RED	YELLOW	
ACCIDENT	(SECURE AGAINST)	PURPLE	ORANGE	
ACCOMPLICES	(ABILITY TO)	BROWN		
ACCORDANCE	(TO BE IN)	YELLOW		
ACCUMULATION	(MENTAL)	YELLOW	GREEN	
ACCUMULATION	(PHYSICAL)	BLUE	GREEN	
ACCURACY	(TO HAVE)	YELLOW BLUE		
ACCUSATIONS	((R) AGAINST YOU)	YELLOW		
ACCUSATIONS	((R) AGAINST THEM)	YELLOW	WHITE	
ACHES, DULL	((R) YOUR OWN)	BLUE		
ACHES, DULL	((R) OTHERS)	BLUE	WHITE	

23

ACHES, SHARP ((R) YOUR OWN)	YELLOW	BLUE	
ACHES, SHARP ((R) OTHERS)	WHITE	YELLOW	
ACHIEVE (FOR YOURSELF)	ORANGE	RED	
ACHIEVE (TO HELP OTHERS)	WHITE	RED	
ACREAGE (TO OBTAIN)	BLUE	GREEN	
ACREAGE (TO RETAIN)	ORANGE	BLUE	
ACROBAT (ABILITY TO BECOME)	YELLOW	ORANGE	
ACTION (TO INSURE)	RED		
ACTIVATION (MENTAL)	RED	YELLOW	
ACTIVATION (MECHANICAL)	BLUE	RED	
ACTIVE (TO BE)	RED	YELLOW	
ACTIVITY (MENTAL)	YELLOW		
ACTIVITY (PHYSICAL)	RED	YELLOW	
ACTOR /ACTRESS (TO BE AN)	YELLOW	BLUE	
ACTUARY (TO BECOME AN)	YELLOW		
AD WRITER (TO BECOME)	YELLOW	BLUE	
ADAPTABILITY (TO HAVE)	BLUE	YELLOW	
ADDICTION ((R) YOURSELF)	BLUE	WHITE	ORANGE
ADJOURN (TO)	BLUE		
ADJUSTER, CLAIMS (FAVOR)	YELLOW	GREEN	
ADJUSTER, CLAIMS (OTHERS)	GREEN		
ADJUSTMENTS (MENTAL)	YELLOW	BLUE	
ADJUSTMENT (PHYSICAL)	RED	YELLOW	
ADMIRATION (TO HAVE)	WHITE	YELLOW	
ADOLESCENCE (HELP CALM)	BLUE		
ADOPTED, BROTHERS (TO HELP)	YELLOW	WHITE	
ADOPTED, SISTERS (TO HELP)	WHITE	PINK	
ADOPTED, BROTHERS (TO OBTAIN)	YELLOW	BLUE	
ADOPTED, SISTERS (TO OBTAIN)	PINK	YELLOW	
ADOPTED, CHILDREN (TO HELP)	PURPLE		
ADOPTED, CHILDREN (PROTECT)	BLUE	PURPLE	
ADOPTION (ABILITY TO OBTAIN)	BLUE	WHITE	PINK
ADORATION (SAFETY)	PURPLE		
ADORNMENT (TO HAVE)	BLUE	PURPLE	
ADRENAL GLANDS (TO STIMULATE)	BLUE		
ADRENALIN (TO HAVE)	YELLOW	BLUE	
ADULTERY (TO DETRACT)	WHITE	BLACK	

24

ADULTERY (TO COMMIT)	BLUE	YELLOW
ADULTERATION (R)	WHITE	
ADULTS (TO HELP)	YELLOW	BLUE
ADVANCEMENTS (PERSONAL)	BLUE	
ADVANCEMENTS (BUSINESS)	GREEN	BLUE
ADVENTURES (TO HAVE)	WHITE	BLUE
ADVENTUROUS DESIRES (OWN)	BROWN	YELLOW
ADVERSARIES (TO CONCUR)	WHITE	RED
ADVERTISING (SUCCESS)	GREEN	YELLOW
ADVICE (TO GIVE)	YELLOW	WHITE
ADVICE (TO RECEIVE)	YELLOW	
ADVISOR (TO BE AN)	YELLOW	PURPLE
ADVOCATE (TO)	WHITE	YELLOW
AERODYNAMICS (SAFETY/FLYING)	WHITE	
AESTHETIC SENSE (ABILITY)	YELLOW	
AESTHETICS (SAFETY WITH)	YELLOW	BLUE
AFFABLE (TO BECOME)	YELLOW	PURPLE
AFFECTATIONS (TO HAVE)	WHITE	YELLOW
AFFECTION (TO GIVE)	PINK	
AFFECTION (TO RECEIVE)	PINK	YELLOW
AFFIDAVITS (HONEST)	YELLOW	ORANGE
AFFIDAVITS (DISHONEST)	BLACK	BROWN YELLOW
AFFILIATION (TO JOIN)	YELLOW	
AFFILIATION (TO QUIT)	YELLOW	BROWN
AFFINITIES (TO OBTAIN)	PINK	WHITE
AFFINITIES (R)	YELLOW	WHITE
AFFLUENT (TO BE)	BLUE	
AGED PERSON (TO HELP)	YELLOW	ORANGE
AGED PERSON (TO PROTECT)	PURPLE	YELLOW
AGENCIES (TO GAIN EMPLOYMENT)	GREEN	
AGENCIES (POSITIVE DEALINGS)	YELLOW	BLUE
AGENCIES, FOREIGN (DEALINGS)	YELLOW	RED
AGGRESSOR (TO BE)	BLUE	WHITE
AGGRESSORS (DEALINGS WITH)	YELLOW	WHITE
AGREEMENTS (WRITTEN)	GREEN	BLUE
AGREEMENTS (VERBAL)	GREEN	YELLOW
AILMENT (TO RELEASE)	BROWN	

Term	Col1	Col2	Col3
AILING (MENTAL)	YELLOW		
AILING (PHYSICAL)	PHYSICAL	BLUE	
AILMENTS CHRONIC (R)	BLUE	WHITE	ORANGE
AIMS (ONE'S)	PURPLE	WHITE	
AIR (PURE)	WHITE	ORANGE	
AIR (CONDITIONING)	YELLOW		
AIRCRAFT (CONSTRUCTION)	YELLOW	BLUE	
AIRCRAFT (REPAIR)	BLUE	YELLOW	
AIR CREW (SAFETY)	YELLOW	WHITE	
AIR DROP (FOOD)	YELLOW	BLUE	
AIR DROP (MEDICINE)	BLUE	WHITE	
AIR EXPRESS (SUCCESSFUL)	YELLOW		
AIRFIELD (SAFETY)	BLUE	WHITE	
AIR FLOW (NATURAL)	BLUE	ORANGE	
AIR FLOW (ARTIFICIAL)	BROWN		
AIR FORCE (TO INSURE PEACE)	YELLOW	BLUE	
AIRLESS (R)	YELLOW	BLUE	
AIRLIFT (TO SECURE)	BLUE	PURPLE	
AIRMAIL (TO RECEIVE)	YELLOW		
ALABAMA (SAFETY IN)	BLUE		
ALASKA (SAFETY IN)	BLUE	WHITE	
ALCOHOL ((R) SELF-ADDICTION)	RED	WHITE	
ALCOHOL ((R) ADDICTION, OTHERS)	WHITE	BLUE	YELLOW
ALERTNESS (MENTAL)	YELLOW		
ALERTNESS (PHYSICAL)	ORANGE		
ALIENATION (OF YOURSELF)	BLUE	YELLOW	WHITE
ALIMONY (TO RECEIVE)	GREEN		
ALIMONY ((R) PAYMENTS	YELLOW	BLUE	
ALLERGIES (TO DISCERN)	YELLOW		
ALLERGIES (R)	WHITE	YELLOW	
ALLIANCES (TO HAVE)	PINK		
ALLIANCES (COVERT)	ORANGE		
ALLIANCES (SOCIAL)	BLUE	YELLOW	
ALOOFNESS ((R) IN YOURSELF)	YELLOW		
ALOOFNESS ((R) IN OTHERS)	WHITE	YELLOW	
ALTARS (PURIFY)	WHITE		
ALTERCATIONS (R)	WHITE	YELLOW	

26

ALTER EGO (HEALTHY)	BLUE	WHITE
ALTER EGO (R)	RED	WHITE
ALTERNATE (TO BECOME AN)	YELLOW	BLUE
ALTERATION (TO ACHIEVE)	BLUE	
ALTITUDE ((R) FEAR OF)	YELLOW	BLUE
ALTOGETHER (TO BRING THINGS)	PINK	YELLOW
ALTRUISM (R)	WHITE	RED
ALTRUISM (TO ACHIEVE)	WHITE	
ALTRUISTIC (TO BECOME)	YELLOW	
AMBUSHES (R)	WHITE	
ANGER (R)	WHITE	YELLOW
ANGINA (R)	WHITE	PINK
ANXIETIES (R)	WHITE	YELLOW
APARTMENT (TO OBTAIN)	BLUE	
APARTMENT (TO MAINTAIN)	BLUE	YELLOW
APOLOGIES (TO RECEIVE)	YELLOW	PINK
APPRECIATION (TO RECEIVE)	WHITE	
APPRECIATION (TO GIVE)	PINK	
APPREHENSION (R)	RED	WHITE
ARGUMENTS (R)	YELLOW	
ARIZONA (SAFETY IN)	YELLOW	
ARKANSAS (SAFETY IN)	YELLOW	
ARREST (R)	YELLOW	RED
ARRIVALS (TO INSURE)	WHITE	PINK
ASPIRATIONS (TO OBTAIN)	PINK	YELLOW
ASSAULTS (R)	RED	WHITE
ATHLETE (TO BECOME AN)	WHITE	PURPLE
ATHLETICS (TO ACHIEVE IN)	BLUE	PURPLE
ATTACHMENTS (TO OBTAIN)	WHITE	YELLOW
ATTACHMENTS (R)	RED	PINK
ATTITUDE (POSITIVE)	YELLOW	WHITE
ATTITUDE ((R) NEGATIVE)	WHITE	RED
ATTITUDES (TOWARD OTHERS)	WHITE	
ATTORNEY (TO OBTAIN AN)	WHITE	YELLOW
ATTORNEYS (POSITIVE DEALINGS)	PINK	PURPLE

27

ATTRACTIONS (TO OBTAIN)	PINK	
ATTRACTIONS (R)	YELLOW	ORANGE
AUNT (FATHER'S SIDE)	PINK	
AUNT (FATHER'S SIDE, MONEY)	GREEN	
AUNT (FATHER'S SIDE, HOME)	BROWN	WHITE
AUNT (FATHER'S SIDE, LEGACIES)	GREEN	BLUE
AUNT (MOTHER'S SIDE)	YELLOW	PINK
AUNT (MOTHER'S SIDE, MONEY)	GREEN	WHITE
AUNT (MOTHER'S SIDE, HOME)	WHITE	BROWN
AUNT (MOTHER'S SIDE, LEGACIES)	BLUE	GREEN
AUSTERITY (R)	BROWN	
AUTHORITY (DEALINGS)	YELLOW	
AUTHOR (TO BECOME AN)	BLUE	GREEN
AUTOMOBILES (TO MAINTAIN)	YELLOW	
AUTOMOBILES (TO PURCHASE)	BLUE	YELLOW
AUTOMOBILES (TO SELL)	YELLOW	GREEN
AWARDS (TO RECEIVE)	BLUE	
AWARDS (R)	YELLOW	
AWKWARDNESS (R)	YELLOW	

- B -

BABIES (TO HAVE)	PINK	
BABIES (TO HAVE MALE)	BLUE	
BABIES (BROTHERS, HELP)	WHITE	BLUE
BABIES (BROTHERS, PROTECT)	PURPLE	WHITE
BABIES (BROTHERS, HOME)	BLUE	YELLOW
BABIES (TO HAVE FEMALE)	PINK	
BABIES (SISTERS, HELP)	WHITE	PINK
BABIES (SISTERS, PROTECT)	PURPLE	PINK
BABIES (SISTERS, HOME)	PINK	YELLOW
BABYSITTERS (TO FIND)	BLUE	
BACHELORS (TO REMAIN)	WHITE	BLUE
BACHELORS (TO OBTAIN)	WHITE	PINK

28

BACK ((R) PAIN)	ORANGE	
BACK ((R) LOWER)	YELLOW	WHITE
BACK ((R) UPPER)	YELLOW	ORANGE
BACKERS (FINANCIAL)	YELLOW	GREEN
BACKERS (PHYSICAL)	BROWN	YELLOW
BACTERIA (R)	ORANGE	BLUE
BAIL (TO OBTAIN)	GREEN	
BALANCE (TO OBTAIN)	YELLOW	
BALANCE (TO BE IN)	BLUE	
BALDNESS (R)	BLUE	
BALDNESS (STOP)	BLUE	ORANGE
BALL GAMES (TO PLAY)	WHITE	YELLOW
BALL GAMES (TO WIN)	BLUE	
BALL GAMES (TO LOSE)	BROWN	
BANDS (MUSIC, TO BELONG)	YELLOW	
BANDS (MUSIC, TO PLAY)	YELLOW	GREEN
BANISHMENT (OF YOURSELF)	BLUE	WHITE
BANISHMENT (OF OTHERS)	YELLOW	BLUE
BANKS (POSITIVE DEALINGS)	YELLOW	GREEN
BANK NOTES (TO OBTAIN)	YELLOW	GREEN
BANKRUPTCY (TO OBTAIN)	WHITE	
BAPTISM (PURITY)	PINK	WHITE
BAR (TO OWN)	YELLOW	BLUE
BARBER (TO BECOME A)	BROWN	GREEN
BARBER (TO BE A SUCCESSFUL)	GREEN	
BARGAINS (TO GIVE)	BLUE	
BARGAINS (TO RECEIVE)	WHITE	YELLOW
BASHFULNESS (R)	WHITE	PINK
BEACH (TO GO TO A)	YELLOW	GREEN
BEAUTY (TO OBTAIN)	PINK	
BEAUTY (TO OTHERS)	YELLOW	PINK
BEGGARS (R)	YELLOW	BROWN
BEGINNINGS (NEW)	WHITE	YELLOW
BEGINNINGS (SUCCESSFUL)	YELLOW	GREEN
BEHAVIOR (CHANGE)	YELLOW	
BEHAVIOR (POSITIVE)	YELLOW	BLUE

29

BELIEF SYSTEM (STRENGTHEN)	ORANGE	BLUE
BELIEVERS (OBTAIN)	BLUE	
BELITTLING (OTHERS)	YELLOW	
BELITTLING ((R) YOURSELF)	BLUE	YELLOW
BENEDICTIONS (TO PERFORM)	PURPLE	WHITE
BENEFACTORS (TO BECOME)	BROWN	GREEN
BENEFITS (TO OBTAIN)	GREEN	
BEREAVEMENT (R)	WHITE	
BEST (TO BE THE)	YELLOW	BLUE
BEST (TO OBTAIN THE)	YELLOW	GREEN
BETRAYED ((R) TO BE)	WHITE	PINK
BETRAY (TO)	BROWN	RED
BETTERMENT (OF MANKIND)	WHITE	BLUE
BETTING ((R) NEED TO BET)	ORANGE	PURPLE
BILLS (THE ABILITY TO PAY)	GREEN	YELLOW
BILLS ((R) FEAR)	WHITE	GREEN
BIRTH ((R) PAIN)	PINK	
BIRTH ((R) FEAR)	WHITE	PINK
BI-SEXUALITY (TO DEAL WITH)	YELLOW	
BI-SEXUALITY (ABILITY TO RELATE)	BLUE	
BI-SEXUALITY (WITHIN OTHERS)	YELLOW	BLUE
BI-SEXUALITY (WITHIN YOURSELF)	BLUE	WHITE
BITES (ANIMAL (R) INFECTION)	ORANGE	
BITES (INSECT (R) INFECTION)	ORANGE	
BITES (HUMAN (R) INFECTION)	ORANGE	
BITTERNESS (R)	YELLOW	WHITE
BLACK MAGICIAN (TO BECOME)	BLACK	WHITE
BLACK MAGICIAN (R) YOURSELF)	WHITE	
BLACKMAIL (R)	WHITE	YELLOW
BLEMISHES, SKIN (R)	ORANGE	BLUE
BLESSINGS (TO HAVE)	BLUE	
BLISS (TO HAVE)	PINK	
BLOATING (R)	WHITE	YELLOW
BOATING (OPEN WATER/SUCCESS)	BLUE	
BOATING (RIVERS/SUCCESS)	WHITE	BLUE
BOATS (TO OBTAIN)	YELLOW	
BOATS (TO SELL)	YELLOW	GREEN

BOATS (FISHING)	WHITE	BLUE
BODY (PHYSICAL, HEALTH)	BLUE	ORANGE
BOILS (R)	WHITE	ORANGE
BOLDNESS (TO OBTAIN)	RED	
BONDAGE ((R) FROM OTHERS)	YELLOW	WHITE
BONDS (TO OBTAIN)	GREEN	
BONDS (TO SELL)	YELLOW	BLUE
BOOKS (TO WRITE)	YELLOW	
BOOKS (TO SELL)	BLUE	YELLOW
BOREDOM (R)	WHITE	BLUE
BORROWING (THINGS)	WHITE	
BORROWING (MONEY)	GREEN	
BOSS (TO BE A SUCCESSFUL)	YELLOW	BLUE
BOSS (TO RELATE TO YOUR)	YELLOW	
BOUNDARIES ((R) TO)	RED	YELLOW
BOYFRIENDS (TO OBTAIN)	YELLOW	PINK
BOYFRIENDS (R)	WHITE	BLUE
BRAIN (TO STIMULATE)	YELLOW	BLUE
BRAVERY (TO OBTAIN)	RED	YELLOW
BRAVERY (TO SECURE)	RED	WHITE
BREAKAGE (R)	BLUE	
BREASTS (TO ENLARGE)	BLUE	ORANGE
BREASTS (TO REDUCE)	WHITE	
BREASTS (INSURE HEALTHY)	ORANGE	WHITE
BREATH (BREATHING)	YELLOW	BLUE
BREATH (FRESH)	BLUE	WHITE
BREATH ((R) BAD)	YELLOW	BROWN
BREEDING (TO BREED DOGS)	BLUE	
BREEDING (TO BREED CATS)	YELLOW	
BREEDING (TO BREED HORSES)	BROWN	
BREEDING (TO BREED CATTLE)	BLUE	BROWN
BRIDE (TO BE A)	PINK	WHITE
BRIDEGROOM (TO BE A)	BLUE	WHITE
BRIDESMAID (TO BE A)	WHITE	YELLOW
BRIEF (TO BE)	BLUE	
BRILLIANT (TO BECOME)	YELLOW	BLUE
BRILLIANCE (TO MAINTAIN)	YELLOW	BROWN

31

BROADCASTER (TO BECOME)	YELLOW	BLUE
BROKERS (TO DEAL WITH)	YELLOW	
BROKER (TO BECOME A)	YELLOW	GREEN
BROKERS (TO EXPOSE)	RED	WHITE
BROTHERS (OVER 12, HEALTH)	WHITE	
BROTHERS (OVER 12, TO HELP)	BLUE	
BROTHERS (OVER 12, TO PROTECT)	WHITE	PURPLE
BROTHERS (OVER 35, HEALTH)	WHITE	ORANGE
BROTHERS (OVER 35, TO HELP)	YELLOW	BLUE
BROTHERS (OVER 35, TO PROTECT)	PURPLE	
BROTHERS-IN-LAW (TO HELP)	PINK	WHITE
BROTHERS-IN-LAW (TO PROTECT)	BLUE	PURPLE
BROTHERS-IN-LAW (HEALTH)	BLUE	ORANGE
BRUISES (R)	ORANGE	
BRUTALITY (R)	WHITE	
BUDGETS (TO MAINTAIN)	GREEN	WHITE
BUILD (TO BUILD)	BROWN	
BUILD (HOUSE, SUCCESSFULLY)	GREEN	BROWN
BUILD (BUILDING, SUCCESSFULLY)	BROWN	
BUILDER (TO BE)	YELLOW	
BUILDER (TO FIND)	YELLOW	GREEN
BULLHEADEDNESS ((R) YOURSELF)	WHITE	
BULLHEADEDNESS ((R) IN OTHERS)	PINK	WHITE
BURDEN ((R) FOR YOURSELF)	WHITE	YELLOW
BURN OUT ((R) FOR YOURSELF)	WHITE	YELLOW
BURN OUT ((R) FOR OTHERS)	BROWN	WHITE
BUSINESS (CREDIT, GOOD)	YELLOW	GREEN
BUSINESS (INCREASE)	GREEN	
BUSINESS (TO BUILD)	BLUE	
BUSINESS (TO BUY)	BLUE	GREEN
BUSINESS (TO SELL)	YELLOW	GREEN

32

- C -

CANAL (TO BELONG)	WHITE	
CABALA (TO UNDERSTAND)	WHITE	YELLOW
CABINET MAKER (TO BE)	BROWN	GREEN
CABINET MAKER (FIND THE BEST)	YELLOW	
CABINET MAKER (TO FINISH A JOB)	BLUE	
CAFES (TO BUY)	WHITE	GREEN
CAFES (TO SELL)	YELLOW	GREEN
CAFFEINE (R)	BROWN	
CALAMITY (R)	YELLOW	
CALIFORNIA (SAFETY IN)	YELLOW	
CALL (FROM A MAN)	YELLOW	
CALL (FROM A WOMAN)	YELLOW	PINK
CALM (TO MAINTAIN)	WHITE	
CALM (TO OBTAIN)	YELLOW	WHITE
CAMP (TO GO TO)	BLUE	
CAMP (TO BUY)	YELLOW	BROWN
CAMP (TO SELL)	YELLOW	GREEN
CANCEL (CONTRACT)	YELLOW	BROWN
CANCER ((R) CARCINOMA)	ORANGE	BLUE
CANCER ((R) MELANOMA)	GREEN	BLUE
CANDID (TO BE)	YELLOW	
CANDIDATE (TO BE A)	YELLOW	
CANDOR (TO HAVE)	YELLOW	WHITE
CAPTIVATE (TO)	BLUE	WHITE
CAPTIVITY (R)	BLUE	
CARDS (TO PLAY)	YELLOW	
CARDS (TO READ)	PURPLE	WHITE
CAREER (TO OBTAIN A)	YELLOW	WHITE
CAREFREE (TO BE)	WHITE	YELLOW
CAREFUL (TO BE)	YELLOW	
CARELESSNESS (R)	WHITE	
CARESSED (TO BE)	PINK	
CARPENTERS (TO BE)	BROWN	
CARPENTER (TO FIND A)	WHITE	GREEN

33

CAR (TO BUY)	YELLOW	
CAR (TO SELL)	GREEN	
CAR (TO FIX)	BLUE	
CASH (TO SAVE)	PINK	GREEN
CASH (TO MAKE)	GREEN	YELLOW
CASH (TO REPLACE)	BROWN	GREEN
CASINOS (TO VISIT)	GREEN	
CASINOS (TO WIN)	GREEN	PURPLE
CASTAWAY (TO BE)	YELLOW	
CASTAWAY (TO FIND)	WHITE	YELLOW
CASTING (FISHING SUCCESSFUL)	BLUE	
CASUALTIES (TO LESSEN)	WHITE	
CAT (TO FIND)	YELLOW	
CAT (INSURE GOOD HEALTH)	ORANGE	BROWN
CASUAL (TO BE)	BLUE	
CAUTION (TO ACT WITH)	BLUE	WHITE
CAUTIOUS (TO BE)	BLUE	WHITE
CAVEAT EMPTOR (TO LET)	YELLOW	
CAVE-IN (TO PREVENT)	BLUE	
CEASE-FIRE (TO HAVE A)	BLUE	PINK
CEDE (WITH GRACE)	PINK	
CELEBRATE (TO)	BLUE	PINK
CELEBRITY (TO BECOME)	WHITE	YELLOW
CELIBACY (TO OBTAIN)	WHITE	
CELIBACY (R)	WHITE	RED
CELIBATE (TO MAINTAIN)	WHITE	YELLOW
CELIBATE (R)	PURPLE	WHITE
CERTIFICATION (TO OBTAIN)	BLUE	YELLOW
CHALLENGE (TO WIN A)	BLUE	
CHAMPION (TO BE THE)	YELLOW	ORANGE
CHANCE (TO HAVE A)	WHITE	BLUE
CHANGELING (TO RECOGNIZE)	YELLOW	
CHANT (TO)	WHITE	
CHARACTER (TO OBTAIN)	BLUE	YELLOW
CHARITY (TO GIVE)	WHITE	
CHARITY (TO RECEIVE)	BLUE	GREEN
CHARM (TO HAVE)	YELLOW	

34

CHECK (TO RECEIVE)	GREEN	
CHEERFUL (TO BE)	PINK	
CHILDISH (TO BECOME)	YELLOW	BLUE
CHOICE (TO HAVE A)	YELLOW	
CLEMENCY (TO HAVE)	PURPLE	
CLEVER (TO BE)	YELLOW	
CLOSURE (TO GIVE)	YELLOW	WHITE
COFFEE ((R) ADDICTION)	BLUE	RED
COLLECT (MONEY)	GREEN	
COLORADO (SAFETY IN)	BLUE	
COMBAT (R)	WHITE	
COMMENTATOR (TO BE A)	YELLOW	
COMMISERATE (R)	WHITE	BLUE
COMMIT (THE ABILITY TO)	YELLOW	
COMMUNICATE (THE ABILITY TO)	YELLOW	
COMMUNICATION (CONTINUING)	BLUE	YELLOW
COMPULSION (R)	BLUE	BROWN
COMPULSIVENESS (R)	YELLOW	RED
CONCEIVE (THE ABILITY TO)	YELLOW	
CONCENTRATE (THE ABILITY TO)	YELLOW	BLUE
CONCEPTUALIZE (THE ABILITY TO)	YELLOW	
CONCESSIONS (ABILITY TO MAKE)	BLUE	
CONFRONT (STRENGTH TO)	RED	WHITE
CONNECTICUT (SAFETY IN)	PINK	
CONSCIENCE (STRENGTHENED)	PURPLE	
CONSCIOUSNESS (EXPANSION)	BLUE	
CONSPIRACIES (R)	WHITE	YELLOW
CONSTANCY (TO MAINTAIN)	BROWN	
CONSTIPATION (R)	BLUE	ORANGE
CONTEST (TO WIN)	BLUE	WHITE
CONTRACTS (FAVORABLE)	GREEN	
CONTROL (TO MAINTAIN)	YELLOW	
CONTROL (TO OBTAIN)	ORANGE	WHITE
CONTROVERSY (R)	BLACK	WHITE
CONTUSION (R)	ORANGE	
CONVALESCENCE (SPEEDY)	WHITE	YELLOW
CONVENTION (TO ATTEND)	BLUE	WHITE

35

CONVERSATION ((R) SHYNESS)	BLUE	YELLOW
CONVERSE (ABILITY TO)	YELLOW	WHITE
CONVICTION (TO GET A)	PURPLE	
CONVICTION (R)	BLUE	PURPLE
CONVULSION (R)	YELLOW	
COOK (TO LEARN TO)	BLUE	YELLOW
COOPERATE (ABILITY TO)	BLUE	GREEN
COPE (ABILITY TO)	YELLOW	
COPULATE (ABILITY T0)	RED	
COPYRIGHT (TO OBTAIN)	YELLOW	
CORDIAL (TO BE)	YELLOW	BLUE
CORRESPONDENT (R)	PURPLE	GRAY
CORNUCOPIA (MAGIC)	PURPLE	ORANGE
COST (OF LIVING REDUCED)	YELLOW	GRAY
COUNSELOR (TO BECOME)	YELLOW	
COUNSELOR (SUCCESSFUL)	YELLOW	ORANGE
COUNTRY (TO LIVE IN)	BLUE	
COUNTRY CLUB (TO BELONG)	YELLOW	GREEN
COUNTRY HOUSE (TO OBTAIN)	WHITE	GREEN
COUNTRY HOUSE (TO BUY)	BROWN	
COUNTRY HOUSE (TO SELL)	GREEN	YELLOW
COUPLE (TO BECOME A PART OF)	YELLOW	PINK
COURAGE (TO HAVE)	BLUE	WHITE
COURAGEOUS (TO BE)	BLUE	
COURT (SUCCESS IN)	PURPLE	
COURTEOUS (TO BE)	PINK	BLUE
COURTLY (TO BE)	PINK	
COUSIN (FATHER SIDE, BOY)	BLUE	
COUSIN (FATHER SIDE, BOY, HEALTH)	GREEN	YELLOW
COUSIN (FATHER SIDE, BOY, LUCK)	GREEN	
COUSIN (FATHER SIDE, GIRL)	PINK	
COUSIN (FATHER SIDE, GIRL HEALTH)	PINK	ORANGE
COUSIN (FATHER SIDE, GIRL, LUCK)	GREEN	PINK
COUSIN (MOTHER SIDE, BOY)	BLUE	YELLOW
COUSIN (MOTHER SIDE, BOY, HEALTH)	ORANGE	BLUE
COUSIN (MOTHER SIDE, BOY, LUCK)	WHITE	YELLOW
COUSIN (MOTHER SIDE, GIRL)	PINK	

COUSIN (MOTHER SIDE, GIRL HEALTH)PINK		ORANGE
COUSIN (MOTHER SIDE, GIRL, LUCK) GREEN		YELLOW
COVERAGE (TO GET)	WHITE	GRAY
COVERAGE (POSITIVE)	YELLOW	PINK
COVERAGE (TO KEEP)	GRAY	YELLOW
COWARDICE (R)	BLACK	WHITE
CRAMP (R)	ORANGE	
CRASH ((R) FEAR OF)	WHITE	
CRAVING ((R) NEED FOR)	YELLOW	ORANGE
CRAWL (LEARN TO)	BLUE	
CRAZY ((R) NEED TO BE)	BLUE	YELLOW
CREATE (THE ABILITY TO)	YELLOW	PURPLE
CREATIVE (ABILITY TO BE)	YELLOW	ORANGE
CREDIBILITY (TO HAVE)	WHITE	
CREDIT (TO HAVE)	GREEN	
CREDIT (TO OBTAIN)	YELLOW	
CREDITABLE (TO BE)	GREEN	
CREDIT CARD (TO OBTAIN)	ORANGE	BROWN
CREDIT CARD (TO RETAIN)	GREEN	YELLOW
CROP (TO HAVE A HEALTHY)	BROWN	GREEN
CROSSOVER (PEACEFUL)	PURPLE	WHITE
CROWD (TO ATTRACT)	BROWN	
CRUEL (R)	YELLOW	
CRY (THE ABILITY TO)	YELLOW	WHITE
CURIOUS (TO BE)	YELLOW	BLUE
CUSTODY (TO OBTAIN)	BLUE	
CUSTODY (TO RETAIN)	GREEN	YELLOW
CUSTOMER (TO ATTRACT)	GREEN	
CUTE (TO BE)	YELLOW	PINK

- D -

DAD (TO HEAR FROM)	YELLOW	
DAD (TO FIND)	BLUE	GREEN

37

DAD (TO INSURE GOOD HEALTH)	BLUE	GRAY
DAD (TO BECOME)	PINK	BLUE
DAMAGE (R)	WHITE	
DANCE (ABILITY TO)	BLUE	
DANCE (TO BE INVITED TO)	YELLOW	BLUE
DANCER (TO BECOME A)	BLUE	PINK
DANGER (R)	PURPLE	
DANGER (PROTECTION FROM)	YELLOW	BLUE
DARK ((R) FEAR OF)	WHITE	
DATA (TO OBTAIN)	YELLOW	
DATE (TO OBTAIN)	BLUE	YELLOW
DAUGHTER (TO INSURE SAFETY)	PURPLE	
DAUGHTER (GOOD HEALTH)	ORANGE	
DAUGHTER (MONEY SUCCESS)	GREEN	YELLOW
DEADLINE (TO MEET)	YELLOW	
DEATH (ABILITY TO DEAL WITH)	WHITE	
DEBATE (ABILITY TO)	YELLOW	BLUE
DEBIT (TO DECREASE)	BLUE	
DEBT (ABILITY TO PAY)	GREEN	
DELAY (ABILITY TO DEAL WITH)	YELLOW	PINK
DELAY (R)	BLUE	
DELICATE (TO BE)	PINK	
DELIGHT (TO EXPERIENCE)	PINK	WHITE
DELUSION (DISPEL)	WHITE	YELLOW
DEMAND (ABILITY TO)	WHITE	PINK
DEMON (TO RELEASE)	BLACK	WHITE
DEMONIC (TO DISPEL)	BLACK	WHITE
DEMOTE (ABILITY TO)	WHITE	YELLOW
DENIAL ((R) WITHIN YOURSELF)	YELLOW	BLUE
DENIAL ((R) WITHIN OTHERS)	YELLOW	WHITE
DEPOSIT (TO RECEIVE)	GREEN	
DEPRESSED (R)	YELLOW	BLUE
DEPRESSION ((R) YOURSELF)	WHITE	BLUE
DEPRESSION ((R) OTHERS)	YELLOW	PINK
DEPARTURE (SUCCESSFUL)	GREEN	PINK
DEPEND (ABILITY TO)	YELLOW	GRAY
DEPENDABILITY (FOR YOURSELF)	WHITE	

38

DEPENDABILITY (FOR OTHERS)	YELLOW	BLUE
DEPENDENCY (FOR YOURSELF)	BLUE	GREEN
DEPICT (ABILITY TO)	BLUE	
DEPLORABLE ((R) ACTS BY YOU)	BLACK	WHITE
DEPLORABLE ((R) ACTS BY OTHERS)	PINK	WHITE
DEPORT ((R) CONDITIONS)	BLACK	WHITE
DESIRE (ABILITY TO OBTAIN)	BLUE	ORANGE
DESPAIR ((R) IN YOURSELF)	YELLOW	BLUE
DESPAIR ((R) IN OTHERS)	YELLOW	GRAY
DESPERATE ((R) THE NEED TO BE)	WHITE	
DESPONDENT ((R) IN YOURSELF)	PINK	YELLOW
DESPONDENT ((R) IN OTHERS)	BLUE	YELLOW

- E -

EAGER (TO BE)	YELLOW	RED
EARLY (TO BE)	WHITE	RED
EARN (THE ABILITY TO)	GREEN	BROWN
EARTHQUAKE (SAFETY FROM)	WHITE	PURPLE
EASE (TO LIVE WITH)	YELLOW	BLUE
EASILY (TO OBTAIN)	YELLOW	BLUE
ECONOMY (TO STIMULATE)	GREEN	YELLOW
EDGE (TO LIVE ON THE)	BLUE	GRAY
EDUCATION (TO OBTAIN)	YELLOW	
EFFORTLESSLY (TO OBTAIN)	WHITE	GREEN
EGO (TO OBTAIN HEALTHY)	YELLOW	
ELECTION (TO WIN)	BLUE	WHITE
ELEGANT (TO BE)	BLUE	
ELIGIBLE (TO BECOME)	GREEN	
EMBRACE (FREEDOM TO)	PINK	
EMBRYO (HEALTHY)	BLUE	WHITE
EMERALD (TO BUY)	GREEN	YELLOW
EMERALD (TO OWN)	BLUE	GREEN
EMERALD (TO SELL)	YELLOW	WHITE
EMERGENCY (TO RELEASE)	PINK	PURPLE
EMOTION (FUNCTIONAL)	WHITE	PINK

EMOTION (HEALTHY)	YELLOW	WHITE
EMPATHY (TO FEEL)	PINK	
EMPHASIS (TO PLACE)	WHITE	
EMPOWER (TO)	BLUE	
ENCHANT (TO)	WHITE	PINK
ENDOWMENT (TO RECEIVE)	GREEN	
ENDURE (THE ABILITY TO)	RED	BLUE
ENERGY (TO OBTAIN)	RED	
ENERGY (TO USE)	RED	WHITE
ENFORCE (THE ABILITY TO)	BLUE	RED
ENGAGED (TO BECOME)	PINK	BLUE
ENJOY (TO)	YELLOW	BLUE
ENLIGHTENED (TO BECOME)	ORANGE	YELLOW
ENVIRONMENT (POSITIVE)	WHITE	
ERADICATE (TO)	WHITE	BLACK
ESCAPE (THE ABILITY TO)	BLUE	WHITE
ESPECIAL (TO BECOME)	WHITE	YELLOW
ETHICAL (TO BE)	GREEN	
EVASIVE (THE ABILITY TO BE)	WHITE	YELLOW
EVIDENCE (TO OBTAIN)	GREEN	GRAY
EXAM (TO PASS)	BLUE	YELLOW
EXCEPTION (TO LIVE BY)	WHITE	
EXCESS (TO HAVE GOOD HEALTH)	BLUE	ORANGE
EXCESS (AMOUNTS OF MONEY)	YELLOW	GREEN
EXCESS (AMOUNTS OF FRIENDS)	BLUE	
EXCESS (AMOUNTS OF PATIENTS)	ORANGE	
EXCESS (AMOUNTS OF CLIENTS)	YELLOW	ORANGE
EXCITEMENT (TO EXPERIENCE)	PINK	RED
EXEMPT (TO BE)	BLUE	
EXHAUSTION (R)	GRAY	WHITE
EXPLAIN (THE ABILITY TO)	YELLOW	
EXPLORE (FREEDOM TO)	RED	YELLOW
EXPRESSION (THE FREEDOM OF)	YELLOW	BLUE
EXTRA (TO HAVE)	BLUE	GREEN

- **F** -

FABULOUS (TO BECOME)	YELLOW	WHITE
FACE (THE ABILITY TO)	WHITE	
FACE-LIFT (A SUCCESSFUL)	ORANGE	PINK
FACE-VALUE (TO SEE THINGS AT)	WHITE	BLUE
FACILITATE (THE ABILITY TO)	BLUE	
FACILITY (POWER TO HAVE)	YELLOW	BLUE
FACT (TO GET THE)	PINK	BLUE
FACTORY (TO BUILD)	GREEN	BLUE
FACTORY (TO BUY)	YELLOW	GREEN
FACTORY (TO SELL)	WHITE	GREEN
FACULTY (OF THE BODY)	YELLOW	
FACULTY (OF THE MIND)	YELLOW	BLUE
FAD (TO CREATE A)	YELLOW	RED
FAIL (SECURITY AGAINST)	WHITE	BLACK
FAIL-SAFE (TO BE)	WHITE	
FAILURE (R)	YELLOW	BLUE
FAINT HEARTED (R)	BLUE	WHITE
FAIR (TO BE)	BLUE	
FAITH (TO HAVE)	PURPLE	
FAITHFUL (TO BE)	PINK	PURPLE
FAKE (TO SEE THAT WHICH IS)	YELLOW	GRAY
FALLACY (TO RELEASE)	YELLOW	
FALLOUT (TO GUARD AGAINST)	RED	YELLOW
FALSE (TO BE)	BLACK	YELLOW
FALSE (TO GUARD AGAINST)	YELLOW	BLUE
FAME (TO HAVE)	PINK	YELLOW
FAMED (TO BE)	YELLOW	BLUE
FAMILY (TO HAVE A)	BLUE	
FAMILY (TO HAVE A CLOSE)	BLUE	
FAMILY (TO HAVE A GOOD)	YELLOW	PURPLE
FAMOUS (TO BE)	PINK	YELLOW
FAMOUS (TO MEET)	PURPLE	YELLOW
FAN (TO HAVE)	YELLOW	BLUE
FANATICISM (TO RELEASE)	YELLOW	RED

41

FANCY (TO BE)	BLUE	
FANCY-FREE (TO BE)	PINK	WHITE
FANCY-FREE ((R) TO LIVE)	YELLOW	BLUE
FANTASY (R)	BLACK	WHITE
FARM (TO HAVE A)	GREEN	
FARM (TO WORK)	YELLOW	
FARMER (TO BE A)	GREEN	
FARMLAND (RICH)	BROWN	ORANGE
FAR-REACHING (TO BE)	YELLOW	WHITE
FAR-SEEING (ABILITY TO BE)	YELLOW	
FAST (TO BE)	RED	
FAT (TO RELEASE BEING)	BROWN	PINK
FATALIST (TO BE A)	BROWN	
FATALIST (R)	WHITE	YELLOW
FATHER (INSURE GOOD HEALTH)	BLUE	
FATHER-IN-LAW (GOOD HEALTH)	GREEN	WHITE
FATHER-IN-LAW (SUCCESS)	BLUE	WHITE
FATIGUE (R)	WHITE	BLACK
FAVOR (TO FIND)	WHITE	
FAVORITE (TO BE THE)	PINK	YELLOW
FEAR (R)	RED	WHITE
FEARLESS (TO BE)	BROWN	WHITE
FEED (THE ABILITY TO)	BLUE	
FEEL (THE ABILITY TO)	PINK	WHITE
FEELINGS (TO HAVE)	BLUE	
FEELINGS (EMOTIONAL)	PINK	BLUE
FEELINGS (PASSIONATE)	RED	PINK
FELLOWSHIP (TO HAVE)	GREEN	BLUE
FELONY (TO FORGIVE)	PINK	BLACK
FEMININITY (TO EXPRESS)	PINK	YELLOW
FERTILE (TO BECOME)	YELLOW	GREEN
FERTILITY (TO ENHANCE)	BLUE	
FETUS (INSURE THE SAFETY OF)	YELLOW	WHITE
FEUD (R)	BLACK	WHITE
FEVER (TO LOWER)	ORANGE	
FEVER (TO RAISE)	YELLOW	
FIANCÉ (TO HAVE A)	BLUE	

42

FIANCÉ (TO BE A)	BLUE	WHITE
FIANCEE (TO HAVE A)	PINK	
FIANCEE (TO BE A)	PINK	WHITE
FICKLE (TO BE)	YELLOW	BROWN
FIGHT (ABILITY TO)	RED	
FIGHT ((R) THE NEED TO)	WHITE	YELLOW
FIGHT (TO AVOID)	WHITE	
FIGURE (TO MAINTAIN A GOOD)	PINK	BLUE
FIGUREHEAD (TO BE A)	BLUE	GRAY
FILM (TO BE IN A)	BLUE	GREEN
FINAL (TO PUT CLOSURE TO)	PURPLE	WHITE
FINALIZE (A BUSINESS DEAL)	GREEN	YELLOW
FINALIZE (A RELATIONSHIP)	PINK	PURPLE
FINANCES (TO INCREASE)	GREEN	
FINANCES (TO STABILIZE)	PURPLE	GREEN
FIND (TO)	WHITE	
FIRST (TO BE)	YELLOW	
FISHING (TO BE SUCCESSFUL)	BROWN	YELLOW
FIT (TO BECOME)	GREEN	BLUE
FLAMBOYANT (TO BECOME)	BLUE	GREEN
FLAWLESS (TO BECOME)	YELLOW	
FLEXIBLE (TO BE)	BLUE	YELLOW
FLIGHT (TO TAKE A)	WHITE	BLUE
FLORIDA (SAFETY IN)	PINK	WHITE
FLOURISH (THE ABILITY TO)	GREEN	PURPLE
FOCUS (THE ABILITY TO)	YELLOW	ORANGE
FOLLOWER (ABILITY TO BE A)	GRAY	
FORBID (TO)	WHITE	BLACK
FORCEFUL (THE ABILITY TO BE)	YELLOW	GRAY
FORGIVE (THE ABILITY TO) WHITE		
FORGIVING (TO BE)	YELLOW	
FORWARD (TO GO)	BLUE	WHITE
FRANCHISE (TO BUY)	GREEN	
FRANCHISE (TO OWN)	YELLOW	GREEN
FRANCHISE (TO SELL)	PURPLE	GREEN
FRATERNITY (TO BELONG TO)	WHITE	YELLOW
FRATERNITY (TO JOIN A)	ORANGE	

FRATERNIZE (ABILITY TO)	YELLOW	WHITE
FRAUD (TO RELEASE)	RED	WHITE
FREE (TO GET)	WHITE	
FREE (TO BE)	YELLOW	BLUE
FREEDOM (TO HAVE)	BLUE	
FREELANCE (TO)	BLUE	GREEN
FRUSTRATION (R)	RED	YELLOW
FULFILLMENT (TO FEEL)	YELLOW	
FUN (TO HAVE)	BLUE	

- G -

GAIN (THE ABILITY TO)	GREEN	WHITE
GALLSTONE (R)	ORANGE	
GAMBLE (SUCCESSFUL)	YELLOW	
GATHER (TO)	BLUE	YELLOW
GATHERING (TO HAVE A)	YELLOW	WHITE
GENEROUS (TO BE)	YELLOW	
GENIUS (TO BECOME)	WHITE	YELLOW
GENTLE (TO BE)	PINK	
GEORGIA (SAFETY IN)	BLUE	
GET (TO OBTAIN)	GREEN	
GIFT (TO GIVE)	WHITE	YELLOW
GIFT (TO RECEIVE)	BLUE	YELLOW
GIRL (TO HAVE A)	PINK	WHITE
GIRLFRIEND (TO FIND A)	YELLOW	BLUE
GIRLFRIEND (TO GET RID OF)	BLACK	WHITE
GIVE (THE ABILITY TO)	GREEN	PINK
GIVE UP (THE ABILITY TO)	BLACK	YELLOW
GLAD (TO BE)	PINK	
GLAMOROUS (TO BE)	PINK	BLUE
GLOOM (R)	BLACK	WHITE
GO (TO)	GREEN	
GO ALONG (TO)	GREEN	YELLOW
GO BEHIND (OTHERS)	BLUE	BROWN

44

GOAL (TO ACCOMPLISH)	PURPLE	
GOD (TO WORSHIP)	WHITE	
GODCHILD (BOY)	BLUE	
GODCHILD (BOY, HEALTHY)	BLUE	ORANGE
GODCHILD (BOY, SAFETY)	BLUE	WHITE
GODCHILD (GIRL)	PINK	
GODCHILD (GIRL, HEALTHY)	PINK	ORANGE
GODCHILD (GIRL, SAFETY)	PINK	WHITE
GODFATHER (HONOR)	PURPLE	PINK
GODLIKE (TO BE)	PINK	WHITE
GODMOTHER (TO HONOR)	PINK	PURPLE
GODSPEED (TO DO WITH)	GREEN	BLUE
GO-GETTER (TO BE A)	BLUE	GREEN
GOLD (TO OBTAIN)	YELLOW	GREEN
GOLDEN RULE (TO LIVE BY)	BLUE	
GOLF (LEARN TO PLAY)	GREEN	
GOLF (TO HAVE TIME TO PLAY)	YELLOW	BLUE
GOOD (TO BE)	WHITE	
GOOD NIGHT (TO HAVE A)	GRAY	
GOSSIP (TO STOP)	WHITE	BLACK
GRACEFUL (TO BE)	WHITE	PINK
GRADE (TO PASS)	YELLOW	
GRANDEUR (TO LIVE A LIFE OF)	BLUE	YELLOW
GREAT (TO BE)	YELLOW	
GREED (R)	BLACK	YELLOW
GREEDY (R)	YELLOW	
GRIEF (R)	YELLOW	
GROW (TO)	GREEN	WHITE
GROWTH (TO STOP)	WHITE	
GUARANTEE (TO GET A)	GREEN	BLUE
GUESS (HAVING THE ABILITY TO)	YELLOW	
GUESTS (TO HAVE)	BLUE	YELLOW

- H -

HABIT (TO RELEASE A)	YELLOW	PINK
HAIR (TO STRENGTHEN)	ORANGE	

45

HAIR (FOR GROWTH)	YELLOW		
HALLUCINATION (R)	ORANGE	YELLOW	
HAMPER (TO OTHERS)	WHITE	BROWN	
HANDFUL (TO HAVE A)	BROWN		
HANDFUL (R)	YELLOW	WHITE	
HANGOVER (TO RELEASE)	PINK	GREEN	
HAPPEN (TO MAKE IT)	WHITE	RED	
HAPPINESS (TO FIND)	PINK	WHITE	
HAPPY (TO BE)	YELLOW	PINK	
HARM (TO GUARD AGAINST)	YELLOW	PURPLE	
HARMONY (TO HAVE)	PINK		
HARVEST (TO HAVE A GOOD)	GREEN	BROWN	
HASTY (TO BE)	RED		
HATE (THE ABILITY TO)	BLACK	BROWN	
HATE (TO RELEASE)	WHITE	BLACK	
HAUNT (TO RELEASE)	WHITE	BLACK	PURPLE
HAVE (TO)	YELLOW		
HAVOC (R)	WHITE	YELLOW	
HEADACHE (R)	WHITE	GRAY	
HEADSTRONG (TO BE)	BLUE		
HEALTH (GOOD)	BLUE	ORANGE	
HEAVEN (TO GO TO)	YELLOW	PURPLE	
HELP (TO GET)	BLUE		
HELPFUL (TO BE)	WHITE	PINK	
HERMIT (TO BE A)	YELLOW	BLUE	
HERMIT (TO LIVE LIKE A)	ORANGE	YELLOW	
HERO (TO BE A)	PURPLE	BLUE	
HEROINE (TO BE A)	PURPLE	BLUE	
HIDE (THE ABILITY TO)	WHITE		
HIDEAWAY (TO FIND A)	BLUE	YELLOW	
HINDER (THE ABILITY TO)	GREEN	GRAY	
HITCH (TO GO OFF WITHOUT A)	YELLOW	ORANGE	
HOBBY (TO FIND A)	PINK	GREEN	
HOLD OUT (THE ABILITY TO)	BLACK	YELLOW	
HOLY (TO BECOME)	PINK	PURPLE	
HOME (TO HAVE A)	BLUE	GREEN	
HOMECOMING (TO HAVE A)	YELLOW		

HONEST (TO BE)	BLUE	
HONOR (TO FIND)	YELLOW	BLUE
HOPE (TO HAVE)	PINK	PURPLE
HOPEFUL (TO BE)	PURPLE	YELLOW
HORROR (TO RELEASE)	YELLOW	WHITE
HOST (TO BE A GOOD)	WHITE	BLUE
HOSTAGE (R)	RED	WHITE
HOSTILITY (R)	WHITE	
HOUSE (TO HAVE A)	BLUE	
HUMANE (ABILITY TO BE)	BLUE	WHITE
HUMOR (TO FIND)	PINK	YELLOW
HUMOR (TO HAVE)	WHITE	YELLOW
HUNGER (R)	BLUE	
HURRY (TO BE IN A)	RED	
HURRY (TO LIVE IN A)	RED	WHITE
HURT (TO RELEASE)	YELLOW	WHITE
HYPERACTIVE (R)	BLUE	
HYPERSENSITIVITY (UNDERSTAND)	YELLOW	BLUE
HYPERTENSION (R)	ORANGE	
HYSTERIA (TO CONTROL)	BLUE	

- I -

ICONOCLASM (TO MAINTAIN)	WHITE	PURPLE
ID (TO STRENGTHEN)	YELLOW	WHITE
IDAHO (SAFETY IN)	BLUE	
IDEA (TO HAVE AN)	YELLOW	BLUE
IDEAL (TO HAVE THE)	YELLOW	
IDEALISM (ABILITY TO)	BLUE	
IDEALIST (TO BE AN)	PINK	YELLOW
IDENTITY (TO MAINTAIN ONES)	BLUE	
IDLE (TO RELEASE)	RED	BLUE
IDLER ((R) FROM YOUR LIFE)	PINK	
IDOLIZE (THE ABILITY TO)	BLUE	YELLOW
IGNOBLE (R)	GRAY	WHITE
IGNORAMUS ((R) THOSE WHO ARE)	WHITE	BLACK

47

IGNORANCE (R)	YELLOW	BLUE
IGNORE (THE ABILITY TO)	YELLOW	WHITE
ILLINOIS (SAFETY IN)	BLUE	PURPLE
ILLITERACY (R)	YELLOW	
ILLNESS (R)	BLUE	ORANGE
ILLUSION (TO LIVE AN)	WHITE	GRAY
IMAGERY (ABILITY FOR GUIDED)	YELLOW	BLUE
IMAGINATION (HAVING AN)	YELLOW	
IMAGINATIVE (TO BE)	BLUE	YELLOW
IMBALANCE (TO RELEASE)	BLUE	
IMBUE (ABILITY TO)	WHITE	PURPLE
IMMACULATE (TO BE)	ORANGE	YELLOW
IMMACULATELY (TO LIVE)	BLUE	PURPLE
IMMATURE (TO BE)	PINK	
IMMATURITY (TO RELEASE)	YELLOW	PINK
IMMEDIATE (TO HAVE)	BLUE	
IMMOBILE (R)	BLACK	GRAY
IMMORTAL (TO BE)	YELLOW	PURPLE
IMMORTALITY (TO HAVE)	WHITE	PURPLE
IMMUNE (TO BE)	ORANGE	YELLOW
IMPACT (TO MAKE AN)	BLUE	BLACK
IMPART (TO OTHERS)	WHITE	
IMPARTIAL (TO BE)	BLUE	PINK
IMPORTANT (TO BE)	YELLOW	BLUE
IMPOTENT (GUARD AGAINST)	ORANGE	BLUE
IMPRESS (ABILITY TO)	PINK	YELLOW
IMPRESSION (LEAVING A LASTING)	YELLOW	PINK
IMPROVE (TO)	WHITE	YELLOW
IMPULSIVE (TO BE)	RED	
IMPULSIVENESS (R)	WHITE	RED
INABILITY (R)	BLACK	WHITE
INACTIVE (R)	RED	
INADEQUACY (R)	YELLOW	BLUE
INCARNATE (THE ABILITY TO BE)	BLUE	GREEN
INCLINE (TO BE)	YELLOW	
INCLUDE (TO)	PINK	
INCOME (TO INCREASE)	GREEN	YELLOW

48

INCORRIGIBLE ((R) BEHAVIOR)	BLUE	
INCUBUS (R)	WHITE	
INDEPENDENT (TO BE)	YELLOW	GREEN
INDESTRUCTIBLE (TO BE)	ORANGE	BLUE
INDIFFERENT (TO BE)	YELLOW	
INDIVIDUALISTIC (TO BE)	WHITE	
INFAMY (R)	GRAY	WHITE
INFERIORITY COMPLEX (R)	WHITE	PURPLE
INFLATION (TO REDUCE)	WHITE	GREEN
INFORMAL (TO BE)	PINK	
INFORMATION (TO GAIN)	YELLOW	GRAY
INFORMER (TO BE AN)	BLUE	YELLOW
INFORMER (TO FIND AN)	BLUE	YELLOW
INSIGHT (TO HAVE)	GREEN	PURPLE
INSPIRE (THE ABILITY TO)	YELLOW	
INTEGRATE (THE ABILITY TO)	PINK	YELLOW
INTELLECTUAL (TO BE AN)	BLUE	
INTROVERTED (R)	YELLOW	WHITE
INTRUST (ABILITY TO)	YELLOW	
INTUITION (TO HAVE)	ORANGE	
INTUITIVE (TO BE)	YELLOW	
IOWA (SAFETY IN)	BLUE	
IRRITABILITY ((R) YELLOW/ FEAR)	PINK	WHITE
ISOLATE (TO)	BLUE	
ISSUE (TO PURSUE AN)	YELLOW	BLUE

- J -

JACKPOT (TO WIN)	GREEN	YELLOW
JAIL (TO GET OUT OF)	YELLOW	PINK
JAIL (TO STAY OUT OF)	WHITE	PURPLE
JEALOUS (TO RELEASE)	WHITE	YELLOW
JEOPARDIZE (TO)	YELLOW	
JOB (TO FIND)	BLUE	
JOB (TO KEEP)	YELLOW	BLUE
JOIN (TO)	WHITE	

49

JOLLY (TO BE)	YELLOW	
JOURNEY (TO TAKE A)	GREEN	YELLOW
JOURNEY (A MENTAL)	YELLOW	PURPLE
JOY (TO HAVE)	YELLOW	BLUE
JOY (TO GIVE)	ORANGE	YELLOW
JOYFUL (TO BE)	BLUE	
JUDGMENT (TO RELEASE)	BLUE	
JUSTICE (TO HAVE)	YELLOW	GRAY
JUSTICE (TO UPHOLD)	PURPLE	
JUSTIFY (ABILITY TO)	YELLOW	WHITE

- K -

KANSAS (SAFETY IN)	YELLOW	BLUE
KARMA (POSITIVE)	WHITE	
KEEN (TO BE)	YELLOW	ORANGE
KEEP (THE ABILITY TO)	PINK	YELLOW
KENTUCKY (SAFETY IN)	BLUE	
KIND (TO BE)	YELLOW	
KNOW (TO)	BLUE	YELLOW
KNOW-HOW (TO HAVE)	YELLOW	GREEN
KNOWLEDGE (TO HAVE)	YELLOW	
KNOWLEDGE (TO RETAIN)	YELLOW	BLUE
KNOWLEDGEABLE (TO BE)	YELLOW	ORANGE
KNOWN (TO BE)	BLUE	

- L -

LABOR (EASY)	YELLOW	
LACERATION (LESS PAIN)	ORANGE	BLUE
LACK (TO RELEASE)	BLUE	
LACKING (TO RELEASE)	BLUE	GREEN
LADY (TO BE)	PINK	WHITE

LADY (TO FIND)	PINK	
LANDLORD (TO BE A)	ORANGE	
LANDLORD (TO DEAL WITH)	YELLOW	
LAND OWNER (TO BE)	YELLOW	BROWN
LARGE (TO HAVE ABUNDANCE)	GREEN	
LAST (ABILITY TO MAKE THINGS)	PURPLE	
LAST RITES (TO ADMINISTER)	PURPLE	WHITE
LAW (TO LIVE WITHIN)	PURPLE	
LAZINESS (R)	ORANGE	
LEARN (THE ABILITY TO)	YELLOW	
LEASE (TO RENEW)	BLUE	
LEASE (TO SIGN)	YELLOW	BLUE
LEFT (TO BE)	BROWN	
LEISURE (TIME)	BLUE	WHITE
LESSON (TO LEARN)	BLUE	YELLOW
LICENSE (TO OBTAIN)	YELLOW	
LIFE (POSITIVE)	GREEN	
LOCATE (THE ABILITY TO)	BROWN	YELLOW
LOUISIANA (SAFETY IN)	BLUE	
LOSS (R)	BLUE	
LOVE (TO FEEL)	YELLOW	PINK
LOVER (TO HAVE)	PINK	YELLOW
LUCK (TO HAVE)	YELLOW	
LUXURY (TO HAVE)	BLUE	GREEN
LUXURY (TO LIVE A LIFE OF)	BLUE	PINK

- M -

MACHO (TO BE)	BLUE	BLACK
MAD (TO RELEASE)	YELLOW	
MAGIC (TO PERFORM)	BROWN	YELLOW
MAGICAL (TO BE)	PURPLE	
MAGICIAN (TO BE A)	YELLOW	BLUE
MAGNIFICENT (TO BE)	YELLOW	

MAID (TO BE A)	BROWN	
MAID (TO HAVE A)	BROWN	YELLOW
MAIL (TO RECEIVE)	WHITE	
MAINE (SAFETY IN)	RED	
MAKE-BELIEVE (ABILITY TO)	YELLOW	BLUE
MALEFIC (TO RELEASE)	WHITE	
MALICIOUS (TO BE)	YELLOW	WHITE
MANAGE (TO)	GREEN	
MANEUVER (ABILITY TO)	WHITE	BROWN
MANIFEST (ABILITY TO)	BLUE	PURPLE
MANIPULATE (ABILITY TO)	YELLOW	PINK
MANNERED (WELL)	BLUE	GREEN
MARRIED (TO BE)	PINK	
MARTYR (TO BE A)	PURPLE	
MARYLAND (SAFETY IN)	RED	
MASSACHUSETTS (SAFETY IN)	BLUE	WHITE
MATERIALISTIC (TO BE)	YELLOW	
MEDITATION (ABILITY TO)	YELLOW	BLUE
MELANCHOLIA (TO RELEASE)	RED	WHITE
MELANCHOLY (TO BE)	YELLOW	BLUE
MELLOW (TO BE)	BLUE	
MEMORY (TO HAVE A GOOD)	YELLOW	
MESSAGE (TO RECEIVE)	YELLOW	
MICHIGAN (SAFETY IN)	BLUE	
MIND (TO HAVE A GOOD)	YELLOW	BLUE
MIND-READER (ABILITY TO BE A)	WHITE	RED
MINNESOTA (SAFETY IN)	WHITE	
MISCHIEVOUS (TO BE)	YELLOW	
MISFORTUNE (R)	BLUE	
MISSISSIPPI (SAFETY IN)	PINK	
MISSOURI (SAFETY IN)	GREEN	
MISTRESS (TO RELEASE)	PINK	WHITE
MISTRESS (TO HAVE A)	PINK	YELLOW
MONEY (TO HAVE)	GREEN	
MONEY (TO KEEP)	GREEN	YELLOW
MONTANA (SAFETY IN)	GREEN	WHITE
MOOD (TO BE IN A GOOD)	BLUE	

MORE (TO HAVE)	YELLOW	
MORTGAGE (TO OWN)	BLUE	GREEN
MOTHER (GOOD HEALTH)	BLUE	PINK
MOTHER (PEACE OF MIND)	YELLOW	BLUE
MOTHER (MONEY SUCCESS)	GREEN	BLUE
MOTHER-IN-LAW (GOOD HEALTH)	BLUE	YELLOW
MOTHER-IN-LAW (PEACE OF MIND)	YELLOW	PINK
MOTHER-IN-LAW (MONEY SUCCESS)	GREEN	
MOVE (TO)	BLUE	YELLOW
MUSICIAN (TO BE A)	BLUE	ORANGE
MYSELF (TO BE)	YELLOW	
MYSTICAL (TO BE)	YELLOW	ORANGE

- N -

NAG ((R) THE NEED TO BE)	YELLOW	
NAMESAKE (TO HAVE A)	PINK	BLUE
NARCISSISM ((R) OBSESSIONS)	PURPLE	BLUE
NARCOTIC ((R) THE NEED)	YELLOW	ORANGE
NARROW-MINDED (R)	BLUE	
NASTY ((R) THE NEED TO BE)	YELLOW	
NATURAL (TO BE)	YELLOW	BROWN
NATURE (TO LIVE IN)	BROWN	
NEAT (TO BE)	WHITE	
NEBRASKA (SAFETY IN)	YELLOW	
NEEDS (TO MEET)	GREEN	WHITE
NEGATIVE ((R) THE NEED TO BE)	YELLOW	
NEGLIGENCE (R)	WHITE	BLUE
NEGOTIATE (THE ABILITY TO)	YELLOW	BLUE
NEIGHBOR (TO GET ALONG WITH)	WHITE	BLUE
NEPHEW (GOOD HEALTH)	WHITE	
NEPHEW (FOR PROTECTION)	PURPLE	WHITE
NEPOTISM (R)	BLUE	
NERVOUS BREAKDOWN (R)	WHITE	YELLOW
NERVOUS SYSTEM (STRENGTHEN)	ORANGE	
NETWORK (ABILITY TO)	GREEN	

NEUROSIS (R)	ORANGE	
NEUROTIC ((R) THE NEED TO BE)	ORANGE	WHITE
NEVADA (SAFETY IN)	GREEN	
NEW HAMPSHIRE (SAFETY IN)	BROWN	
NEW JERSEY (SAFETY IN)	YELLOW	
NEW MEXICO (SAFETY IN)	WHITE	
NEW YORK (SAFETY IN)	BLACK	WHITE
NICE (TO BE)	PINK	
NICOTINE ((R) ADDICTION FROM)	ORANGE	BROWN
NIECE (GOOD HEALTH)	PINK	WHITE
NIECE (FOR PROTECTION)	PINK	ORANGE
NON-COMMITTAL (TO BE)	YELLOW	
NON-DESCRIPT (TO BE)	WHITE	
NON-STOP (TO GO)	GREEN	
NON-VIOLENT (TO BE)	YELLOW	PINK
NORMAL (TO BE)	BLUE	
NORTH CAROLINA (SAFETY IN)	BLUE	
NORTH DAKOTA (SAFETY IN)	YELLOW	
NOW (TO OBTAIN)	GREEN	
NUISANCE ((R) THE NEED TO BE)	YELLOW	ORANGE
NURTURE (THE ABILITY TO)	YELLOW	

- O -

OATH (TO TAKE AND KEEP)	YELLOW	
OBEDIENT (TO BE)	BLUE	WHITE
OBESE (TO RELEASE)	PINK	BROWN
OBEY (TO)	YELLOW	
OBJECT (TO BECOME AN)	PINK	
OBJECTIVE (TO BE)	BLUE	WHITE
OBJECTIVITY (TO HAVE)	BLUE	GREEN
OBLIGATE (THE ABILITY TO)	PINK	BLUE
OBLIGATION (TO UPHOLD AN)	YELLOW	GREEN
OBLIVION (TO DISAPPEAR INTO)	WHITE	YELLOW
OBSCENITY (TO RELEASE)	WHITE	
OBSEQUIOUS (THE ABILITY TO BE)	YELLOW	GREEN

OBSERVANT (ABILITY TO BE)	YELLOW	
OBSESSION (RELEASE)	YELLOW	PINK
OBSTACLE (TO RELEASE)	WHITE	GREEN
OBTAIN (TO)	GREEN	BLUE
OBVIOUS (TO BE)	YELLOW	
OBVIOUS (NOT TO BE)	GRAY	YELLOW
OCCULT (TO UNDERSTAND)	YELLOW	
OCCULT ((R) YOURSELF FROM)	PINK	YELLOW
OCCULT (TO BELONG TO)	YELLOW	WHITE
OCEAN (TO GO TO)	BLUE	
OCEAN (TO MOVE TO)	BLUE	GREEN
ODD (TO BE)	GRAY	
ODD (NOT TO BE)	YELLOW	
ODDS (TO BE AT)	GRAY	
ODDS (NOT BE AT)	YELLOW	GRAY
ODOR (TO RELEASE)	WHITE	
OFFEND (NOT TO)	YELLOW	PINK
OFFENSIVE (NOT TO BE)	PINK	
OFFER (THE ABILITY TO)	GREEN	
OFFICE (TO HAVE AN)	BLUE	YELLOW
OFFICER (TO BE AN)	YELLOW	GREEN
OFFICIAL (DEAL WELL WITH AN)	YELLOW	
OHIO (SAFETY IN)	WHITE	
OKLAHOMA (SAFETY IN)	ORANGE	GREEN
OLD AGE (PEACEFUL)	BLUE	
OLOGY (ABILITY TO UNDERSTAND)	YELLOW	
OMIT (THE ABILITY TO)	YELLOW	BLUE
ON (TO BE)	YELLOW	
ONENESS (WITH YOURSELF)	YELLOW	PURPLE
ONESELF (TO BE)	YELLOW	
ONGOING (TO HAVE THINGS)	YELLOW	BROWN
ONWARD (TO BE)	YELLOW	GRAY
OPEN (TO BE)	PINK	YELLOW
OPEN-MINDED (TO BE)	BLUE	
OPERATION (SUCCESSFUL)	BLUE	ORANGE
OPERATIVE (TO BE)	BLUE	
OPINIONS (TO ACCEPT OTHERS')	WHITE	YELLOW

OPPORTUNIST (TO BE AN)	BROWN	
OPPORTUNIST (NOT TO BE)	WHITE	BROWN
OPPORTUNITY (TO HAVE AN)	BLUE	
OPPRESSION (TO RELEASE)	BLUE	ORANGE
OPTIMIST (TO BE AN)	YELLOW	
OPTIMISTIC (TO BE)	YELLOW	WHITE
OPTION (TO HAVE)	BLUE	
OPULENCE (TO HAVE)	GREEN	YELLOW
OPULENT (TO BE)	GREEN	
ORATION (ABILITY TO GIVE)	YELLOW	
ORDER (TO HAVE)	BLUE	
ORDERLY (TO BE)	BLUE	WHITE
OREGON (SAFETY IN)	WHITE	
ORGANIZE (ABILITY TO)	YELLOW	
ORIGINAL (TO BE)	WHITE	BLUE
ORTHODOX (TO BE)	WHITE	
ORTHODOX (NOT TO BE)	YELLOW	WHITE
OSCAR (TO WIN)	YELLOW	PURPLE
OSMOSIS (TO LEARN BY)	YELLOW	
OUTCOME (A PEACEFUL)	BLUE	
OUTGOING (TO BE)	RED	WHITE
OUTLANDISH (TO BE)	RED	YELLOW
OUTLOOK (TO HAVE A GOOD)	PINK	
OUTRAGE ((R) NEED TO BE)	WHITE	BLACK
OVERJOYED (TO BE)	GREEN	BLUE
OVERSLEEP ((R) THE NEED TO)	RED	WHITE
OWN (TO)	BLUE	GREEN

- P -

PACE (YOURSELF)	BLUE	
PACIFIC (TO BE)	PINK	
PACIFIST (TO BE A)	YELLOW	PINK
PACIFY (TO)	PINK	
PAGEANT (TO WIN)	GREEN	BLUE
PAIN (TO RELEASE)	BLUE	ORANGE

56

PAINSTAKING (TO BE)	YELLOW	WHITE
PAL (TO BE A)	BLUE	
PALMISTRY (TO UNDERSTAND)	YELLOW	RED
PANIC (NOT TO)	YELLOW	GRAY
PANTHEON (TO UNDERSTAND)	WHITE	YELLOW
PAPER MONEY (TO HAVE)	GREEN	YELLOW
PAPER PROFITS (TO HAVE)	YELLOW	
PAPER WORK (TO FINISH)	BLUE	
PARADISE (TO LIVE A LIFE OF)	WHITE	BLUE
PARAPSYCHOLOGY (UNDERSTAND)	YELLOW	ORANGE
PARASITE (R)	ORANGE	
PARENT (TO RESPECT)	YELLOW	WHITE
PAROLED (TO BE)	GREEN	
PART (TO BECOME A)	YELLOW	RED
PART (THE ABILITY TO)	PINK	WHITE
PARTAKE (THE ABILITY TO)	BLUE	
PARTAKE (THE OPPORTUNITY TO)	YELLOW	BLUE
PARTICIPANT (TO BE A)	BLUE	
PARTNER (TO BE A GOOD)	BLUE	YELLOW
PARTY (TO BE INVITED)	YELLOW	
PARTY (TO HAVE A GOOD TIME)	BLUE	YELLOW
PASSION (TO FEEL)	PINK	RED
PASSIONATE (TO BE)	RED	
PASSIVE (TO BE)	WHITE	BLUE
PAY (THE ABILITY TO)	GREEN	
PAYCHECK (TO RECEIVE A)	BLUE	GREEN
PAYMENT (TO MAKE A)	GREEN	
PEACE (TO MAKE)	PINK	
PEACE (TO HAVE)	PINK	YELLOW
PEACEFUL (TO BE)	BLUE	
PENSION (TO RECEIVE)	GREEN	
PENNSYLVANIA (SAFETY IN)	YELLOW	
PERCEIVE (THE ABILITY TO)	YELLOW	BLUE
PERCEPTIVE (TO BE)	ORANGE	
PERFECT (TO BE)	PINK	BLUE
PERFORM (THE ABILITY TO)	BLUE	
PERPLEXITY (TO RELEASE)	WHITE	

PERSONALITY (TO HAVE A GOOD)	BLUE	YELLOW
PERSPECTIVE (TO HAVE A GOOD)	YELLOW	BLUE
PERSUASIVE (TO BE)	WHITE	YELLOW
PET (TO HAVE A)	BROWN	YELLOW
PHILOSOPHICAL (TO BE)	YELLOW	
PHILOSOPHY (TO UNDERSTAND)	YELLOW	BLUE
PHYSICAL (TO BE)	BLUE	RED
PLAY (THE ABILITY TO)	YELLOW	
PLENTY (TO HAVE)	BLUE	GREEN
POLICY (TO LIVE UP TO)	BLUE	
POLITE (TO BE)	YELLOW	
POLITICAL (TO BE)	BLUE	GRAY
POLITICS (TO UNDERSTAND)	YELLOW	
POLLUTION (TO STOP)	WHITE	
POLTERGEISTS (RID YOURSELF)	WHITE	PURPLE
POVERTY ((R) NEED TO BE)	GREEN	
POPULAR (TO BE)	PINK	YELLOW
POSITIVE (TO BE)	BLUE	
POSSESSIVE ((R) NEED	BLACK	WHITE
POTENTIAL (TO HAVE)	WHITE	
POTENTIAL (TO LIVE UP TO)	GREEN	BLUE
POWER (TO HAVE)	RED	
POWERFUL (TO BE)	WHITE	RED
PRACTICAL (TO BE)	BLUE	
PREGNANT (ABILITY TO BECOME)	YELLOW	PINK
PRETTY (TO BE)	PINK	
PREVENT (THE ABILITY TO)	RED	WHITE
PROGRESS (THE ABILITY TO)	GREEN	
PROJECT (ABILITY TO FINISH)	RED	
PROMISE (ABILITY TO KEEP)	YELLOW	WHITE
PROMOTION (TO GET)	BLUE	WHITE
PROSPERITY (TO HAVE)	GREEN	
PROUD (TO BE)	YELLOW	
PRUDENT (TO BE)	GREEN	BLUE
PSYCHIC (TO BE)	YELLOW	ORANGE
PUBLISH (ABILITY TO)	YELLOW	
PURPOSE (TO SEE YOUR OWN)	BLUE	

58

- Q -

QUALIFIED (TO BE)	YELLOW	
QUALIFY (TO)	BLUE	
QUALITY (TO HAVE)	GREEN	YELLOW
QUALM (TO RELEASE)	WHITE	RED
QUARREL ((R) THE NEED TO)	WHITE	
QUEST (TO HAVE A)	BLUE	YELLOW
QUESTIONS (TO HAVE ANSWERS)	YELLOW	ORANGE
QUICK (TO DO)	RED	
QUIET (TO HAVE SOME)	WHITE	
QUIT (ABILITY TO DO SO)	BLUE	PURPLE
QUOTA (TO MEET YOUR)	YELLOW	RED

- R -

RABBLE-ROUSER (TO BE A)	YELLOW	
RABBLE-ROUSER (NOT TO BE A)	BLUE	YELLOW
RACE (TO WIN)	GREEN	
RADIANT (TO BE)	WHITE	
RADIATE (THE ABILITY TO)	YELLOW	BLUE
RADICAL (TO BE)	BROWN	
RADICAL (NOT TO BE)	WHITE	BROWN
RAFFLE (TO WIN)	GREEN	
RAISE (TO GET A)	BLUE	GREEN
RANCH (TO BUY)	YELLOW	GREEN
RANCH (TO OWN)	GREEN	BROWN
RANCH (TO SELL)	YELLOW	BLUE
RANK (TO GAIN)	RED	
RATE (TO LOWER)	YELLOW	WHITE
RATE (TO RAISE)	BLUE	RED
REASONABLE (TO BE)	YELLOW	
REASSURE (TO BE)	YELLOW	GRAY
RECOGNITION (TO GAIN)	GREEN	BLUE
RECOMMEND (TO)	YELLOW	

RECOMMENDATION (FAVORABLE)	BLUE	
RECONCILIATION (TO HAVE A)	PINK	BLUE
RECONSIDER (ABILITY TO)	BLUE	
RECOURSE (TO TAKE)	GRAY	
RECOVER (ABILITY TO)	ORANGE	BLUE
RECOVERY (SPEEDY)	PINK	ORANGE
RECREATE (ABILITY TO)	BLUE	
RECREATE (CHANCE TO)	WHITE	BLUE
RECTIFY (THE ABILITY TO)	GRAY	YELLOW
RECTIFY (OPPORTUNITY TO)	YELLOW	BLUE
REDEEM (ONE'S SELF)	WHITE	
REFLECT (ABILITY TO)	WHITE	PINK
REFORM (TO)	BLUE	
REFRAIN (TO)	YELLOW	GRAY
REFUND (TO GET A)	GREEN	
REGRET ((R) THE NEED TO)	YELLOW	WHITE
REJOICE (TO)	YELLOW	BLUE
RELIGION (TO BELIEVE)	WHITE	
REMEMBER (THE ABILITY TO)	YELLOW	
REPRESENTATION (TO HAVE)	BLUE	
REPRODUCE (ABILITY TO)	BLUE	
RESPONSIBLE (TO BE)	BLACK	WHITE
REST (TO HAVE SOME)	WHITE	
RETURN (ABILITY TO)	WHITE	
RETURN (CHANCE TO)	WHITE	BLUE
RHODE ISLAND (SAFETY IN)	GREEN	
RICH (TO BECOME)	GREEN	YELLOW
RIGHT (TO BE)	YELLOW	
RIGHTEOUS (TO BE)	WHITE	PURPLE
ROTTEN (TO BE)	BROWN	

- S -

SABBATH (TO HONOR THE)	WHITE	
SABOTAGE (TO)	GRAY	BLACK
SABOTAGE (NOT TO)	GRAY	WHITE

60

SAD (TO RELEASE)	WHITE	
SAFE (TO BE)	WHITE	
SAFETY (TO LIVE IN)	WHITE	YELLOW
SAIL (OPPORTUNITY TO)	BLUE	WHITE
SALARY (TO GET AN INCREASE)	GREEN	
SALVAGEABLE (TO BE)	WHITE	
SANE (TO BE)	YELLOW	
SAVE (THE ABILITY TO)	BLUE	
SCARCE (TO MAKE YOURSELF)	BROWN	
SECLUSION (TO FIND)	WHITE	PINK
SECRET (TO KEEP)	WHITE	BLUE
SECURITY (TO HAVE)	YELLOW	
SEDUCE (OPPORTUNITY TO)	RED	PINK
SELECTIVE (TO BE)	YELLOW	BLUE
SELF-ASSERTIVE (TO BE)	RED	WHITE
SELF-ASSURANCE (TO HAVE)	BLUE	
SELF-CENTERED (TO BE)	YELLOW	
SELF-CONFIDENCE (TO HAVE)	RED	YELLOW
SELF-CONTAINED (TO BE)	WHITE	
SELF-CONTROL (TO HAVE)	WHITE	BLUE
SELF-DECEPTION (TO RELEASE)	BLACK	WHITE
SELF-DETERMINATION (TO HAVE)	WHITE	
SELF-DETERMINATION (TO KEEP)	BLUE	YELLOW
SELF-ESTEEM (TO HAVE)	ORANGE	
SELFISH (TO RELEASE)	WHITE	BLACK
SENSIBLE (TO BE)	YELLOW	
SENSITIVE (TO BE)	BLUE	
SENSUAL (TO BE)	PINK	RED
SENSUOUS (TO BE)	PINK	RED
SEPARATE (WITHOUT PAIN)	WHITE	YELLOW
SERENE (TO FEEL)	PINK	
SERVICE (TO BE ACCEPTED)	BLUE	YELLOW
SETTLEMENT (TO RECEIVE)	GREEN	
SETTLEMENT (TO REACH A)	YELLOW	GREEN
SEX (TO HAVE)	RED	
SEXUAL (TO BE)	PINK	
SHAKE (TO GET A FAIR)	BLUE	

SHARE (THE ABILITY TO)	BLUE	
SHINE (THE ABILITY TO)	YELLOW	PINK
SHORTAGE (TO RELEASE)	WHITE	ORANGE
SICKNESS (TO RELEASE)	YELLOW	ORANGE
SILENT (TO BE)	WHITE	PINK
SIMPLE (TO BE)	YELLOW	
SING (THE ABILITY TO)	PINK	BLUE
SINGLE (TO BE)	PINK	WHITE
SISTER (GOOD HEALTH)	BLUE	
SISTER (SUCCESS)	GREEN	BLUE
SISTER (INSURE PEACE OF MIND)	YELLOW	GREEN
SKEPTICISM (TO RELEASE)	BLACK	WHITE
SLEEP (THE ABILITY TO)	PINK	
SMART (TO BE)	YELLOW	PURPLE
SMILE (THE ABILITY TO)	BLUE	WHITE
SOCIAL (THE ABILITY TO BE)	WHITE	BLUE
SOPHISTICATED (TO BE)	BLUE	
SORROW (TO RELEASE)	WHITE	PURPLE
SOUTH CAROLINA (SAFETY IN)	BLUE	
SOUTH DAKOTA (SAFETY IN)	YELLOW	
SPACE (TO HAVE)	WHITE	YELLOW
SPEAK (ABILITY TO FREELY)	YELLOW	BLUE
SPECULATE (THE ABILITY TO)	YELLOW	GREEN
SPEECH (TO GIVE A)	BLUE	
SPIRIT (TO HAVE)	PINK	PURPLE
SPOILED (TO BE)	PINK	
SPONTANEOUS (TO BE)	GREEN	
STEP-BROTHER (GOOD HEALTH)	BLUE	GREEN
STEP-BROTHER (SUCCESS)	GREEN	WHITE
STEP-DAUGHTER (GOOD HEALTH)	GREEN	PINK
STEP-DAUGHTER (SUCCESS)	GREEN	PINK
STEP-FATHER (SUCCESS)	GREEN	WHITE
STEP-MOTHER (GOOD HEALTH)	PINK	ORANGE
STEP-MOTHER (SUCCESS)	GREEN	YELLOW
STEP-SISTER (GOOD HEALTH)	GREEN	YELLOW
STEP-SISTER (SUCCESS)	GREEN	PINK
STEP-SON (GOOD HEALTH)	ORANGE	BLUE

STEP-SON (SUCCESS)	BLUE	
STIMULATE (ABILITY TO)	BLACK	GREEN
STOP (TO GET SOMEONE TO)	BLACK	WHITE
STRUCTURE (TO HAVE)	YELLOW	BLUE
SUCCEED (IN LIFE)	GREEN	PINK
SUPER (TO BE)	BLUE	
SUPPORT (TO RECEIVE)	BLUE	GREEN
SURPASS (IN LIFE)	YELLOW	

- T -

TABLOID (TO BE IN A)	YELLOW	GREEN
TABLOID (NOT TO BE IN A)	BLACK	WHITE
TACIT (TO BE)	WHITE	
TACT (TO USE)	PINK	YELLOW
TACTFUL (TO BE)	YELLOW	
TACTLESS (TO BE)	YELLOW	GRAY
TAKE (TO)	BLUE	YELLOW
TAKEOVER (TO)	BLACK	GREEN
TALENT (TO HAVE)	BLUE	YELLOW
TALK (THE ABILITY TO)	YELLOW	
TALK ((R) THE FEAR TO)	PINK	YELLOW
TAN (TO GET A)	BROWN	WHITE
TANGIBLE (TO MAKE)	PINK	ORANGE
TANTALIZE (ABILITY TO)	BLUE	
TANTRUM (TO RELEASE)	YELLOW	
TAOISM (TO UNDERSTAND)	PURPLE	
TAPE (TO MAKE A)	YELLOW	BLUE
TAPE RECORDING (TO MAKE A)	YELLOW	BLUE
TASK (TO STAY ON)	BROWN	YELLOW
TEACH (THE ABILITY TO)	YELLOW	WHITE
TEACHER (ABILITY TO BE)	YELLOW	
TEACHER (PATIENCE TO BE A)	BLUE	YELLOW
TECHNIQUE (TO DEVELOP A NEW)	WHITE	YELLOW
TELEPATHIC (TO BE)	YELLOW	ORANGE
TELEPATHY (ABILITY TO USE)	YELLOW	

63

TELEVISION (TO BE ON THE)	BLUE	WHITE
TEMPER (TO CONTROL)	WHITE	PINK
TEMPTATION (TO RESIST)	WHITE	PURPLE
TENNESSEE (SAFETY IN)	ORANGE	
TERRIBLE (TO RELEASE)	WHITE	
TEST (TO PASS)	YELLOW	
TEST (TO TAKE)	YELLOW	WHITE
TESTIFY (TO)	YELLOW	
TESTIFY (GET SOMEONE ELSE TO)	BLUE	
TEXAS (SAFETY IN)	PINK	
THANK (THE ABILITY TO)	YELLOW	BLUE
THANKFUL (TO BE)	BLUE	PINK
THIEF (TO CATCH A)	RED	WHITE
THIEF (TO CONVICT A)	BLUE	RED
THIN (TO BE)	PINK	BROWN
THINK (ABILITY TO)	YELLOW	
THOUGHTFUL (TO BE)	BLUE	WHITE
THRESHOLD (TO CROSS)	PINK	
THRIFTY (TO BE)	YELLOW	BROWN
THYROID (TO STIMULATE)	YELLOW	
TIME (TO HAVE)	RED	
TIME (TO MAKE)	RED	YELLOW
TOGETHER (TO BE)	PINK	
TOGETHERNESS (TO HAVE)	PINK	WHITE
TOLERANT (TO BE)	BROWN	
TOLERANT (OF OTHERS)	YELLOW	BROWN
TOMORROW (TO SEE)	YELLOW	
TOOTHACHE ((R) PAIN)	WHITE	BLUE
TOUCH (TO BE IN)	YELLOW	
TOY (TO HAVE)	RED	PINK
TRACK (TO BE ON)	BLUE	
TRADE (ABILITY TO)	RED	YELLOW
TRAVEL (THE ABILITY TO)	BLUE	YELLOW
TROUT (TO CATCH)	GREEN	BLUE
TRUE (TO BE)	WHITE	
TRUSTWORTHY (TO BE)	BLUE	WHITE
TYPICAL (TO BE)	WHITE	

64

- U -

UGLY (NOT TO BE)	PINK	
ULTIMATE (THE)	WHITE	
ULTIMATUM (TO GIVE AN)	BLUE	GREEN
ULTRA-AMBITIOUS (TO BE)	GREEN	
ULTRA-CONFIDENT (TO BE)	BLUE	YELLOW
ULTRA-CONSERVATIVE (TO BE)	WHITE	
ULTRA-MODERN (TO BE)	RED	YELLOW
UNATTACHED (TO BE)	YELLOW	
UNAWARE (TO BE)	BROWN	
UNDERSTANDING (TO BE)	YELLOW	
UNEMPLOYMENT (TO RELEASE)	GREEN	
UNMARRIED (TO BE)	WHITE	
UNSELFISH (TO BE)	YELLOW	WHITE
UPHOLD (THE ABILITY TO)	BLUE	GREEN
UPSTANDING (TO BE)	PINK	
UPWARD (TO MOVE)	WHITE	GREEN
USEFUL (TO BE)	GREEN	RED
UTAH (SAFETY IN)	RED	WHITE

- V -

VACANCY (TO HAVE A)	BLUE	
VACATE (TO)	RED	GREEN
VACATION (TO GO ON)	YELLOW	WHITE
VACILLATE (THE ABILITY TO)	PINK	YELLOW
VAGABOND (TO BE A)	BLUE	
VAGUE (TO BE)	GRAY	
VAGUE (NOT TO BE)	YELLOW	
VAIN (TO BE)	PINK	YELLOW
VAIN (NOT TO BE)	PINK	
VALUABLE (TO BE)	GREEN	
VALUABLES (TO HAVE)	GREEN	BROWN
VALUE (TO HAVE)	GREEN	

65

VARIETY (TO HAVE A)	YELLOW	PINK
VEGETARIAN (TO BE A)	GREEN	BROWN
VEHICLE (TO BE A)	PURPLE	
VEHICLE (TO HAVE A)	YELLOW	
VENERABLE (TO BE)	GREEN	PINK
VENERABLE (NOT TO BE)	PINK	
VENTUROUS (TO BE)	YELLOW	RED
VERDICT (A POSITIVE)	BLUE	

- V -

VERMONT (SAFETY IN)	PINK	GREEN
VIBRATION (TO FEEL)	YELLOW	ORANGE
VICTORY (TO HAVE)	BLUE	GREEN
VIEW (TO HAVE A GOOD)	YELLOW	
VINDICATE (TO)	PURPLE	PINK
VINDICTIVE (TO BE)	BLUE	
VIRGINIA (SAFETY IN)	BLUE	
VIRTUE (TO HAVE)	WHITE	
VISION (TO HAVE CLEAR)	YELLOW	
VISITOR (TO HAVE A)	BLUE	

- W -

WAGE (TO EARN A GOOD)	GREEN	
WAIT (THE ABILITY TO)	RED	WHITE
WALK (THE ABILITY TO)	YELLOW	
WANDERLUST (DESIRE TO)	YELLOW	BLUE
WANT (THE ABILITY TO)	BLUE	
WARM (TO BE)	RED	YELLOW
WARM-HEARTED (TO BE)	PINK	
WARN (TO)	RED	YELLOW
WARRANTY (TO GET A)	YELLOW	
WARRIOR (TO BE A)	WHITE	RED
WASH (ABILITY TO)	BLUE	WHITE

WASHINGTON (SAFETY IN)	WHITE	
WASHINGTON, D.C. (SAFETY IN)	RED	
WASTE (NOT TO)	ORANGE	
WATER (TO HAVE PLENTY OF)	BLUE	
WAY (TO KNOW)	BLUE	
WEAK (NOT TO BECOME)	ORANGE	
WEALTHY (TO BE)	GREEN	
WEDDING (TO HAVE A)	PINK	BLUE
WEIGHT (TO REDUCE)	PINK	BROWN
WELCOME (TO BE)	BLUE	WHITE
WEST VIRGINIA (SAFETY IN)	PURPLE	
WHOLESALE (TO BUY)	GREEN	
WIFE (TO HAVE A)	PINK	
WINDFALL (TO HAVE A)	PINK	
WISCONSIN (SAFETY IN)	WHITE	PINK
WISH (TO GET YOUR)	PINK	
WONDERMENT (TO EXPERIENCE)	BLUE	PURPLE
WRITE (THE ABILITY TO)	GREEN	YELLOW
WYOMING (SAFETY IN)	PINK	

- X -

X-RAY (TO GET GOOD RESULTS)	WHITE	
X-RAY ASTRONOMY (UNDERSTAND)	YELLOW	GREEN

- Y -

YACHT (TO BUY)	WHITE	GREEN
YACHT (TO SELL)	YELLOW	RED
YEARN (RELEASE)	RED	YELLOW
YOGA (THE ABILITY TO DO)	ORANGE	
YOUNG (THE ABILITY TO REMAIN)	PINK	ORANGE
YOURSELF (TO BE)	BLUE	
YOURSELF (TO FIND)	YELLOW	BLUE

67

YOUTH (TO MAINTAIN YOUR)	PINK	
YOUTHFUL (TO BE)	BLUE	

- Z -

ZEALOUS (TO BE)	BLUE	PINK
ZEST (TO HAVE)	YELLOW	
ZOO (TO GO TO THE)	GREEN	

STATES

To ensure you that your travel will be productive, giving you the satisfaction that you need to enjoy yourself on any trip, you may wish to light the appropriate candle representing your destination. Light your candle within two days of your trip, sit back, and enjoy your time away.

ALABAMA	BLUE	
ALASKA	RED	WHITE
ARIZONA	YELLOW	
ARKANSAS	YELLOW	
ARKANSAS	YELLOW	
CALIFORNIA	ORANGE	
COLORADO	WHITE	
CONNECTICUT	BLUE	
DELAWARE	WHITE	
FLORIDA	PINK	WHITE
GEORGIA	BLUE	
HAWAII	YELLOW	
IDAHO	GREEN	
ILLINOIS	PINK	BLUE
INDIANA	GREEN	
IOWA	ORANGE	BLUE
KANSAS	WHITE	
KENTUCKY	YELLOW	

68

LOUISIANA	BLUE	
MAINE	WHITE	YELLOW
MARYLAND	GREEN	
MASSACHUSETTS	BLUE	WHITE
MICHIGAN	BLUE	
MINNESOTA	WHITE	
MISSISSIPPI	PINK	
MISSOURI	GREEN	WHITE
MONTANA	BLUE	
NEBRASKA	YELLOW	
NEVADA	GREEN	
NEW HAMPSHIRE	BROWN	
NEW JERSEY	YELLOW	
NEW MEXICO	WHITE	
NEW YORK	BLACK	WHITE
NORTH CAROLINA	BLUE	
NORTH DAKOTA	YELLOW	
OHIO	WHITE	
OKLAHOMA	ORANGE	GREEN
OREGON	WHITE	
PENNSYLVANIA	YELLOW	
RHODE ISLAND	GREEN	
SOUTH CAROLINA	BLUE	
SOUTH DAKOTA	YELLOW	
TENNESSEE	ORANGE	
TEXAS	PINK	
UTAH	RED	WHITE
VERMONT	PINK	GREEN
VIRGINIA	BLUE	
WASHINGTON, D.C.	RED	
WASHINGTON	WHITE	
WEST VIRGINIA	PURPLE	
WISCONSIN	WHITE	PINK
WYOMING	PINK	

To ensure peace of mind in your day to day life, you may wish to light a candle on the first day of each month. The twelve months of the year vibrate at their own unique vibrational rate. This vibrational rate can also be referred to as a vibrational frequency, thus emanating color. When you light a colored candle indicative of the specific month that you are approaching, you will be instilling within yourself an innate sense of balance.

JANUARY	RED	BROWN
FEBRUARY	BLUE	GREEN
MARCH	WHITE	GREEN
APRIL	WHITE	PINK
MAY	RED	YELLOW
JUNE	RED	BLUE
JULY	GREEN	BROWN
AUGUST	RED	GREEN
SEPTEMBER	YELLOW	BLACK
OCTOBER	BLACK	BLUE
NOVEMBER	BROWN	BLACK
DECEMBER	YELLOW	RED

DAYS OF THE WEEK

When anticipating a slow or frustrating day, you may want to light a small candle in the morning to get yourself started. A small stick or votive candle would be ideal in this case. Keep in mind, never leave a small candle unattended. When timing is a problem, you may want to light your candle for the next day at night before you go to sleep. This candle can serve a dual purpose. It will make a great mood setter for the evening, and it will also provide you with a great start for the next day.

MONDAY	WHITE	**TUESDAY**	RED
WEDNESDAY	YELLOW	**THURSDAY**	BLUE

FRIDAY	GREEN	
SUNDAY	ORANGE	

SATURDAY	BROWN

PARTS OF THE BODY

When lighting candles to obtain a wish, let's not forget to include the grandest wish of them all: to be in good physical health, with a strong body and mind. When lighting a candle with the parts of the body in mind, light the appropriate color knowing as the candle is lit that rejuvenating energy will be filling your body, specifically that part of the body that you have lit the candle to stimulate. Light your candles for the parts of the body during the bring time frame in your ephemeral timing guide.

ABDOMEN	BLUE	YELLOW
ARMS	YELLOW	
BACK (LOWER HALF)	GREEN	
BACK (UPPER HALF)	RED	
BRAIN	YELLOW	ORANGE
BUTT	BLUE	
CHEST	YELLOW	
EAR (LEFT)	RED	
EAR (RIGHT)	BLUE	
EYE (MALE, RIGHT)	BLUE	
EYE (MALE, LEFT)	YELLOW	
EYE (FEMALE, RIGHT)	BLUE	
EYE (FEMALE, LEFT)	YELLOW	
FACE	RED	
FEET	RED	YELLOW
FINGERS	GREEN	YELLOW
FOREHEAD	ORANGE	YELLOW
HANDS	YELLOW	BLUE
HEAD	RED	BROWN
HIPS	BROWN	
JAW (LOWER)	GREEN	
JAW (UPPER)	RED	
LEGS (LOWER)	YELLOW	
LEGS (UPPER)	BLUE	

LIPS (LOWER)	BLUE	
LIPS (UPPER)	RED	
MOUTH	GREEN	YELLOW
NAILS	ORANGE	YELLOW
NECK	GREEN	
TOES	BLUE	

WHITE

ABDUCTIONS (RELEASE)	
ABRUPTNESS (TO RELEASE)	
ABSURD (NOT TO BE)	AND PINK
ABUSE (RELEASE)	AND BLUE
ABUSIVE (TO RELEASE)	
ACHES, SHARP (RELEASE, OTHERS)	AND YELLOW
ACHIEVE (TO HELP OTHERS)	AND RED
ADMIRATION (TO HAVE)	AND YELLOW
ADOPTED, SISTER (TO HELP)	AND PINK
ADULTERY (TO DETRACT)	AND BLACK
ADULTERATION (RELEASE)	
ADVENTURES (TO HAVE)	AND BLUE
ADVERSARIES (TO CONCUR)	AND RED
ADVOCATE (TO)	AND YELLOW
AERODYNAMICS (SAFETY IN FLYING)	
AFFECTATIONS (TO HAVE)	AND YELLOW
AIR (PURE)	AND ORANGE
ALCOHOL ((R) ADDICTIONS, OTHERS)	AND BLUE, YELLOW
ALLERGIES (RELEASE)	AND YELLOW
ALOOFNESS ((R) IN OTHERS)	AND YELLOW
ALTERS (PURIFY)	
ALTERCATIONS (RELEASE)	AND YELLOW
ALTRUISM (RELEASE)	AND RED
ALTRUISM (TO BECOME)	
AMBUSHERS (RELEASE)	
ANGER (RELEASE)	AND YELLOW
ANGINA (RELEASE)	AND PINK
ANXIETIES (RELEASE)	AND YELLOW

72

APPRECIATION (TO RECEIVE)
ARRIVALS (TO INSURE)   AND PINK
ATHLETES (TO BECOME)   AND PURPLE
ATTACHMENTS (RELEASE NEGATIVE)   AND RED
ATTITUDE (RELEASE NEGATIVE)   AND RED
ATTITUDES (TOWARDS OTHERS)
ATTORNEYS (TO OBTAIN)   AND YELLOW
AUNT (MOTHER'S, HOME)   AND BROWN

WHITE

BABIES (BROTHERS, HELP)   AND BLUE
BABIES (SISTERS, HELP)   AND PINK
BACHELORS (TO REMAIN)   AND BLUE
BACHELORS (TO OBTAIN)   AND PINK
BALL GAMES (TO PLAY)   AND YELLOW
BANKRUPTCY (TO OBTAIN)
BARGAIN (TO RECEIVE)   AND YELLOW
BASHFULNESS (RELEASE)   AND PINK
BEGINNINGS (NEW)   AND YELLOW
BEREAVEMENT (RELEASE)
BETRAYAL (RELEASE)   AND PINK
BETTERMENT (OF MANKIND)   AND BLUE
BILLS ((R) FEAR)   AND PINK
BIRTH (RELEASE FEAR)   AND PINK
BLACK MAGICIAN ((R) YOURSELF)
BLACKMAIL (RELEASE)   AND YELLOW
BLOATING (RELEASE)   AND YELLOW
BOATING (RIVERS, SUCCESSFUL)   AND BLUE
BOATS (FISHING)   AND BLUE
BOILS (RELEASE)   AND ORANGE
BOREDOM (RELEASE)   AND BLUE
BORROWING (THINGS)

73

BOYFRIENDS (RELEASE)   AND BLUE

BREASTS (TO REDUCE)

BRIDESMAID (TO BE A)   AND YELLOW

BROTHERS (OVER 12 GOOD HEALTH)

BROTHERS (OVER 12 TO PROTECT)   AND PURPLE

BROTHERS (OVER 35 GOOD HEALTH) AND ORANGE

BRUTALITY (RELEASE)

BULLHEADNESS ((R) IN YOURSELF)

BURDEN (RELEASE FOR YOURSELF)   AND YELLOW

BURN OUT ((R) FOR YOURSELF)   AND YELLOW

CABAL (TO BELONG)

CABALS (TO UNDERSTAND)   AND YELLOW

CAFES (TO BUY)   AND GREEN

CALM (TO MAINTAIN)

CAREFREE (TO BE)   AND YELLOW

CARELESSNESS (RELEASE)

CARPENTER (TO FIND)   AND GREEN

CASTAWAY (TO FIND)   AND YELLOW

CASUALTIES (TO LESSEN)

CELEBRITY (TO BECOME)   AND YELLOW

CELIBACY (TO OBTAIN)

CELIBACY (RELEASE)   AND RED

CELIBATE (TO MAINTAIN)   AND YELLOW

CHANCE (TO HAVE A)   AND BLUE

CHANT (TO)

CHARITY (TO GIVE)

COLORADO (SAFETY IN)

COMBAT (RELEASE)

COMMISERATE (RELEASE)   AND BLUE

CONSPIRACIES (RELEASE)   AND YELLOW

CONTROL (RELEASE)   AND YELLOW

CONVALESCENCE (SPEEDY)   AND YELLOW

COUNTRY HOUSE (TO OBTAIN)   AND GREEN

COUSIN (MOTHER'S SIDE BOY,LUCK) AND YELLOW

COVERAGE (TO GET)   AND GRAY

CRASH (RELEASE FEAR OF)

CREDIBILITY (TO HAVE)

DAMAGE (RELEASE)

DARK (RELEASE FEAR OF)

DEATH (ABILITY TO DEAL WITH)

DELAWARE (SAFETY IN)

DELUSION (DISPEL)   AND YELLOW

DEMAND (ABILITY TO)   AND PINK

DEMOTE (ABILITY TO)   AND YELLOW

DEPRESSION (RELEASE YOURSELF)   AND BLUE

DEPENDABILITY (FOR YOURSELF)

DESPERATE ((R) THE NEED TO BE)

EARLY (TO BE)   AND RED

EARTHQUAKE (SAFETY FROM)   AND PURPLE

EFFORTLESS (TO OBTAIN)   AND GREEN

EMOTION (FUNCTIONAL)   AND PINK

EMPHASIS (TO PLACE)

ENCHANT (TO)   AND PINK

ENVIRONMENT (POSITIVE)

ERADICATE (TO)   AND BLACK

ESPECIAL (TO BECOME)   AND YELLOW

EVASIVE (THE ABILITY TO BE)   AND YELLOW

EXCEPTION (TO LIVE BY)

FACE (THE ABILITY TO)

FACE-VALUE (TO SEE THINGS AT)   AND BLUE

FACTORY (TO SELL)   AND GREEN

FAIL (SECURITY AGAINST)   AND BLACK

FAIL-SAFE (TO BE)

FAMILY (TO HAVE A)   AND YELLOW

FATALIST (RELEASE)   AND YELLOW

FATIGUE (RELEASE)   AND BLACK

FAVOR (TO FIND)

FIGHT ((R) THE NEED TO)   AND YELLOW

FIGHT (TO AVOID)

FIND (TO)

FIGHT (TO TAKE A)   AND BLUE

FORBID (TO)   AND BLACK

FORGIVE (THE ABILITY TO)

FRATERNITY (TO BELONG)   AND YELLOW

FREE (TO GET)

GENIUS (TO BECOME)   AND YELLOW

GIFT (TO GIVE)   AND YELLOW

GOD (TO WORSHIP)

GOOD (TO BE)

GOSSIP (TO STOP)   AND BLACK

GRACEFUL (TO BE)   AND PINK

GROW (TO STOP)

HAMPER (TO OTHERS)   AND BROWN

HAPPEN (TO MAKE IT)   AND RED

HATE (TO RELEASE)   AND BLACK

HAUNT (TO RELEASE)   AND BLACK, PURPLE

HAVOC (TO RELEASE)   AND YELLOW

HEADACHE (TO RELEASE)   AND GRAY

HELPFUL (TO BE)   AND PINK

HIDE (THE ABILITY TO)

HOST (TO BE A GOOD)   AND BLUE

HOSTILITY (TO RELEASE)

HUMOR (TO HAVE)   AND YELLOW

ICONOCLASM (TO MAINTAIN)   AND PURPLE

IGNORAMUS ((R) THOSE WHO ARE)   AND BLACK

ILLUSION (TO LIVE AN)   AND GRAY

IMBUE (ABILITY TO)   AND PURPLE

IMMORTALITY (TO HAVE)   AND PURPLE

IMPART (TO OTHERS)

IMPROVE (TO)   AND YELLOW

IMPULSIVENESS (RELEASE)   AND RED

INCUBUS (RELEASE)

INDIVIDUALISTIC (TO BE)

INFERIORITY COMPLEX (RELEASE) AND PURPLE

INFLATION (TO REDUCE)   AND GREEN

JAIL (TO STAY OUT)   AND PURPLE

JEALOUSY (TO RELEASE)   AND YELLOW
JOIN (TO)
KANSAS (SAFETY IN)
KARMA (POSITIVE)
MAIL (TO RECEIVE)
MAINE (SAFETY IN)   AND YELLOW
MALEFIC (TO RELEASE)
MANEUVER (THE ABILITY TO)   AND BROWN
MIND-READER (ABILITY TO BE A) AND RED
MINNESOTA (SAFETY IN)
NEAT (TO BE)
NEGLIGENCE (RELEASE)   AND BLUE
NEIGHBOR (TO GET ALONG WITH) AND BLUE
NEPHEW (GOOD HEALTH)
NERVOUS BREAKDOWN (RELEASE) AND YELLOW
NEW MEXICO (SAFETY IN)
NONDESCRIPT (TO BE)
OBLIVION (TO DISAPPEAR INTO) AND YELLOW
OBSCENITY (TO RELEASE)
OBSTACLE (TO RELEASE)   AND GREEN
ODOR (TO RELEASE)
OFFICIAL (TO BE AN)   AND YELLOW
OHIO (SAFETY IN)
OPINION (TO ACCEPT OTHERS) AND YELLOW
OPPORTUNIST (NOT TO BE AN) AND BROWN
OREGON (SAFETY IN)
ORIGINAL (TO BE)   AND BLUE
ORTHODOX (TO BE)
OUTRAGE ((R) THE NEED TO BE) AND BLACK
PANTHEON (TO UNDERSTAND) AND YELLOW
PARADISE (TO LIVE A LIFE OF) AND BLUE
PASSIVE (TO BE)   AND BLUE
PERPLEXITY (TO RELEASE)
PERSUASIVE (TO BE)   AND YELLOW
POLLUTION (TO STOP)

77

POLTERGEIST (RID YOURSELF)   AND PURPLE

POTENTIAL (TO HAVE)

POWERFUL (TO BE)   AND RED

QUALM (TO RELEASE)   AND RED

QUARREL ((R) THE NEED TO)

QUIET (TO HAVE SOME)

RADIANT (TO BE)

RADICAL (NOT TO BE)   AND BROWN

RECREATE (CHANCE TO)   AND BLUE

REDEEM (ONESELF)

REFLECT (ABILITY TO)   AND PINK

RELIGION (TO BELIEVE)

REST (TO HAVE SOME)

RETURN (THE ABILITY TO)

RETURN (THE CHANCE TO)   AND BLUE

RIGHTEOUS (TO BE)   AND PURPLE

SABBATH (TO HONOR THE)

SAD (TO RELEASE)

SAFE (TO BE)

SAFETY (TO LIVE IN)   AND YELLOW

SALVAGEABLE (TO BE)

SECLUSION (TO FIND)   AND PINK

SECRET (TO KEEP)   AND BLUE

SELF-CONTAINED (TO BE)

SELF-CONTROL (TO HAVE)   AND BLUE

SELF-DETERMINATION (TO HAVE)

SELFISH (TO RELEASE)   AND BLACK

SEPARATE (WITHOUT PAIN)   AND YELLOW

SHORTAGE (TO RELEASE)   AND ORANGE

SILENT (TO BE)   AND PINK

SOCIAL (ABILITY TO BE)   AND BLUE

SORROW (TO RELEASE)   AND PURPLE

SPACE (TO HAVE)   AND YELLOW

STEP-FATHER (GOOD HEALTH)   AND YELLOW

TACIT (TO BE)

78

TECHNIQUE (TO DEVELOP A NEW)   AND YELLOW
TEMPER (TO CONTROL)   AND PINK
TEMPTATION (TO RESIST)   AND PURPLE
TERRIBLE (TO RELEASE)
TOOTHACHE ((R) PAIN)   AND BLUE
TRUE (TO BE)
TYPICAL (TO BE)
ULTIMATE (THE)
ULTRA-CONSERVATIVE (TO BE)
UNMARRIED (TO BE)
UPWARD (TO MOVE)   AND GREEN
VIRTUE (TO HAVE)
WARRIOR (TO BE)   AND RED
WASHINGTON (SAFETY IN)
WISCONSIN (SAFETY)   AND PINK
X-RAY (TO GET GOOD RESULTS)
YACHT (TO BUY)   AND GREEN

BLUE

ABNORMAL BEHAVIOR (RELEASE)   AND YELLOW
ABNORMALITIES (RELEASE)   AND WHITE
ABRASIONS (RELEASE PAIN)
ACADEMIC (FREEDOM)   AND YELLOW
ACCEDE (TO)
ACCUMULATION (PHYSICAL)   AND GREEN
ACHES, DULL (RELEASE YOUR OWN)
ACHES, DULL (RELEASE OTHERS)   AND WHITE
ACREAGE (TO OBTAIN)   AND GREEN
ACTIVATION (MECHANICAL)   AND RED
ACTORS/ACTRESSES (TO PERFECT)   AND RED
ADAPTABILITY (TO HAVE)   AND YELLOW
ADDICTS (RELEASE, YOURSELF)   AND WHITE, ORANGE

79

ADJOURNMENTS (TO)

ADOLESCENCE (TO KEEP CALM)

ADOPTED, CHILDREN (PROTECT)   AND PURPLE

ADOPTION (ABILITY TO)   AND WHITE, PINK

ADORNMENT (TO HAVE)   AND PURPLE

ADRENAL GLANDS (TO STIMULATE)

ADULTERY (TO COMMIT)   AND YELLOW

ADVANCEMENTS (PERSONAL)

AFFLUENT (TO BE)

AGGRESSORS (TO BE)   AND WHITE

AILMENTS CHRONIC (RELEASE)   AND WHITE, ORANGE

AIRCRAFT (REPAIR)   AND YELLOW

AIR DROP (MEDICINE)   AND WHITE

AIRFIELD (SAFETY)   AND WHITE

AIR FLOW (NATURAL)   AND ORANGE

AIRLIFT (TO SECURE)   AND PURPLE

ALABAMA (SAFETY IN)

ALIENATION (OF YOURSELF)

ALIENATION (OF OTHERS)   AND YELLOW, WHITE

ALLIANCES (SOCIAL)   AND YELLOW

ALTER EGO (HEALTHY)   AND WHITE

ALTERATION (TO ACHIEVE)

APARTMENT (TO OBTAIN)

ATHLETES (TO OBTAIN)   AND PURPLE

AUNT (MOTHER'S SIDE, LEGACIES)   AND GREEN

AUTHORS (TO BECOME)   AND GREEN

AUTOMOBILES (TO PURCHASE)   AND YELLOW

AWARDS (TO RECEIVE)

BABIES (BOYS)

BABIES (BROTHERS, HOME)   AND YELLOW

BABY SISTERS (TO FIND)

BALANCE (TO BE IN)

BALDNESS (RELEASE)

BALDNESS (TO STOP)   AND ORANGE

BALL GAMES (TO WIN)

BANISHMENT (OF YOURSELF)   AND WHITE

BARGAIN (TO GIVE)

BELIEVERS (OBTAIN)

BELITTLING (RELEASE YOURSELF)   AND YELLOW

BI-SEXUALITY (ABILITY TO RELATE)

BI-SEXUALITY (WITHIN YOURSELF) AND WHITE

BLESSINGS (TO HAVE)

BOATING (OPEN WATER, SUCCESSFUL)

BODY (PHYSICAL, HEALTH)   AND ORANGE

BOOKS (TO SELL)   AND YELLOW

BREAKAGE (RELEASE)

BREASTS (TO ENLARGE)   AND ORANGE

BREATH (FRESH)   AND WHITE

BREEDING (TO BREED DOGS)

BREEDING (TO BREED CATTLE)   AND BROWN

BRIDEGROOM (TO BE A)   AND WHITE

BRIEF (TO BE)

BROTHERS (OVER 12, TO HELP)

BROTHERS-IN-LAW (TO PROTECT) AND PURPLE

BROTHERS-IN-LAW (GOOD HEALTH) AND ORANGE

BUSINESS (TO BUILD)

BUSINESS (TO BUY)   AND GREEN

CABINET MAKER (TO FINISH A JOB)

CAMP (TO GO TO)

CAPTIVATE (TO)   AND WHITE

CAPTIVITY (RELEASE)

CAR (TO FIX)

CASTING (FISHING SUCCESSFUL)

CASUAL (TO BE)

CAUTION (TO ACT WITH)   AND WHITE

CAUTIOUS (TO BE)   AND WHITE

CAVE-IN (TO PREVENT)

CEASE-FIRE (TO HAVE A)   AND PINK

CELEBRATE (TO)   AND PINK

CERTIFICATION (TO OBTAIN)   AND YELLOW

81

CHALLENGE (TO WIN)
CHARACTER (TO OBTAIN)   AND YELLOW
CHARITY (TO RECEIVE)   AND GREEN
COFFEE (RELEASE ADDICTION)   AND RED
COMMUNICATION (CONTINUING)   AND YELLOW
COMPULSION (RELEASE)   AND BROWN
CONCESSION (ABILITY TO MAKE)
CONNECTICUT (SAFETY IN)
CONSCIOUSNESS (EXPANSION)
CONSTIPATION (RELEASE)   AND ORANGE
CONTEST (TO WIN)   AND WHITE
CONVENTION (TO ATTEND)   AND WHITE
CONVERSATION ((R) SHYNESS)   AND YELLOW
CONVICTION (RELEASE)   AND PURPLE
COOK (TO LEARN TO)   AND YELLOW
COOPERATE (ABILITY TO)   AND GREEN
COUNTRY (TO LIVE IN THE)
COURAGE (TO HAVE)   AND WHITE
COURAGEOUS (TO BE)
COUSIN (FATHER'S SIDE, BOY)
COUSIN (MOTHER'S SIDE, BOY)   AND YELLOW
CRAWL (LEARN TO)
CRAZY (RELEASE NEED TO BE)   AND YELLOW
CUSTODY (TO OBTAIN)
DAD (TO FIND)   AND GREEN
DAD (TO INSURE GOOD HEALTH)   AND GRAY
DANCE (ABILITY TO)
DANCER (TO BECOME A)   AND PINK
DATE (TO HAVE A)   AND YELLOW
DEBIT (TO DECREASE)
DELAY (RELEASE)
DEPENDENCY (FOR YOURSELF)   AND GREEN
DEPICT (ABILITY TO)
DESIRE (ABILITY TO OBTAIN)   AND ORANGE
DESPONDENT (RELEASE IN OTHERS) AND YELLOW

EDGE (TO LIVE ON THE)   AND GRAY
ELECTION (TO WIN)   AND WHITE
ELEGANT (TO BE)
EMBRYO (HEALTHY)   AND WHITE
EMERALD (TO OWN)   AND GREEN
EMPOWER (TO)
ENFORCE (THE ABILITY TO)   AND RED
ESCAPE (ABILITY TO)   AND WHITE
EXAM (TO PASS)   AND YELLOW
EXCESS (TO HAVE, GOOD HEALTHY) AND ORANGE
EXCESS (AMOUNTS OF FRIENDS)
EXEMPT (TO BE)
EXTRA (TO HAVE)   AND GREEN
FACILITATE (THE ABILITY TO)
FAINT-HEARTED (RELEASE)   AND WHITE
FAIR (TO BE)
FAMILY (TO HAVE A CLOSE)
FANCY (TO BE)
FATHER (INSURE GOOD HEALTH)
FATHER-IN-LAW (GOOD HEALTH)   AND WHITE
FEED (THE ABILITY TO)
FEELINGS (TO HAVE)
FERTILITY (TO ENHANCE)
FIANCÉ (TO HAVE A)
FIANCEE (TO BE A)   AND WHITE
FIGUREHEAD (TO BE A)   AND GRAY
FILM (TO BE IN A)   AND GREEN
FLAMBOYANT (TO BECOME)   AND GREEN
FLEXIBLE (TO BE)   AND YELLOW
FORWARD (TO GO)   AND WHITE
FREEDOM (TO HAVE)
FREELANCE (TO)   AND GREEN
FUN (TO HAVE)
GATHER (TO)   AND YELLOW
GEORGIA (SAFETY IN)

83

GIFT (TO RECEIVE)	AND YELLOW
GO BEHIND (OTHERS)	AND BROWN
GODCHILD (BOY)	
GODCHILD (BOY, HEALTHY)	AND ORANGE
GODCHILD (BOY, SAFETY)	AND WHITE
GO-GETTER (TO BE A)	AND GREEN
GOLDEN RULE (TO LIVE BY)	
GRANDEUR (TO LIVE A LIFE OF)	AND YELLOW
GUESTS (TO HAVE)	
HEADSTRONG (TO BE)	
HEALTH (GOOD)	AND ORANGE
HELP (TO GET)	
HIDE AWAY (TO FIND A)	AND YELLOW
HOME (TO HAVE A)	AND GREEN
HONEST (TO BE)	
HOUSE (TO HAVE A)	
HUMANE (ABILITY TO BE)	AND WHITE
HUNGER (RELEASE)	
HYPERACTIVITY (RELEASE)	AND WHITE
HYSTERIA (TO CONTROL)	
IDEALISM (ABILITY TOWARDS)	
IDENTITY (TO MAINTAIN ONES')	
IDOLIZE (THE ABILITY TO)	AND YELLOW
ILLNESS (RELEASE)	AND ORANGE
IMAGINATIVE (TO BE)	AND YELLOW
IMBALANCE (TO RELEASE)	
IMMACULATELY (TO LIVE)	AND PURPLE
IMMEDIATELY (TO HAVE)	
IMPACT (TO MAKE AN)	AND BLACK
IMPARTIAL (TO BE)	AND PINK
INCARNATE (THE ABILITY TO BE)	AND GREEN
INCORRIGIBLE ((R) BEHAVIOR)	
INFORMER (TO FIND AN)	AND YELLOW
INTELLECTUAL (TO BE)	
ISOLATE (TO)	

84

JOB (TO FIND)
JOYFUL (TO BE)
JUDGMENT (TO RELEASE)
KNOW (ABILITY TO)   AND YELLOW
KNOWN (TO BE)
LACK (TO RELEASE)
LACKING (TO RELEASE)   AND GREEN
LEASE (TO RENEW)
LEISURE (TIME)   AND WHITE
LESSON (TO LEARN)   AND YELLOW
LOSS (RELEASE)
LOUISIANA (SAFETY IN)
LUXURY (TO HAVE)   AND GREEN
LUXURY (TO LIVE A LIFE OF)   AND PINK
MACHO (TO BE)   AND BLACK
MANIFEST (ABILITY TO)   AND PURPLE
MANNERED (WELL)   AND GREEN
MASSACHUSETTS (SAFETY IN)   AND WHITE
MELLOW (TO BE)
MICHIGAN (SAFETY IN)
MISFORTUNE (RELEASE)
MONTANA (SAFETY IN)
MOOD (TO BE IN A GOOD)
MORTGAGE (TO OWN)   AND GREEN
MOTHER (GOOD HEALTH)   AND PINK
MOTHER-IN-LAW (GOOD HEALTH)   AND YELLOW
MOVE (TO)   AND YELLOW
MUSICIAN (TO BE A)   AND ORANGE
NARROW-MINDED (RELEASE)
NEPOTISM (RELEASE)
NORMAL (TO BE)
NORTH CAROLINA (SAFETY IN)
OBEDIENT (TO BE)   AND WHITE
OBJECTIVE (TO BE)   AND WHITE
OBJECTIVITY (TO HAVE)   AND GREEN

85

OCEAN (TO GO TO)

OCEAN (TO MOVE TO)   AND GREEN

OFFICE (TO HAVE AN)   AND YELLOW

OLD AGE (PEACEFUL)

OPEN-MINDED (TO BE)

OPERATION (SUCCESSFUL)   AND ORANGE

OPERATIVE (TO BE)

OPPORTUNITY (TO HAVE AN)

OPPRESSION (TO RELEASE)   AND ORANGE

OPTION (TO HAVE)

ORDER (TO HAVE)

ORDERLY (TO BE)   AND WHITE

OUTCOME (A PEACEFUL)

OWN (TO)

PACE (YOURSELF)

PAIN (TO RELEASE)   AND ORANGE

PAL (TO BE A)

PAPERWORK (TO FINISH)

PARTAKE (THE ABILITY TO)

PARTICIPANT (TO BE A)

PARTNER (TO BE A GOOD)   AND YELLOW

PARTY (TO HAVE A GOOD TIME)   AND YELLOW

PAYCHECK (TO RECEIVE A)   AND GREEN

PEACEFUL (TO BE)

PERFORM (THE ABILITY TO)

PERSONALITY (TO HAVE A GOOD) AND YELLOW

PHYSICAL (TO BE)   AND RED

PLENTY (TO HAVE)   AND GREEN

POLICY (TO LIVE UP TO)

POLITICAL (TO BE)

POSITIVE (TO BE)

PRACTICAL (TO BE)

PROMOTION (TO GET)   AND WHITE

PURPOSE (TO SEE YOUR OWN)

QUALIFY (TO)

86

QUEST (TO HAVE A)	AND YELLOW
QUIT (ABILITY TO)	AND PURPLE
RABBLE-ROUSER (NOT BE A)	AND YELLOW
RAISE (TO GET A)	AND GREEN
RATE (TO RAISE)	AND RED
RECOMMENDATION (FAVORABLE)	
RECONSIDER (ABILITY TO)	
RECREATE (ABILITY TO)	
REFORM (TO)	
REPRESENTATION (TO HAVE)	
REPRODUCE (ABILITY TO)	
SAIL (OPPORTUNITY TO)	AND WHITE
SAVE (THE ABILITY TO)	
SELF-ASSURANCE (TO HAVE)	
SELF-DETERMINATION (TO KEEP)	AND YELLOW
SENSITIVE (TO BE)	
SERVICE (TO BE ACCEPTED)	AND YELLOW
SHAKE (TO GET A FAIR)	
SHARE (THE ABILITY TO)	
SISTER (GOOD HEALTH)	
SMILE (THE ABILITY TO)	AND WHITE
SOPHISTICATED (TO BE)	
SOUTH CAROLINA (SAFETY IN)	
SPEECH (TO GIVE A)	
STEP-BROTHER (GOOD HEALTH)	AND GREEN
STEP-SON (SUCCESS)	
SUPER (TO BE)	
SUPPORT (TO RECEIVE)	AND GREEN
TAKE (TO)	AND YELLOW
TALENT (TO HAVE)	AND YELLOW
TANTALIZE (ABILITY TO)	
TEACHER (PATIENCE TO BE A)	AND YELLOW
TELEVISION (TO BE ON)	AND WHITE
TESTIFY (GET SOMEONE ELSE TO)	
THANKFUL (TO BE)	AND PINK

BLUE

THIEF (TO CONVICT A)	AND RED
THOUGHTFUL (TO BE)	AND WHITE
TRACK (TO BE ON)	
TRAVEL (THE ABILITY TO)	AND YELLOW
TRUSTWORTHY (TO BE)	AND WHITE
ULTIMATUM (TO GIVE AN)	AND GREEN
ULTRA-CONFIDENT (TO BE)	AND YELLOW
UPHOLD (THE ABILITY TO)	AND GREEN
VACANCY (TO HAVE A)	
VAGABOND (TO BE A)	
VERDICT (A POSITIVE)	
VICTORY (TO HAVE)	AND GREEN
VINDICTIVE (TO BE)	
VIRGINIA (SAFETY IN)	
VISITOR (TO HAVE A)	
WANT (THE ABILITY TO)	
WARM (TO BE)	
WASH (ABILITY TO)	AND WHITE
WATER (TO HAVE PLENTY)	
WAY (TO KNOW THE)	
WELCOME (TO BE)	AND WHITE
WONDERMENT (TO EXPERIENCE)	AND PURPLE
YOURSELF (TO BE)	
YOUTHFUL (TO BE)	
ZEALOUS (TO BE)	AND PINK

BLACK

AFFIDAVITS (DISHONEST)	AND BROWN, YELLOW
BLACK MAGICIAN (TO BECOME)	AND WHITE
CONTROVERSY (RELEASE)	AND WHITE
COWARDICE (RELEASE)	AND WHITE
DEMON (TO RELEASE)	AND WHITE

88

DEMONIC (TO DISPEL)	AND WHITE
DEPLORABLE ((R) ACTS BY YOU)	AND WHITE
DEPORT ((R) CONDITIONS)	AND WHITE
FALSE (TO BE)	AND YELLOW
FANTASY (RELEASE)	AND WHITE
FEUD (RELEASE)	AND WHITE
GIRLFRIEND (TO GET RID OF)	AND WHITE
GIVE UP (THE ABILITY TO)	AND YELLOW
GLOOM (RELEASE)	AND WHITE
GREED (RELEASE)	AND YELLOW
GUILTY (TO BE FOUND)	
HATE (THE ABILITY TO)	AND BROWN
HATE (RELEASE THE NEED TO)	AND WHITE
IMMOBILE (RELEASE)	AND GRAY
INABILITY (RELEASE)	AND WHITE
NEW YORK (SAFETY IN)	AND WHITE
POSSESSIVE (RELEASE THE NEED)	AND WHITE
RESPONSIBLE (TO BE)	AND WHITE
SELF-DECEPTION (TO RELEASE)	AND WHITE
SKEPTICISM (TO RELEASE)	AND WHITE
STIMULATE (ABILITY TO)	AND GREEN
STOP (TO GET SOMEONE TO)	AND WHITE
TABLOID (NOT TO BE IN A)	AND WHITE
TAKEOVER (ABILITY TO)	AND GREEN

ORANGE

ABORTIONS (SAFE)	AND YELLOW
ACHIEVE (FOR YOURSELF)	AND RED
ACREAGE (TO RETAIN)	AND BLUE
AD WRITER (TO BECOME)	AND YELLOW
ALERTNESS (PHYSICAL)	

89

ALLIANCES (COVERT)

BACK (RELEASE, PAIN)

BACTERIA (RELEASE)   AND BLUE

BELIEF SYSTEM (STRENGTHEN)   AND BLUE

BET (RELEASE THE NEED TO)   AND PURPLE

BITES (ANIMAL, (R) INFECTION)

BITES (INSECT, (R) INFECTION)

BITES (HUMAN, (R) INFECTION)

BLEMISHES, SKIN (RELEASE)   AND BLUE

BREAST (INSURE HEALTHY)   AND WHITE

BRUISES (RELEASE)

CALIFORNIA (SAFETY IN)

CANCER (RELEASE CARCINOMA)   AND BLUE

CAT (TO INSURE GOOD HEALTH)   AND BROWN

CONTROL (TO OBTAIN)   AND WHITE

CONTUSION (RELEASE)

COOPERATION (TO OBTAIN)   AND GREEN

COUSIN (MOTHER SIDE BOY HEALTH)AND BLUE

CRAMP (RELEASE)

CREDIT CARD (TO OBTAIN)   AND BROWN

DAUGHTER (GOOD HEALTH)

ENLIGHTEN (TO BECOME)   AND YELLOW

EXCESS (AMOUNTS OF PATIENTS)

FACELIFT (SUCCESSFUL)   AND PINK

FEVER (LOWER)

FRATERNITY (TO JOIN)

GALLSTONE (RELEASE)

HAIR (TO STRENGTHEN)

HALLUCINATION (TO RELEASE)   AND YELLOW

HERMIT (TO LIVE LIKE A)   AND YELLOW

HYPERTENSION (RELEASE)

IMMACULATE (TO BE)   AND YELLOW

IMMUNE (TO BE)   AND YELLOW

90

IMPOTENT (GUARD AGAINST)	AND BLUE
INDESTRUCTIBLE (TO BE)	AND BLUE
INTUITION (TO HAVE)	
IOWA (SAFETY IN)	AND BLUE
JOY (TO GIVE)	AND YELLOW
LACERATION (LESS PAIN)	AND BLUE
LANDLORD (TO BE A)	
LAZINESS (RELEASE)	
NERVOUS SYSTEM (STRENGTHEN)	
NEUROSIS (RELEASE)	
NEUROTIC ((R) THE NEED TO BE)	AND WHITE
NICOTINE (RELEASE, ADDICTION)	AND BROWN
OKLAHOMA (SAFETY IN)	AND GREEN
PARASITE (RELEASE)	
PERCEPTIVE (TO BE)	
RECOVER (THE ABILITY TO)	AND BLUE
SELF-ESTEEM (TO HAVE)	
STEP-SON (GOOD HEALTH)	AND BLUE
TENNESSEE (SAFETY IN)	
WASTE (NOT TO)	
WEAK (NOT TO BECOME)	
YOGA (THE ABILITY TO DO)	

RED

ABANDON (TO)	
ABRUPT (TO BE)	
ABSURD (TO BE)	
ACCELERATION (PHYSICAL)	AND YELLOW
ACTION (TO INSURE)	
ACTIVATION (MENTAL)	AND YELLOW
ACTIVE (TO BE)	AND YELLOW

ACTIVITY (PHYSICAL)	AND YELLOW
ADJUSTMENTS (PHYSICAL)	AND YELLOW
ALASKA (SAFETY IN)	AND WHITE
ALCOHOL ((R) OWN ADDICTION)	AND YELLOW
ALTER EGO (RELEASE)	AND WHITE
APPREHENSION (RELEASE) AND WHITE	
ASSAULT (RELEASE)	AND WHITE
ATTACHMENTS (RELEASE)	AND PINK
BOLD (TO BE)	
BOUNDARIES (TO RELEASE)	AND YELLOW
BRAVERY (TO OBTAIN)	AND YELLOW
BRAVERY (TO SECURE)	AND WHITE
BROKERS (TO EXPOSE)	AND WHITE
CONFRONT (STRENGTH TO)	AND WHITE
COPULATE (ABILITY TO)	
ENDURE (THE ABILITY TO)	AND BLUE
ENERGY (TO OBTAIN)	
ENERGY (TO USE)	AND WHITE
EXPLORE (FREEDOM TO)	AND YELLOW
FALLOUT (TO GUARD AGAINST)	AND YELLOW
FAST (TO BE)	
FEAR (RELEASE)	AND WHITE
FEELINGS (PASSIONATE)	AND PINK
FIGHT (ABILITY TO)	
FRAUD (TO RELEASE)	AND WHITE
FRUSTRATION (RELEASE)	AND YELLOW
HASTY (TO BE)	
HOSTAGE (RELEASE)	AND WHITE
HURRY (TO BE IN A)	
HURRY (TO LIVE IN A)	AND WHITE
IDLE (TO RELEASE)	AND BLUE
IMPULSIVE (TO BE)	
INACTIVE (RELEASE)	
MELANCHOLIA (TO RELEASE)	AND WHITE
OUTGOING (TO BE)	AND WHITE

92

OUTLANDISH (TO BE)	AND YELLOW
OVERSLEEP ((R) THE NEED TO)	AND WHITE
PASSIONATE (TO BE)	
POWER (TO HAVE)	
PREVENT (THE ABILITY TO)	AND WHITE
PROJECT (ABILITY TO FINISH)	AND BLUE
QUICK (T0 D0)	
RANK (TO GAIN)	
SEDUCE (OPPORTUNITY TO)	AND PINK
SELF-ASSERTIVE (TO BE)	AND WHITE
SELF-CONFIDENCE (TO HAVE)	AND YELLOW
SEX (TO HAVE)	
THIEF (TO CATCH A)	AND WHITE
TIME (TO HAVE)	
TIME (TO MAKE)	AND YELLOW
TOY (TO HAVE)	AND PINK
TRADE (ABILITY TO)	AND YELLOW
ULTRA-MODERN (TO BE)	AND YELLOW
UTAH (SAFETY IN)	AND WHITE
VACATE (TO)	AND GREEN
WAIT (THE ABILITY TO)	AND WHITE
WARN (TO)	AND YELLOW
WASHINGTON, D.C. (SAFETY IN)	
YEARN (RELEASE)	AND YELLOW

GREEN

ABUNDANCE (TO HAVE AN)	AND YELLOW
ADJUSTERS (FAVOR/OTHERS)	
ADVANCEMENTS (BUSINESS)	AND BLUE
ADVERTISING (SUCCESS)	AND YELLOW
AGENCIES (TO GAIN EMPLOYMENT)	
AGREEMENTS (WRITTEN)	AND BLUE

93

GREEN

AGREEMENTS (VERBAL)	AND YELLOW
ALIMONY (TO RECEIVE)	
AUGUST (POSITIVE)	
AUNT (FATHER'S SIDE, MONEY)	
AUNT (FATHER'S SIDE, LEGACIES)	AND BLUE
AUNT (MOTHER'S SIDE, MONEY)	AND WHITE
BAIL (TO OBTAIN)	
BARBER (TO BE SUCCESSFUL)	
BENEFITS (TO OBTAIN)	
BILLS (THE ABILITY TO PAY)	AND YELLOW
BONDS (TO OBTAIN)	
BORROWING (MONEY)	
BUDGETS (TO MAINTAIN)	AND WHITE
BUILD (A HOUSE, SUCCESSFULLY)	AND BROWN
BUSINESS (INCREASE)	
CANCER (RELEASE MELANOMA)	AND BLUE
CAREER (TO IMPROVE)	
CAR (TO SELL)	
CASH (TO MAKE)	AND YELLOW
CASINOS (TO VISIT)	
CASINOS (TO WIN)	AND PURPLE
CHECK (TO RECEIVE)	
COLLECT (MONEY)	
CONTRACTS (FAVORABLE)	
COUNTRY HOUSE (TO SELL)	AND YELLOW
COUSIN (FATHER SIDE, BOY,LUCK)	
COUSIN (FATHER SIDE,BOY,HEALTH)	AND YELLOW
COUSIN (FATHER SIDE, GIRL LUCK)	AND PINK
COUSIN (MOTHER SIDE, GIRL LUCK)	AND YELLOW
CREDIT (TO HAVE)	
CREDITABLE (TO BE)	
CREDIT CARD (TO RETAIN)	AND YELLOW
CUSTODY (TO RETAIN)	AND YELLOW
CUSTOMER (TO ATTRACT)	
DAUGHTER (MONEY SUCCESS)	AND YELLOW

94

DEBT (ABILITY TO PAY)
DEPOSIT (TO RECEIVE)
DEPARTURE (SUCCESSFUL)   AND PINK
EARN (THE ABILITY TO)   AND BROWN
ECONOMY (TO STIMULATE)   AND YELLOW
ELIGIBLE (TO BECOME)
EMERALD (TO BUY)   AND YELLOW
ENDOWMENTS (TO RECEIVE)
ETHICAL (TO BE)
EVIDENCE (TO OBTAIN)   AND GRAY
FACTORY (TO BUILD)   AND BLUE
FARM (TO HAVE A)
FARMER (TO BE A)   AND BROWN
FATHER (INSURE SUCCESS)   AND BLUE
FATHER-IN-LAW (SUCCESS)   AND WHITE
FELLOWSHIP (TO HAVE)   AND BLUE
FINALIZE (A BUSINESS DEAL)   AND YELLOW
FINANCES (TO INCREASE)
FIT (TO BECOME)   AND BLUE
FLOURISH (THE ABILITY TO)   AND PURPLE
FRANCHISE (TO BUY)
GAIN (THE ABILITY TO)   AND WHITE
GET (TO OBTAIN)
GIVE (THE ABILITY TO)   AND PINK
GO (TO)
GO ALONG (TO)   AND YELLOW
GODSPEED (TO DO WITH)   AND BLUE
GOLF (TO LEARN TO PLAY)
GROW (TO)   AND WHITE
GUARANTEE (TO GET A)   AND BLUE
HARVEST (TO HAVE A GOOD)   AND BROWN
HINDER (THE ABILITY TO)   AND GRAY
IDAHO (SAFETY IN)
INCOME (TO INCREASE)   AND YELLOW

95

INDIANA (SAFETY IN)
INHERITANCE (TO RECEIVE)   AND YELLOW
INSIGHT (TO HAVE)   AND PURPLE
JACKPOT (TO WIN)   AND YELLOW
JOURNEY (TO TAKE A)   AND YELLOW
LARGE (TO HAVE ABUNDANCE)
LIFE (POSITIVE)
MANAGE (TO)
MARYLAND (SAFETY IN)
MISSOURI (SAFETY IN)   AND WHITE
MONEY (TO HAVE)   AND YELLOW
MOTHER (MONEY SUCCESS)   AND BLUE
MOTHER-IN-LAW (MONEY SUCCESS)
NEED (TO MEET)   AND WHITE
NEIGHBORLY (TO BE)   AND BLUE
NETWORK (ABILITY TO)
NEVADA (SAFETY IN)
NONSTOP (TO GO)
NOW (TO OBTAIN)
OBTAIN (TO)   AND BLUE
OFFER (THE ABILITY TO)
OPULENCE (TO HAVE)   AND YELLOW
OPULENT (TO BE)
OVERJOYED (TO BE)   AND BLUE
PAGEANT (TO WIN)   AND BLUE
PAPER MONEY (TO HAVE)   AND YELLOW
PAROLED (TO BE)
PAY (THE ABILITY TO)
PAYMENT (TO MAKE A)
PENSION (TO RECEIVE)
POOR (RELEASE YOURSELF FROM)
POTENTIAL (TO LIVE UP TO)   AND BLUE
PROGRESS (THE ABILITY TO)
PROSPERITY (TO HAVE)
PRUDENT (TO BE)   AND BLUE

96

QUALITY (TO HAVE)	AND YELLOW
RACE (TO WIN)	
RAFFLE (TO WIN)	
RANCH (TO OWN)	AND BROWN
RECOGNITION (TO GAIN)	AND BLUE
REFUND (TO GET A)	
RHODE ISLAND (SAFETY IN)	
RICH (TO BECOME)	AND YELLOW
SALARY (TO GET AN INCREASE)	
SETTLEMENT (TO RECEIVE)	
SISTER (SUCCESS)	AND WHITE
SPONTANEOUS (TO BE)	
STEP-BROTHER (SUCCESS)	AND WHITE
STEP-DAUGHTER (GOOD HEALTH)	AND PINK
STEP-DAUGHTER (SUCCESS)	AND PINK
STEP-FATHER (SUCCESS)	AND WHITE
STEP-MOTHER (SUCCESS)	AND YELLOW
STEP-SISTER (GOOD HEALTH)	AND YELLOW
STEP-SISTER (SUCCESS)	AND PINK
SUCCEED (IN LIFE)	AND PINK
TROUT (TO CATCH)	AND BLUE
ULTRA-AMBITIOUS (TO BE)	
UNEMPLOYMENT (TO RELEASE)	
USEFUL (TO BE)	AND RED
VALUABLE (TO BE)	
VALUABLES (TO HAVE)	AND BROWN
VALUE (TO HAVE)	
VEGETARIAN (TO BE A)	AND BROWN
VENERABLE (TO BE)	AND PINK
WAGE (TO EARN A GOOD)	
WEALTHY (TO BE)	
WHOLESALE (TO BUY)	
WINDFALL (TO HAVE A)	
WRITE (THE ABILITY TO)	AND YELLOW

ZOO (TO GO TO THE)

ABUSE (RELEASE FOR CHILDREN)   AND WHITE
ADOPTED, SISTER (TO OBTAIN)   AND YELLOW
AFFECTION (TO GIVE)
AFFECTION (TO RECEIVE)   AND YELLOW
AFFINITIES (TO OBTAIN)   AND WHITE
ALLIANCES (TO HAVE)
ALTOGETHER (TO BRING THINGS)   AND YELLOW
APPRECIATION (TO GIVE)
ASPIRATIONS (TO OBTAIN)   AND YELLOW
ATTORNEYS (POSITIVE DEALINGS)   AND PURPLE
ATTRACTIONS (TO OBTAIN)
AUNT (FATHER'S SIDE)
BABIES (TO HAVE)
BABIES (GIRLS)
BABIES (SISTER, HOME)   AND YELLOW
BAPTISM (PURITY)   AND WHITE
BEAUTY (TO OBTAIN)
BIRTH (RELEASE PAIN)
BLISS (TO HAVE)
BRIDE (TO BE A)   AND WHITE
BROTHER-IN-LAW (TO HELP)   AND WHITE
BULLHEADEDNESS ((R) IN OTHERS)   AND WHITE
CARESSED (TO BE)
CASH (TO SAVE)   AND GREEN
CEDE (WITH GRACE)
CHEERFUL (TO BE)
COURTEOUS (TO BE)   AND BLUE
COURTLY (TO BE)
COUSIN (FATHER SIDE, GIRL)
COUSIN (FATHER SIDE, GIRL HEALTH)AND ORANGE

98

COUSIN (MOTHER SIDE, GIRL)

COUSIN (MOTHER SIDE,HEALTH,GIRL)AND ORANGE

DAD (TO BECOME)   AND BLUE

DELICATE (TO BE)

DELIGHT (TO EXPERIENCE)   AND WHITE

DEPENDENCY (FOR OTHERS)   AND GREEN

DEPLORABLE ((R) ACTS BY OTHERS) AND WHITE

DESPONDENT ((R) IN YOURSELF)   AND YELLOW

EMBRACE (FREEDOM TO)

EMERGENCY (TO RELEASE)   AND PURPLE

EMPATHY (TO FEEL)

ENGAGED (TO BECOME)   AND BLUE

EXCITEMENT (TO EXPERIENCE)   AND RED

FACT (TO GET THE)   AND BLUE

FAITHFUL (TO BE)   AND PURPLE

FAME (TO HAVE)   AND YELLOW

FAMOUS (TO BE)   AND YELLOW

FANCY-FREE (TO BE)   AND WHITE

FAVORITE (TO BE THE)   AND YELLOW

FEEL (THE ABILITY TO)   AND WHITE

FEELINGS (EMOTIONAL)   AND BLUE

FELONY (TO FORGIVE)   AND BLACK

FEMININITY (TO EXPRESS)   AND YELLOW

FIANCEE (TO HAVE A)

FIANCEE (TO BE A)   AND WHITE

FIGURE (TO MAINTAIN A GOOD)   AND BLUE

FINALIZE (A RELATIONSHIP)   AND PURPLE

FLORIDA (SAFETY IN)   AND WHITE

GENTLE (TO BE)

GIRL (TO HAVE A)   AND WHITE

GLAD (TO BE)

GLAMOROUS (TO BE)   AND BLUE

GODCHILD (GIRL)

GODCHILD (GIRL, HEALTHY)   AND ORANGE

GODCHILD (GIRL, SAFETY)   AND WHITE

99

GODLIKE (TO BE)	AND WHITE
GODMOTHER (TO HONOR)	AND PURPLE
HANGOVER (TO RELEASE)	AND GREEN
HAPPINESS (TO FIND)	AND WHITE
HARMONY (TO HAVE)	
HOBBY (TO FIND A)	AND GREEN
HOLY (TO BECOME)	AND PURPLE
HOPE (TO HAVE)	AND PURPLE
HUMOR (TO FIND)	AND YELLOW
IDEALIST (TO BE AN)	AND YELLOW
IDLER ((R) FROM YOURSELF)	
ILLINOIS (SAFETY IN)	AND BLUE
IMMATURE (TO BE)	
IMPRESS (ABILITY TO)	AND YELLOW
INCLUDE (TO)	
INFORMAL (TO BE)	
INTEGRATE (THE ABILITY TO)	AND YELLOW
IRRITABILITY ((R) YELLOW/FEAR)	AND WHITE
KEEP (THE ABILITY TO)	AND YELLOW
LADY (TO BE)	AND WHITE
LADY (TO FIND)	
LOVER (TO HAVE)	AND YELLOW
MARRIED (TO BE)	
MISSISSIPPI (SAFETY IN)	
MISTRESS (TO RELEASE)	AND WHITE
MISTRESS (TO HAVE A)	AND YELLOW
NAMESAKE (TO HAVE A)	AND BLUE
NICE (TO BE)	
NIECE (GOOD HEALTH)	AND WHITE
NIECE (FOR PROTECTION)	AND ORANGE
OBESE (TO RELEASE)	AND BROWN
OBJECT (TO BECOME AN)	
OBLIGATE (THE ABILITY TO)	AND BLUE
OCCULT ((R) YOURSELF FROM)	AND YELLOW
OFFENSIVE (NOT TO BE)	

100

OPEN (TO BE)	AND YELLOW
OUTLOOK (TO HAVE A GOOD)	
PACIFIC (TO BE)	
PACIFY (TO)	
PART (THE ABILITY TO)	AND WHITE
PASSION (TO FEEL)	AND RED
PEACE (TO MAKE)	
PEACE (TO HAVE)	AND YELLOW
PERFECT (TO BE)	AND BLUE
POPULAR (TO BE)	AND YELLOW
PRETTY (TO BE)	
RECONCILIATION (TO HAVE A)	AND BLUE
RECOVERY (SPEEDY)	AND ORANGE
SENSUAL (TO BE)	AND RED
SENSUOUS (TO BE)	AND RED
SERENE (TO FEEL)	
SEXUAL (TO BE)	
SING (THE ABILITY TO)	AND BLUE
SINGLE (TO BE)	AND WHITE
SLEEP (THE ABILITY TO)	
SPIRIT (TO HAVE)	AND PURPLE
SPOILED (TO BE)	
STEP-MOTHER (GOOD HEALTH)	AND ORANGE
TACT (TO USE)	AND YELLOW
TALK (RELEASE THE FEAR TO)	AND YELLOW
TANGIBLE (TO MAKE)	AND ORANGE
TEXAS (SAFETY IN)	
THIN (TO BE)	AND BROWN
THRESHOLD (TO CROSS)	
TOGETHER (TO BE)	
TOGETHERNESS (TO HAVE)	AND WHITE
UGLY (NOT TO BE)	
UPSTANDING (TO BE)	
VACILLATE (THE ABILITY TO)	AND YELLOW
VAIN (TO BE)	

101

VENERABLE (NOT TO BE)
VERMONT (SAFETY IN)   AND GREEN
WARM-HEARTED (TO BE)
WEDDING (TO HAVE A)   AND BLUE
WEIGHT (TO REDUCE)   AND BROWN
WIFE (TO HAVE A)
WISH (TO GET YOUR)
WYOMING (SAFETY IN)
YOUNG (THE ABILITY TO REMAIN)   AND ORANGE
YOUTH (TO MAINTAIN YOUR)

BROWN

ABSENT (TO BE)
ACCOMPLICES (THE ABILITY TO)
ADVENTUROUS DESIRES (OWN)   AND YELLOW
AGUES (TO RELEASE)
AIR FLOW (ARTIFICIAL)
AUNT (FATHER SIDE, HOME)   AND WHITE
AUSTERITY (RELEASE)
BACKERS (PHYSICAL)   AND YELLOW
BALL GAMES (TO LOSE)
BARBER (TO BECOME A)   AND GREEN
BENEFACTORS (TO BECOME)   AND GREEN
BETRAYAL (TO BETRAY)   AND RED
BREEDING (TO BREED HORSES)
BUILD (TO BE ABLE TO)
BUILD (A BUILDING SUCCESSFUL)
BURDEN ((R) FOR OTHERS)   AND WHITE
CABINET MAKER (TO BE)   AND GREEN
CAFFEINE (RELEASE)
CARPENTERS (TO BE)   AND BROWN
CASH (TO REPLACE)   AND GREEN

102

CONSTANCY (TO MAINTAIN)

COUNTRY HOUSE (TO BUY)

CROP (TO HAVE A HEALTHY)   AND BROWN, GREEN

CROWD (TO ATTRACT)

FARMLAND (RICH)   AND BROWN, ORANGE

FAT (TO RELEASE BEING)   AND PINK

FATALIST (TO BE A)

FEARLESS (TO BE)   AND WHITE

FISHING (SUCCESSFUL)   AND YELLOW

HANDFUL (TO HAVE A)

LEFT (TO BE)

LOCATE (THE ABILITY TO)   AND YELLOW

MAGIC (TO PERFORM)   AND YELLOW

MAID (TO BE A)

MAID (TO HAVE A)

NATURE (TO LIVE IN)

NEW HAMPSHIRE (SAFETY IN)

OPPORTUNIST (TO BE AN)

PET (TO HAVE A)   AND BROWN, YELLOW

RADICAL (TO BE)

ROTTEN (TO BE)

SCARCE (TO MAKE YOURSELF)

TAN (TO GET A)   AND BROWN, WHITE

TASK (TO STAY ON)   AND YELLOW

TOLERANT (TO BE)

UNAWARE (TO BE)

GRAY

COVERAGE (TO KEEP)   AND YELLOW

EXHAUSTION (RELEASE)   AND WHITE

FOLLOWER (ABILITY TO BE A)

GOOD NIGHT (TO HAVE A)

GRAY

IGNOBLE (RELEASE)	AND WHITE
INFAMY (RELEASE)	AND WHITE
OBVIOUS (NOT TO BE)	AND YELLOW
ODD (TO BE)	
ODDS (TO BE AT)	
RECOURSE (TO TAKE)	
RECTIFY (THE ABILITY TO)	AND YELLOW
SABOTAGE (TO)	AND BLACK
SABOTAGE (NOT TO)	AND WHITE
VAGUE (TO BE)	

PURPLE

ACCIDENT (SECURE AGAINST)	AND ORANGE
ADOPTED CHILDREN (TO HELP)	
ADORATION (SAFETY)	
ADULTS (TO PROTECT)	
AGED PERSON (TO PROTECT)	AND YELLOW
AIMS (ONES)	AND WHITE
BABIES (BROTHERS, PROTECT)	AND WHITE
BABIES (SISTERS, PROTECT)	AND PINK
BENEDICTIONS (TO PERFORM)	AND WHITE
BROTHERS (OVER 35, TO PROTECT)	
CARDS (TO READ)	AND WHITE
CELIBATE (RELEASE)	AND WHITE
CLEMENCY (TO HAVE)	
CONSCIENCE (STRENGTHENED)	
CONVICTION (TO GET A)	
CORRESPONDENT (RELEASE)	AND GRAY
CORNUCOPIA (MAGIC)	AND ORANGE
COURT (SUCCESS IN)	

CROSSOVER (PEACEFUL)	AND WHITE
DANGER (RELEASE)	
DAUGHTER (TO INSURE SAFETY)	
FAITH (TO HAVE)	
FAMOUS (TO MEET THEM)	AND YELLOW
FINAL (TO PUT CLOSURE TO)	AND WHITE
FINANCES (TO STABILIZE)	AND GREEN
FRANCHIISE (TO SELL)	AND GREEN
GOAL (TO ACCOMPLISH)	
GODFATHER (HONOR)	AND PINK
HERO (TO BE A)	AND BLUE
HEROINE (TO BE A)	AND BLUE
HOPEFUL (TO BE)	AND YELLOW
JUSTICE (TO UPHOLD)	
LAST (ABILITY TO MAKE THINGS)	
LAST RITES (TO ADMINISTER)	AND WHITE
LAW (TO LIVE WITHIN)	
MAGICAL (TO BE)	
MARTYR (TO BE A)	
NARCISSISM ((R) OBSESSIONS)	AND BLUE
NEPHEW (FOR PROTECTION)	AND WHITE
TAOISM (TO UNDERSTAND)	
VEHICLE (TO BE A FOR)	
VINDICATE (TO)	AND PINK
WEST VIRGINIA (SAFETY IN)	

YELLOW

ABANDONED (NOT TO BE)	AND BLUE
ABDICATE (TO)	
ABILITIES (TO HAVE)	AND ORANGE
ABILITIES (TO USE)	
ABSENT-MINDED (RELEASE)	

ABSTRACT (TO BE)	
ACADEMIC (TO BE)	
ACCELERATE (TO)	
ACCELERATION (MENTAL)	
ACCORDANCE (TO BE IN)	
ACCUMULATION (MENTAL)	AND GREEN
ACCURACY (TO HAVE)	AND BLUE
ACCUSATIONS ((R) AGAINST YOU)	
ACCUSATIONS ((R) AGAINST OTHER)	AND WHITE
ACHES, **SHARP** ((R) YOUR OWN)	AND BLUE
ACROBAT (ABILITY TO BECOME)	AND ORANGE
ACTIVITY (MENTAL)	
ACTORS/ACTRESS (TO BECOME)	AND BLUE
AD WRITERS (TO BECOME)	AND BLUE
ADDICTS ((R) TO HELP OTHERS)	AND WHITE
ADJUSTERS, CLAIMS (YOUR FAVOR)	AND GREEN
ADJUSTMENTS (MENTAL)	AND BLUE
ADOPTED BROTHERS (TO HELP)	AND WHITE
ADOPTED BROTHERS (TO OBTAIN)	AND BLUE
ADRENALIN (TO HAVE)	AND BLUE
ADULTS (TO HELP)	AND BLUE
ADVICE (TO GIVE)	AND WHITE
ADVICE (TO RECEIVE)	
ADVISOR (TO BE AN)	AND PURPLE
AESTHETIC SENSE (ABILITY)	
AESTHETICS (SAFETY WITH)	AND BLUE
AFFABLE (TO BECOME)	AND PURPLE
AFFIDAVITS (HONEST)	AND ORANGE
AFFILIATION (TO JOIN)	
AFFILIATION (TO QUIT)	AND BROWN
AFFINITIES (RELEASE)	AND WHITE
AGED PERSON (TO HELP)	AND ORANGE
AGENCIES (POSITIVE DEALINGS)	AND BLUE
AGENCIES, FOREIGN (DEALINGS)	AND RED
AGGRESSORS (DEALINGS)	AND WHITE

106

AILING (MENTAL)	
AILING (PHYSICAL)	AND BLUE
AIR (CONDITIONING)	
AIRCRAFT (CONSTRUCTION)	AND BLUE
AIR CREW (SAFETY)	AND WHITE
AIR DROP (FOOD)	AND BLUE
AIR EXPRESS (SUCCESSFUL)	
AIR FORCE (TO INSURE PEACE)	AND BLUE
AIRLESS (RELEASE)	AND WHITE
AIRMAIL (TO RECEIVE)	
ALERTNESS (MENTAL)	
ALIMONY (RELEASE PAYMENT)	AND BLUE
ALLERGIES (TO DISCERN)	
ALOOFNESS ((R) IN YOURSELF)	
ALTERNATE (TO BECOME)	AND BLUE
ALTITUDE (RELEASE FEAR OF)	AND BLUE
ALTRUIST (TO BECOME)	
APOLOGIES (TO RECEIVE)	AND PINK
ARGUMENTS (RELEASE)	
ARIZONA (SAFETY IN)	
ARKANSAS (SAFETY IN)	
ARREST (RELEASE)	AND RED
ATTITUDE (POSITIVE)	AND WHITE
ATTRACTIONS (RELEASE)	AND ORANGE
AUNT (MOTHER'S SIDE)	AND PINK
AUTHORITY (DEALINGS)	
AUTOMOBILES (TO MAINTAIN)	
AUTOMOBILES (TO SELL)	AND GREEN
AWARDS (RELEASE)	AND YELLOW
AWKWARD (RELEASE)	
BACK (RELEASE PAIN, LOWER)	AND WHITE
BACK (RELEASE PAIN, UPPER)	AND ORANGE
BACKERS (FINANCIAL)	AND GREEN
BALANCE (TO OBTAIN)	

107

BANDS (MUSIC, TO BELONG)	
BANDS (MUSIC, TO PLAY)	AND GREEN
BANISHMENT (OF OTHERS)	AND BLUE
BANKS (POSITIVE DEALINGS)	AND GREEN
BANK NOTES (TO OBTAIN)	AND GREEN
BAR (TO OWN)	AND BLUE
BEACH (TO GO TO)	AND GREEN
BEAUTY (TO OTHERS)	AND PINK
BEGGARS (RELEASE)	AND BROWN
BEGINNINGS (SUCCESSFUL)	AND GREEN
BEHAVIOR (CHANGE)	
BEHAVIOR (POSITIVE)	AND BLUE
BELITTLING (OTHERS)	
BEST (TO BE)	AND BLUE
BEST (TO OBTAIN)	AND GREEN
BI-SEXUALITY (TO DEAL WITH)	
BI-SEXUALITY (WITH OTHERS)	AND BLUE
BITTERNESS (RELEASE)	AND WHITE
BOATS (TO OBTAIN)	
BOATS (TO SELL)	AND GREEN
BONDAGE (RELEASE FROM OTHERS)	AND WHITE
BONDS (TO SELL)	AND BLUE
BOOKS (TO WRITE)	
BOSS (TO BE SUCCESSFUL)	AND BLUE
BOSS (TO RELATE TO YOU)	
BOYFRIENDS (TO OBTAIN)	AND PINK
BRAIN (TO STIMULATE)	AND BLUE
BREATH (BREATHING)	AND BLUE
BREEDING (TO BREED CATS)	
BRILLIANT (TO BECOME)	AND BLUE
BRILLIANCE (TO MAINTAIN)	AND BROWN
BROADCASTERS (TO BECOME)	AND BLUE
BROKERS (TO DEAL WITH)	
BROKERS (TO BECOME)	AND GREEN
BROTHERS (OVER 35, TO HELP)	AND BLUE

108

BUILDER (TO BE)

BUILDER (TO FIND)   AND GREEN

BURN OUT (RELEASE FOR OTHERS)

BUSINESS (CREDIT, GOOD)   AND GREEN

BUSINESS (TO SELL)   AND GREEN

CABINET MAKER (FIND THE BEST)

CAFES (TO SELL)   AND GREEN

CALAMITY (RELEASE)

CALL (FROM A MAN)

CALL (FROM A WOMAN)   AND PINK

CALM (TO OBTAIN)   AND WHITE

CAMP (TO BUY)   AND BROWN

CAMP (TO SELL)   AND GREEN

CANCEL (CONTRACT)   AND BROWN

CANDID (TO BE)

CANDIDATE (TO BE A)

CANDOR (TO HAVE)   AND WHITE

CARDS (TO PLAY)

CAREER (TO OBTAIN)   AND WHITE

CAREFUL (TO BE)

CAR (TO BUY)

CASTAWAY (TO BE)

CAT (TO FIND)

CAVEAT EMPTOR (LET THE)

CHAMPION (TO BE THE)   AND ORANGE

CHANGELING (TO RECOGNIZE)

CHARM (TO HAVE)

CHILDISH (TO BECOME)   AND BLUE

CHOICE (TO HAVE A)

CLEVER (TO BE)

CLOSURE (TO GIVE)   AND WHITE

COMMENTATOR (TO BE A)

COMMIT (THE ABILITY TO)

COMMUNICATE (ABILITY TO)

COMPULSIVENESS (RELEASE)   AND RED

CONCEIVE (THE ABILITY TO)	
CONCENTRATE (ABILITY TO)	AND BLUE
CONCEPTUALIZE (ABILITY TO)	
CONTROL (TO MAINTAIN)	
CONVERSE (ABILITY TO)	AND WHITE
CONVULSION (RELEASE)	
COPE (ABILITY TO)	
COPYRIGHT (TO OBTAIN)	
CORDIAL (TO BE)	AND BLUE
COST (OF LIVING REDUCED)	AND GRAY
COUNSELOR (TO BECOME)	
COUNSELOR (SUCCESSFUL)	AND ORANGE
COUNTRY CLUB (TO BELONG)	AND GREEN
COUPLE (TO BECOME PART OF)	AND PINK
COVERAGE (POSITIVE)	AND PINK
CRAVING (RELEASE NEED FOR)	AND ORANGE
CREATE (ABILITY TO)	AND PURPLE
CREATIVE (ABILITY TO BE)	AND ORANGE
CREDIT (TO OBTAIN)	
CRUEL (TO RELEASE)	
CRY (ABILITY TO)	AND WHITE
CURIOUS (TO BE)	AND BLUE
CUTE (TO BE)	AND PINK
DAD (TO HEAR FROM)	
DANCE (TO BE INVITED TO A)	AND BLUE
DANGER (PROTECTION FROM)	AND BLUE
DATA (TO OBTAIN)	
DEADLINE (TO MEET)	
DEBATE (ABILITY TO)	AND BLUE
DELAY (ABILITY TO DEAL WITH)	AND PINK
DENIAL ((R) WITHIN YOURSELF)	AND BLUE
DENIAL ((R) WITHIN OTHERS)	AND WHITE
DEPRESSED (RELEASE)	AND BLUE
DEPRESSION ((R) IN OTHERS)	AND PINK
DEPEND (ABILITY TO)	AND GRAY

110

DEPENDABILITY (FOR OTHERS)	AND BLUE
DESPAIR (RELEASE IN YOURSELF)	AND BLUE
DESPAIR (RELEASE IN OTHERS)	AND GRAY
EAGER (TO BE)	AND RED
EASE (TO LIVE WITH)	AND BLUE
EASILY (TO OBTAIN)	AND BLUE
EDUCATION (TO OBTAIN)	
EGO (TO OBTAIN HEALTHY)	
EMERALD (TO SELL)	AND WHITE
EMOTION (HEALTHY)	AND WHITE
ENJOY (TO)	AND BLUE
EXCESS (AMOUNTS OF MONEY)	AND GREEN
EXCESS (AMOUNTS OF CLIENTS)	AND ORANGE
EXPLAIN (THE ABILITY TO)	
EXPRESSION (FREEDOM OF)	AND BLUE
FABULOUS (TO BECOME)	AND WHITE
FACILITATE (POWER TO)	AND BLUE
FACTORY (TO BUY)	AND GREEN
FACULTY (OF THE BODY)	
FACULTY (OF THE MIND)	AND BLUE
FAD (TO CREATE A)	AND RED
FAILURE (RELEASE)	
FALSE (TO GUARD AGAINST)	AND BLUE
FAMED (TO BE)	AND BLUE
FAMILY (TO HAVE A GOOD)	AND PURPLE
FAN (TO HAVE)	AND BLUE
FANATICISM (TO RELEASE)	AND RED
FANCY-FREE (TO LIVE)	AND BLUE
FARM (TO WORK)	
FAR-REACHING (TO BE)	AND WHITE
FAIR-SEEING (ABILITY TO BE)	
FERTILE (TO BECOME)	AND GREEN
FETUS (INSURE THE SAFETY OF)	AND WHITE
FEVER (TO RAISE)	
FICKLE (TO BE)	AND BROWN

111

FIRST (TO BE)

FLAWLESS (TO BECOME)

FOCUS (THE ABILITY TO)   AND ORANGE

FORCEFUL (THE ABILITY TO BE)   AND GRAY

FORGIVING (TO BE)

FRANCHISE (TO OWN)   AND GREEN

FRATERNIZE (ABILITY TO)   AND WHITE

FREE (TO BE)   AND BLUE

FULFILLMENT (TO FEEL)

GAMBLE (SUCCESSFUL)

GATHERING (TO HAVE A)   AND WHITE

GENEROUS (TO BE)

GIRLFRIEND (TO FIND A)   AND BLUE

GOLD (TO OBTAIN)   AND GREEN

GOLF (TO HAVE TIME TO PLAY)   AND BLUE

GRADE (TO PASS)

GREAT (TO BE)

GREEDY (RELEASE)

GRIEF (TO RELEASE)

GUESS (HAVING THE ABILITY TO)

GUIDE (COMMUNICATE WITH)   AND PURPLE

GUILTY (TO RELEASE)   AND ORANGE

HABIT (TO RELEASE A)   AND PINK

HAIR (FOR GROWTH)

HANDFUL (TO RELEASE)   AND WHITE

HAPPY (TO BE)   AND PINK

HARM (TO GUARD AGAINST)   AND PURPLE

HAVE (TO)

HEAVEN (TO GO TO)   AND PURPLE

HERMIT (TO BE A)   AND BLUE

HITCH (GO WITHOUT A)   AND ORANGE

HOMECOMING (HAVE A)

HONOR (TO FIND)   AND BLUE

HORROR (RELEASE)   AND WHITE

HURT (RELEASE TO)   AND WHITE

112

HYPERSENSITIVITY (KNOW)	AND BLUE
ID (TO STRENGTHEN)	AND WHITE
IDEA (TO HAVE AN)	AND BLUE
IDEAL (TO HAVE THE)	
IGNORANCE (RELEASE)	AND BLUE
IGNORE (ABILITY TO)	AND WHITE
ILLITERACY (RELEASE)	
IMAGERY (GUIDED)	AND BLUE
IMAGINATION (HAVING AN)	
IMMATURITY (RELEASE)	AND PINK
IMMORTAL (TO BE)	AND PURPLE
IMPORTANT (TO BE)	AND BLUE
IMPRESSION (LASTING)	AND PINK
INADEQUACY (RELEASE)	AND BLUE
INCLINE (TO BE)	
INDEPENDENT (TO BE)	AND GREEN
INDIFFERENT (TO BE)	
INFORMATION (TO GAIN)	AND GREEN
INFORMER (TO BE AN)	
INSPIRE (ABILITY TO)	
INTROVERTED (RELEASE)	AND WHITE
INTRUST (ABILITY TO)	
INTUITIVE (TO BE)	
ISSUE (TO PURSUE AN)	AND BLUE
JAIL (TO GET OUT OF)	AND PINK
JEALOUSY (RELEASE)	AND WHITE
JEOPARDIZE (TO)	
JOB (TO KEEP)	AND BLUE
JOLLY (TO BE)	
JOURNEY (A MENTAL)	AND PURPLE
JOY (TO HAVE)	AND BLUE
JUSTICE (TO HAVE)	AND GRAY
JUSTIFY (ABILITY TO)	AND WHITE
KEEN (TO BE)	AND ORANGE
KENTUCKY (SAFETY IN)	

KIND (TO BE)

KNOW HOW (TO HAVE)   AND GREEN

KNOWLEDGE (TO HAVE)

KNOWLEDGE (TO RETAIN)   AND BLUE

KNOWLEDGEABLE (TO BE)   AND ORANGE

LABOR (EASY)

LANDLORD (TO DEAL WITH)

LANDOWNER (TO BE)

LEASE (TO SIGN)   AND BLUE

LICENSE (TO OBTAIN)

LOVE (TO FEEL)   AND PINK

LUCK (TO HAVE)

MAD (TO RELEASE)

MAGICIAN (TO BE A)   AND BLUE

MAGNIFICENT (TO BE)

MAKE BELIEVE (ABILITY TO)   AND BLUE

MALICIOUS (TO BE)   AND WHITE

MANIPULATE (ABILITY TO) AND PINK

MATERIALISTIC (ABILITY TO)

MEDITATION (ABILITY TO)   AND BLUE

MELANCHOLY (TO BE)   AND BLUE

MEMORY (TO HAVE A GOOD)

MESSAGE (TO RECEIVE)

MIND (TO HAVE A GOOD)   AND BLUE

MISCHIEVOUS (TO BE)

MORE (TO HAVE)

MOTHER (PEACE OF MIND)   AND BLUE

MOTHER-IN-LAW (PEACE OF MIND) AND PINK

MYSELF (TO BE)

MYSTICAL (TO BE)   AND ORANGE

NAG (RELEASE NEED)

NARCOTIC (RELEASE)   AND ORANGE

NASTY (RELEASE NEED TO BE)

NATURAL (TO BE)   AND BROWN

NEBRASKA (SAFETY IN)

114

NEGATIVE (RELEASE NEED TO BE)

NEGOTIATE (ABILITY TO)   AND BLUE

NEW JERSEY (SAFETY IN)

NONCOMMITTAL (TO BE)

NONVIOLENT (TO BE)   AND PINK

NORTH DAKOTA (SAFETY IN)

NUISANCE (RELEASE NEED TO BE)   AND ORANGE

NURTURE (ABILITY TO)

OATH (TO TAKE AND KEEP)

OBEY (TO)

OBLIGATION (TO UPHOLD AN)   AND GREEN

OBSEQUIOUS (ABILITY TO BE)   AND GREEN

OBSERVANT (ABILITY TO BE)

OBSESSION (RELEASE)   AND PINK

OBVIOUS (TO BE)

OCCULT (TO UNDERSTAND)

OCCULT (TO BELONG)   AND WHITE

ODD (NOT TO BE)

ODDS (NOT TO BE AT)   AND GRAY

OFFEND (NOT TO)   AND PINK

OFFICER (TO BE AN)   AND GREEN

OFFICIAL (DEAL WITH AN)

OLOGY (ABILITY TO UNDERSTAND)

OMIT (ABILITY TO)   AND BLUE

ON (TO BE)

ONENESS (WITH YOURSELF)   AND PURPLE

ONESELF (TO BE)

ONGOING (TO HAVE THINGS)   AND BROWN

ONWARD (TO BE)   AND GRAY

OPTIMIST (TO BE AN)

OPTIMISTIC (TO BE)   AND WHITE

ORATION (ABILITY TO GIVE)

ORGANIZE (ABILITY TO)

ORTHODOX (NOT TO BE)   AND WHITE

OSCAR (TO WIN)   AND PURPLE

115

OSMOSIS (TO LEARN BY)

PACIFIST (TO BE A)   AND PINK

PAINSTAKING (TO BE)   AND WHITE

PALMISTRY (TO UNDERSTAND)   AND RED

PANIC (NOT TO)   AND GRAY

PAPER PROFITS (TO HAVE)

PARAPSYCHOLOGY (UNDERSTAND) AND ORANGE

PARENTS (TO RESPECT)   AND WHITE

PART (TO BECOME A)   AND RED

PARTAKE (OPPORTUNITY TO)   AND BLUE

PARTY (TO BE INVITED TO)

PENNSYLVANIA (SAFETY IN)

PERCEIVE (ABILITY TO)   AND BLUE

PERSPECTIVE (TO HAVE A GOOD)   AND BLUE

PHILOSOPHICAL (TO BE)

PHILOSOPHY (TO UNDERSTAND)   AND BLUE

PLAY (THE ABILITY TO)

POLITE (TO BE)

POLITICS (UNDERSTAND)

PREGNANT (ABILITY TO BECOME)   AND PINK

PROMISE (ABILITY TO KEEP)   AND WHITE

PROUD (TO BE)

PSYCHIC (TO BE)   AND ORANGE

PUBLISH (ABILITY TO)

QUALIFIED (TO BE)

QUESTIONS (TO HAVE ANSWERS)   AND ORANGE

QUOTA (TO MEET YOUR)   AND RED

RABBLE-ROUSER (TO BE A)

RADIATE (ABILITY TO)   AND BLUE

RANCH (TO BUY)   AND GREEN

RANCH (TO SELL)   AND BLUE

RATE (TO LOWER)   AND WHITE

REASONABLE (TO BE)

REASSURE (TO BE)   AND GRAY

RECOMMEND (TO)

RECTIFY (OPPORTUNITY TO)   AND BLUE
REFRAIN (TO)   AND GRAY
REGRET (RELEASE THE NEED TO)   AND WHITE
REJOICE (TO)   AND BLUE
REMEMBER (ABILITY TO)
RIGHT (TO BE)
SANE (TO BE)
SECURITY (TO HAVE)
SELECTIVE (TO BE)   AND BLUE
SELF-CENTERED (TO BE)
SENSIBLE (TO BE)
SETTLEMENT (TO REACH A)   AND GREEN
SHINE (THE ABILITY TO)   AND PINK
SICKNESS (TO RELEASE)   AND ORANGE
SIMPLE (TO BE)
SISTER (INSURE PEACE OF MIND)   AND GREEN
SMART (TO BE)   AND PURPLE
SOUTH DAKOTA (SAFETY IN)
SPEAK (ABILITY TO FREELY)   AND BLUE
SPECULATE (THE ABILITY TO)   AND GREEN
STRUCTURE (TO HAVE)   AND BLUE
SURPASS (IN LIFE)
TABLOID (TO BE IN A)   AND GREEN
TACTFUL (TO BE)
TACTLESS (TO BE)   AND GRAY
TALK (THE ABILITY TO)
TANTRUM (TO RELEASE)
TAPE (TO MAKE A)   AND BLUE
TAPE RECORDING (TO MAKE A)   AND BLUE
TEACH (THE ABILITY TO)   AND WHITE
TEACHER (ABILITY TO BE A)
TELEPATHIC (TO BE)   AND ORANGE
TELEPATHY (ABILITY TO USE)
TEST (TO PASS)
TESTIFY (TO)

THANK (THE ABILITY TO)	AND BLUE
THINK (ABILITY TO)	
THRIFTY (TO BE)	AND BROWN
THYROID (TO STIMULATE)	
TOLERANT (OF OTHERS)	AND BROWN
TOMORROW (TO SEE)	
TOUCH (TO BE IN)	
UNATTACHED (TO BE)	
UNDERSTANDING (TO BE)	
UNSELFISH (TO BE)	AND WHITE
VACATION (TO GO ON)	AND WHITE
VAGUE (NOT TO BE)	
VARIETY (TO HAVE A)	AND PINK
VEHICLE (TO HAVE A)	
VENTUROUS (TO BE)	AND RED
VIBRATION (TO FEEL)	AND ORANGE
VIEW (TO HAVE A GOOD)	
VISION (TO HAVE A CLEAR)	
WALK (THE ABILITY TO)	
WANDERLUST (ABILITY TO)	AND BLUE
WARRANTY (TO GET A)	
WATCH (THE ABILITY TO)	
X-RAY ASTRONOMY (UNDERSTAND)	AND GREEN
YACHT (TO SELL)	AND RED
YOURSELF (TO FIND)	AND BLUE
ZEST (TO HAVE)	

CANDLES, SHAPES AND SIZES

When lighting candles using, the dictionary, any size candle will work. However, the longer the candle stays lit, the more energy you will have at your disposal, ensuring your wish to manifest.

When lighting one tapered candle, you will find that your wish may only

118

partially come to fruition. You will find that in order to obtain enough energy to manifest your desire, at the very least, you will need to light two 12-inch tapered candles.

The operative candle to light will be the five to seven day candles. When these candles are not available, tapered candles will work.

EPHEMERAL GUIDE

The Ephemeral Guide has been written using the exact Greenwich Mean Time (GMT) for the bring and release time cycles.

To determine your corresponding local time, use the time zone table listed below. This table has been written using Standard Time Zones, Meridians, hours, and minutes from Greenwich Mean Time to indicate the beginning and ending of each bring and release cycle.

In the event that Daylight Savings Time (DST) is being observed, you will need to subtract one hour from the original hours indicated representing your particular time zone.

Example: Eastern Standard Time is 5 hours less than Greenwich Mean Time. Under normal circumstances, you will subtract 5 hours from the Greenwich Mean Time. During Daylight Savings Time, you will subtract 4 hours from Greenwich Mean Time.

Eastern Standard Time = 5.
Eastern Daylight Time = 4.

Western Standard Time Zones

Standard Time	Meridian	Hours / Minutes
Greenwich Mean	0W00	0 00
West African	15W00	1 00
Azores	30W00	2 00
Brazil Zone 2	45W00	3 00

119

Newfoundland	52W30	3 00
Atlantic	60W00	4 00
Eastern	75W00	5 00
Central	90W00	6 00
Mountain	105W00	7 00
Pacific	120W00	8 00
Yukon	135W00	9 00
Alaska-Hawaii	150W00	10 00
Hawaiian	157W30	10 30
Nome	165W00	11 00
Bering	165W00	11 00
International Date	180W00	12 00

Eastern Standard Time Zones

Standard Time	Meridian	Hours / Minutes
Central European	15E00	1 00
Middle European	15E00	1 00
Eastern European	30E00	2 00
Baghdad	45E00	3 00
USSR Zone 3	60E00	4 00
USSR Zone 4	75E00	5 00
Indian	82E30	5 00
USSR Zone 5	90E00	6 00
North Sumatra	97E00	6 30
South Sumatra	105E00	7 00
Java	112E30	7 30
China Coast	120E00	8 00
Japan	135E00	9 00
South Australia	142E30	9 30
Guam	150E00	10 00
New Zealand	180E00	12 00

This table will enable you to determine the appropriate days to light your candles. You will have quick reference as to when to light your candles to bring something to you, and, conversely, when to light a candle to release or rid yourself from unwanted situations and things, as well as to release from within yourself dysfunctional personality tendencies and traits.

The traditional definition for eclipse, aside from the fact that it si the relative position between the sun, earth, and the moon is "crisis point." When lighting a candle at the point of an eclipse, it will lessen the effects of the eclipse as this energy manifests in your life.

At the time of a solar eclipse, make a list of all of the things that you want. Light a white candle and burn your list with the white candle. It was believed by the Ancients that God at the time of the solar eclipse had a clear view of all the earth and that one's good intentions would at that time be rewarded by one's desires. By making a list of your desires, you will be focusing your energies, so that your desires will manifest. Solar eclipse will be indicated in the ephemeral guide.

May 2001
From 00:00 on the 1st through 13:53 on the 7th = the bring time frame.

From 13:54 on the 7th through 2:46 on the 23rd = the releasing time frame.

From 2:47 on the 23rd through 24:00 on the 31st = the bring time frame.

June 2001

From 00:00 on the 1st through 1:39 on the 6th = the bring time frame

From 1:40 on the 6th through 12:03 on the 21st = the releasing time frame.

From 12:04 on the 21st through 24:00 on the 30th = the bring time frame

July 2001

From 00:00 on the 1st through 15:04 on the 5th = the bring time frame.

From 15:05 on the 5th through 19:44 on the 20th = the releasing time frame.

From 19:45 on the 20th through 24:00 on the 31st = the bring time frame.

August 2001

From 00:00 on the 1st through 5:56 on the 4th = the bring time frame.

From 5:57 on the 4th through 2:55 on the 19th = the releasing time frame.

From 2:56 on the 19th through 24:00 on the 31st = the bring time frame.

September 2001
From 00:00 on the 1st through 21:43 on the 2nd = the bring time frame.

From 21:44 on the 2nd through 10:27 on the 17th = the releasing time frame.

From 10:28 on the 17th through 24:00 on the 30th = the bring time frame.

October 2001

From 00:00 on the 1st through 13:49 on the 2nd = the bring time frame.
From 13:50 on the 2nd through 19:23 on the 16th = the releasing time frame.

From 19:24 on the 16th through 24:00 on the 31st = the bring time frame.

November 2001

From 00:00 on the 1st through 5:41 on the 1st = the bring time frame.

From 5:42 on the 1st through 6:40 on the 16th = the releasing time frame.

From 6:41 on the 16th through 20:49 on the 30th = the bring time frame.

From 20:50 on the 30th through 24:00 on the 30th = the releasing time frame.

December 2001
From 00:00 on the 1st through 20:52 on the 14th = the releasing time frame.

From 20:53 on the 14th through 10:29 on the 30th = the bring time frame.

From 10:30 on the 30th. through 24:00 on the 30th.= the releasing time frame.

January 2002

From 00:00 on the 1st. through 13:30 on the 13th. =the releasing time frame.

From 20:26 on the 13th. through 22:52 on the 28th.=the bring time frame.

From 20:27 on the 13th. through 24:00 on the 31st.= the releasing time frame.

February 2002

From 00:00 on the 1st. Through 7:41 on the 12th. = the releasing time frame.

From 7:42 on the 12th through 9:17 on the 27th = the bring time frame.

From 9:18 on the 27th through 24:00 on the 28th = the releasing time frame.

March 2002

From 00:00 on the 1st through 2:04 on the 14th = the releasing time frame.

From 2:05 on the 14th through 18:25 on the 28th = the bring time frame.

From 18:26 on the 28th through 24:00 on the 31st. =the releasing time frame.

April 2002

From 00:00 on the 1st through 19:21 on the 12th = the releasing time frame.

From 19:22 on the 12th through 3:00 on the 27th. = the bring time frame.

From 3:01 on the 27th through 24:00 on the 30th.=the releasing time frame.

May 2002

From 00:00 on the 1st. Through 10:45 on the 12th. = the releasing time frame.

From 10:46 on the 12th through 11:51 on the 26th.= the bring time frame.

From 11:52 on the 26th through 24:00 on the 31st.= the releasing time frame.

June 2002

From 00:00 on the 1st through 23:47 on the 10th = the releasing time frame.

124

From 23:48 on the 10th through 21:42 on the 24th = the bring time frame.

From 21:43 on the 24th through 24:00 on the 30th = the releasing time frame.

July 2002

From 00:00 on the 1st through 10:26 on the 10th = the releasing time frame.

From 10:27 on the 10th through 9:08 on the 24th = the bring time frame.

From 9:09 on the 24th through 24:00 on the 31st = the releasing time frame.

August 2002

From 00:00 on the 1st through 19:15 on the 8th = the releasing time frame.

From 19:16 on the 8th through 22:29 on the 22nd = the bring time frame.

From 22:30 on the 22nd through 24:00 on the 31st = the releasing time frame.

September 2002

From 00:00 on the 1st through 3:10 on the 7th = the releasing time frame.

From 3:11 on the 7th through 13:59 on the 21st = the bring time frame.

From 14:00 on the 21st through 24:00 on the 30th = the releasing time frame.

October 2002

From 00:00 on the 1st through 11:18 on the 6th = the releasing time frame.

From 11:19 on the 6th through 7:20 on the 21st = the bring time frame.

From 7:21 on the 21st through 24:00 on the 31st = the releasing time frame.

November 2002

From 00:00 on the 1st through 20:35 on the 4th= the releasing time frame.

From 20:36 on the 4th through 1:34 on the 20th = the bring time frame.

From 1:35 on the 20th through 24:00 on the 30th = the releasing time frame.

December 2002

From 00:00 on the 1st through 7:34 on the 4th = the releasing time frame.

From 7:35 on the 4th through 19:10 on the 19th = the bring time frame.

From 19:11 on the 27th through 24:00 on the 31st = the releasing time frame.

January 2003

From 00:00 on the 1st through 20:23 on the 2nd = the releasing time frame.

From 20:24 on the 2nd through 10:48 on the 18th = the bring time frame.

126

From 10:49 on the 18th through 24:00 on the 31st = the releasing time frame.

February 2003

From 00:00 on the 1st through 10:48 on the 1st = the releasing time frame.

From 10:49 on the 1st through 23:51 on the 16th = the bring time frame.

From 23:52 on the 16th through 24:00 on the 28th = the releasing time frame.

March 2003

From 00:00 on the 1st through 2:35 on the 3rd = the releasing time frame.

From 2:36 on the 3rd through 10:35 on the 18th = the bring time frame.

From 10:36 on the 18th through 24:00 on the 31st = the releasing time frame.

April 2003

From 00:00 on the 1st through on the 1st = the releasing time frame.

From 19:20 on the 1st through 19:36 on the 16th = the bring time frame.

From 10:37 on the 16th through 24:00 on the 30th = the releasing time frame.

May 2003

From 00:00 on the 1st through 12:15 on the 1st = the releasing time frame.

From 12:16 on the 1st through 3:36 on the 16th = the bring time frame.

From 3:37 on the 16th through 4:20 on the 31st = the releasing time frame.

From 4:21 on the 31st through 24:00 on the 31st = the bring time frame.

June 2003

From 00:00 on the 1st through 11:16 on the 14th = the bring time frame.

From 11:17 on the 14th through 18:39 on the 29th = the releasing time frame.

From 18:40 on the 29 through 24:00 on the 30th = the bring time frame.

July 2003

From 00:00 on the 1st through 19:21 on the 13th = the bring time frame.

From 19:22 on the 13th through 6:53 on the 29th = the releasing time frame.

From 6:54 on the 29th through 24:00 on the 31st = the bring time frame.

August 2003
From 00:00 on the 1st through 4:48 on the 12th = the bring time frame.

From 4:49 on the 12th through 17:26 on the 27th = the releasing time frame.

From 17:27 on the 27th through 24:00 on the 31st = the bring time frame.
September 2003

From 00:00 on the 1st through 16:36 on the 10th = the bring time frame

From 16:37 on the 10th through 3:09 on the 26th = the releasing time frame.

From 3:10 on the 26th through 24:00 on the 30th = the bring time frame.
October 2003

From 00:00 on the 1st through 7:28 on the 10th = the bring time frame

From 7:29 on the 10th through 12:50 on the 25th = the releasing time frame.

From 12:51 on the 25th through 24:00 on the 31st = the bring time frame.
November 2003

From 00:00 on the 1st through 1:13 on the 9th = the bring time frame.

From 1:14 on the 9th through 22:59 on the 23rd = the releasing time frame.

From 23:00 on the 23rd through 24:00 on the 30th = the bring time frame.

December 2003
From 00:00 on the 1st through 20:37 on the 8th = the bring time frame.

From 20:38 on the 8th through 9:43 on the 23rd = the releasing time frame.

From 9:44 0n the 23rd through 24:00 on the 31st. = the bring time frame.

January 2004

From 00:00 on the 1st through 15:40 on the 7th = the bring time frame.

From 15:41 on the 7th through 21:05 on the 21st = the releasing time frame.

From 21:06 on the 21st through 24:00 on the 31st= the bring time frame.

February 2004
From 00:00 on the 1st through 8:47 on the 6th = the bring time frame.

From 8:48 on the 6th through 9:18 on the 20th = the releasing time frame.

From 9:19 on the 20th through 24:00 on the 29th = the bring time frame.

March 2004

From 00:00 on the 1st through 23:14 on the 6th = the bring time frame.

From 23:15 on the 6th through 22:41 on the 20th = the releasing time frame.

From 22:42 on the 20th through 24:00 on the 31st = the bring time frame.

April 2004

From 00:00 on the 1st through 11:03 on the 5th = the bring time frame.

From 11:04 on the 5th through 13:21 on the 19th = the releasing time frame.

From 13:22 on the 19th through 24:00 on the 30th = the bring time frame.

May 2004

From 00:00 on the 1st through 20:33 on the 4th = the bring time frame.
From 20:34 on the 4th through 4:52 on the 19th = the releasing time frame.

From 4:53 on the 19th through 24:00 on the 31st = the bring time frame.

June 2004

From 00:00 on the 1st through 4:20 on the 3rd = the bring time frame.

From 4:21 on the 3rd through 20:27 on the 17th = the releasing time frame.

From 20:28 on the 17th through 24:00 on the 30th = the bring time frame.

July 2004
From 00:00 in the 1st through 11:09 on the 2nd = the bring time frame.

From 11:10 on the 2nd through 11:24 on the 17th = the releasing time frame.

From 11:25 on the 17th through 18:05 on the 31st = the bring time frame.

From 18:06 on the 31st through 24:00 on the 31st = the releasing time frame.

August 2004

From 00:00 on the 1st through 1:24 on the 16th = the releasing time frame.

From 1:25 on the 16th through 2:22 on the 30th = the bring time frame.

From 2:23 on the 30th through 24:00 on the 31st = the releasing time frame.

September 2004

From 00:00 on the 1st through 14:29 on the 14th = the releasing time frame.

From 14:30 on the 14th through 13:09 on the 28th = the bring time frame.

From 13:10 on the 9th through 24:00 on the 30th = the releasing time frame.

October 2004

From 00:00 on the 1st through 2:48 on the 14th = the releasing time frame.

From 2:49 on the 14th through 3:07 on the 28th = the bring time frame.

From 3:08 on the 28th through 24:00 on the 31st = the releasing time frame.

November 2004

From 00:00 on the 1st through 14:27 on the 12th = the releasing time frame.

From 14:28 on the 12th through 20:07 on the 26th = the bring time frame.

132

From 20:08 on the 26th through 24:00 on the 30th = the releasing time frame.

December 2004

From 00:00 on the 1st through 1:29 on the 12th = the releasing time frame.

From 1:30 on the 12th through 15:06 on the 26th = the bring time frame.

From 15:07 on the 26th through 24:00 on the 31st = the releasing time frame.

January 2005

From 00:00 on the 1st through 12:03 on the 10th = the releasing time frame.

From 12:04 on the 10th through 10:32 on the 25th = the bring time frame.

From 10:33 on the 25th through 24:00 on the 31st = the releasing time frame.

February 2005

From 00:00 on the 1st through 22:28 on the 8th = the releasing time frame.

From 22:29 on the 8th through 4:54 on the 24th = the bring time frame.

From 4:55 on the 24th through 24:00 on the 28th = the releasing time frame.

March 2005

From 00:00 on the 1st through 9:11 on the 10th = the releasing time frame.

From 9:12 on the 10th through 20:59 on the 25th = the bring time frame.

From 21:00 on the 25th through 24:00 on the 31st = the releasing time frame.

April 2005

From 00:00 on the 1st through 20:32 on the 8th = the releasing time frame.

From 20:33 on the 8th through 10:06 on the 24th = the bring time frame.

From 10:07 on the 24th through 24:00 on the 30th = the releasing time frame.

May 2005

From 00:00 on the 1st through 8:46 on the 8th = the releasing time frame.

From 8:47 on the 8th through 20:18 on the 23rd = the bring time frame.

From 20:19 on the 23rd through 24:00 on the 31st = the releasing time frame.

June 2005

From 00:00 on the 1st through 21:55 on the 6th = the releasing time frame.

From 21:56 on the 6th through 4:14 on the 22nd = the bring time frame.

134

From 4:14 on the 22nd through 24:00 on the 30th = the releasing time frame.

July 2005

From 00:00 on the 1st through 12:03 on the 6th = the releasing time frame.

From 12:04 on the 6th through 11:00 on the 21st = the bring time frame.

From 11:01 on the 21st through 24:00 on the 31st = the releasing time frame.

August 2005

From 00:00 on the 1st through 3:05 on the 5th = the releasing time frame.

From 3:06 on the 5th through 17:53 on the 19th = the bring time frame.

From 17:54 on the 19th through 24:00 on the 31st = the releasing time frame.

September 2005

From 00:00 on the 1st through 18:45 on the 3rd = the releasing time frame.

From 18:46 on the 3rd through 2:01 on the 18th = the bring time frame.

From 2:02 on the 18th through 24:00 on the 30th = the releasing time frame.

October 2005

From 00:00 on the 1st through 10:28 on the 3rd = the releasing time frame.

From 10:29 on the 3rd through 12:14 on the 17th = the bring time frame.

From 12:15 on the 17th through 24:00 on the 31st = the releasing time frame.

November 2005

From 00:00 on the 1st through 1:25 on the 2nd = the releasing time frame.

From 1:26 on the 2nd through 0:58 on the 16th = the bring time frame.

From 0:59 on the 16th through 24:00 on the 30th = the releasing time frame.

December 2005

From 00:00 on the 1st through 15:01 on the 1st = the releasing time frame.

From 15:02 on the 1st through 16:16 on the 15th = the bring time frame.

From 16:17 on the 15th through 3:12 on the 31st = the releasing time frame.

From 3:13 on the 31st through 24:00 on the 31st = the bring time frame.

January 2006

From 00:00 on the 1st through 9:48 on the 14th = the bring time frame.

136

From 9:49 on the 14th through 14:15 on the 29th = the releasing time frame.

From 14:16 on the 29th through 24:00 on the 31st = the bring time frame.

February 2006

From 00:00 on the 1st through 4:44 on the 13th = the bring time frame.

From 4:45 on the 13th through 0:31 on the 28th = the releasing time frame.

From 0:32 on the 28th through 24:00 on the 28th = the bring time frame.

March 2006

From 00:00 on the 1st through 23:36 on the 14th = the bring time frame.

From 23:37 on the 14th through 10:15 on the 29th = the releasing time frame.

From 10:16 on the 29th through 24:00 on the 31st = the bring time frame.

April 2006

From 00:00 on the 1st through 16:40 on the 13th = the bring time frame.

From 16:41 on the 13th through 19:44 on the 27th = the releasing time frame.

From 19:45 on the 27th through 24:00 on the 30th = the bring time frame.

May 2006

137

From 00:00 on the 1st through 6:51 on the 13th = the bring time frame.

From 6:52 on the 13th through 5:26 on the 27th = the releasing time frame.

From 5:27 on the 27th through 24:00 on the 31st = the bring time frame.

June 2006

From 00:00 on the 1st through 18:03 on the 11th = the bring time frame.

From 18:04 on the 11th through 16:05 on the 25th = the releasing time frame.

From 16:06 on the 25th through 24:00 on the 30th = the bring time frame.

July 2006

From 00:00 on the 1st through 3:02 on the 11th = the bring time frame.

From 3:03 on the 11th through 4:31 on the 25th = the releasing time frame.

From 4:32 on the 25th through 24:00 on the 31st = the bring time frame.

August 2006

From 00:00 on the 1st through 10:54 on the 9th = the bring time frame.

138

From 10:55 on the 9th through 19:10 on the 23rd = the releasing time frame.

From 19:11 on the 23rd through 24:00 on the 31st = the bring time frame.

September 2006

From 00:00 on the 1st through 18:42 on the 7th = the bring time frame.

From 18:43 on the 7th through 11:45 on the 22nd = the releasing time frame.

From 11:46 on the 22nd through 24:00 on the 30th = the bring time frame.

October 2006

From 00:00 on the 1st through 3:13 on the 7th = the bring time frame.

From 3:14 on the 7th through 5:14 on the 22nd = the releasing time frame.

From 5:15 on the 22nd through 24:00 on the 31st = the bring time frame.

November 2006

From 00:00 on the 1st through 12:58 on the 5th = the bring time frame.

From 12:59 on the 5th through 22:18 on the 20th = the releasing time frame.

From 22:19 on the 20th through 24:00 on the 30th = the bring time frame.

December 2006

From 00:00 on the 1st through 0:25 on the 5th = the bring time frame.

From 0:26 on the 5th through 14:01 on the 20th = the releasing time frame.

From 14:02 on the 20th through 24:00 on the 31st = the bring time frame.

January 2007
From 00:00 on the 1st through 13:58 on the 3rd = the bring time frame.

From 13:59 on the 3rd through 4:01 on the 19th = the releasing time frame.

From 4:02 on the 19th through 24:00 on the 31st = the bring time frame.

February 2007

From 00:00 on the 1st through 5:45 on the 2nd = the bring time frame.

From 5:46 on the 2nd through 16:14 on the 17th = the releasing time frame.

From 16:15 on the 17th through 24:00 on the 28th = the bring time frame.

March 2007

From 00:00 on the 1st through 23:17 on the 3rd = the bring time frame.

140

From 23:17 on the 3rd through 2:43 on the 19th = the releasing time frame.

From 2:44 on the 19th through 24:00 on the 31st = the bring time frame

April 2007

From 00:00 on the 1st through 17:15 on the 2nd = the bring time frame.

From 17:16 on the 2nd through 11:36 on the 17th = the releasing time frame

From 11:37 on the 17th through 24:00 on the 30th = the bring time frame.

May 2007

From 00:00 on the 1st through 10:09 on the 2nd = the bring time frame.

From 10:10 on the 2nd through 19:27 on the 16th = the releasing time frame.

From 19:29 on the 16th through 24:00 on the 31st = the bring time frame.

June 2007

From 00:00 on the 1st through 1:04 on the 1st = the bring time frame.

From 1:05 on the 1st through 3:13 on the 15th = the releasing time frame.

From 3:14 on the 15th through 13:49 on the 30th = the bring time frame.

From 13:50 on the 30th through 24:00 on the 30th = the releasing time frame.

July 2007

From 00:00 on the 1st through 12:04 on the 14th = the releasing time frame.

From 12:05 on the 14th through 0:48 on the 30th = the bring time frame.

From 0:49 on the 30th through 24:00 on the 31st = the releasing time frame.

August 2007

From 00:00 on the 1st through 23:03 on the 12th = the releasing time frame.

From 23:04 on the 12th through 10:35 on the 28th = the bring time frame.

From 10:6 on the 28th through 24:00 on the 31st = the releasing time frame.

September 2007

From 00:00 on the 1st through 12:44 on the 11th = the releasing time frame.

From 12:45 on the 11th through 19:45 on the 26th = the bring time frame.

From 19:46 on the 26th through 24:00 on the 30th = the releasing time frame.

October 2007

From 00:00 on the 1st through on the 11th = the releasing time frame.

From 5:02 on the 11th through 4:52 on the 26th = the bring time frame.

From 4:53 on the 26th through 24:00 on the 31st = the releasing time frame.

November 2007

From 00:00 on the 1st through 23:03 on the 9th = the releasing time frame.

From 23:04 on the 9th through 14:30 on the 24th = the bring time frame.

November 2007 continued

From 14:31 on the 24th through 24:00 on the 30th = the releasing time frame.

December 2007

From 00:00 on the 1st through 17:40 on the 9th = the releasing time frame.

From 17:41 on the 9th through 1:16 on the 24th = the bring time frame.

From 1:17 on the 24th through 24:00 on the 31st = the releasing time frame.

January 2008

From 00:00 on the 1st through 11:37 on the 8th = the releasing time frame.

143

From 11:38 on the 8th through 13:35 on the 22nd = the bring time frame.

From 13:36 on the 22nd through 24:00 on the 31st = the releasing time frame.

February 2008

From 00:00 on the 1st through 3:45 on the 7th = the releasing time frame.

From 3:46 on the 7th through 3:31 on the 21st = the bring time frame.

From 3:32 on the 21st through 24:00 on the 29th = the releasing time frame.

March 2008
From 00:00 on the 1st through 17:14 on the 7th = the releasing time frame.

From 17:15 on the 7th through 18:40 on the 21st = the bring time frame.

From 18:41 on the 21st through 24:00 on the 31st = the releasing time frame.

April 2008

From 00:00 on the 1st through 3:55 on the 6th = the releasing time frame.

From 3:56 on the 6th through 10:25 on the 20th = the bring time frame.

144

From 10:26 on the 20th through 24:00 on the 30th = the releasing time frame.

May 2008

From 00:00 on the 1st through 12:18 on the 5th = the releasing time frame.

From 12:19 on the 5th through 2:11 on the 20th = the bring time frame.

From 2:12 on the 20th through 24:00 on the 31st = the releasing time frame.

June 2008

From 00:00 on the 1st through 19:23 on the 3rd = the releasing time frame.

From 19:24 on the 3rd through 17:31 on the 18th = the bring time frame.

From 17:32 on the 18 through 24:00 on the 30th = the releasing time frame.

July 2008

From 00:00 on the 1st through 2:19 on the 3rd = the releasing time frame.

From 2:20 on the 3rd through 7:59 on the 18th = the bring time frame.

From 8:00 on the 18th through 24:00 on the 31st = the releasing time frame.

August 2008

145

From 00:00 on the 1st through 10:13 on the 1st = the releasing time frame.

From 10:14 on the 1st through 21:17 on the 16th = the bring time frame.

From 21:18 on the 16th through 19:58 on the 30th = the releasing time frame.

From 19:59 on the 30th through 24:00 on the 31st = the bring time frame.

September 2008

From 00:00 on the 1st through 9:13 on the 15th = the bring time frame.

From 9:14 on the 15th through 8:12 on the 29th = the releasing time frame.

From 8:13 on the 29th through 24:00 on the 30th = the bring time frame.

October 2008
From 00:00 on the 1st through 20:02 on the 14th = the bring time frame.

From 20:03 on the 14th through 23:14 on the 28th = the releasing time frame.

From 23:15 on the 28th through 24:00 on the 31st = the bring time frame.

November 2008
From 00:00 on the 1st through 6:17 on the 13th = the bring time frame.

From 6:18 on the 13th through 16:55 on the 27th = the releasing time frame.

From 16:56 on the 27th through 24:00 on the 30th = the bring time frame.

December 2008

From 00:00 on the 1st through 16:37 on the 12th = the bring time frame.

From 16:38 on the 12th through 12:22 on the 27th = the releasing time frame.

From 12:23 on the 27th through 24:00 on the 31st = the bring time frame.

January 2009
From 00:00 on the 1st through 3:27 on the 11th = the bring time frame.

From 3:28 on the 11th through 7:55 on the 26th = the releasing time frame.

From 7:56 on the 26th through 24:00 on the 31st = the bring time frame.

February 2009

From 00:00 on the 1st through 14:49 on the 9th = the bring time frame.

From 14:50 on the 9th through 1:35 on the 25th = the releasing time frame.

From on the 25th through 24:00 on the 28th = the bring time frame.

March 2009

From 00:00 on the 1st through 2:38 on the 11th = the bring time frame.

From 2:39 on the 11th through 16:06 on the 26th = the releasing time frame.

From 16:07 on the 26th through 24:00 on the 31st = the bring time frame.

April 2009

From 00:00 on the 1st through 14:56 on the 9th = the bring time frame.

From 14:57 on the 9th through 3:23 on the 25th = the releasing time frame.

From 3:24 on the 25th through 24:00 on the 30th = the bring time frame.

May 2009

From 00:00 on the 1st through 4:02 on the 9th = the bring time frame.

From 4:03 on the 9th through 12:11 on the 24th = the releasing time frame.

From 12:12 on the 24th through 24:00 on the 31st = the bring time frame.

June 2009
From 00:00 on the 1st through 18:12 on the 7th = the bring time frame.

From 18:13 on the 7th through 19:35 on the 22nd = the releasing time frame.

From 19:36 on the 22nd through 24:00 on the 30th = the bring time frame.

July 2009

From 00:00 on the 1st through 9:22 on the 7th = the bring time frame.

From 9:23 on the 7th through 2:35 on the 22nd = the releasing time frame.

From 2:36 on the 22nd through 24:00 on the 31st = the bring time frame.

August 2009

From 00:00 on the 1st through 0:55 on the 6th = the bring time frame.

From 0:56 on the 6th through 10:02 on the 20th = the releasing time frame.

From 10:03 on the 20th through 24:00 on the 31st = the bring time frame.

September 2009

From 00:00 on the 1st through 16:03 on the 4th = the bring time frame.

From 16:04 on the 4th through 18:44 on the 18th = the releasing time frame.

From 18:45 on the 18th through 24:00 on the 30th = the bring time frame.

149

October 2009

From 00:00 on the 1st through 6:10 on the 4th = the bring time frame.

From 6:11 on 4th through 5:33 on the 18th = the releasing time frame.

From 5:34 on the 18th through 24:00 on the 31st = the bring time frame.

November 2009
From 00:00 on the 1st through 19:14 on the 2nd = the bring time frame.

From 19:15 on the 2nd through 19:14 on the 16th = the releasing time frame.

From 19:15 on the 16th through 24:00 on the 30th = the bring time frame.

December 2009

From 00:00 on the 1st through 7:31 on the 2nd = the bring time frame.

From 7:32 on the 2nd through 12:02 on the 16th = the releasing time frame.

From 12:03 on the 16th through 19:13 on the 31st = the bring time frame.

From 19:14 on the 31st through 24:00 on the 31st = the releasing time frame.

January 2010

From 00:00 on the 1st through 7:11 on the 15th = the releasing time frame.

From 7:12 on the 15th through 6:18 on the 30th = the bring time frame.

From 6:19 on the 30th through 24:00 on the 31st = the releasing time frame.

February 2010

From 00:00 on the 1st through 2:51 on the 14th = the releasing time frame.

From 2:52 on the 14th through 16:38 on the 28th = the bring time frame.

From 16:39 on the 28th through 24:00 on the 28th = the releasing time frame.

March 2010

From 00:00 on the 1st through 21:01 on the 15th = the releasing time frame.

From 21:02 on the 15th through 2:26 on the 30th = the bring time frame.

From 2:27 on the 30th through 24:00 on the 31st = the releasing time frame.

April 2010

From 00:00 on the 1st through 12:29 on the 14th = the releasing time frame.

From 12:30 on the 14th through 12:19 on the 28th = the bring time frame.

From 12:20 on the 28th through 24:00 on the 30th = the releasing time frame.

May 2010

From 00:00 on the 1st through 1:04 on the 14th = the releasing time frame.

From 1:05 on the 14th through 23:07 on the 27th = the bring time frame.

From 23:08 on the 27th through 24:00 on the 31st = the releasing time frame.

June 2010

From 00:00 on the 1st through 11:15 on the 12th = the releasing time frame.

From 11:16 on the 12th through 11:30 on the 26th = the bring time frame.

From 11:31 on the 26th through 24:00 on the 30th = the releasing time frame.

July 2010

From 00:00 on the 1st through 19:41 on the 11th = the releasing time frame.

From 19:42 on the 11th through 1:37 on the 26th = the bring time frame.

From 1:38 on the 26th through 24:00 on the 31st = the releasing time frame.

August 2010

From 00:00 on the 1st through 3:08 on the 10th = the releasing time frame.

From 3:09 on the 10th through 17:05 on the 24th = the bring time frame.

From 17:06 on the 24th through 24:00 on the 31st = the releasing time frame.

September 2010

From 00:00 on the 1st through 10:30 on the 8th = the releasing time frame.

From 10:31 on the 8th through 9:17 on the 23rd = the bring time frame.

From 9:18 on the 23rd through 24:00 on the 30th = the releasing time frame.

October 2010

From 00:00 on the 1st through 18:45 on the 7th = the releasing time frame.

From 18:46 on the 7th through 1:37 on the 23rd = the bring time frame.

From 1:38 on the 23rd through 24:00 on the 31st = the releasing time frame.

November 2010

From 00:00 on the 1st through 4:52 on the 6th = the releasing time frame.

153

From 4:53 on the 6th through 17:27 on the 21st = the bring time frame.

From 17:28 on the 21st through 24:00 on the 30th = the releasing time frame.

December 2010

From 00:00 on the 1st through 17:36 on the 5th = the releasing time frame.

From 17:37 on the 5th through 8:14 on the 21st = the bring time frame.

From 8:15 on the 21st through 24:00 on the 31st = the releasing time frame.

January 2011

From 00:00 on the 1st through 9:03 on the 4th = the releasing time frame.

From 9:04 on the 4th through 21:21 on the 19th = the bring time frame.

From 21:22 on the 19th through 24:00 on the 31st = the releasing time frame.

February 2011

From 00:00 on the 1st through 2:31 on the 3rd = the releasing time frame.

From 2:32 on the 3rd through 8:36 on the 18th = the bring time frame.

COEXISTING CYCLES

Within each cycle, there are coexistent cycles. Each cycle will effect your feelings and emotions in conjunction with each other.

The following numbered days will dictate your feelings and emotions on each particular issue. The Bring and Release Time Frame will dictate your mood or perception on the cycle. During the Bring Time Frame to enhance your cycle, light the colored candle that represents your mood. During the Release Time Frame, light a red candle upside down to release your emotions if you wish to keep the issue, waiting for it to work itself out. Light the colored candle that represents the situation, if your wish is to release yourself from the issue altogether.

The shaded area - indicates the Release Time Frame, with the non-shaded indicates the Bring Time Frame.

1st, 13th, 25th	+ Confidence and positive contracts. - Personal conflicts.
2nd, 14th, 26th	+ Good day to ask for a raise. - Problems with money.
3rd, 15th, 27th	+ Good day to write and publish. - Communication problems with others.
4th, 16th, 28th	+ Good feelings about accomplishments. - The urge to move or get away.
5th, 17th, 29th	+ Creative and expressive. - Problems expressing yourself.
6th, 18th, 30th	+ Good for new job or relationships. - Problems with coworkers.
7th, 19th, 31st	+ Start new business out of your home. - You think the world is against you.
8th, 20th	+ Days to reap what you have sown. - Everyone wants what you have.
9th, 21st	+ Good day for travel. - Problem with your car.
10th, 22nd	+ Good day for bonding. - Childhood dredging.
11th, 23rd	+ Days to enjoy life. - Problems with plans.
12th, 24th	+ Days you will not hurt yourself. - Days you might sabotage yourself.

155

WHO NEEDS TO LIGHT CANDLES

Lighting candles is a personal preference. Anyone wishing to live on the American Dream, in the pursuit of happiness, should light candles. Anyone with the religious belief and the understanding that God, the Father; God, the Son; and God, the Holy Ghost, will assist you in your time of need should light candles. Anyone wanting to improve the quality of their life should light candles. Anyone who cannot conceive that lighting a candle can improve the quality of life should light candles. Anyone who wishes to incite changes into their life should light candles. Anyone needing money, or anyone wanting to be loved, or who has a desire to love someone else, should light candles. Anyone with a need to study who possesses a lack of concentration should light candles ... and the list goes on and on.

The simple fact of the matter is that civilized people have a tendency to allow society and culture to dictate their wishes, but not their hearts, their minds and even perhaps, their souls; thus, ending up living the life that is socially acceptable, but going against what they inherently want for themselves.

Light your candles! Your life can be better and you can thank a friend for it.

CANDLES DO MAKE A DIFFERENCE

Not everyone can go into a bookstore, pick out a book on candles, and become "candle literate." For some, the road to the understanding of candles has been covered by downed power lines. His is Stephen's story.

Stephen had a problem. He was an account representative at a mid-sized computer firm and felt unappreciated. He had not received a raise in over two years. He hated his boss. Several coworkers had quit, leaving him covered with extra work. His wife had run off with his neighbor's butler, and Stephen had a heart problem, making it all but impossible to quit his job, the health benefits were too good. To top it all off, a recent storm had downed power lines, stranding him at home with no electricity. "No problem," he grumbled to himself, grabbing a handful of candles from under the sink. "Might just as well make the best of it."

156

Stephen lit a yellow candle, then sank into his favorite chair to read some book his wife had "graciously" left behind. Oddly enough, it was on candles.

The soft light and silence set in. He was soon fast asleep.

He awoke with the book still in his hand. It was dark and he saw a warm glow in the east. Daylight soon. The candle had burnt out. His watch showed 5:45 A.M.

Matter-of-factly, he mumbled, "Time to get to work." The lights were still out, so he shaved with a hand razor, washed his face, and ate a leisurely breakfast.

Stephen somehow thought he felt wonderfully different. Activities seemed to flow. Even the boss smiled, and asked Stephen's opinion about something, and took the time to listen about Stephen's need for help. "I'll check into that," he said, sliding into his office. The boss had said that before, but, for some reason, this time it felt more sincere.

Arriving at home that evening, Stephen found that the lights had come back on. He did not, however, run to the T.V. set - his usual habit. Instead, he picked up the same book that he had started the night before, and continued to read about candles.

"Yellow, yellow, yellow - here it is - communication and contracts," he mumbled. "Well, I'll be ..." Enthralled, Stephen spent hours that night pouring over the book that would become his constant companion.

He asked for and got a raise after lighting a green candle. He received added support on the job after lighting a blue candle. No problem! And now, he has a new relationship. "Red candles work wonders, " the book said, "for passion." Plus, his heart hasn't given him any problems since the lights went out.

Hopefully, you won't have to wait until the lights go out to discover the accuracy behind lighting candles, but if you do, remember to always keep a handful under the sink ...

When lighting candles for a specific reason, it is called "lighting candles to purpose." When your "purpose" has been established, you will then be able to ascertain the proper color, the perfect time, and the correct methodology for your wish to come true. In this section, we will discuss all of these principles.

Now that you have experimented and experienced the effectiveness of candle lighting through the last section, you are ready to expand your experience by diversifying the techniques in which you will be lighting your candles to purpose. In this section, there will be such examples as how to flip candles to release negative energy, and how to intensify the energy of the candles that you will be lighting, as well as how to determine whether or not your wish will come to pass as you expect. Candle lighting will become an important part of your life; thus, there will be no room for error.

You may also wish to make your own candles, establishing purpose for your candle from the beginning. This will enable your intent to be much stronger.

With your newfound knowledge of color, with correct timing and candles, there will be no stopping you ...

LIGHTING A CANDLE TO GET YOUR WISH

When lighting a candle for a specific wish, there are a number of exercises that you might want to try. These exercises will enable you to obtain your wish, as well as help you phrase your desire, in order for your wish to manifest.

EXERCISE #1

The first exercise will be to light a pink candle to represent your desire, with full intent for your wish to manifest. Light your candle during the time frame that is indicated in this book under the BRING column, assuming that your wish is to bring you something or someone. If your wish is to rid yourself from something or someone, light your pink candle during the time frame indicated by the RELEASE column.

EXERCISE #2

158

The second wish candle exercise will be to write your wish on a piece of parchment paper. Wrap your paper around your pink tapered candle with a small piece of string or ribbon. If your paper burns completely with your candle, your wish will come true. If your paper only partially burns, this is an indication that your wish will interfere with the free will of another; thus, you will have to rephrase your wish or desire and try your candle exercise again.

CANDLE LIGHTING TO GET YOUR WISH

EXERCISE #3

Your third wish candle exercise will be to choose the color of candle that will best represent your wish: pink, for love; green, for money; orange, for good health; purple, for spiritual insight, etc. Write your wish in the wax of your candle. If your candle burns all the way down and does not put itself out, your wish will come true. If your candle goes out before it has had a chance to burn all the way down, you must rephrase your desire. Your wish cannot and will not manifest if your intent is to interfere with the free will of another. Rephrase your wish and try again.

EXERCISE #4

The fourth wish candle exercise will be to light three pink seven-day candles, one each day for three days. On the fourth day, light a brown seven-day candle. If the brown candle goes out before the last pink candle, your wish will soon come to pass.

THERE IS NO CANDLE EXERCISE THAT YOU CAN DO TO INTERFERE WITH THE FREE WILL OF OTHERS.

LIGHTING CANDLES TO RELEASE FINANCIAL DIFFICULTIES

When lighting a candle, you are allowing your concerns to burn away from the flame of the candle. Not everyone will grasp the concept that lighting a colored candle can aid in the quality of their life, and so be it. For those who do, life will be waiting to grant them their every whim.

159

As you begin to light candles to release financial difficulties, there is one thing that you must do. And, for some with financial problems, this may be hard, but you must invest anywhere between three and four dollars to get yourself started. This cost will be for your first candle. This candle should be designed to stay lit for five to seven days.

When buying a green candle, and lighting it between the time frame marked BRING in your timing guide, your candle will incite much more than your three dollar investment to come to you.

LIGHTING CANDLES TO ACCEPT MONEY

Everyone over the age of twelve has experienced the need for money. When applying for a job, we all know what is needed in order to make ends meet. However, how can you ask for the amount of money that you need? You see, when unemployment sets in, insecurity is a tendency that follows close behind.

When seeking employment to assure yourself that you will receive the amount of money that you need, first light a red candle that you have designed to release negative energy. When you find your self-esteem low and there seems to be an inability to see your own worth, it may be that you are holding on to dysfunctional thought patterns connected to your worth, thus keeping you from achieving your goals. These red candles will aid in the release of these thought patterns, as well as release negative energy. Light your red candle upside down during the release time frame.

Secondly, on the first day of the bring time frame, light one green candle, one blue candle, and one yellow candle. Your green, blue, and yellow candles should be designed to stay lit for five to seven days. This will ensure you a healthy self-esteem, a positive self-worth, and the income that you need. The blue candle will aid in maintaining your balance, while the yellow candle will allow the communications to remain open so you will receive the money (green candle) that you're seeking.

MONEY DRAWING EXERCISES

When your cash flow is low and there seems to be no relief in sight, there is a candle exercise that you can do to ensure that your money will be plentiful for your expenses.

First, light one red candle upside down to release any negative energy connected to your having money.

The second thing you do is light one green candle on the first day of the BRING column in your timing guide. On the second day, you light another green candle, and, on the third day, you light the third green candle. On the fourth day, light one green candle and one yellow candle. The green will keep the money flowing and the yellow will keep the communication open, so that the money may continue.

MONEY DRAWING EXERCISES

On the fifth day, light one more red candle upside down, releasing all negative energy connected to your having money, as well as any blocks that you may have on a subconscious level, that has prevented you from succeeding on a financial level.

RELEASING YOURSELF FROM UNWANTED ENERGY

Negative energy continues to live and breathe as you do. The only difference is that negative energy seems to breed and multiply.

Have you ever noticed that your fear (negative energy) grows through your thoughts, as you communicate with others? When you have this negative energy around you, you will attract others with the same negative energy around them; thus, the breeding of negative energy has begun.

We all know that candle lighting will enable you to succeed in your endeavors. This is known, but how many people actually have experienced or understand the mechanics behind lighting candles to release things, people, situations, and negative energy from them?

Lighting a candle to release yourself from something will not lessen your active involvement in life. It will not only enable you to live a freer, more harmonious life of your choosing, releasing you from negative people, we well as releasing you from negative energy which causes you to attract negative people in the first place.

161

RELEASING IS IMPORTANT. Matter can only occupy one space at one time, thus releasing is essential. Use the following exercises to do your releasing.

Remember to always use your timing guide in this book. To properly release, you should **NEVER** do a releasing exercise, other than flipping candles, during the **BRING** time frame.

FLIPPING CANDLES

Have you ever had a day that makes you wish you had just stayed in bed? Well, those days can now be remedied.

If red stick candles bring energy, is it not safe to say that if you flip that same candle and light it from the bottom, that the energy will go away? Fortunately, it does.

The world is full of negative energy. When you have a bad day, it is because some of that negative energy has attached itself to you. You can't see negative energy. Just like you can't see happiness, you merely feel it. This negative energy exists nonetheless.

The term "flipping a candle" first started with the gypsies in Brussels, then in the northeastern regions of the United States. Gypsies would "flip" dandles to ensure that they would not get caught committing a crime, or that they would be exonerated, if they were caught, thus keeping them from incarceration.

The same will apply today. If you want something to go away, something that you apparently have no control over, take a red stick candle, (a red candle that has been designed to be laced in a candle stick holder), and cut the top of the candle, so that you can properly place it in a candle stick holder. Cut the wax around the bottom of the candle, so that the wick is exposed. Place the candle upside down in your candle stick holder. Light the wick that you have exposed, releasing all negative energy around you. Ouila'! A good day.

Flipping red candles with the intent to release negative energy can be done at any time. There is never a bad time to flip a red candle.

162

RELEASE COMPETITION IN A RELATIONISHIP

When you are actively involved in a relationship, you must always work at keeping that relationship alive.

When you feel as if there is an outside interference, light a red candle using the flipping method. This exercise can be done at anytime.

When there is another person actively pursuing the one who you are involved with, light a red candle upside down. The only difference here is that you will be writing the name of the person who is interfering into the wax of the candle. This exercise can be done anytime.

CANDLE EXERCISE

There are certain times when candle lighting is more powerful than any other time of the year. During these times, you will benefit immensely by building up the energies of your candle lighting.

This is done by lighting one candle to purpose a day, repeating it for seven days. For instance, if you light a pink candle to bring you a new love, you would light a pink candle every day for seven days. To stabilize your energy and your intent, on the eighth day, you will need to light a pink candle, as well as a brown candle, to give you the consistency and the stabilizing flow from the pink candles.

With this same concept in mid when looking for money, you need to light seven green candles, one a day for seven days, and on the eighth day, you light one green candle and one yellow candle. This will allow the energy to continue the open communications that will allow the money to flow.

The same will apply when lighting candles for good health. Light orange candles for seven days, with blue and orange candles lit on the eighth day. This will allow the balance to continue to flow through the orange candles.

This same principle will apply with any candle you light during this special time. On the eighth day, light a complementary candle with the same color that you have been lighting for the last seven days.

163

The ephemeral guide will give you the dates on which these candles exercises will be most effective.

MAKING CANDLES TO PURPOSE

Making your own candles will give you hours of rich and rewarding experiences. S you begin to melt your wax, your thoughts and concentration will be on your desired result.

When money is a necessity, it is hard to keep from thinking about what you need. The same tends to apply when it has been some time since your last date.

In this book, you will learn such things as how to add household spices, dried flowers, and yard shrubs to your candles to increase the intent of your purpose.

EQUIPMENT YOU WILL NEED BEFORE YOU BEGIN

1.Heavy gauge sauce pan or double boiler
2.Metal strainer
3.Thin wire wick
4.Candle molds
5.Long metal rod
6.Colored dyes for candle wax
7.Candle wax hardener
8.9/10ths paraffin
9.1/10th bees wax
10.Candle making thermometer

WARNINGS: WHEN MAKING CANDLES

NEVER leave candle wax to melt unattended. **WAX IS HIGHLY FLAMMABLE AND CAN COMBUST,** if it gets too hot. **NEVER:** allow wax to boil. **ALWAYS** follow directions on your paraffin package when melting wax.

164

MAKING CANDLES FOR PURPOSE

Using a heavy gauge sauce pan or double boiler, melt 9/10ths paraffin with 1/10th bees wax. Melt your wax on low heat. (When the wax has melted, you may add your spices and oils.)

As your wax is melting, put your "wick end" on your wick. (A "wick end" is a flat piece of metal that will weigh the end of your wick to the bottom of your candle.) Wrap the top end of your wick to a pencil. After you pouryour wax, lay the pencil across the top of your glass jar or mold, keeping your wick straight.

For candles made in a plastic or plaster mold, heat your wax to 160 to 180 degrees. Glass molded candle wax should be heated to 170 to 200 degrees. For acrylic and clay molded candles, heat your wax to 180 to 200 degrees. Use a candle making thermometer to determine the proper degree of your candle wax.

When following these directions, your candle will not sink in the middle. Sinking may be a problem if your wax does not heat to the proper temperature.

Stir in your hardener and add the color of your choice. Pour the wax into the molds of choice (there are none that are better than others).

After you pour the wax into the molds, run a long metal rod down the side of your wick. Allow the wax to begin to set up. Take the rod out and continue to run it down the center of your candle, at least four to five times, as your wax is beginning to harden. This will allow the air to be released from your wax.

Your last step is to light your candles during the appropriate times for your purpose.

When making candles to purpose, you can add colored dyes to make the color of your choice. There are also kitchen spices, fresh flowers, and shrub clippings that you can add to your candle wax to intensify the energy of your candles. Your intent, in conjunction with your candle, will expedite your desire.

165

When using spices and flowers, add them when the wax is melting. Always strain your wax through a metal strainer when adding anything to wax, so as to not have residue in your candle that may interfere with the burning of your candle.

LOVE DRAWING RECIPES

Melt 9/10ths paraffin with 1/10th bees wax. Add pink colored dye to get your desired color results. (When adding color to your candle wax, the more vibrant the color, the happier you will be with your new love.)
Add 1 teaspoon of pulverized cinnamon.
Add two drops of clove oil.
Add one fourth more hardener than your hardener package indicates.
Strain your wax through a metal strainer when pouring your candles.
Allow the new love drawing candle to set up.

Light your candle during the first available date indicated on your timing guide to bring things to you.
Sit back and get excited!

Cinnamon and clove oil, harmoniously working in conjunction with your pink color, will give you a long-term love. Cinnamon added to any candle base will give you the harmony of which fairy tales are made. The clove oil in this candle will ensure that if there is an end to your newfound relationship, it will not be painful.

INCREASING YOUR SEXUAL PROWESS

In the sixties, sexual promiscuity was on the rise.

During the seventies and the eighties, there seemed to be a hush of silence regarding the once freely given acts of love, with open displays of lust and passion. Lust and passion, I might add, never died - only the blatantness of the promiscuity subsided.

As we enter the 1990s, once again we begin to hear open conversations about the sexual relationships between men and women. Sexual comments and sexual innuendoes seem to be a common topic again.

However, talking is not enough to ensure you a sexual partner. Sexually-transmitted diseases have made sexual adventures a frightening pastime.

Women can discuss their sexual preferences, but even this will not ensure that there will be someone out there for them. Now that sex is no longer a religious experience, isn't it time for those with the desire to explore and experience to have the opportunity to do so, thus attracting that perfect

INCREASING YOUR SEXUAL PROWESS

healthy mate for as long as you care to keep him? This exercise has been written primarily for women. Isn't it fun, now that the tables have turned? Now, men are the objects of animalistic lust and sexual advances, as opposed to women, as it had been for years!

In order to attract a sexual partner, make five red candles. In these red candles, put two drops of lavender extract and one drop of almond oil. The red candle will ensure that the lust will continue for as long as you are interested in the man who you have attracted. The lavender will bring him to you without effort, and the almond oil gives you the power without the emotional attachment.

Light the red candles one a day for five days, beginning on the first day listed under the BRING column. Now, sit back and wait for that hunk to be yours.

ENSURING A LOVE WITH PROTECTION

When your intent is to bring in a love who is warm and tender, the ingredients that you need to add to your pink candles are a lot different than those previously listed. With tenderness and sensitivity being your main objective, you need to add the following ingredients to your basic candle: one teaspoon of pulverized lavender and two drops of vanilla extract.

Light three pink candles designed to bring love, one a day for three days, starting on the second day of your BRING column. On the fourth day, light one brown candle that you have made to purpose for protection (see recipe for protection).

When lighting one candle, it will ensure your love for thirty days. Three candles will ensure the same love for ninety days. During this same ninety-day period, should you find that you no longer with to continue the relationship that your candle has brought to you, you will have the remaining time for another love to come to you. By lighting a brown candle, this love energy will last four times longer, giving you three hundred and sixty days to explore your love possibilities.

These candles should only be lit during the times indicated in your timing guide under the BRING column. If you light these same candles at the

ENSURING A LOVE WITH PROTECTION

wrong time, your love will be detoured for the same three hundred and sixty days. Even though there will be a second chance to light your candles during the appropriate time, you will still be under the conflict that you have set up by lighting them incorrectly.

SECURING YOUR RELATIONSHIP

Cathy had been dating Johnny for three years. Their relationship had gone through the usual ups and downs, but for the most part, she felt they had a really good relationship.

Cathy was still in school, and Johnny worked for a local newspaper as a press mechanic. Their plans were to marry upon Cathy's graduation.

One evening, Johnny was working late, so Cathy went to dinner with some friends from school. As Cathy and her friends were being seated, Cathy noticed a friend of hers having dinner in the same restaurant.

When she approached her friend, she noticed that her friend's date was none other than her boyfriend, Johnny. Shocked, yes. Amazed, a bit.
Mad, a lot!

Cathy had always had the reputation of being a lady and was not about to create a scene. She said hi to her friend and ignored Johnny. Cathy, losing her appetite, left with her friends.

Cathy was sure that Johnny had a good excuse, and she would go home and he would call. Two days passed, no call.

The next week, Cathy - a nervous wreck - cried every night. Johnny was gone and her plans for the future were over.

Cathy talked to a friend of hers. Her friend told her that if she would call Johnny, she could clear the whole thing up, and they could get back together. Since Cathy had too much pride, she couldn't do such a thing.

Talking to another friend, Cathy discovered that if she made seven pink candles and put two teaspoons of dried chives in the candle wax as it melted, Johnny would call her and the relationship could then continue.

SECURING YOUR RELATIONSHIP

This was something that seemed absurd to Cathy, but she did want Johnny back. Cathy concluded that she would make and light the candles, as long as Johnny would come back, and that he never found out she had done anything as bizarre as make candles to get him back.

Cathy's friend told her that in order to get what she wanted, she wouldhave to light the candles on a certain day, and, if she didn't light them at the right time, Johnny would never come back. This wasn't what Cathy wanted, so she lit her candles on the exact day indicated by her friend.

To give a happy ending to this common story, Cathy lit the candles, Johnny called, and they are happier now than they have ever been.

Sometimes women need to swallow their pride and light candles to encourage those things that they want, or to ensure themselves that the man they want will be theirs.

The time frame of this candle exercise is to light one candle a day for seven days beginning on the first day of the BRING column indicated in the timing guide.

169

ATTRACTING AN AFFAIR WITHOUT COMMITMENTS

There are people who have a resistance to full time relationships. This exercise is for all of you looking for only a brief affair.

When making a love drawing candles, use the basic candle recipe, adding a red candle dye and two teaspoons of dried magnolia petals. This wil bring to you a brief interlude with no strings or commitments.

When making candles to purpose, you must always project, as well as centralize, your emotions and thoughts on your wish. Candle exercises are not new. They have been around since ancient times. American Indian medicine men use similar flowers, shrubs, and plants to gain the same results.

Light your red candle to purpose on the first day listed under the BRING time frame in your timing guide.

ATTRACTING A RELATIONSHIP THAT WILL COMPLEMENT YOUR PERSONALITY

Use the basic candle recipe. Add pink dye (pink will represent the love you are looking for). Pulverize one teaspoons of allspice from your kitchen. Add the allspice and one teaspoon of ground basil to your candle wax. This will give you a love relationship that will be on the same intellectual level that you function on, with no competition or communication problems.

Light your pink candle on the first day listed under the BRING column in your timing guide. By following these directions properly, you will receive the love that you have been seeking.

ATTRACTING A LOVE FOR THE EVENING

Since the beginning of time, women have used the essence of lavender to attract a man. In the oldest profession, women would wear lavender perfume to attract a gentleman for the evening.

When making a candle to purpose, and that purpose is love, use a pink

170

dye and two drops of pure lavender essence. When the candle burns out, expect that new love to soon follow.

When using the actual lavender flower, dry the flower and add two teaspoons of pulverized lavender to your pink dyed candle wax. Remember to always strain your candle wax before pouring it into your molds, as not to have any residue from the flower in your candle.

Light your pink love drawing candle on the second day of the BRING column indicated in your timing guide.
SUBSTITUTE: If you do not make your own candle, you may substitute a pink candle that you buy with the **"INTENT"** to bring in love as expressed in this exercise. Remember, the intent will be stronger, if you make your own candle.

CANDLES TO BRING LOVE

As you melt your wax to make candles to attract love, there is one ingredient that you women may want to include - "PATCHOULY." By adding two drops of patchouly oil to a love drawing candle, you will attract a man with money. (When adding oils to your candles, add only the amount specified. More is not better.) You may also use two drops of patchouly on the top of a pink candle that you have purchased with the intent to bring in a new love.

For you gentlemen lighting candles, you may also desire to attract a new love who is financially secure. Your magic ingredient will be two drops of **"MUSK OIL."** Add two drops of musk oil to your pink candles to ensure that your new lady is not in need of your financial support; thus, ensuring you a financially free relationship.

ATTRACTING LOVE, NOT NEED

Love is a feeling and an emotion that seems to be lacking in a number of young relationships. So many relationships have been based on need and a sense of insecurity rather than love.

In order to establish a new (or renew an existing) relationship based on

171

love, desire, and passion, there are a number of flowers and spices that will bring this to you. One of these flowers is honeysuckle.

When pulverizing and adding two teaspoons of honeysuckle to your pink candle wax, you will be ready to light your love drawing candle under the proper time frame to bring i a new love. This will give you the security to just sit back and relax, while waiting for that new love to come into your life.

Make two pink honeysuckle candles. Light the first candle on the second day indicated in your timing guide under the first BRING column of the month. Light your second candle on the second day of the second BRING column of the same month. If there is only one BRING time frame during the month that you want to light your candles, you must wait for a month with two BRING time frames in order for this exercise to work.

BLENDING FAMILIES

We all know that in the fifties, planning and establishing a family was a "forever" concept. Since then, times and people have changed.

Free-willed people, with the lust for adventure and change, have surfaced among the ranks of young Americans. Adventure allows the vitality of your youth to continue, giving you that zest which so commonly is missing from relationships.

For some people, having an affair on the side allows them to maintain that zest for life which, in turn, allows them to continue in their relationship with their spouse.

For others, the morality that has taken them into their adulthood will not allow them an affair. For these people, leaving their home and families to establish new families is their only hope.

Young married couples cannot accept the concept that they, too, may grow older and have different views on life and industry. The concept that one spouse will outgrow the other is beyond their realm of comprehension; yet not all people who marry at the tender age of seventeen will still hold their original goals and objectives at the age of

172

thirty-five. Having already established a home and a family, these families have a tendency to fall apart.

The separation of such families can be devastating on the part of one or, at times, all parties involved. Parting will cause changes in the lifestyles of all affected. These changes, even though devastating at first, in the end, will always prove to be best for all concerned.

As a result of these positive changes, there should never be blame on anyone's part. The concept has always applied and will always continue to apply, that no one can break up a happy home; thus, there can be no blame. There is no fault. There is only **"ISNESS."** It isn't right and it isn't wrong, it just is.

People, inherently will feel sorry and guilty far longer for things that they have not done, than they will for things that they have done. The reasoning behind this is that you can always justify your actions; whereas, it is impossible to justify your inaction.

As you begin your new life, you will be establishing new relationships and new families, bringing together new and different personalities. When blending families, as these new people come together, there are personality clashes and conflicts. These conflicts stem from the fact that not all people raise their children the same way. In the beginning, no one in a blended family knows what is expected from them.

Your new family is now young, exciting, and interesting. Oftentimes, people look to the blended family as another opportunity in life to succeed in love, lust, and passion. To ensure an easy transition, with peace of mind, no guilt, and no remorse, make three yellow candles. Add one drop of almond oil and two teaspoons of dried pulverized chives. The lust for your new life, coupled with a smooth transition, will make blending families easier. Life is replete with change, and while the change will be wonderful, these candles will ensure happiness within your new family, as well as peace of mind connected to the family you might have left behind.

Life must continue, and you must live your own life. The best line written to exemplify this situation has to be: **"I DON'T WANT TO WAKE UP SOMEDAY AND BE AT THE END OF SOMEONE**

ELSE'S LIFE." This is clearly what you will be doing, if you stay in a dysfunctional relationship because of your fear of how your existing partner will act or react.

Light your first yellow candle on the first day of the second BRING column in your timing guide under the BRING time frame. Light your second yellow candle on the second day of the same BRING cycle and the third candle on the third day of the same BRING cycle. As you know, not all months have two BRING time frames. Plan your move accordingly.

MONEY DRAWING CANDLE EXERCISES

All of the following candle recipes will be made with the basic candle base.

Parsley has always been an ingredient that can be added to a candle base to ensure money. Parsley is also a stabilizer. When adding this component to your candles, a beneficial, unanticipated result in the form

MONEY DRAWING CANDLE EXERCISES

of stability will be yours. This stability will be mental, physical, and spiritual.

Add one and one half teaspoons of dried parsley to your vibrantly green candle base. You may light as many of these green candles as your wish. However, light them only during the BRING time frame.

Parsley is an ingredient that has a tendency to invoke the monkey's paw syndrome. When lighting a candle to bring in money with the intensity that parsley has, you must also light a candle made to purpose to add protection from the monkey's paw. This candle should be blue in color, made with two teaspoons of pulverized bay leaves, and lit on the fourth day of the BRING time frame.

174

ATTRACTING MONEY WITH THE ABILITY TO ACCEPT IT

When drawing money to themselves, some people have the concept that having money will change their personal identity; thus, they ask for money with an inability to accept it.

When making candles that will bring the money that you want and need, there is a special ingredient that you must add, enabling your candles to ensure your intent to manifest. This ingredient is aloe.

Aloe has been used for centuries to ensure the influx of money. Aloe has also been used to heal emotional and physical distress, as well as financial uncertainties. Add two drops of pure aloe extract to your candles that you have made to purpose to bring money to you.

When you are using the aloe plant, you must first cut the plant into small pieces. Dry the aloe and add one teaspoon of the dried aloe to your candle. The color of your candle base should be green.

If your intent is for material wealth, light your candle on the sixth day during the BRING time frame; for spiritual wealth, light your green candle on the seventh day during the same time; for emotional wealth, light your green candle on the third day of the same time frame.

INVESTMENT EXERCISE

Nine to five may bring security and satisfaction to some; however, this type of structure and impersonal lifestyle solicits stagnation and boredome for the rest. The feeling of selling one's soul for minimum wage seems to be the consensus among these other people, and the answer for them has always been self-employment of some sort, coupled with investing or marketing. When this is the case, fear has a tendency to slip in. To release yourself from this insecurity, allowing you the capability to make sound and rational decisions in conjunction with trading, there is a candle to purpose that you can make and light. This candle will give you what you want, as well as what you need, and to succeed in the market once again.

Consult your timing guide. When the timing guide indicates that you are under a BRING cycle, light a red candle that you have designed to release negative energy.

Your next step is to make seven green candles. These candles should be made to last for five to seven days. He wick must be the thinnest wire wick that you can find. After you melt your wax, add two teaspoons of kitchen allspice (pulverized), one teaspoon of nutmeg, and one teaspoon of poppy seeds that you have also pulverized.

On the first day of the BRING time frame, light your first green candle. On the second day, light your second green candle. Continue daily until you have lit all seven green candles consecutively. Your mind will be clear and sound investments will be made, allowing your money to flow once again.

WARNING ...... Light these candles only during the BRING time frame indicated on your timing guide. Making a mistake with this candle exercise can be devastating. If you are from the school of skepticism, please do not try to prove the author wrong with this exercise. Do yourself a favor - try something less traumatic!

ACCUMULATION OF MONEY

When money comes in freely, there is also the tendency to allow the same money to flow freely in the opposite direction. His never allows the money to accumulate; consequently, one never has great wealth, only the freedom to spend money at will.

This can be fun, but only for a short time. After awhile, old age and financial insecurity creeps in. "Where is it?" And "Where did it go?" are two common questions among people who make easy money.

Yes, we have the answer for this, too..... When financial protection for old age and the preservation of monies accumulated seem to be your goals, and the abundance of great wealth is your desire, then almond oil, aloe, and ginger are your answers.

Make three vibrantly green colored candles, using the thinnest wire wick possible to ensure the longevity of your candles. When your wax has melted, add two drops of almond oil, two drops of aloe extract, and one teaspoon of ginger to your candle wax. When adding oils to your wax, you also need to add one fourth more hardener than called for on the hardener package. Not only will this allow your candles to harden, it will also give a high gloss sheen to them, adding to the brilliance of your color. The combination of these ingredients in the green dye of the wax will ensure the accumulation of great wealth.

Light your three green candles while concentrating on your purpose in the following manner. During the BRING time frame, light one green candle. Wait one day and light your second green candle. Wait one more day and light your third green candle.

All candle exercises are designed to bring the maximum amount of success when followed properly.

INTELLECT AND CONCENTRATION

When studying becomes redundant - to the point that it seems school is all that life has to offer - the consensus among students is that there has to be relief somewhere, or, at the very least, someday.

The average public school will instruct students three hundred minutes a day, five days a week, nine months per year. That is fifty-four thousand minutes of in-house instruction every year.

In most states, homework is required, adding another low average of eight hundred minutes of home study. We now have millions of young minds spending fifty-four thousand, eight hundred minutes every year involved with instructional learning of some sort. This has to instill pressure within a vast majority of these children and young adults.

To help you and your child study, learn, and comprehend, yellow candles will aid you in all of your educational endeavors. They also aid your concentrated efforts toward keeping your child in school, as well as help you maintain your composure when assisting your child with his required homework.

Yellow is the color that, on a psychological level, stimulates your intellect.

During the active times of the American Indian, sage was burnt and the smoke was waved over the sick to send the evil spirit out of the body of the sick. This method was implemented to ensure that the sick could then return home with a health mind and a strong body.

When hours of concentration is spent on studying, oftentimes, the body will become weak; thus, the color for studying is yellow and the ingredient is sage.

When making candles to purpose, make two yellow candles, adding two teaspoons of dried sage. Light the first yellow candle on the first day of the first BRING column of the month, with the second yellow candle to be lit on the first day of the second BRING column of the month.

"ROAD TRIP" - VACATION PLANS THAT WORK

Is it any wonder that annual vacations are a necessity in this troubled time that we live? Work, pressure, war, perplexity, and countless hours of suspicion within relationships and at work are just a few of the common conditions of daily life. But, what happens when you start to make those vacation plans?

You plan for nearly a year - money, travel agents, tickets, hotel accommodations, the list goes on and on - well, enough of that.

Let's go on a camping trip. You get a tent, a bit of food, and put those darling little children in the back of the Ford. "Road trip" - oh, what a nightmare! You find a camp site and the cooking begins, three squares around the open fire and poison ivy for dessert. Well, let's not go camping.

How about the Motel Six at the end of the block? The kids can still play with the neighborhood children and you won't have to strap the stingray to the back of the car! If the corner motel is the best that your physical and emotional psyche can endure, there is, most certainly, a candle made to purpose for you.

Before you begin to plan that long-awaited holiday, make two orange candles, adding two drops of red hot pepper juice. Light one candle on the first day of the BRING column, and the second orange candle on the first day of the second BRING column, and continue this exercise every month while planning your vacation. The orange color of the candle will help you keep your wits about you, and the red hot pepper juice will ensure that the vital energy, which is a must during a vacation, is there for you to enjoy.

RELEASING NEGATIVE ENERGY EXERCISE

When you desire is to release negative energy, your exercise wil be relativity simple in nature.

First, you will need four gray candles. These candles should be designed to stay lit for five to seven days.

Light your first gray candle on the first day of the first RELEASE time frame of the month. Light your second gray candle on the fourth day of the first RELEASE time frame. Your next step is to light your third ray candle on the first day of the second RELEASE time frame of the month, and your fourth gray candle will be lit on the fourth day of the second RELEASE time frame of the same month.

Lighting gray candles to release negative energy is the most effective method of releasing. When releasing anything that has taken time to produce, you must put forth effort in order for your release to be effective. An example: When having problems in a relationship, these problems seem to surface overnight; however, we know that they seldom do. These problems have brewed under the surface for some time, thus the release will take some time, as well. (One month to be exact.)

While there are exercises that will give you instant results, you will still have to light your gray candles to release the core of your problem.

STIMULATING YOUR INTELLECT AS YOU PROTECT YOUR EMOTIONS

When you live in Georgia, everything is a peach. There are over thirty-five

Peachtree Streets in the metro-Atlanta area alone. But, how many people actually know how much a peach can do for them? (Note: Exclude the peach seed. When making candles, you never use toxic or poisonous ingredients.)

One of the most unique facets of the peach, when dried and added to candles, is that it facilitates your intellect and ability to reason.

When residing in close proximity to other people, you have a tendency to pick up the energies and feelings of those around you. When you are making candles to purpose and lighting candles to stimulate your mental facilities, and you need to safeguard yourself against the emotional energy of those around you, make one yellow candle. Add two teaspoons of dried peaches. Thus, you will be killing two birds with one stone, so to speak.

The peach is the most versatile of all fruits. It can be used in candles for intellect, and you can add one teaspoon of dried peaches to green candles for money. It is not uncommon to add two teaspoons of dried peaches to a brown candle to ensure protection and safety, while on a hunting trip in the country.

When lighting a candle for intellect and protection from the energy of those around you, the most effective time to light your candle will be on the third day indicated under the BRING column. You will then notice yourself feeling good and thinking very clearly.

SOMETIMES PEACE AND QUIET IS ALL YOU NEED

Sandy is a flight attendant with three small children. Recently divorced, she just opened her own business in addition to her job with the airline.

This kind of enterprising vitality is not uncommon. The 1990s have proven to be the continuation of the liberation of American women.

In the sixties, when burning your bra was fashionable, women had something to prove. They were strong and wanted people to treat them justly. In the 1990s, there are also things that women have to prove, but the

180

difference now is there is no one to whom to prove it. Single, productive women are achieving success, but they can't care who knows it - or if anyone <u>does</u> know it. This is liberation - productivity, with a healthy ego.

This liberation, like in the sixties, has a price that must be paid, as liberation in any form has a price. The price in the sixties was equal pay for equal work, couple with ridicule and oppression.

The price in the nineties is a bit different. Now, all Sandy wants is peace and quiet. Everything that needs to be handled is - and, I might add - with style and grace. However, as life goes on, the need for rest and solitude is inevitable. Meditation works well, but twenty minutes a day is often too much time to spend not being constructively productive, when lighting a candle takes only seconds and continues to work as you continue with everything else.

For peace of mind, solitude, and relaxation on the run, light one yellow candle on the first day of the BRING column. In this yellow candle, add two teaspoons of pulverized Queen Ann's lace and two drops of pure lime juice. The yellow candle will allow your mind to stay clear. The Queen Ann's lace will give you power, while the lime juice allows you to maintain your youthful vitality. Light and enjoy.

MOTHERING

Every little girl grows up playing house and wanting to be a mommy. Toy high heels, mommy's make-up, and dolls to change and feed fill hours of playing grown up, getting parental experiences, and giving your real mom time off from the constant, "What are you doing, Mommy?" syndrome.

Continuing on into life, how many times - as a parent - have you felt secure that your children were fast asleep in the other room, only to look in on those little darlings to find that the powder has somehow come out of its shaker and thrown itself all over your child's room? Or, how many times has someone broken into your home, just to mess up your child's room? You see, children seldom do such dastardly things themselves. Well, you asked for this parental, <u>mommy</u> position through your dreams and aspirations as a child. Now, it's time for help.

Children are a wonder with their inquisitive and imaginative minds, and they add to the spice of life. However, for the constant endurance required when you have - children, there is one more spice you need - kitchen allspice.

This spice will be added to an orange candle since orange is the color of endurance and emotional stability. Pulverize the allspice and add two teaspoons to your candle. As your wax begins to melt, add two teaspoons of ground lemon peel and one teaspoon of dried lime peel, as well.

Light our candle on the third day under the BRING column in your timing guide. Since three is the number that represents communication and relaxation, you will light an orange candle that you have made to purpose on the third day of the BRING column each month to ensure your endurance as a mother.

SAFETY IN TRAVEL

In the 199s, travel is on the rise - by car, train, plane, and boat - just to name a few.

We all know, during the time of the Vietnam War, more Americans lost their lives on U.S. highways, than died in Vietnam. With this in mind, it's a wonder that - in good faith - the majority of Americans buy automobiles. Is it transportation that they need, or do Americans have a death wish? With the high speed of the American energy, there are only a few protective shields that one can implement to ensure safety on the American highways and county byways.

The Catholic saint, St. Christopher, is the patron saint of safety in speed and in travel. Within the last decade, theologians have revealed that perhaps St. Christopher may not have existed; however, the belief in him has been in existence for centuries. Nonetheless, lighting a candle in St. Christopher's honor, plus making a candle to purpose for protection and safety in travel, may be your only hope on the road.

When making a candle to purpose, melt your wax, adding a brilliant blue dye. When your wax has melted, add two teaspoons of dried heather and two teaspoon of dried pulverized mistletoe. Remember to strain your wax

182

as you pour it into your molds.

Light your protection candle during the BRING time frame in the timing guide.

CAUTION WHEN USING MISTLETOE: When used in a candle, mistletoe must be strained carefully, making sure all stems and leaves have been removed before pouring your wax into the candle mold. When burning a candle, any part of the actual plant that gets into your candle wax and burns can make you sick.

MISTLETOE IS POISONOUS WHEN IT IS ON FIRE.

WHATEVER HAPPENED TO THAT PERFECT JOB?

Money can't buy happiness. This is common knowledge. However, when you're accustomed to having money and that flow stops, there is a lot of insecurity which develops. With the onset of insecurity, there is often the disappearance of self-confidence and self-esteem. Thus, your dilemma begins.

The big job search has begun and there is no job to be found. There is an answer to your prayer. When the application of this candle exercise is followed properly, the opportunity to land that big job will be yours.

On the first day of the BRING time frame, light a green candle designed to stay lit for five to seven days. In this candle, put two teaspoons of pulverized pecan nuts. On the second day of this same time frame, light one yellow five to seven-day candle to which you have added one teaspoon of ginger and one drop of almond oil. Repeat this cycle for eight days.

On the eighth day, you will have lit four green candles and four yellow candles, which re-establishes your confidence and self-esteem. This, in turn, opens the money flow once again, allowing you to prosper financially. To continue this exercise, on the first day of the RELEASE time frame, light one red candle that you have designed to flip, thus releasing any and all negative energy that has kept you from succeeding.

RELIEF FOR THE LOSS OF A LOVED ONE

Who can ever say how or why someone will depart from this life? We only know that - even if it comes expectedly - there is emotional pain that seems to hold on and last forever.

When my little sister died, I thought she had abandoned me and that my life had ended with hers. The pain, I thought, was going to last for the rest of my life. I had no energy, as well as no passion for life - nor any incentive to continue to life. (This is not an exclusive response. For time and eternity, the most religious and spiritual people have mourned the loss of their loved ones.) In my opinion, God had given me more than my share of heartache and pain. On the other hand, He also gave me the insight to do something about it.

I wanted the pain and the bitterness to go away and, after awhile, I decided I would do anything to make them disappear. So, I did. I made two white candles. "One," I said, "is for my sister and the other is for me." Both were made with two drops of lemon oil and two teaspoons of fennel seeds.

On the first day in the timing guide to BRING things, I lit both candles and went to sleep. For the first time since my sister had died, I dreamed she was happy; and when I awoke, I was too.

The pain and suffering people will endure as they mourn the loss of someone dear to them can be compared to nothing else. I do thank God that there is at least something that can help.

MONEY DOES NOT HAVE TO BE THE ROOT OF ALL EVIL

We all have heard the age old saying that "money is the root of all evil," yet there are candle recipes you can make that will bring money to you that will not be associated with problems.

First, melt your wax, adding one teaspoon of sea salt and one half teaspoon

184

of oregano from your kitchen. The sea salt will purity your intent for money and the oregano will bring it to you. Remember, money doesn't have to be evil.

Always remember to light your candle under the appropriate time frame. If you light candles to bring money, use your timing guide to light your candles during the dates specified "to bring." The last thing you want is to light that candle at the wrong time and have all your money disappear!

When your wish is for money, make your candles green. When you are willing to make your money through your present profession, make your money candles yellow, using the same ingredients and following the same directions.

Light your money candles on the second day indicated in your timing guide under the BRING column.

CONTINUED FINANCIAL SUCCESS

Temporary solutions for financial distress appear to be the only answers that some people seem to demonstrate. If this is your dilemma, then almond oil may be your answer. When adding one and a half drops of almond oil to your candles, which you have poured with the intent for continued financial success, success will be yours.

When almond oil is added to vibrantly green colored candles made with the intent to bring money, the money seems to have no end. With the aid of the candles that you have made, excessive amounts of energy will answer all your questions about money, giving you everything you need to make all the money that you have been waiting for.

This endless amount of monies will not come in the form of an inheritance or thousands of dollars in gifts. Rather, this will be easily made money.

For easy money, light your green candle on the second day indicated in your timing guide under the BRING column.

SUCCESS, POWER, AND MONEY

185

Success, power, and money. Is this the new American Dream? As times change, so do the people who participate. American people have always adjusted their ways, as well as their means, to accommodate the socio-economical trends of their time. However, many people have outgrown their time, going beyond their means and adjusting their lifestyles accordingly. They have found, while conventional ways complement conventional lifestyles, unconventional ways solicit much more.

There has been an increased number of new millionaires in the United States just within the past decade. People are striking out - growing beyond their fears, traveling beyond their comfort zones - realizing that life certainly has much more to offer. The concept that one can ask and the answer will appear has apparently proven to be applicable, especially in these modern times.

You too can release your fears, thus inciting a free, uninhibited lifestyle, which induces power, strength, flexibility and competence. To incite all of this into your life, make two purple candles. Add two teaspoons of kitchen allspice, one drop of almond oil, one fourth extra hardener and one teaspoon of parsley. (Pulverize your allspice and parsley.)

The purple color will connect your conscious mind with your subconscious mind, thus enhancing your insight. The allspice will bring you power. The almond oil, in conjunction with the purple color, will give you strength and endurance. The parsley will ensure you more money than you have ever possessed.

Light both of your purple candles on the second day indicated in your timing guide under the BRING column. Success and all of its encompassing aspects will be yours.

WHAT TO DO FOR THAT EMOTIONAL UPLIFT

When times are hard, there has to be something that we can do to maintain a good self-image and that high self-esteem is very much needed in this world we call home.

We have gone through the Industrial Revolution. There was the care and concern for the farmers and the American farmland. There was the health craze of the eighties.

Presently, we are focusing our attention on the emotional stability/instability of our country: addictions, dependency, co-dependency, borderline disorders, women's issues, and male issues. During "Operation Desert Storm," there was a concentrated effort - on the behalf of thousands of independent doctors, therapists, and counselors volunteering their time - to ensure emotional stability of American children whose parents took part in the Desert Storm operation. This sounds like the beginning of the Emotional Revolution. At no other time in the history of the United States has the public been as concerned about the emotional well-being of our nation.

To ensure your emotional well-being, as well as a good self-esteem and a positive mental attitude, make four yellow candles to purpose. This purpose will be "a healthy mental attitude." In your candles, put two teaspoons of dried oranges. Citric juices will eliminate negative self-esteem and a poor emotional attitude.

Light these candles during the time frame that will ensure what you want will come to you. This is the BRING column. Light one candle a day for four days. Four is the number of stability and foundations: mental, physical, and spiritual.

PROTECTION FOR SINGLE WOMEN AND SINGLE PARENTS

The American Dream of mon, dad, two cars in the driveway,, and two point five children, commonly conceived in the fifties and the sixties, seem not to apply in the nineties. Divorced couples and single parent families are on the rise; thus, leaving women - who grew up thinking that there was a man out there somewhere who would take care of her - living on her own with small and/or numerous children.

We have come a long way from the conventional thought process of the American Dream. But, where do we go from here? Who is left to care for, protect, and defend these women, vulnerable and alone?

Women of the nineties are becoming hard. They see life for what it is and for what they have made it, recognizing that the macho role, deemed upon the male species by society, had ever brought happiness to the American family i the way that it had been designed. Thus, men are little boys wanting toys, not responsibilities, and women are little girls, looking for a fairy tale. Where do these two meet? This is the realization of the feminine consensus of the nineties.

Finding protection for themselves, women often seek unconventional methods. These methods come in the form of making candles to purpose and lighting them under the correct time frame to protect themselves.

If this is your story, make two brown candles, adding two teaspoons of pulverized fennel seeds. Light your candle during the BRING time frame and relax in your home. Protection will be yours.

THE MONKEY'S PAW SYNDROME

A long time ago - far, far away - there lived a simple family. A man and a woman with one small child. They made their home in a small village outside the kingdom of a very powerful and very wealthy king. They worked hard to make ends meet.

One morning, on his way to work, the father met an old woman just sitting by the side of the road, counting stones that she had placed in front of her. When the father stopped to see if the old woman needed any help, she was so surprised and grateful that anyone had stopped, she told him that she was really a princess and that she could grant him any three wishes that his heart desired.

The father, forgetting all about going to work, ran home to tell his wife of his encounter with the old woman and the wishes that she had granted to him. His wife was ecstatic in her excitement. She said, "I want a lot of money for our first wish." So, money is what they asked for.

Seconds later, there was a knock on their door. It was a representative from the kingdom. "The King was hunting and accidentally killed your son," he said, then continued, "The King feels badly about this and wants me to give you all this money."

The man left the couple alone with their pain and disbelief. The wife just looked at the money. They had wished for money and they did receive their first wish, but they never wanted, not were they willing to accept money for the life of their son.

The wife, realizing what she had done, wanted to use the second wish to bring their son back to life. The father, in shock and disbelief, stopped his wife before the made the second wish, saying, "If our son returns to us, are we willing to see his soul less, mangled body? Are we right in bringing our son back from his death?"

With questions in his heart and tears in his eyes, he stopped his wife as she made the second wish by saying, "I want all of the wishes to go away." Thus, using all of their wishes, the money was gone, and their son was again playing in the forest, healthy and strong, as he had been the morning before the man came from the King. The moral of this story is to be sure that what you want is more important than any price you may be willing to pay.

To protect yourself from the monkey's paw, make the most vibrantly blue colored candle that you have ever seen. In this candle, put two teaspoons of pulverized bay leaves. Light your candle on the fourth day listed under the BRING column. (This protection will last for one month.)

PROTECTION FROM YOUR EXTERNAL ENVIRONMENT

Life is full of uncertainties. When you try to live the best way you know how, while the influence and the influx of so many people dictate the opposite, life gets hard. When living on a mountaintop or in a cave in the heart of America's Midwest starts to look appealing, there is most certainly a problem in your life.

These problems, conspicuously external in the beginning, soon become internal, as your external environment will always dictate the emotional well-being of your internal self-worth. It is now time to protect yourself from this apparently destructive external environment, so that the life you live - even in the heart of the city - can be your own.

Start by making four white candles to purpose. Your purpose will be for protection. The ingredients that you will add to your candles are two teaspoons of ground basil, one teaspoon of anise, and two teaspoons of dried and ground barley. The basic allows your money to continue to flow. (Oftentimes, when one pulls away from external influences, there is a tendency to withdraw from the main sources that keeps one alive.) The anise allows you to maintain a healthy perspective on your life, while the barley protects you against negative energy from others.

These four candles should be lit starting on the first day listed under the BRING column in your timing guide. Light one candle a day for four days. Four is the number for stability and strong foundations; thus, by lighting these four candles, you will be restoring your life and bypassing your previously disjointed foundation.

HOW TO MAINTAIN POWER WITH A HEALTHY EGO

Power and ego are two trans-personal emotions that have the most violent oppositions. Power, when used correctly, is constructive and an asset to anyone's character. Ego is the healthiest of all forms of self-confidence and self-esteem. However, misdirected power causes chaos, and always an inflated ego. Being a derivative of misdirected power, an inflated ego can only be controlled through the constructive power of the individual. Once an inflated ego takes hold, the power turns into misdirected, devastating energy, which oftentimes takes a negative turn, and frequently destroys the person through his own means.

When you find yourself in a position of power, you must safeguard against the onset of such chaos and destruction. The candle color for balance, as well as protection in this case, is blue. The blue candle will keep your emotions in check, allowing only positive and constructive power to flow through you.

You must also make your candle to purpose by adding one and one half teaspoons of ginger. The ginger will deter the misuse of power, as well as deter the ego from becoming unjustifiably inflated. This candle should only be lit under the BRING time frame to insure that the protection will come to you and not be released from you.

PROFESSIONAL PROTECTION

When securing a career position, there is a feeling of relief and a sense of accomplishment and well-being. But, what about professional protection - the protection that says you will remain in that position until you're ready to leave? With early retirement, the economy, and major companies filing Chapter Eleven or even Chapter Thirteen everyday, insecurity has become a common emotion amongst the professional work forces. This is not a comforting thought.

Your degree seems not to be worth the paper that it is printed on, not to mention the hours, years, and the cost of your education that you have sacrificed for your accomplishment.

No one wants to be addicted to lighting candles. Thus, when the insecurities being, you should light your protection candles.

When making candles for professional protection, make nine green and three blue candles. To each of these candles, you need to add two drops of coconut oil, one fourth more hardener than the hardener package calls for and two teaspoons of curry powder.

The coconut oil will give you the vitality and the enthusiasm you had the day you got your job; allowing those holding superiority over you to see your worth. The curry powder will ostracize all adversaries standing in your way of success. On the first day under the BRING column, light one blue candle and one green candle. Continue to light your green candles every day for nine days, lighting your second blue candle five days after the first, and the third blue candle will be lit five days after the second.

The candles you have made to purpose will work for you, even if they have been sitting on your shelf for years.

LOVE CANDLES TO PURPOSE EXERCISES:

LOVE DRAWING:
1 Pink candle
1 Teaspoon pulverized cinnamon
2 Drops clove oil
1/4 Extra hardener
Light: 1st day BRING column

SEXUAL PROWESS:
5 Red candles
2 Drops lavender extract
1 Drop almond oil
1/4 Extra hardener
Light: 1 a day for 5 days
Begin on the 1st day of BRING column

LOVE WITH PROTECTION:
3 Pink candles
1 Brown candle
1 Teaspoon of pulverized lavender
2 Drops of vanilla
Light 1 pink a day for 3 days
Start on the 2nd day of the BRING column
On fourth day light brown

SECURING A RELATIONSHIP:
7 Pink candles
2 Teaspoons dried chives
Light: 1 candle a day for 7 days
Starting on the 1st day of BRING column

AN AFFAIR WITH NO COMMITMENT:
1 Red candle
2 Teaspoons of dried magnolia petals
Light: 1st day of BRING column

ATTRACTING LOVE TO COMPLEMENT YOUR PERSONALITY:

1 Pink candle
1 Teaspoon of allspice
1 Teaspoon of ground basil
Light: 1st day of BRING column

ATTRACTING LOVE FOR THE EVENING:
1 Pink candle
2 Drops of lavender extract/or
2 Teaspoons of dried pulverized lavender
Light: 2nd day of BRING column

BRING LOVE (FOR WOMEN):
1 Pink candle
2 Drops of patchouly
Light: 3rd day of BRING column

BRING LOVE (FOR MEN):
1 Pink candle
2 Drops of musk
Light: 3rd day of BRING column

ATTRACTING LOVE, NOT NEED:
2 Pink candles
2 Teaspoons of dried pulverized honeysuckle
Light: 1st on 2nd day of 1st BRING column
Light: 2nd on 2nd day of 2nd BRING column, same month

BLENDING FAMILIES:
3 Yellow candles
1 Drop almond oil
1/4 Extra hardener
2 Teaspoons dried chives
Light: 1 candle on first day second BRING column
2nd candle on second day, 3rd on 3rd day

MONEY CANDLES TO PURPOSE EXERCISES:

MONEY DRAWING CANDLES:
1 Green candle
1 and ½ Teaspoons parsley
Light: any time during the BRING time frame

MONEY WITH THE ABILITY TO ACCEPT IT:
1 Green candle
2 Drops of pure aloe extract
Light; 6th day of the BRING column

INVESTMENT EXERCISES:
1 Red candle upside down
Light: now
CONTINUE:
7 Green candles
2 Teaspoons allspice
1 Teaspoon nutmeg
1 Teaspoon poppy seeds
Light: 1st candle on the 1st day
2nd candle on the 2nd day and so on
Lighting all 7 candles consecutively
Under the BRING cycle

ACCUMULATION OF MONEY:
3 Green candles
2 Drops almond oil
2 Drops aloe extract
1 Teaspoon ginger
1/4 Extra hardener
Light: starting on the 1st day of the BRING column light
1 candle every other day

MONEY WITH NO EVIL INTENT
1 Green candle (new job)
1 Teaspoon sea sales
½ Teaspoon oregano
Light: any time during the BRING time frame

MONEY WITH NO EVIL INTENT

1 Yellow candle (money from present employment)
1 Teaspoon sea sales
½ Teaspoon oregano
Light: any time during the BRING time frame

CONTINUED FINANCIAL SUCCESS:

1 Green candle
1 and ½ Drops almond oil
Light: 2nd day of BRING column

SUCCESS, POWER, AND MONEY:

2 Purple candles
2 Teaspoons allspice
1 Drop almond oil
1 Teaspoon parsley
1/4 Extra hardener
Light: both candles on the 2nd day of the BRING column

PROTECTION CANDLES TO PURPOSE:

PROTECTING YOUR EMOTIONS:

1 Yellow candle
2 Teaspoons dried peaches
Light: 3rd day of BRING column

PROTECTION WHILE HUNTING:

1 Brown candle
2 Teaspoons dried peaches
Light: 3rd day of BRING column

PROTECTION WITH MONEY:

1 Green candle
2 Teaspoons dried peaches
Light: 3rd day of BRING column

RELEASING NEGATIVE ENERGY:

4 Gray candles
Light: 1st Gray on first day of RELEASE column, light 2nd on 4th day, light 3rd on 1st day of second RELEASE cycle, and light 4th candle on 4th day of

second RELEASE time frame.

PROTECTION FOR PERFECT JOB:

4 Green candles

2 Teaspoons pulverized pecan nuts

1/4 Extra hardener

Light: 1st, 3rd, 5th, and 7th days during the BRING column

IN CONJUNCTION WITH:

4 Yellow candles

1 Teaspoon of ginger

1 Drop of almond oil

Light: 2nd, 4th, 6th, and 8th days during the BRING column

MONKEY'S PAW SYNDROME:

1 Blue candle

2 Teaspoons bay leaves

Light: 4th day of BRING column

PROTECTION FOR SINGLE WOMEN:

2 Brown candles

2 Teaspoons fennel seed

Light: any time during BRING column

PROTECTION FOR EXTERNAL ENVIRONMENT:

4 White candles

2 Teaspoons ground basil

1 Teaspoon anise

2 Teaspoons dried barley

Light: 1st day through the 4th during BRING column

PROFESSIONAL PROTECTION:

9 Green candles

3 Blue candles

2 Drops coconut oil

1/4 Extra hardener

2 Teaspoons curry powder

Light: 1 blue and 1 green on the 1st day of the BRING column. Continue with the green, lighting them every day for 9 days.

Light: blue every 5 days

196

EMOTIONAL STABILITY CANDLES TO PURPOSE

INTELLECT AND CONCENTRATION:
2 Yellow candles
2 Teaspoons sage
Light: The 1st candle on the 1st day of the BRING column.
Light: 2nd on the 1st day of the next BRING column

"ROAD TRIP" EMOTIONAL STABILITY:
2 Orange candles
2 Drops red hot pepper juice
1/4 Extra hardener
Light: 1st candle on the 1st day of the BRING column
Light: 2nd candle on the 1st day of the 2nd BRING column

PEACE AND QUIET IS ALL YOU NEED:
1 Yellow candle
2 Teaspoons Queen Anne's lace
2 Drops pure lime juice
Light: any time during BRING column

MOTHERING:
1 Orange candle
2 Teaspoons dried lemon peel
1 Teaspoon dried lime peel
2 Teaspoons dried allspice
Light: 3rd day of BRING column

SAFETY IN TRAVEL:
1 Blue candle
2 Teaspoons dried heather
2 Teaspoons dried pulverized mistletoe
Light: during the BRING column time frame

THE LOSS OF A LOVED ONE:
2 White candles
2 Drops lemon juice
2 Teaspoons fennel seeds
Light: any time

EMOTIONAL UPLIFT:
4 Yellow candles
2 Teaspoons dried oranges
Light: 1 Candle a day for 4 days beginning on the 1st day of the BRING column

POWER WITH A HEALTHY EGO:
1 Blue candle
1 and ½ teaspoons ginger
Light: any time during BRING column

PERSONALIZING YOUR CANDLE LIGHTING

Throughout history, candle lighting has brought forth spiritual and emotional comfort. Continuing with this premise, we will now add a form of personalized candle lighting, thus, giving you the spiritual, emotional, and financial comfort that you need. We will take this ephemeral guide one step further in its use to determine the correct day on which to light a candle.

Each day of the month will be represented by a feeling, an emotion, or a situation, beginning with the first day of the month and continuing on to the last day of the month. We will "add down" the day of the month to make it a single digit and then give the digit a personality of its own. This personality will then give you a more in-depth understanding of how candles work; and how picking your own day, corresponding to the personality of the single digit will incite your purpose, bringing to you or releasing from you, your intent.

Each number is listed below with the definition of the single digit. (Example: the 23rd day of the month can be added down like so: $2 + 3 = 5$.)

$1 = 1. 2 = 2. 3 = 3. 4 = 4. 5 = 5. 6 = 6. 7 = 7. 8 = 8. 9 = 9. 10 = 1. 11 = 2. 12 = 3. 13 = 4. 14 = 5. 15 = 5. 16 = 7. 17 = 8. 18 = 9. 19 = 1. 20 = 2. 21 = 3. 22 = 4. 23 = 5. 24 = 6. 25 = 6. 26 = 8. 27 = 9. 28 = 10 = 1. 29 = 11 = 2. 30 = 3. 31 = 4.$

When lighting a candle, the candle you choose will emanate the vibrational energy, via the color to incite what you are seeking. The same principle wil apply when you pick the day on which you light your candle. The following is a brief description of each of the single digits:

1.	One is the number of individuality, leadership, independence, self-reliance, willpower, domination, beginnings and creations - anything you exert physical energy to comprise. When lighting a candle during the BRING time frame, you will be bringing these things to you. When lighting the same candle on a one (1) day during the RELEASE time frame, you will be releasing these things from you. Always keep in mind your intent for lighting the candle. If you light a candle with intent to bring leadership, the same candle will not incite willpower. You must have the intent in order for your desire to manifest.

2.	Two is the number of duality, change, travel, emotions, moods, flexibility, sensitivity, psychic attraction or interest, money, capacity to acquire wealth. If your intent is to acquire wealth, the optimum time to light a green candle is during a BRING time frame on a day that equals a two. (Example: The 2nd or the 20th both equal 2.) To release yourself from your fear of travel, you would light a yellow candle on a two day falling during a RELEASE time frame.

3.	Three is the number for communication, contracts, increase, optimism, good fortune, short distance travel, early childhood education, neighbors, your immediate environment. When looking for good fortune, and a three day falls within a BRING time frame, light a yellow candle. If you are having problems with your neighbor, light a yellow candle on a three day during a RELEASE time frame, in order to release your problems with your neighbor.

4.	Four is the number of solidarity, balance, consistency, foundation, the base in which you exist, your home, your belief system, your family, mental and emotional stability, a four day is the best day under the BRING time frame. When a four day falls within a RELEASE time frame, releasing a problem with your family would be optimal.

5.	Five is the number for creativity, intellect, conscious mind, logic, winning money, sex, affairs, children, love, marriage, social life, idealism, art, beauty, gambling, and creative writing. In order to

199

have an affair, you need to light a red candle on a five day under the BRING time frame; whereas, a five day falling within the RELEASE time frame would be adequate for releasing your fear of creative writing.

6. Six is the number for work, health, services performed for others, operations, menial jobs, hard labor, illnesses of the lungs, and what you must do in order to survive. When you're looking for a ob, light a blue candle during the BRING time frame on a six day. To release the need for hard work, light a blue candle on a six day during a RELEASE time frame.

7. Seven is the number of social relationships, long-term relationships, husbands and wives, visibility to the public, what other people think of you, drive, energy, resourcefulness, wisdom, power, your ability or inability to understand. When releasing a long-term relationship, light a pink candle on a seven day during a RELEASE time frame.

8. Eight is the number that represents your ability to obtain great wealth from others, inheritance, legacies, charisma, sex appeal, banks, increase in income, stocks, bonds, dividends and profits, death, insurance, taxes, association with the underground, subways. This is the "wish number" - what you will want come to you. When your will is to obtain your long-awaited insurance settlement, light a green candle on an eight day under a BRING time frame. To release problems with taxes or with banks, light a yellow candle on an eight day under a RELEASE time frame.

9. Nine is the number that symbolizes endings and with each ending, there is a beginning. Nine is publishing, higher education, long distance travel, philosophy, universities, concentration, parents, in-laws, extended family, money from your career. A nine day falling within a BRING time frame is a perfect time to light a green candle to obtain more money from your career. When a nine day falls within a RELEASE time frame, you may wish to light a yellow candle to release your fear of being accepted into a certain university or college.

Long before the psychology of color held any merit in the Western World, people throughout religious history sought refuge and comfort in God. This comfort came in the form of religious holy men and patron saints. In this section, we will continue to put our faith in the tried and true religious doctrines from the past, thus, allowing us to continue to put our hopes for a substantial, or even subservient lifestyle in God's Hands.

Some religions believe that only through Christ will one's prayers be answered by God. Catholic parishioners, believing in and understanding angels, patron saints, martyrs, and holy men, know that by asking their loved ones who have gone on before them for assistance, God will, in fact, hear their prayer. There are two special days when you may light a candle to ask for the assistance of a loved one. These two days are the day of their birth and the anniversary of their passing from this life.

You may light a candle and receive aid from any saint or loved one at any time. Included here, however, is a list of proper days to ask for assistance from the saints, as well as all other holy men.

When lighting candles to the saints, martyrs, and holy men, it may be hard for some to know which saint will be the most appropriate to light your candle to. When this is the case, you should light your candles to the saint with whom you have a personal affinity. The example for this is: If your name is Christina, light your candles to Christina on July 24th, or if your birthday is March 18th, light your candles to Cyril of Jerusalem on the 18th of March. Find your personal saint for those times of need. ALL saints, martyrs, and holy religious figureheads have the capability to assist you in any endeavor.

When requesting assistance from the saints, light the color candle that best represents your wish. Use the candle lighting dictionary guide to choose your color. (A few examples are: for money, light green; for love, light pink; for passion, light red. If there is a problem in your family and your desire is to mend and bring your family closer together, light blue for peace of mind and balance.)

If lighting a candle to the saints and loved ones, you do not need to use the timing guide. However, if you are not lighting a candle to a saint, you must certainly use the timing guide to obtain your wish.

When lighting a candle to a loved one, patron saint, or holy figurehead, recite the following prayer:

"O LORD, HEAR YOUR PEOPLE, WHO HUMBLY SUPPLICATE YOU UNDER THE PROTECTION OF YOUR SAINTS, THAT YOU MAY GRANT US TO ENJOY PEACE DURING THIS LIFE AND TO FIND COMFORT OF LIFE ETERNAL. THROUGH OUR LORD, (THE CLOSING OF YOUR RELIGIOUS PREFERENCE) AMEN."

Allow yourself a few moments of silence when lighting your candles.

SAINTS, MARTYRS AND HOLY MEN

ABACHUM (MARTYR)	JANUARY 19TH
ABDON (MARTYR)	JULY 30TH
ACHILLEUS (MARTYR)	MAY 12TH
ADAUCTUS (MARTYR)	AUGUST 30TH
ADRIAN (MARTYR)	SEPTEMBER 8TH
AGAPITUS M. (MARTYR)	AUGUST 6TH
AGAPITUS M. (MARTYR)	AUGUST 18TH
AGATHA (MARTYR)	FEBRUARY 5TH
AGNES (MARTYR)	JANUARY 21ST
AGRICOLA (MARTYR)	NOVEMBER 4TH
ALBERT The Great (CONFESSOR)	NOVEMBER 15TH
ALEXANDER 1 (MARTYR)	MAY 3RD
ALEXIUS (CONFESSOR)	JULY 17TH
ALOYSIUS Gonzaga (CONFESSOR)	JUNE 21ST
ALPHONSUS Mary de Liguori (CONFESSOR)	AUGUST 2nd
AMBROSE (CONFESSOR)	DECEMBER 7th
ANACLETUS (MARTYR)	JULY 14TH
ANASTASIA (MARTYR)	DECEMBER 25th
ANASTASIUS (MARTYR)	JANUARY 22nd
ANDREW (APOSTLE)	NOVEMBER 30TH
ANDREW Avellino (CONFESSOR)	NOVEMBER 10TH
ANDREW Corsini (CONFESSOR)	FEBRUARY 4TH
ANGELA Merice (VIRGIN)	JUNE 1ST
ANICETUS (MARTYR)	APRIL 17TH
ANNE (PATRONESS)	JULY 26TH
ANSELM (MARTYR)	APRIL 21ST
ANTHONY, (ABBOT, (PATRIARCH OF MONKS)	JANUARY 17TH
ANTHONY Mary Zaccaria (CONFESSOR)	JULY 5TH
ANTHONY of Padua (CONFESSOR)	JUNE 13TH
ANTONINUS (CONFESSOR)	MAY 10TH
APOLLINARIS (MARTYR)	JULY 23rd
APOLLONIA (MARTYR)	FEBRUARY 9th

202

APULEIUS (CONFESSOR)	MAY 2ND
AUDIFAX (MARTYR)	JANUARY 19TH
AUGUSTINE OF CANTERBURY (CONFESSOR)	MAY 28TH
AUGUSTINE OF HIPPO (CONFESSOR)	AUGUST 28TH
BACCHUS (MARTYR)	OCTOBER 7TH
BARBARA (MARTYR)	DECEMBER 4TH
BARNABAS (APOSTLE)	JUNE 11TH
BARTHOLOMEW (APOSTLE)	AUGUST 24TH
BASIL (CONFESSOR)	JUNE 14TH
BASILIDE (MARTYR)	JUNE 12TH
BEATRICE (MARTYR)	JULY 29TH
BEDE (CONFESSOR)	MAY 27TH
BENEDICT (ABBOT)	MARCH 21ST
BERNADETTE, Marie (VIRGIN)	FEBRUARY 18TH
BERNARD (ABBOT)	AUGUST 20TH
BERNARDINE OF SIENA (CONFESSOR)	MAY 20TH
BABIANA (VIRGIN, MARTYR)	DECEMBER 2ND
BLAISE (MARTYR)	FEBRUARY 3RD
BONAVENTURE (CONFESSOR)	JULY 14TH
BONIFACE, M. (MARTYR)	MAY 14TH
BONIFACE, B.M. (MARTYR)	JUNE 5TH
BRIDGET (HOLY WOMAN)	OCTOBER 8TH
BRUNO (CONFESSOR)	OCTOBER 6TH
CAIUS (MARTYR)	APRIL 22ND
CAJETAN (CONFESSOR)	AUGUST 7TH
CALLISTUS (MARTYR)	OCTOBER 14TH
CAMILLUS OF LELLIS (CONFESSOR)	JULY 18TH
CANTUE (MARTYR)	JANUARY 19TH
CASIMIR (CONFESSOR)	MARCH 4TH
CASSIAN (MARTYR)	AUGUST 13TH
CATHERINE, WM. (VIRGIN, MARTYR)	NOVEMBER 25TH
CATHERINE, Laboure V. (VIRGIN)	NOVEMBER 28TH
CATHERINE OF SIENA (VIRGIN)	APRIL 30TH
CECILIA (MARTYR)	NOVEMBER 22ND
CELSUS (MARTYR)	JULY 28TH
CHARLES, Barromeo (CONFESSOR)	NOVEMBER 4TH
CHRISTINA (VIRGIN, MARTYR)	JULY 24TH
CHRISTOPHER (MARTYR)	JULY 25TH
CHRYSANTHUS (MARTYR)	OCTOBER 25TH
CHRYSOGONUS (MARTYR)	NOVEMBER 24TH
CLARE (VIRGIN)	AUGUST 12TH
CLEMENT (MARTYR)	NOVEMBER 23RD
CLETUS (MARTYR)	APRIL 26TH
CORNELIUS (MARTYR)	SEPTEMBER 16TH
COSMAS (MARTYR)	SEPTEMBER 27TH
CRESCENTIA (MARTYR)	JUNE 15TH
CYRPIAN (MARTYR)	SEPTEMBER 16TH
CYRPRIAN (MARTYR)	SEPTEMBER 26TH
CRYIACUS (MARTYR)	AUGUST 8TH
CYRIL, B. (CONFESSOR)	JULY 7TH

CYRIL OF ALEXANDRIA (CONFESSOR)	FEBRUARY 9TH
CYRIL OF JERUSALEM (CONFESSOR)	MARCH 18TH
CYRINUS (MARTYR)	JUNE 12TH
DAMASUS (CONFESSOR)	DECEMBER 11TH
DAMIAN (MARTYR)	SEPTEMBER 27TH
DARIA (MARTYR)	OCTOBER 25TH
DIDACUS (CONFESSOR)	NOVEMBER 13TH
DIONYSIUS (MARTYR)	OCTOBER 9TH
DOMINIC (CONFESSOR)	AUGUST 4TH
DOMITILLA (MARTYR)	MAY 12TH
DONATUS (MARTYR)	AUGUST 7TH
DOROTHY (VIRGIN, MARTYR)	FEBRUARY 6TH
EDWARD (CONFESSOR)	OCTOBER 13TH
ELEUTHERIUS (MARTYR)	OCTOBER 9TH
ELEURHERIUS (POPE, MARTYR)	MAY 26TH
ELIZABETH (HOLY WOMAN)	NOVEMBER 19TH
ELIZABETH, Queen of Portugal (HOLY WOMAN)	JULY 8TH
EMERENTIANA (VIRGIN, MARTYR)	JANUARY 23RD
EPHREM (CONFESSOR)	JUNE 18TH
EPHIMACHUS (MARTYR)	MAY 10TH
ERASMUS (MARTYR)	JUNE 2ND
EUPHEMIA (VIRGIN, MARTYR)	SEPTEMBER 16TH
EUSEBIUS (CONFESSOR)	AUGUST 14TH
EUSEBIUS, B.M. (MARTYR)	DECEMBER 16TH
EUSTACE (MARTYR)	SEPTEMBER 20TH
EVARISTUS (MARTYR)	OCTOBER 26TH
EVENTIUS (MARTYR)	MAY 3RD
FABIAN (MARTYR)	JANUARY 20TH
FAUSTINUS (MARTYR)	FEBRUARY 15TH
FAUSTINUS (MARTYR)	JULY 29TH
FELICIAN (MARTYR)	JUNE 9TH
FELICISSIMUS (MARTYR)	AUGUST 6TH
FELICITAS (MARTYR)	NOVEMBER 23RD
FELICITAS (MARTYR)	MARCH 6TH
ST. FELIX I (MARTYR)	MAY 30TH
FELIX II (MARTYR)	JULY 29TH
FELIX (MARTYR)	JANUARY 14TH
FELIX (MARTYR)	JULY 12TH
FELIX M. (MARTYR)	AUGUST 30TH
FELIX OF VALOIS (CONFESSOR)	NOVEMBER 20TH
FIDELIS OF SIGMARINGEN (CONFESSOR)	APRIL 24TH
FRAMCSE OF ROME (HOLY WOMAN)	MARCH 9TH
FRANCIS XAVIER CABRINI (VIRGIN)	DECEMBER 22ND
FRANCIS OF ASSISI (CONFESSOR)	OCTOBER 4TH
FRANCIS BORGIA (CONFESSOR)	OCTOBER 10TH
FRANCIS CARACCIOLO (CONFESSOR)	JUNE 4TH
FRANCIS OF PAULA (CONFESSOR)	APRIL 2ND
FRANCIS DE SALES (CONFESSOR)	JANUARY 29TH
FRANCIS XAVIER (CONFESSOR)	DECEMBER 3RD
GABRIEL (ARCHANGEL)	MARCH 24TH

GABRIEL OF OUR LADY OF SORROWS	FEBRUARY 27th
GEMINIANUS (MARTYR)	SEPTEMBER 16TH
GEORGE (MARTYR)	APRIL 23RD
GERTRUDE (VIRGIN)	NOVEMBER 16TH
GERVASE (MARTYR)	JUNE 19TH
GILES (ABBOT)	SEPTEMBER 1ST
GORDIAN (MARTYR)	MAY 10TH
GORGONIUS (MARTYR)	SEPTEMBER 9TH
GREGORY VII (CONFESSOR)	MAY 25TH
GREGORY THE GREAT (CONFESSOR)	MARCH 12TH
GREGORY OF NAZIANZEN (CONFESSOR)	MAY 9TH
GREGORY WONDER WORKER (CONFESSOR)	NOVEMBER 17TH
HEDWIG (HOLY WOMAN)	OCTOBER 16TH
HENRY (CONFESSOR)	JULY 15TH
HERMENGILD (MARTYR)	APRIL 13TH
HERMES (MARTYR)	AUGUST 28TH
HALARION (ABBOT)	OCTOBER 21ST
HILARY (CONFESSOR)	JANUARY 14TH
HIPPOLYTUS (MARTYR)	AUGUST 13TH
HIPPOLYTUS (MARTYR)	AUGUST 22ND
HYCINTH (CONFESSOR)	AUGUST 17TH
HYACINTH (MARTYR)	SEPTEMBER 11TH
HYGINUS (MARTYR)	JANUARY 11TH
IGNATIUS (MARTYR)	FEBRUARY 1ST
IGNATIUS OF LOYOLA (CONFESSOR)	JULY 31ST
INNOCENT I (CONFESSOR)	JULY 28TH
IRENAEBUS (MARTYR)	JUNE 28TH
ISAAC, Jogues (MARTYR)	SEPTEMBER 26TH
ISIDORE (CONFESSOR)	APRIL 24TH
ISIDORE (CONFESSOR)	MARCH 22ND
JAMES (APOSTLE)	JULY 25TH
JAMES THE LESS (APOSTLE)	MAY 11TH
JANE, Frances De Chantal	AUGUST 21ST
JANUARIUS (MARTYR)	SEPTEMBER 19TH
JEROME, Emillian (CONFESSOR)	JULY 20TH
JEROME (CONFESSOR)	SEPTEMBER 30TH
JOACHIM (CONFESSOR)	AUGUST 16TH
JOHN (APOSTLE)	DECEMBER 27TH
JOHN THE BAPTIST (PERCURSOR)	JUNE 24TH
JOHN BOSCO (CONFESSOR)	JANUARY 31ST
JOHN DE BREBEUF (MARTYR)	SEPTEMBER 26TH
JOHN CANTIUS (CONFESSOR)	OCTOBER 20TH
JOHN OF CAPISTRAN (CONFESSOR)	MARCH 28TH
JOHN CHRYSOSTOM (CONFESSOR)	JANUARY 27TH
JOHN OF THE CROSS (CONFESSOR)	NOVEMBER 24TH
JOHN DAMASCENE (CONFESSOR)	MARCH 27TH
JOHN EUDES (CONFESSOR)	AUGUST 19TH
JOHN OF SAINT FACUNDO (CONFESSOR)	JUNE 12TH
JOHN OF GOD (CONFESSOR)	MARCH 8TH
JOHN GUALBERT (ABBOT)	JULY 12TH

205

JOHN, Leonard (CONFESSOR)	OCTOBER 9TH
JOHN, Mary Vianney (CONFESSOR)	AUGUST 9TH'
JOHN OF MATHA (CONFESSOR)	FEBRUARY 8TH
JOHN (MARTYR)	JUNE 26TH
JOHN I (POPE, MARTYR)	MAY 27TH
JOSAPHAT (MARTYR)	NOVEMBER 14TH
JOSEPH (PATRON, CONFESSOR)	MARCH 19TH
JOSEPH CALASANCTIUS (CONFESSOR)	AUGUST 27TH
JOSEPH OF CUPERTINO (CONFESSOR)	SEPTEMBER 18TH
JOVITA (MARTYR)	FEBRUARY 15TH
JUDE (APOSTLE)	OCTOBER 28TH
JULIANA FALCONIERI (VIRGIN)	JOHN 19TH
JULIE BILLIART (VIRGIN)	APRIL 8TH
JUSTIN (MARTYR)	APRIL 14TH
JUSTINA (VIRGIN, MARTYR)	SEPTEMBER 26TH
JUVENAL (CONFESSOR)	MAY 3RD
LARGUS (MARTYR)	AUGUST 8TH
LAWERENCE (MARTYR)	AUGUST 10TH
LAWERENCE JUSTINIAN (CONFESSOR)	SEPTEMBER 5TH
LEO I (POPE, CONFESSOR)	APRIL 11TH
LEO II (POPE, CONFESSOR)	JULY 3RD
LIBORIUS (BISHOP, CONFESSOR)	JULY 23RD
LINUS (POPE, MARTYR)	SEPTEMBER 23RD
LOUIS (KING, CONFESSOR)	AUGUST 25TH
LOUISE DE MARILLAC (HOLY WOMAN)	MARCH 15TH
LUCIUS (POPE, MARTYR)	MARCH 4TH
LUCY (VIRGIN, MARTYR)	DECEMBER 13TH
LUCY (MARTYR)	SEPTEMBER 16TH
LUKE (EVENGELIST)	OCTOBER 18TH
MADELINE SOPHIE BARAT (VIRGIN)	JUNE 18TH
MARCELLIANUS (MARTYR)	JUNE 18TH
MARCELLINUS (POPE, MARTYR)	APRIL 26TH
MARCELLINUS (MARTYR)	JUNE 2ND
MARCELLUS (MARTYR)	OCTOBER 7TH
MARCELLUS (POPE, MARTYR)	JANUARY 16TH
MARGARET (VIRGIN, MARTYR)	JULY 20TH
MARGRET Mary Alacoque (VIRGIN)	OCTOBER 17TH
MARGRET, Queen of Scotland (HOLY WOMAN)	JUNE 10TH
MARIUS (MARTYR)	JANUARY 19TH
MARK (EVANGELIST)	APRIL 25TH
MARK (MARTYR)	JUNE 18TH
MARK (POPE, CONFESSOR)	OCTOBER 7TH
MARTHA (VIRGIN)	JULY 29TH
MARTHA (MARTYR)	JANUARY 19TH
MARTIN I (POPE, MARTYR)	NOVEMBER 11TH
MARTIN DE PORRES (CONFESSOR)	NOVEMBER 3RD
MARTINA (VIRGIN, MARTYR)	NOVEMBER 3RD
MARTINIAN (MARTYR)	JULY 2ND
MARY MAGDALEN (PENITENT)	JULY 22ND
MARY MAGDALEN DEI PAZZI (VIRGIN)	MAY 29TH

MATTHEW (APOSTLE, EVANGELIST)	SEPTEMBER 21ST
MATTHIAS (APOSTLE)	FEBRUARY 24TH
MAURRCE (MARTYR)	SEPTEMBER 22ND
MARUS (ABBOT)	JANUARY 15TH
MAXIMUS (MARTYR)	APRIL 14TH
MELCHIADES (POPE, MARTYR)	DECEMBER 10TH
MENNAS (MARTYR)	NOVEMBER 11TH
METHODIUS (BISHOP, CONFESSOR)	JULY 7TH
MODESTUS (MARTYR)	JUNE 15TH
MONICA (HOLY WOMAN)	MAY 4TH
NABOR (MARTYR)	JUNE 12TH
NABOR (MARTYR)	JULY 12TH
NAZARIUS (MARTYR)	JULY 28TH
NAZARIUS (MARTYR)	JUNE 12TH
NEREUS (MARTYR)	MAY 12TH
NICHOLAS (BISHOP, CONFESSOR)	DECEMBER 6TH
NICHOLAS OF TOLENTINE (CONFESSOR)	SEPTEMBER 10TH
NICOMEDES (MARTYR)	SEPTEMBER 15TH
NORVERT (BISHOP, CONFESSOR)	JUNE 6TH
NYMPHA (VIRGIN, MARTYR)	NOVEMBER 10TH
PANCRAS (MARTYR)	MAY 12TH
PANTALEON (MARTYR)	JULY 27TH
PASCHAL BAYLON (CONFESSOR)	MAY 17TH
PATRICK (BISHOP, CONFESSOR)	MARCH 17TH
PAUL (APOSTLE)	JUNE 29TH
PAUL OF THE CROSS (CONFESSOR)	APRIL 28TH
PAUL, THE HERMIT (CONFESSOR)	JANUARY 15TH
PAUL (MARTYR)	JUNE 26TH
PAULINUS (BISHOP, CONFESSOR)	JUNE 22ND
PERPETUA (MARTYR)	MARCH 6TH
PETER AND PAUL (APOSTLES)	JUNE 29TH
PETER (MARTYR)	JUNE 2ND
PETER OF ALCANTARA (CONFESSOR)	OCTOBER 19TH
PETER OF ALEXANDRAI (BISHOP, MARTYR)	NOVEMBER 26TH
PETER CANISIUS (CONFESSOR)	APRIL 27TH
PETER CELESTINE (POPE, CONFESSOR)	MAY 19TH
PETER CHRYSOLOGUS (BISHOP, CONFESSOR)	DECEMBER 4TH
PETER CLAVER (CONFESSOR)	SEPTEMBER 9TH
PETER DAMIAN (BISHOP, CONFESSOR)	FEBRUARY 23RD
PETER IOLASCO (CONFESSOR)	JANUARY 28TH
PETER OF VERONA (MARTYR)	APRIL 29TH
PETRONILLA (VIRGIN)	MAY 31ST
PHILIP (APOSTLE)	MAY 11TH
PHILIP BENIZI (CONFESSOR)	AUGUST 23RD
PHILIP NERI (CONFESSOR)	MAY 26TH
PHILLIPPINE DUCHESNE (VIRGIN)	NOVEMBER 17TH
PIUS I (POPE, MARTYR)	JULY 11TH
PIUS V (POPE, CONFESSOR)	MAY 5TH
PIUS X (POPE, CONFESSOR)	SEPTEMBER 3RD
PLACIDUS (MARTYR)	OCTOBER 5TH

POLYCARP (BISHOP, MARTYR)	JANUARY 26TH
PONTIANUS (POPE, MARTYR)	NOVEMBER 19TH
PRAXEDES (VIRGIN)	JULY 21ST
PRIMUS (MARTYR)	JUNE 9TH
PRISCA (VIRGIN, MARTYR)	JANUARY 18TH
PROCESSUS (MARTYR)	JULY 2ND
PROTASE (MARTYR)	JUNE 19TH
PROTUS (MARTYR)	SEPTEMBER 11TH
PUDENTIANA (VIRGIN)	MAY 19TH
RAPHAEL (ARCHANGEL)	OCTOBER 24TH
RAYMOND OF PENNAFORT (CONFESSOR)	JANUARY 23RD
RAYMUND NONNATUS (CONFESSOR)	AUGUST 31ST
REMIGIUS (BISHOP, CONFESSOR)	OCTOBER 1ST
RESPICIUS (MARTYR)	NOVEMBER 10TH
ROBERT BELLARMINE (BISHOP, CONFESSOR)	MAY 13TH
ROMANUS (MARTYR)	AUGUST 9TH
ROMUALD (ABBOT)	FEBRUARY 7TH
ROSE OF LIMA (VIRGIN)	AUGUST 30TH
RUFINA (VIRGIN, MARTYR)	JULY 10TH
RUSTICUS (MARTYR)	OCTOBER 9TH
SABBAS (ABBOT)	DECEMBER 5TH
SABINA (MARTYR)	AUGUST 29TH
SATURNINUS (MARTYR)	NOVEMBER 29TH
SCHOLASTICA (VIRGIN)	FEBRUARY 10TH
SEBASTIAN (MARTYR)	JANUARY 20TH
SECCUNDA (VIRGIN, MARTYR)	JULY 10TH
SENNEN (MARTYR)	JULY 30TH
SERGIUS (MARTYR)	OCTOBER 7TH
SILVERIUS (POPE, MARTYR)	JUNE 20TH
SIMERON (BISHOP, MARTYR)	FEBRUARY 18TH
SIMON (APOSTLE)	OCTOBER 28TH
SIMPLICIUS (MARTYR)	JULY 29TH
SIXTUS II (POPE, MARTYR)	AUGUST 6TH
SMARAGDUS (MARTYR)	AUGUST 8TH
SOTER (POPE, MARTYR)	APRIL 22ND
STANISLAUS (BISHOP, MARTYR)	MAY 7TH
STEPHEN I (MARTYR)	DECEMBER 26TH
STEPHEN I (POPE, MARTYR)	AUGUST 2ND
STEPHEN (KING, CONFESSOR)	SEPTEMBER 2ND
SUSANNA (VIRGIN, MARTYR)	AUGUST 11TH
SYLVESTER (ABBOT)	NOVEMBER 26TH
SYLVESTER I (POPE, CONFESSOR)	DECEMBER 31ST
SYMPHORIAN (MARTYR)	AUGUST 22ND
TELESPHORUS (POPE, MARTYR)	JANUARY 5TH
TERESA (VIRGIN)	OCTOBER 15TH
THECLA (VIRGIN, MARTYR)	SEPTEMBER 23RD
THERESA (OF THE CHILD JESUS)	OCTOBER 3RD
THEODORE (MARTYR)	NOVEMBER 9TH
THEODULUS (MARTYR)	MAY 3RD
THOMAS (APOSTLE)	DECEMBER 21ST

THOMAS AQUIANAS (CONFESSOR)	MARCH 7TH
THOMAS (BISHOP, MARTYR)	DECEMBER 29TH
THOMAS OF VILLANOVA (BISHOP, CONFESSOR)	SEPTEMBER 22ND
TIBURTIUS (MARTYR)	APRIL 14TH
TIBURTIUS (MARTYR)	AUGUST 11TH
TIMOTHY (BISHOP, MARTYR)	JANUARY 24TH
TIMOTHY (MARTYR)	AUGUST 22ND
TITUS (CONFESSOR, BISHOP)	FEBRUARY 6TH
TYPHON (MARTYR)	NOVEMBER 10TH
UBALDUS (BISHOP, CONFESSOR)	MAY 16TH
URBAN I (POPE, MARTYR)	MAY 25TH
URSULA (VIRGIN, MARTYR)	OCTOBER 21ST
VALENTINE (PRIEST, MARTYR)	FEBRUARY 14TH
VALERIAN (MARTYR)	APRIL 14TH
VENANTIUS (MARTYR)	MAY 18TH
VICTOR (POPE, MARTYR)	JULY 28TH
VINCENT FERRER (CONFESSOR)	APRIL 5TH
VINCENT DE PAUL (CONFESSOR)	JULY 19TH
VINCENT (MARTYR)	JANUARY 22ND
VITALIS (MARTYR)	APRIL 28TH
VITALIS (MARTYR)	NOVEMBER 4TH
VITUS (MARTYR)	JUNE 15TH
WENCESLAUS (DUKE, MARTYR)	SEPTEMBER 28TH
WILLIAM (ABBOT)	JUNE 25TH
ZEPHYRINUS (POPE, MARTYR)	AUGUST 26TH

THE TWELVE APOSTLES IN CONJUNCTION WITH THE TWELVE MONTHS OF THE YEAR

The twelve apostles seem to hold a remarkable resemblance in relationship to the characteristics of the twelve months of the year, in association with the signs of the zodiac.

Throughout the ages, man has inevitably mastered the technique of masking life - making it appear not as it is, but as man would like it to be, trying and striving to complicate the simplest of all issues - life itself - by twisting and turning, distorting and misusing the God given arts of reason, logic and rationale. Few things can be proven to its absolute, and anything that can be, will soon, through science, be proven not to be. Not man nor beast is safe from the ever proving/disproving science of our time.

Time is cyclical, not linear. The events of the past will always recur on the level of individual conscious acceptance. So many people marvel at the statement that all religions are just and true, that it depends on the level of consciousness of the person as to whether or not they will accept one belief system over another. They act as if they understand, walking away in total agreement, but with questions on their faces. Not everything was meant to be understood by everyone.

The understanding or knowledgeable person will never dispute the truth of someone else, knowing that their truth is individual and does not need to be substantiated or validated by anyone else. The holiest of all people find God within themselves, partaking not in the traditional orthodox dogma. You will not see these people in church on Sundays, not will you hear them preach on television. They believe within and in themselves.

Man has been looking to the heavens for thousands of years. What are they looking for? We have heard of the twelve tribes of Israel and the twelve apostles. The star that shone from the East, guiding the wise men to baby Jesus - was this Halley's Comet? There are as many questions about biblical times as there are people to answer them.

We are not living with the same conditions, nor do we have the same thought processes, as did these people living hundreds of years ago. Thus, we are ill-equipped to interpret the acts, the discretions, or indiscretions of the past. We can only take what has been written and expand upon it, not through interpretation, but through our ability to add to what has been revealed to us throughout time. Given twice more the concept of time being cyclical and not linear, thus giving the spiral effect to past events.

People have dabbled in the past, correlating the twelve apostles and the twelve signs of the zodiac. How many people have actually taken their blinders off long enough to allow such an ancient concept to actually exist? Is the Tropic of Cancer only the Tropic of Cancer? Or, was it named hundreds of years ago after the deadly disease that would some day plague this world? Was the Tropic of Cancer, along with the twelve apostles chosen by Christ to represent what had already been set into motion by God: "The cyclical, biological time clock of the living," compelling all man to act and react on a whim, not always at will?"

We have to ask ourselves, when we get that overwhelming urge to act in a manner that is atypical of our character: "Where is this need to act out coming from?" Is this character destiny or free will? Are you following the compelling energy of the zodiac, as some feel so strongly exist, or is this atypical behavior God's Will and perhaps not your will? So many questions, so few pages to fill.

God's Will is the compelling force that guides all of us. The astrological energy of the universe is that of God. The twelve apostles of Jesus Christ were chosen by Christ through divine guidance from God. The twelve apostles are not only typical of the twelve signs of the zodiac, they are the epitome of the zodiac - and for good reason. God has been allowing man free will through divine guidance. We are being guided and protected as Christ was protected, through the divine order of free will.

When life has gotten to the point that a little help is needed, or that you feel a need for divine intervention, light the appropriate candle to the apostle that will best give, through God, the assistance and insight that you are in need of at the time.

The Apostle's Creed has been, and will always be, the creed of the most holy. When lighting your candles to the apostles, you may recite this creed, thus bringing you comfort as you pay your respects to the apostles.

THE APOSTLE'S CREED

1. I believe in the Father Almighty;
2. Maker of heaven and earth;
3. And, in Jesus Christ, His only son, our Lord;
4. Who was conceived by the Holy Ghost, born of the Virgin Mary;
5. Suffered under Pontius Pilate, was crucified dead and buried;
6. He descended into hell, the third day, He rose again from the dead;
7. He ascended into heaven, sitteth at the right hand of God the Father Almighty;
8. From thence, He shall come to judge the quick and the dead;
9. I believe in the Holy Ghost, the Holy Catholic Church;
10. The communion of the saints, the forgiveness of sins;
11. The resurrection of the body;
12. Life everlasting. Amen.

211

Each apostle has their own timing guide. To ensure your candle lighting is successful, you must follow the apostle lighting guide. This timing guide has been written in CST. Please adjust to your local time by using the timing guide referenced on page 122 to determine your local time.

PETER, THE APOSTLE TO CHRIST
MARCH 21ST THROUGH APRIL 19TH

Peter will be the religious figurehead aiding and assisting you in matters of urgency, lending patience and understanding to your inability to remain calm as you watch the divine order, or God's will, unfold in your life.

Peter is especially sensitive to those people born during the time frame from March 21st through April 19th. These people inherently possess the same intrinsic personality traits of Peter. There is a personal desire, on Peter's behalf, to help all of those people who can identify with him.

Peter was Christ's first apostle. He was headstrong, a good leader, and impulsive to lead in matters of grave urgency. Although Peter was aggressive, he was always admired for his ability to achieve at any task. Setting his stubborn mind to accomplish, his goals were always within his reach.

Peter's real name was Simon Bar-Jona, which translated from Latin means "Simon, son of John." Simon Bar-Jona's name was changed by Christ. The phrase that Christ used was "Thou art Peter, and upon this rock, I shall build my church" (Matt. 16:18). It was originally said that this name was given to Simon in jest, as the name "Peter" translated from Latin is "Petrus" (meaning rock), and Peter's thoughts were as hard and as stubborn as a rock.

Peter preached the Word of God in Judea and was put in prison by Herod. As he lay sleeping, Peter, chained between two guards, was delivered from prison by an angel of God. He then continued his ministry 0 first in Antioch and then in Rome. He established himself in Rome, making it the center of the Church.

Peter died in Rome, during the persecution of Nero (64-68 A.D.), by being crucified head downward. He was persistent in his endeavors and preached the Word of God until the day of his death.

212

Peter, being the first apostle of Christ, will assist you in all of your endeavors to incite something new into your life. He will assist you with patience and give you the energy to achieve. There is no end to the amount of assistance that he can give you.

At times, most people, feel as if life can be overwhelming. God has a divine plan for everyone. Through your ability to identify with Peter, you will receive all that God has to offer you.

No one likes to be patient. Within life, urgency is the name of the game. One common saying is, "He who hesitates is lost." Perhaps this saying substantiates the fact that, without the assurance of divine guidance, we may be wandering through life aimlessly forever. When the assistance of Peter is needed - to buy a new car, to find a lost love, or to get a different job - he will be there to assist you in any matter that requires patience. And, in any situation that you feel an urgency to complete, Peter will direct you in the changes you wish to make in your life.

Use your timing guide to determine when to light your candle to call for the assistance of Peter, the first apostle of Christ. There will be two days per month, at which time he will assist you, granting you divine guidance, patience, and the ability to easily cope with life's issues. While any day is a good day to light a candle out of respect for him, there are certain days that will be better than others to request his assistance in your life.

When following the timing guide, you must light one yellow candle with a small white candle. Snuff out the white candle, but allow your yellow candle to continue to burn until it goes out. Giving thanks to Peter is not a form of worship. You are only giving thanks for the assistance.

When requesting Peter's assistance in starting new projects, the candle color to light is yellow. Before you begin any new undertaking, to ensure success, light one yellow candle in honor of Peter on the dates below. Light one yellow candle on the dates listed, if your desire is to begin a new adventure, or if you plan to initiate a change in your life within thirty days before the dates listed. The operative time to light your candle is between 4:00 A.M. and 6:00 A.M.

Peter Apostle to Jesus
March 21st through April 19th

2001
June 14th 11:02 AM through June 16th 8:36 PM
July 11th 6:35 PM through July 14th 5:10 AM
August 8th 1:04 AM through August 10th 12:21 PM
September 4th 6:57 AM through September 6th 6:16 PM
October 1st 1:07 PM through October 3rd 11:59 PM
October 28th 8:14 PM through October 31st 6:45 AM
November 25th 4:20 AM through November 27th 3:04 PM
December 22nd 12:44 PM through December 25th 0:10 AM

2002
January 18th 8:34 PM through January 21st 8:44 AM
February 15th 3:24 AM through February 17th 3:55 PM
March 14th 9:33 AM through March 16th 9:59 PM
April 10th 3:39 PM through April 13th 3:53 AM
May 7th 10:21 PM through May 10th 10:30 AM
June 4th 5:50 AM through June 6th 6:04 PM
July 1st 1:48 PM through July 4th 2:14 AM
July 28th 9:37 PM through July 31st 10:14 AM
August 25th 4:46 AM through August 27th 5:29 PM
September 21st 11:10 AM through September 23rd 11:52 PM
October 18th 5:12 PM through October 21st 5:54 AM
November 14th 11:36 PM through November 17th 12:21 PM
December 12th 6:57 AM through December 14th 7:41 PM

2003
January 8th 3:14 PM through January 11th 3:46 AM
February 4th 11:43 PM through February 7th 11:56 AM
March 4th 7:29 AM through March 6th 7:34 PM
March 31st 2:03 PM through April 3rd 2:18 AM
April 27th 7:53 PM through April 30th 8:24 AM
May 25th 1:58 AM through May 27th 2:30 PM
June 21st 9:04 AM through June 23rd 9:12 PM
July 18th 5:18 PM through July 21st 4:46 AM
August 15th 1:59 AM through August 17th 12:50 PM
September 11th 10:09 AM through September 13th 8:47 PM
October 8th 5:07 PM through October 11th 4:02 AM
November 11th 11:02 PM through November 7th 10:27 AM
December 2nd 4:56 AM through December 4th 4:28 PM
December 29th 12:08 PM through December 31st 11:00 PM

2004

January 25th 9:05 PM through January 28th 6:44 AM
February 22nd 6:44 AM through February 24th 3:28 PM
March 20th 3:28 PM through March 23rd 0:07 AM
April 16th 10:23 PM through April 19th 7:40 AM
May 14th 4:01 AM through May 16th 1:55 PM
June 10th 9:48 AM through June 12th 7:34 PM
July 7th 5:02 PM through July 10th 1:49 AM
August 4th 1:59 AM through August 6th 9:23 AM
August 31st 11:45 AM through September 2nd 6:14 PM
September 27th 8:56 PM through September 30th 3:22 AM
October 25th 4:24 AM through October 27th 11:35 AM
November 21st 10:10 AM through November 23rd 6:14 PM
December 18th 3:51 PM through December 20th 11:50 PM

2005

January 14th 11:26 PM through January 17th 6:04 AM
February 11th 9:21 AM through February 13th 2:15 PM
March 10th 8:03 PM through March 13th 0:03 AM
April 7th 5:27 AM through April 9th 9:48 AM
May 4th 12:35 PM through May 6th 5:59 PM
May 31st 6:07 through June 3rd 0:17 AM
June 27th 11:51 PM through June 30th 5:43 AM
July 25th 7:22 AM through July 27th 11:52 AM
August 21st 5:01 PM through August 23rd 7:56 PM
September 18th 3:42 AM through September 20th 5:45 AM
October 15th 1:39 PM through October 17th 4:02 PM
November 11th 9:22 PM through November 14th 1:01 AM
December 9th 3:01 AM through December 11th 7:43 AM

2006

January 5th 8:44 AM through January 7th 1:07 PM
February 1st 4:45 PM through February 3rd 7:29 PM
March 1st 3:18 AM through March 3rd 4:21 AM
March 28th 2:30 PM through March 30th 2:59 PM
April 25th 0:12 AM through April 27th 1:25 AM
May 22nd 7:23 AM through May 24th 9:59 AM
June 18th 12:53 PM through June 20th 4:21 PM
July 15th 6:39 PM through July 17th 9:43 PM
August 12th 2:21 AM through August 14th 3:58 AM

September 8th 12:23 PM through September 10th 12:28 PM
October 5th 11:32 PM through October 7th 11:02 PM
November 2nd 9:46 AM through November 4th 10:03 AM
November 29th 5:30 PM through December 1st 7:24 PM
December 26th 11:04 PM through December 29th 2:07 AM

2007
January 23rd 4:52 AM through January 25th 7:27 AM
February 19th 1:06 PM through February 21st 2:02 PM
March 18th 11:42PM through March 20th 11:14 PM
April 15th 10:46 AM through April 17th 10:09 AM
May 12th 8:19 PM through May 14th 8:47 PM
June 9th 3:26 AM through June 11th 5:28 AM
July 6th 8:57 AM through July 8th 11:52 AM
August 2nd 2:43 PM through August 4th 5:14 PM
September 26th 8:22 AM through September 28th 8:15 AM
October 23rd 7:24 PM through October 25th 7:06 PM
November 20th 5:25 AM through November 22nd 6:17 AM
December 17th 12:52 PM through December 19th 3:37 PM

2008
January 13th 6:23 PM through January 15th 10:11 PM
February 10th 0:17 AM through February 12th 3:32 AN
March 8th 8:24 AM through March 10th 10:12 AM
April 4th 6:27 PM through April6th 7:18 PM
May 2nd 4:51 AM through May 4th 5:57 AM
May 29th 1:52 PM through May 31st 4:17 PM
June 25th 8:49 PM through June 28th 0:49 AM
July 23rd 2:22 AM through June 25th 7:13 AM
August 19th 8:10 AM through August 21st 12:37 PM
September 15th 3:39 PM through September 17th 6:55 PM
October 13th 1:07 AM through October 15th 3:29 AM
November 9th 11:26 AM through November 11th 2:04 PM
December 6th 8:44 PM through December 9th 0:51 AM

2009
January 3rd 3:49 AM through January 5th 9:44 AM
January 30th 9:25 AM through February 1st 4:07 PM
February 26th 3:24 PM through February 28th 9:32 PM
March 23rd 3:08 PM through March 25th 11:01 PM

216

April 22nd 8:09 AM through April 24th 12:44 PM
May 19th 5:30 PM through May 21st 10:39 PM
June 16th 1:52 AM through June 18th 8:19 AM
July 13th 8:40 AM through July 15th 4:28 PM
August 9th 2:23 PM through August 11th 10:49 PM
September 5th 8:14 PM through September 8th 4:16 PM
October 3rd 3:20 AM through October 5th 10:32 AM
October 30th 11:56 AM through November 1st 6:43 PM
November 26th 9:10 PM through November 29th 4:32 PM
December 24th 5:39 AM through December 26th 2:25 PM

2010
January 20th 12:35 PM through January 22nd 10:37 PM
February 16th 6:29 PM through February 19th 4:53 AM
March 16th 0:31 AM through March 18th 10:26 AM
April 12th 7:30 AM through April 14th 4:52 PM
May 9th 3:28 PM through May 12th 0:46 AM
June 5th 11:48 PM through June 8 9:38 AM
July 3rd 7:43 AM through July 5th 6:26 PM
July 30th 2:40 PM through August 2nd 2:11 AM
August 26th 8:48 PM through August 29th 8:33 AM
September 23rd 2:46 AM through September 25th 2:13 PM
October 20th 9:22 AM through October 22nd 8:26 PM
November 16th 4:57 PM through November 19th 4:02 AM
December 14th 1:13 AM through December 16th 12:47 PM

SIMON, THE CAANANITE AND THE ZEALOT
APRIL 20TH THROUGH MAY 20TH

Before becoming one of Christ's disciples, Simon started his life with anger and zealousness. He was bullheaded and seemed to know what was best for everyone else. He was politically involved and felt the best way to change someone's way of thinking was to fight with them over their beliefs.

Simon's belief was in force. In his younger years, he was involved with the Canaanites, who sought to overthrow the Roman occupation of Palestine by force. After the invitation to join Christ, Simon found that his uncompromising lifestyle had disappeared, only to be replaced with love,

217

honesty, and compassion. Simon joined Christ and the other apostles to preach the Word of God.

When Simon was involved in the political aspects of his life, he felt that he was doing right by all those he served. However, after studying with Christ, he knew his mission in life was to be kind and in service to others. We all know to be in service to others is at the opposite end of the spectrum from where Simon had started his life.

Simon spent hours and years of his life listening to the Words of Christ. Soon, he, too, was a devout convert, dedicating his life to spreading God's Word. He was martyred in the first century.

There is a kindred emotion between Simon and those people born between April 20th and May 20th. One distinct commonality these people share with Simon is the fact that they have an intrinsic need to serve.

Simon will assist you in your time of need via lighting candles. (The Catholic religion refers to this practice as Novena, lighting candles to summon the aid of a saint.) Simon's passion for spreading God's Word enabled him to not only be of service to others during his life, but through his sainthood enables him to continue to serve you.

In your quiet moments, contemplate the life teachings of Simon. Light one green candle and pray that through God, Simon will assist you in your endeavors to serve others, as well as yourself.

Everyone born between April 20th and May 20th will experience life, as did Simon, as a double-edged sword. With frequent times of all or nothing, coupled with the life tendency of good or bad, they seldom experience the balance which solicits harmony in life. Harmony only comes to these people as they solicit the aid of Simon and expend time in service to others. Through Simon and service to others, these people, as well as anyone lighting a green candle in honor of Simon, will receive balance, harmony, honor, peace of mind, and the ability to prosper on a spiritual and material level.

The time that is best to light a candle to summon the aid of Simon is between 2:00 A.M. and 4:00 A.M. on the dates listed below. Although you may solicit his help on any day at any time, the operative times are listed below.

Simon, the Caananite and the Zealot
April 20th through May 20th.

2001

June 16th 8:38 PM through June 19th 2:39 AM
July 14th 5:12 AM through July 16th 12:24 PM
August 10th 12:22 PM through August 12th 8:57 PM
September 6th 6:18 PM through September 9th 3:39 AM
October 4th 0:01 AM through October 6th 9:10 AM
November 27th 3:05 PM through November 29th 11:02 PM

2002

January 21st 8:46 AM through January 23rd 6:25 PM
February 17th 3:57 PM through February 20th 2:47 AM
March 16th 10:00 PM through March 19th 9:17 AM
April 13th 3:55 AM through April 15th 2:54 PM
May 10th 10:31 AM through May 12th 9:02 PM
June 6th 6:05 PM through June 9th 4:27 AM
July 4th 2:15 AM through July 6th 12:58 PM
July 31st 10:16 AM through August 2nd 9:44 PM
August 27th 5:30 PM through August 30th 5:43 AM
September 23rd 11:53 PM through September 26th 12:24 PM
October 21st 5:55 AM through October 23rd 6:15 PM
November 17th 12:22 PM through November 20th 0:22 AM
December 14th 7:42 PM through December 17th 7:40 AM

2003

January 11th 3:47 AM through July 13th 4:06 PM
February 7th 11:58 AM through February 10th 0:42 AM
March 6th 7:35 PM through March 9th 8:35 AM
April 3rd 2:19 AM through March 5th 3:21 PM
April 30th 8:25 AM through May 2nd 9:25 PM
May 27th 2:31 PM through May 30th 3:28 AM
June 23rd 9:14 PM through June 26th 10:11 AM
July 21st 4:47 through July 23rd 5:40 PM
August 17th 12:52 PM through August 20th 1:39 AM
September 13th 8:49 PM through September 16th 9:30 AM

219

October 11th 4:04 AM through October 13th 4:42 PM
November 7th 10:29 AM through November 9th 11:12 PM
December 4th 4:29 PM through December 7th 5:23 AM

2004
December 31st 2003 11:01 PM through January 3rd 11:55 AM
January 28th 6:45 AM through January 30th 7:16 PM
February 24th 3:29 PM through February 27th 3:19 AM
March 23rd 0:09 AM through March 25th 11:32 AM
April 19th 7:41 AM through April 21st 7:08 PM
May 16th 1:56 PM through May 19th 1:44 AM
June 12th 7:36 PM through June 15th 7:42 AM
July 10th 1:50 AM through July 12th 1:42 PM
August 6th 9:25 AM through August 8th 8:31 PM
September 2nd 6:15 PM through September 5th 4:22 AM
September 30th 3:24 AM through October 2nd 12:53 PM
October 27th 11:37 AM through October 29th 9:09 PM
November 23rd 6:16 PM through November 26th 4:22 AM
December 20th 11:51 PM through December 23rd 10:29 AM

2005
January 17th 6:05 AM through January 19th 4:21 PM
February 13th 2:17 PM through February 15th 11:16 PM
March 13th 0:05 AM through March 15th 7:42 AM
April 9th 9:49 AM through April 11th 4:53 PM
May 6th 6:00 PM through May 9th 1:27 AM
June 3rd 0:19 AM through June 5th 8:34 Am
June 30th 5:44 AM through July 2nd 2:24 PM
July 27th 11:54 AM through July 29th 8:00 PM
August 23rd 7:57 PM through August 26th 2:40 AM
September 20th 5:48 AM through September 22nd 11:05 AM
October 17th 4:03 PM through October 19th 8:42 PM
November 14th 1:02 AM through November 16th 6:08 AM
December 11th 7:45 AM through December 13th 1:57 PM

2006
January 7th 1:09 PM through January 9th 7:56 PM
February 3rd 7:31 PM through February 6th 1:31 AM
March 3rd 4:22 AM through March 5th 8:36 AM
March 30th 3:00 PM through April 1st 5:48 PM

April 27th 1:26 AM through April 29th 3:56 AM
May 24th 10:00 AM through May 26th 1:18 PM
June 20th 4:22 PM through June 22nd 8:48 PM
July 17th 9:44 PM through July 20th 2:36 AM
August 14th 3:59 Am through August 16th 8:06 AM
September 10th 12:30 PM through September 12th 2:57 PM
October 7th 11:04 PM through October 10th 0:05 Am
November 4th 10:05 AM through November 6th 10:44 AM
December 1st 7:25 PM through December 3rd 9:03 PM
December 29th 2:08 AM through December 31st 5:15 AM

2007
January 25th 7:28 AM through January 27th 11:08 AM
February 21st 2:04 PM through February 23rd 4:40 PM
March 20th 11:15 PM through March 23rd 0:05 AM
April 17th 10:11 AM through April 19th 9:50 AM
May 14th 8:48 PM through May 16th 8:32 PM
June 11th 5:29 AM through June 13th 6:22 AM
July 8th 11:54 AM through July 10th 2:08 PM
August 4th 5:16 PM through August 6th 7:59 PM
August 31st 11:35 PM through September 3rd 1:29 AM
September 28th 8:17 AM through September 30th 8:33 AM
October 25th 7:07 PM through October 27th 6:10 PM
November 22nd 6:18 AM through November 24th 5:28 AM
December 19th 3:38 PM through December 21st 4:13 PM

2008
January 15th 10:13 PM through January 18th 0:28 AM
February 12th 3:34 AM through February 14th 6:17 AM
March 10th 10:13 AM through March 12th 11:52 AM
April 6th 7:19 PM through April 8th 7:25 PM
May 4th 5:58 AM through May 6th 5:16 AM
May 31st 4:18 PM through June 2nd 4:05 PM
June 28th 0:50 AM through June 30th 2:10 AM
July25th 7:14 AM through July 27th 9:53 AM
August 21st 12:38 PM through August 23rd 3:47 PM
September 17th 6:56 PM through September 19th 9:15 PM
October 15th 3:31 AM through October 17th 4:24 AM
November11th 2:05 PM through November 13th 2:10 PM
December 9th 0:52 AM through December 11th 1:32 AM

221

2009
January 5th 9:46 AM through January 7th 12:10 PM
February 1st 4:08 PM through February 3rd 8:13 PM
February 28th 9:33 PM through March 3rd 1:57 AM
March 28th 4:09 AM through March 30th 7:34 AM
April 24th 12:46 PM through April 26th 3:00 PM
May 21st 10:40 PM through May 24th 0:33 AM
June 18th 8:21 AM through June 20th 10:59 AM
July 15th 4:30 PM through July 17th 8:40 PM
August 11th 10:50 PM through August 14th 4:24 AM
September 8th 4:17 AM through September 10th 10:16 AM
October 5th 10:33 AM through October 7th 3:45 PM
November 1st 6:44 PM through November 3rd 10:51 PM
November 29th 4:34 AM through December 1st 8:22 AM
December 26th 2:26 PM through December 30th 8:44 PM

2010
January 22nd 10:38 PM through January 25th 5:09 AM
February 19th 4:54 AM through February 21st 12:44 PM
March 18th 10:28 AM through March 20th 6:26 PM
April 14th 4:54 PM through April 17th 0:06 AM
May 12th 0:47 AM through May 14th 7:15 AM
June 8th 9:39 AM through June 10th 4:08 PM
July 5th 6:28 PM through July 8th 1:48 AM
August 2nd 2:12 AM through August 4th 10:51 AM
August 29th 8;34 AM through August 31st 6:16 PM
September 25th 2:15PM through September 28th 0:08 AM
October 22nd 8:28 PM through October 25th 5:44 AM
November 19th 4:03 AM through November 21st 12:43 PM
December 16th 12:48 PM through December 18th 9:35 PM

JAMES THE LESS
MAY 21ST THROUGH JUNE 20TH

James, twin brother to Judas and son of Alpheus, adds character and humor to the twelve apostles. While there are many conflicting stories about his life before he followed Christ, the common consensus among the different religion is that James was the cousin of Jesus.

222

Learning God's Word in his travels with Christ, James, on the first day of his soul journey, listened as Jesus spoke of the gates to heaven being open to all men and women - that all men and women were alike - and the Word of God would be available to everyone, for God did not discriminate.

James was a simple-minded man who loved and admired Christ. He was enamored of Christ, asking very few questions. He traveled with Christ for four years, at which time, Christ met with his death. James went on to write one of the epistles of the New Testament.

James was sensitive and shy, but had a thirst for knowledge. He had a love of travel and was an adventurous man. He wrote and enjoyed the teachings of all things that he had not come into contact with before.

James possessed all the personality traits and led a life that is typical of those people born between May 21st and June 20th. This time frame is characteristic of the twin, as James was a twin, and deals not only with communication, but with travel. Throughout his life, James was led to communicate with millions of people, traveling near and far with the other disciples and their adored teacher.

Another characteristic of this time frame, and of James, is an uncanny ability to hold two faces, giving the impression that they feel and are in accordance with one thing or another, when actually, they may think or feel the exact opposite. This was the personality of James.

When you wish for travel or eloquence in speech and/or writing, James will assist you. Since not everyone has the ability to speak, to be heard, or to be understood, lighting a yellow candle will summon the aid of James.

You can light a candle any day and at any time to summon James' aid; however, there are specific days during the month that are better than others to gain his assistance. Use the timing guide below to light your candle to him, knowing as well that the hours between 12:00 A.M. and 2:00 A.M. are the most appropriate times to light a candle in his honor when seeking his assistance.

When you light your yellow candle, there is nothing you have to say. As when lighting a candle to the saints, your thoughts are known and what you wish will come to you.

Always use this timing guide to light your candles to James the Less, cousin and apostle to Jesus.

James the Less
May 21st through June 20th

2001
June 19th 2:41 AM through June 21st 5:39 AM
July 16th 12:25 PM through July 18th 3:54 PM
August 12th 8:58 PM through August 15th 1:52 AM
September 9th 3:41 AM through September 11th 10:07 AM
October 6th 9:11 AM through October 8th 4:17 PM
November 2nd 3:12 PM through November 4th 9:42 PM
November 29th 11:03 PM through December 2nd 4:27 AM
December 27th 8:39 AM through December 29th 1:38 PM

2002
January 23rd 6:27 PM through January 26th 0:15 AM
February 20th 2:49 AM through February 22nd 10:14 AM
March 19th 9:18 AM through March 21st 6:04 PM
April 15th 2:55 PM through April 17th 11:59 PM
May 12th 9:03 PM through May 15th 5:31 AM
June 9th 4:28 AM through June 11th 12:13 PM
July 6th 12:59 PM through July 8th 8:34 PM
August 2nd 9:45 PM through August 5th 6:00 AM
August 30th 5:44 AM through September 1st 3:12 PM
September 26th 12:25 PM through September 28th 10:58 PM
October 23rd 6:16 PM through October 26th 5:07 AM
November 20th 0:24 AM through November 22nd 10:45 AM
December 17th 7:42 AM through December 19th 5:27 PM

2003
January 13th 4:07 PM through January 16th 1:54 AM
February 10th 0:44 AM through February 12th 11:16 AM
March 9th 8:36 AM through March 11th 8:10 PM
April 5th 3:23 PM through April 8th 3:34 AM
May 2nd 9:27 PM through May 5th 9:39 AM
May 30th 3:30 AM through June 1st 3:25 PM
June 26th 10:12 M through June 28th 9:50 PM
July 23rd 5:41 PM through July 26th 5:21 AM

August 20th 1:40 AM through August 22nd 1:42 PM
September 16th 9:31 AM through September 18th 10:04 PM
October 13th 4:44 PM through October 16th 5:39 AM
November 9th 11:13 PM through November 12th 12:08 PM
December 7th 5:25 AM through December 9th 6:09 PM

2004
January 3rd 11:57 AM through January 6th 0:37 AM
January 30th 7:17 PM through February 2nd 8:01 AM
February 27th 3:21 AM through February 29th 4:10 PM
March 25th 11:34 AM through March 28th 0:21 AM
April 21st 7:09 PM through April 24th 7:54 AM
May 19th 1:46 AM through May 21st 2:23 PM
June 15th 7:43 AM through June 17th 8:35 PM
July 12th 1:44 PM through July 15th 2:39 AM
August 8th 8:32 PM through August 11th 9:17 AM
September 5th 4:24 AM through September 7th 4:48 PM
October 2nd 12:55 PM through October 5th 0:51 AM
October 29th 9:10 PM through November 1st 8:54 AM
November 26th 4:42 AM through November 28th 4:08 PM
December 23rd 10:31 AM through December 25th 10:36 PM

2005
December 30th 2004 11:32 PM through January 2nd 10:17 AM
January 19th 4:23 PM through January 22nd 4:39 AM
February 15th 11:17 PM through February 18th 11:10 AM
March 15th 7:43 AM through March 17th 6:41 PM
April 11th 4:54 PM through April 14th 3:00 AM
May 9th 1:28 AM through May 11th 11:18 AM
June 5th 8:35 AM through June 7th 6:45 PM
July 2nd 2:25 PM through July 5th 1:06 AM
July 29th 8:01 PM through August 1st 6:51 AM
August 26th 2:42 AM through August 28th 12:55 PM
September 22nd 11:06 PM through September 24th 8:09 PM
October 19th 8:43 PM through October 22nd 4:38 AM
November 16th 6:09 AM through November 18th 1:41 PM
December 13th 2:00 PM through December 15th 9:59 PM

2006
January 9th 7:58 PM through January 12th 4:48 AM

225

February 6th 1:32 AM through February 8th 10:32 AM
March 5th 8:37 AM through March 7th 4:36 PM
April 1st 5:49 PM through April 4th 0:13 AM
April 29th 3:57 AM through May 1st 9:16 AM
May 26th 1:19 PM through May 28th 6:32 PM
June 22nd 8:49 PM through June 25th 2:46 AM
July 20th 2:37 AM through July 22nd 9:26 AM
August 16th 8:07 AM through August 18th 3:01 PM
September 12th 2:59 PM through September 14th 8:52 PM
October 10th 0:06 AM through October 12th 4:20 AM
November 6th 10:46 AM through November 8th 1:44 PM
December 3rd 9:04 PM through December 5th 11:59 PM

2007
December 31st 2006 5:16 AM through January 2nd 9:12 AM
January 27th 11:09 AM through January 29th 4:15 PM
February 23rd 4:42 PM through February 25th 9:46 PM
March 23rd 0:06 AM through March 25th 3:47 AM
April 19th 9:51 AM through April 21st 11:49 AM
May 16th 8:33 PM through May 18th 9:37 PM
June 13th 6:24 AM through June 15th 7:43 AM
July 10th 2:10 PM through July 12th 4:39 PM
August 6th 8:01 PM through August 8th 11:34 PM
September 3rd 1:30 AM through September 5th 5:07 AM
October 27th 6:11 PM through October 29th 6:48 PM
November 24th 5:29 AM through November 26th 5:05 AM
December 21st 4:14 PM through December 23rd 4:17 PM

2008
December 30th 2007 7:37 AM through January 1st 7:30 PM
January 18th 0:29 AM through January 20th 2:03 AM
February 14th 6:19 AM through February 16th 9:11 AM
March 12th 11:54 AM through March 14th 2:36 PM
April 8th 7:27 PM through April 10th 8:41 PM
May 6th 5:17 AM through May 8th 5:00 AM
June 2nd 4:06 PM through June 4th 3:15 PM
June 30th 2:03 AM through July 2nd 1:52 AM
July 27th 9:55 AM through July 29th 11:11 AM
August 23rd 3:48 PM through August 25th 6:17 PM
September 19th 9:17 PM through September 21st 11:48 PM

226

October 17th 4:25 AM through October 19th 5:39 AM
November 13th 2:12 PM through November 15th 1:51 PM
December 11th 1:33 AM through December 13th 0:39 AM

2009
January 7th 12:11 PM through January 9th 12:12 PM
March 3rd 2:00 AM through March 5th 5:05 AM
March 30th 7:36 AM through April 1st 10:29 AM
April 26th 3:02 PM through April 28th 4:36 PM
May 24th 0:34 AM through May 26th 0:57 AM
June 20th 11:00 AM through June 22nd 11:11 AM
July 17th 8:41 PM through July 19th 9:49 PM
August 14th 4:25 AM through August 16th 7:12 AM
September 10th 10:17 AM through September 12th 2:18 PM
October 7th 3:46 PM through October 9th 7:47 PM
November 3rd 10:52 PM through November 6th 1:41 AM
December 1st 8:23 AM through December 3rd 10:00 AM
December 28th 7:13 PM through December 30th 8:44 PM
2010
January 25th 5:10 AM through January 27th 7:59 AM
February 21st 12:46 PM through February 23rd 5:26 PM
March 20th 6:27 PM through March 23rd 0:13 AM
April 17th 0:01 AM through April 19th 5:37 AM
May 14th 7:17 AM through May 16th 11:43 AM
June 10th 4:10 PM through June 12th 7:48 PM
July 8th 1:49 AM through July 10th 5:36 AM
August 4th 10:53 AM through August 6th 3:48 PM
August 31st 6:18 PM through September 3rd 0:48 AM
September 28th 0:09 AM through September 30th 7:43 AM
October 25th 5:46 AM through October 27th 1:12 PM
November 21st 12:45 PM through November 23rd 7:12 PM
December 18th 9:36 PM through December 21st 3:20 AM

ANDREW, APOSTLE TO JESUS
JUNE 21ST THROUGH JULY 22ND

The biblical story of Jesus meeting with the two fishermen, saying "Come

227

with me, and I will make you fishers of men" (Matt. 4: 19-20), is a common story memorized in Sunday school by children. Jesus was speaking to Simon, who was called Peter, and his brother Andrew.

Andrew was the oldest of five children (Simon and Andrew had three sisters). Andrew, at this time lived with his brother, Simon Peter, as their father had died.

At Jesus' invitation, Andrew and his brother, Simon Peter, left their nets and followed him. Along the waterfront of the Sea of Galilee, the three came across two other brothers who were mending their father's nets. Jesus again said, "Lay down your nets, and follow me." Following their Master's wishes, they faithfully accompanied the other three. These two brothers were James, son of Zebedee, and his brother, John.

St. Andrew, who was loved and honored through his work with Jesus and St. John the Baptist, suffered martyrdom in Patras, Greece. He was a kind and gentle man. He honored the family and preached this concept throughout Greece and other countries. As well as being a stable man and projecting God's Word through his strengths, Andrew was sensitive, intuitive, and protective of those people who followed him and his other apostles. Andrew loved Jesus because Jesus was consistent in his sincerity.

Andrew held all of the personality traits of those born between June 21st and July 22nd. Being strong, stable, consistent, honorable with his intentions, and possessing a strong sense of intuition were just a fdew of Andrew's impeccable qualities.

Life can wear on the nerves of anyone. When you have a feeling that you cannot shake, or a need for understanding with nowhere to turn, light a blue candle and ask that St. Andrew aid you in your time of need, with stability and security. He will help you stabilize your feelings, emotions, and your home, giving you a feeling that all the basics in life will once again be in sync.

To give you an idea as to the strength and the fortitude of St. Andrew, he was crucified on a cross in the shape of an "X", and he preached for two days on the cross before he met his Creator in heaven, professing his undying love and devotion for Jesus and His Father in Heaven until the last moments of his life. To find the strength to continue your life with the sensitivity and devotion as that possessed by St. Andrew, light a blue candle between the hours of 10:00 P.M. and 12:00 A.M. These hours will best magnify the energy and guidance of St. Andrew.

Use the timing guide below to find the best days to light a candle to St. Andrew, so that you, too, will, as did those a long, long time ago, receive the love, stability, honor, and sensitivity from the martyred St. Andrew.

Andrew, Apostle to Jesus
June 21st through July 22nd

2001
June 21st 5:40 AM through June 23rd 6:52 AM
July 18th 3:55 PM through July 20th 4:41 PM
August 15th 1:54 AM through August 17th 3:23 AM
September 11th 10:09 AM through September 13th 1:13 PM
October 8th 4:18 PM through October 10th 8:52 PM
November 4th 9:43 PM through November 7th 2:31 AM
December 2nd 4:29 AM through December 4th 8:13 AM
December 29th 1:39 PM through December 31st 4:07 PM

2002
January 26th 0:16 AM through January 28th 2:29 AM
February 22nd 10:15 AM through February 24th 1:35 PM
March 21st 6:05 PM through March 23rd 11:11 PM
April 18th 0:01 AM through April 20th 6:19 AM
May 15th 5:32 AM through May 17th 10:50 AM
June 11th 12:14 PM through June 13th 5:37 PM
July 8th 8:36 PM through July 11th 1:06 AM
August 5th 6:01 AM through August 7th 10:25 AM
September 1st 3:13 PM through September 3rd 8:34PM
September 28th 11:00 PM through October 1st 5:67 AM
October 26th 5:09 AM through October 28th 1:18 PM
November 22nd 10:47 AM through November 24th 6:58 PM
December 19th 5:29 PM through December 22nd 0:46 AM

2003
January 16th 1:55 AM through January 18th 8:27 AM
February 12th 11:18 AM through February 14th 6:03 PM

229

March 11th 8:11 PM through March 14th 4:04 AM
April 8th 3:35 AM through April 10th 12:52 PM
May 5th 9:51 AM through May 7th 7:44 PM
June 1st 3:27 PM through June 4th 1:23 AM
June 28th 9:51 PM through July 1st 7:11 AM
July 26th 5:22 AM through July 28th 2:15 PM
August 22nd 1:43 PM through August 24th 10:46 PM
September 18th 10:06 PM through September 21st 8:00 AM
October 16th 5:40 AM through October 18th 4:39 PM
November 12th 12:09 PM through November 14th 11:46 PM
December 9th 6:11 PM through December 12th 5:38 AM

2004
January 6th 0:38 AM through January 8th 11:36 AM
February 2nd 8:02 AM through February 4th 6:48 PM
February 29th 4:11 PM through March 3rd 3:16 AM
March 28th 0:22 AM March 30th 12:05 PM
April 24th 7:55 AM through April 26th 8:12 PM
May 21st 2:34 PM through May 24th 3:04 AM
June 17th 8:36 PM through June 20th 9:03 AM
July 15th 2:40 AM through July 17th 2:54 PM
August 11th 9:19 AM through August 13th 9:27 PM
September 7th 4:49 PM through September 10th 5:04 AM
October 5th 0:53 AM through October 7th 1:20 PM
November 1st 8:52 AM through November 3rd 9:30 PM
November 28th 4:10 PM through December 1st 4:48 AM
December 25th 10:37 PM through December 28th 11:11 AM

2005
January 22nd 4:41 AM through January 24th 5:18 PM
February 18th 11:13 AM through February 20th 11:52 PM
March 17th 6:43 PM through March 20th 7:15 AM
April 14th 3:02 AM through April 16th 3:14 PM
May 11th 11:20 AM through May 13th 11:15 PM
June 7th 6:46 PM through June 10th 6:38 AM
July 5th 1:07 AM through July 7th 1:09 PM
August 1st 6:52 AM through August 3rd 7:08 PM
August 28th 12:56 PM through August 31st 1:12 AM
September 24th 8:10 PM through September 27th 8:01 AM
October 22nd 4:40 through October 24th 3:46 PM

November 18th 1:42 PM through November 21st 0:08 AM
December 15th 10:00 PM through December 18th 8:16 AM

2006
January 12th 4:49 AM through January 14th 3:28 PM
February 8th 10:33 AM through February 10th 9:43 PM
March 7th 4:37 PM through March 10th 3:41 AM
April 4th 0:14 AM through April 6th 10:23 AM
May 1st 9:17 AM through May 3rd 6:15 PM
May 28th 6:33 PM through May 31st 2:49 AM
June 25th 2:47 AM through June 27th 11:07 AM
July 22nd 9:27 AM through July 24th 6:23 PM
August 18th 3:03 PM through August 21st 0:31 AM
September 14th 8:53 PM through September 17th 6:14 AM
October 12th 4:21 AM through October 14th 12:37 PM
November 8th 1:45 PM through November 10th 8:33 PM
December 6th 0:00 AM through December 8th 5:50 AM

2007
January 2nd 9:14 AM through January 4th 3:12 PM
January 29th 4:16 PM through January 31st 11:13 PM
February 25th 9:47 PM through February 28th 5:28 AM
March 25th 3:48 AM through March 27th 11:03 AM
April 21st 11:50 AM through April 23rd 5:37 PM
May 18th 9:38 PM through May 21st 1:54 AM
June 15th 7:45 AM through June 17th 11:23 AM
July 12th 4:39 PM through July 14th 8:41 PM
August 8th 11:36 PM through August 11th 4:40 AM
September 5th 5:08 AM through September 7th 10:58 AM
October 2nd 10:57 AM through October 4th 4:25 PM
October 29th 6:49 PM through October 31st 10:47 PM
November 26th 5:07 AM through November 28th 7:21 AM
December 23rd 4:18 PM through December 25th 5:51 PM

2008
January 20th 2:05 AM through January 22nd 4:18 AM
February 16th 9:12 AM through February 18th 12:50 PM
March 14th 2:37 PM through March 16th 7:02 PM
April 10th 8:43 PM through April 13th 0:27 AM
May 8th 5:02 AM through May 10th 7:08 AM

June 4th 3:16 PM through June 6th 3:58 PM
July 2nd 1:53 AM through July 4th 2:14 AM
August 25th 6:18 PM through August 27th 8:49 PM
September 21st 11:49 PM through September 24th 3:12 AM
October 19th 5:40 AM through October 21st 8:34 AM
November 15th 1L52 PM through November 17th 3:06 PM
December 13th 0:40 AM through December 15th 0:22 AM

2009
January 9th 12:13 PM through January 11th 11:39 AM
February 5th 10:05 PM through February 7th 10:42 PM
March 5th 5:07 AM through March 7th 7:23 AM
April 1st 10:30 AM through April 3rd 1:31 PM
April 28th 4:37 PM through April 30th 6:54 PM
May 26th 0:58 AM through May 28th 1:43 AM
June 22nd 11:12 AM through June 24th 10:49 AM
July 19th 9:51 PM July 21st 9:26 PM
August 16th 7:13 AM through August 18th 7:55 AM
September 12th 2:20 PM through September 14th 4:38 PM
October 9th 7:47 PM through October 11th 11:01 PM
November 6th 1:42 AM through November 8th 4:22 AM
December 3rd 10:01 AM through December 5th 11:05 AM

2010
December 30th 8:45 PM through January 1st 8:38 PM
January 27th 8:00 AM through January 29th 8:08 AM
February 23rd 5:28 PM through February 25th 7:06 PM
March 23rd 0:15 AM through March 25th 3:37 AM
April 19th 5:38 AM through April 21st 9:39 AM
May 16th 11:44 AM through May 18th 3:04 Pm
June 12th 7:49 PM through June 14th 9:52 Pm
July 10th 5:37 AM through July 12th 6:51 AM
August 6th 3:49 PM through August 8th 5:20 PM
September 3rd 0:49 AM through September 5th 3:42 AM
September 30th 7:44 AM through October 2nd 12:18 PM
October 27th 1:13 PM through October 29th 6:36 PM
November 23rd 7:13 PM through November 25th 11:59 PM
December 21st 3:21 AM through December 23rd 6:48 AM

The Apostle John was the youngest of the twelve disciples. His youth and childlike actions did not detract from his eagerness to learn God's Word. With his enthusiasm to be in the presence of Jesus, he kept his youth throughout his life.

John preached the gospel and chronicled the words spoken by Jesus, which were to be read by many long after John departed this life. He was fearless like a child, with the zealousness of the times, preaching throughout Asia Minor.

John was the brother of James, son of Zebedee. Peter, John, and his brother, James, were with Jesus when Jesus transfigured before them. Appearing with Jesus were Moses and Elijah. The two spirits were speaking to Jesus in John, Peter, and James's presence, when a voice came out of a cloud covering them, saying, "This is my Beloved Son, in whom I am well pleased. Listen to Him."

Upon hearing the voice, the three men fell to their faces in fear. Only after Jesus touched them, saying, "Arise and do not be afraid," did they lift their heads, seeing then only Jesus standing there. Jesus went on to say, "Tell no man what you have seen, until the Son of Man has risen again from the dead." John, being a child at the time, witnessed many miracles during his life, while in the company of Jesus.

John possessed all the personality traits and characteristics of a person born between July 23rd and August 22nd. When you follow God's Will, and not your will, your life will be full of adventure, miracles, and leadership qualities. You will be fearless, with the uncanny ability to achieve through your most childlike persona.

John was the disciple closest to Jesus during Christ's pilgrimage on earth, and after the crucifixion of Jesus Christ, he was the disciple closest to Peter. (John went with Peter to prepare the Last Supper, and was depicted in Leonardo Da Vinci's painting of the Last Supper as the young lad leaning over the apostle's shoulder.) Peter and John traveled together throughout Asia Minor, spreading the word of their Master to the Gentiles.

The combative and adventurous spirit of John often emerged when traveling with Peter, as John would inevitability desire to go where Peter said they would meet with the most resistance. Yes, John did have a bit of a gambling spirit.

When the qualities of John are what you are looking for, or you were born during the July 23rd to August 22nd time frame and your desire is to get your life back on track, light a white candle on the appropriate day to remember not only what we might call your roots, but to honor the one who walked before you under such austere circumstances. The best time to light a candle to St. John, the beloved apostle to Jesus, is between the hours of 8:00 P.M. and 10:00 P.M., and on the dates listed below.

John the Beloved
July 23rd through August 22nd

2001
June 23rd 6:54 AM through June 25th 7:55 AM
July 20th 4:42 PM through July 22nd 4:27 PM
August 17th 3:24 AM through August 19th 2:50 AM
September 13th 1:16 PM through September 15th 1:37 PM
October 10th 8:53 PM through October 12th 10:55 PM
November 7th 2:33 AM through November 9th 5:47 AM
December 4th 8:15 AM through December 6th 11:09 AM
December 31st 4:08 PM through January 2nd 5:32 PM

2002
January 28th 2:30 AM through January 30th 2:38 AM
February 24th 1:36 PM through February 26th 1:45 PM
March 23rd 11:12 PM through March 26th 0:41 AM
April 20th 6:20 AM through April 22nd 9:33 AM
May 17th 11:51 AM through May 19th 3:58 PM
June 13th 5:39 PM through June 15th 9:22 PM
July 11th 1:07 AM through July 13th 3:39 AM
August 7th 10:26 AM through August 9th 12:01 PM
September 3rd 8:35 PM through September 5th 10:14 PM
October 1st 5:57 AM through October 3rd 8:50 AM
October 28th 1:19 PM through October 30th 5:57 PM
November 24th 6:59 PM through November 27th 0:40 AM
December 22nd 0:47 AM through December 24th 6:03 AM

2003

January 18th 8:28 AM through January 20th 12:30 PM
February 14th 6:04 PM through February 16th 9:20 PM
March 14th 4:06 AM through March 16th 7:51 AM
April 10th 12:53 PM through April 12th 6:05 PM
May 7th 7:46 PM through May 10th 2:29 AM
June 4th 1:24 AM through June 6th 8:48 AM
July 1st 7:12 AM through July 3rd 2:14 PM
July 28th 2:16 PM through July 30th 8:24 PM
August 24th 10:47 PM through August 27th 4:25 AM
September 21st 8:02 AM through September 23rd 2:03 PM
October 18th 4:40 PM through October 20th 11:59 PM
November 14th 11:47 PM through November 17th 8:34 AM
December 12th 5:40 AM through December 14th 3:04 PM

2004

January 8th 11:37 AM through January 10th 8:36 PM
February 4th 6:49 PM through February 7th 3:01 AM
March 3rd 3:17 AM through March 5th 11:15 AM
March 30th 12:06 PM through April 1st 8:44 PM
April 26th 8:13 PM through April 29th 5:57 AM
May 24th 3:06 AM through May 26th 1:50 PM
June 20th 9:05 AM through June 22nd 8:08 PM
July 17th 2:55 PM through July 20th 1:42 AM
August 13th 9:29 PM through August 16th 7:47 AM
September 10th 5:05 AM through September 12th 3:14 PM
October 7th 1:22 PM through October 9th 11:58 PM
November 3rd 9:31 PM through November 6th 8:58 AM
December 1st 4:49 AM through December 3rd 4:58 PM
December 28th 11:13 AM through December 30th 11:31 PM

2005

January 24th 5:20 PM through January 27th 5:21 AM
February 20th 11:54 PM through February 23rd 11:41 AM
March 20th 7:16 AM through March 22nd 7:08 PM
April 16th 3:16 PM through April 19th 3:24 AM
May 13th 11:16 PM through May 16th 11:45 AM
June 10th 6:39 AM through June 12th 7:19 PM
July 7th 1:10 PM through July 10th 1:55 AM
August 3rd 7:09 PM through August 6th 7:52 AM

August 31st 1:14 AM through September 2nd 1:54 PM
September 27th 8:02 AM through September 29th 8:41 PM
October 24th 3:48 PM through October 27th 4:26 AM
November 21st 0:09 AM through November 23rd 12:39 PM
December 18th 8:17 AM through December 20th 8:37 PM

2006
January 14th 3:30 PM through January 17th 3:47 AM
February 10th 9:44 PM through February 13th 10:12 AM
March 10th 3:42 AM through March 12 4:22 PM
April 6th 10:24 AM through April 8th 10:56 PM
May 3rd 6:17 PM through May 6th 6:17 AM
May 31st 2:51 AM through June 2nd 2:16 PM
June 27th 11:08 AM through June 29th 10:12 PM
July 24th 6:24 PM through July 27th 5:37 AM
August 21st 0:33 AM through August 23rd 12:06 PM
September 17th 6:15 AM through September 19th 6:04 PM
October 14th 12:38 PM through October 17th 0:14 AM
November 10th 8:33 PM through November 13th 7:17 AM
December 8th 5:51 AM through December 10th 3:29 PM

PHILIP, APOSTLE TO JESUS
AUGUST 23RD THROUGH SEPTEMBER 22ND

Philip, the most meticulous of Jesus's apostles, was full of tenacity. He was young, vibrant, and eager to learn, with the leadership qualities needed to organize the travel, lodging, and the all encompassing care of his Master and fellow disciples. Philip was in for the time of his life and enjoyed every adventurous moment.

Philip was enthusiastic about being in the company of Jesus, and was enamored of Christ. He spent many hours recounting his life with Jesus through writing, recording the memorable experiences for all the world to read long after his death.

Philip, meticulous in his thinking with the capacity for concentration to details, was the perfect one to tend to all aspects of the apostles' travels throughout Christ's mission on Earth. An example of this is recorded in St. John 6:1-6, in the conversation between Jesus and Philip while at the sea of

Galilee with the multitude of five thousand, as the Feast of Passover drew near. Jesus turned to Philip and said, "Now are we going to feed all these people?" It was only natural, even though Christ knew it would take a miracle to feed them, for him to consult with his "business manager," so to speak, for dining arrangements. It was also very fitting in John 12:20-21 for the Greeks, who wished to speak to Jesus, to approach Philip with their request.

Philip chose to hold steadfast to his inquisitive mind, with his never ending attention to detail. In John 14:8, he said to Jesus, "Lord, show us the Father, and we shall be satisfied." Philip had known for years the satisfaction, not physical proof. Philip lived to stimulate his intellect and his ability to reason, comprising facts and organizing them, finding Jesus to be just and true in his remarkable ability to know God's Law though Jesus had no formal training on such a vast topic.

In Acts 8:6-40, Philip went to the city of Samaria and proclaimed Christ to the citizens of that city. When they heard His Words and witnessed His great acts, unclean spirits came out of those who had been possessed and those who were paralyzed or lame were healed. The voice of God's angel was heard on many occasions in Philip's life, and when the Lord's angel spoke to him, there was never a question as to whom was speaking.

When the angel of God said to Philip, "Go south to the road that goes down from Jerusalem to Gaza," Philip went. There he met a eunuch, a minister of Candace, Queen of the Ethiopians, who had come to Jerusalem to worship, and was returning home. He was sitting in his chariot, reading the Prophet Isaiah. The spirit told Philip to go to the chariot and join the man. In his conversation with the eunuch, Philip asked him if he understood what he was reading. The man replied, "With no one to guide me, how can I understand?" so Philip began to tel him of Christ. Since the men were beside a body of water, the eunuch asked Philip if he would baptize him. As they both came out of the water, the angel of God picked up Philip and put him in Azotus, leaving the eunuch there alone.

Philip, through his association with Christ and the disciples, lived a full and spiritually-rewarding life, following his Master through a life of enlightenment. The personality traits of Philip are typical of those people born between August 23rd and September 22nd.

Your ability to serve others, in conjunction with profoundly meticulous thought processes, will be enhanced by lighting a candle to Philip. The best time to light your candle is between the hours of 6:00 P.M. and 8:00 P.M. Use the timing guide listed below to light your candle for the most effective outcome.

Philip Apostle to Jesus
August 23rd through September 22nd

2001
June 25th 7:57 AM through June 27th 10:09 AM
July 22rd 4:28 PM through July 24th 5:05 PM
August 19th 2:52 AM through August 21st 2:17 AM
September 15th 1:38 PM through September 17th 12:58 PM
October 12th 10:57 PM through October 14th 11:24 PM
November 9th 5:48 AM through November 11th 7:51 AM
December 6th 11:10 AM through December 8th 1:55 PM

2002
January 2nd 5:33 PM through January 4th 7:22 PM
January 30th 2:39 AM through February 1st 2:43 AM
February 26th 1:46 PM through February 28th 12:44 PM
March 26th 0:43 AM through March 28th 0:02 AM
April 22nd 9:34 AM through April 24th 10:20 AM
May 19th 4:00 PM through May 21st 6:17 PM
June 15th 9:23 PM through June 18th 0:08 AM
July 13th 3:40 AM through July 15th 5:37 AM
August 9th 12:02 PM through August 11th 12:36 PM
September 5th 10:15 PM through September 7th 9:54 PM
October 3rd 8:51 AM through October 5th 8:49 AM
October 30th 5:58 PM through November 3rd 7:08 PM
November 27th 0:41 AM through November 29th 3:52 AM
December 24th 6:04 AM through December 26th 9:51 AM

2003
January 20th 12:31 PM through January 22nd 3:21 PM
February 16th 9:21 PM through February 18th 10:45 PM
March 16th 7:52 AM through March 18th 8:41 AM
April 12th 6:06 PM through April 14th 7:40 PM
May 10th 2:31 AM through May 12th 5:40 AM

June 6th 8:50 AM through June 8th 1:28 PM
July 3rd 2:15 PM through July 5th 7:18 PM
July 30th 8:26 PM through August 2nd 0:46 AM
August 27th 4:26 AM through August 29th 7:39 AM
September 23rd 2:04 PM through September 25th 4:46 PM
October 21st 0:00 AM through October 23rd 3:25 AM
November 17th 8:36 AM through November 19th 1:39 PM
December 14th 3:06 PM through December 16th 9:45 PM

2004
January 10th 8:37 PM through January 13th 3:36 AM
February 7th 3:02 AM through February 9th 9:10 AM
March 5th 11:17 AM through March 7th 4:29 PM
April 1st 8:45 PM through April 4th 1:50 AM
April 29th 6:00 AM through May 1st 12:01 PM
May 26th 1:51 PM through May 28th 9:20 PM
June 22nd 8:09 PM through June 25th 4:48 AM
July 20th 1:43 AM through July 22nd 10:37 AM
August 16th 7:48 AM through August 18th 4:08 PM
September 12th 3:16 PM through September 14th 10:51 PM
October 9th 11:59 PM through October 12th 7:30 AM
November 6th 8:59 AM through November 8th 5:20 PM
December 3rd 4:59 PM through December 6th 2:45 AM

2005
December 30th 2004 11:32 PM through January 2nd 10:17 AM
January 27th 5:23 AM through January 29th 4:11 PM
February 23rd 11:43 AM through February 25th 9:57 PM
March 22nd 7:09 PM through March 25th 4:58 AM
April 19th 3:27 AM through April 21st 1:25 PM
May 16th 11:46 AM through May 18th 10:27 PM
June 12th 7:21 PM through June 15th 6:56 AM
July 10th 1:57 AM through July 12th 2:06 PM
August 6th 7:53 AM through August 8th 8:07 PM
September 2nd 1:55 PM through September 5th 1:50 AM
September 29th 8:43 PM through October 2nd 8:21 AM
October 27th 4:28 AM through October 29th 4:13 PM
November 23rd 12:41 PM through November 28th 10:31 AM
December 20th 8:38 PM through December 23rd 9:24 AM

2006
January 17th 3:48 AM through January 19th 4:47 PM
February 13th 10:13 AM through February 15th 11:07 PM
March 12th 4:23 PM through March 15th 5:11 AM
April 8th 10:58 PM through April 11th 11:44 AM
May 6th 6:19 AM through May 8th 7:08 PM
June 2nd 2:17 PM through June 5th 3:06 AM
June 29th 10:14 PM through July 2nd 11:03 AM
July 27th 5:36 AM through July 29th 6:26 PM
August 23rd 12:07 PM through August 26th 1:00 AM
September 19th 6:06 PM through September 22nd 7:04 AM
October 17th 0:15 AM through October 19th 1:18 PM
November 313th 7:18 AM through November 15th 8:12 PM
December 10th 3:30 PM through December 13th 3:59 AM

2007
January 7th 0:18 AM through January 9th 12:13 PM
February 3rd 8:34 AM through February 5th 8:14 PM
March 2nd 3:31 PM through March 5th 3:23 AM
March 29th 9:26 PM through April1st 9:42 AM
April 26th 3:24 AM through April 28th 3:43 PM
May 23rd 10:26 AM through May 25th 10:14 PM
June 19th 6:45 PM through June 22nd 5:42 AM
July 17th 3:39 AM through July 19th 1:51 PM
August 13th 12:03 PM through August 15th 10:03 PM
September 9th 7:09 PM through September 12th 5:30 AM
October 7th 1:03 AM through October 9th 11:55 AM
November 3rd 6:44 AM through November 5th 4:46 PM
November 30th 1:44 PM through December 3rd 0:00 AM
December 27th 10:44 PM through December 30th 7:35 AM

2008
January 24th 8:48 AM through January 26th 4:34 PM
February 20th 6:06 PM through February 23rd 1:43 AM
March 19th 1:25 AM through March 21st 9:44 AM
April 15th 7:06 AM through April 17th 4:09 PM
May 12th 12:48 PM through May 14th 9:45 PM
June 8th 8:01 PM through June 11th 3:54 AM
July 6th 5:04 AM through July 8th 11:29 AM
August 2nd 2:59 PM through August 4th 8:26 PM

August 30th 0:18 AM through September 1st 5:43 AM
September 26th 7:52 AM through September 28th 2:04 PM
October 23rd 1:40 PM through October 25th 8:46 PM
November 19th 7:12 PM through November 22nd 2:19 AM
December 17th 2:35 AM through December 19th 8:21 AM

2009
January 13th 12:33 PM through January 15th 4:29 PM
February 9th 11:38 PM through February 12th 2:31 AM
March 9th 9:34 AM through March 11th 12:45 PM
April 5th 5:01 PM through April 7th 9:21 PM
May 2nd 10:37 PM through May 5th 3:50 AM
May 30th 4:17 AM through June 1st 9:16 AM
June 26th 11:47 AM through June 28th 3:23 PM
July 23rd 9:23 PM through July 25th 11:24 PM
August 20th 8:00 AM through August 22nd 9:10 AM
September 16th 5:56 PM through September 18th 7:25 PM
October 14th 1:45 AM through October 16th 4:28 AM
November 10th 7:30 AM through November 12th 11:21 AM
December 7th 1:06 PM through December 9th 4:45 PM

2010
January 3rd 8:51 PM through January 5th 10:55 PM
January 31st 7:22 AM through February 2nd 7:40 AM
February 27th 6:51 PM through March 1st 6:29 PM
March 27th 4:56 AM through March 29th 5:19 AM
April 23rd 12:23 PM through April 25th 2:14 PM
May 20th 5:57 PM through May 22nd 8:48 PM
June 16th 11:40 PM through June 19th 2:11 AM
July 14th 7:14 AM through July 16th 8:22 AM
August 10th 5:00 PM through August 12th 4:40 PM
September 7th 3:51 AM through September 9th 2:58 AM
October 4th 1:59 PM through October 6th 1:49 PM
October 31st 9:50 PM through November 2nd 11:16 PM
November 28th 3:33 AM through November 30th 6:13 AM
December 25th 9:13 AM through December 27th 11:36 AM

BARTHOLOMEW / NATHANAEL
SEPTEMBER 23RD THROUGH OCTOBER 22ND

Bartholomew was the most educated of all of the apostles. When he was taken to Jesus by Philip, Jesus said, (in St. John 1: 47-49), "Behold a true Israelite, in whom there is no guile!" In response, Nathanael (as Bartholomew was called) asked Jesus, "How do you know me?" Jesus answered him, saying, "Before Philip called you, when you were under the fig tree, I saw you." Nathanael then answered, "Rabbi, you are the son of God! You are the King of Israel!" Bartholomew had experienced many doubts while on his way with Philip to meet Jesus. However, when in the company of Jesus Christ, all of Bartholomew's questions seemed to be answered.

These same characteristics are indicative of people born during the time frame of September 23rd through October 22nd. They may doubt your words forever, but when you give them enough facts on which to base their conclusion, they establish hasty and precise convictions that will last forever. These people, as with Bartholomew, have a passion for learning and high moral standards. The astrological name for this time frame is Libra, meaning balance and fair.

While there are a lot of specifics for this time frame, the constellation of Libra says it all - two scales. Some say that the scales balance good against evil. The ancient Egyptians believed that the king of the underworld used the scales to weigh the hearts of men when deciding their ultimate fate.

With the scales of balance being indicate of Bartholomew and those born during this time frame, is it any wonder their character traits are synonymous with these words: fair, just, honorable, kind, loving, compassionate, harmonious, and beauty? Is it any wonder, as demonstrated by Bartholomew and others representing this sign, that they inevitably have a tendency to over-evaluate, giving the illusion they believe in nothing, or they believe everything, until they finally make that decisive commitment, as Bartholomew did with Jesus?

A question that may baffle many of these people is found in Matthew 19:28. Jesus said, "Truly, I say to you, when the Son of Man shall sit on His glorious throne, you who have followed me will also sit on twelve thrones, judging the twelve tribes of Israel." Was Jesus referring to the twelve signs of the zodiac as the twelve thrones, or the (now) twelve planets as the twelve tribes of Israel? In the beginning of Verse 28, Jesus makes reference to "you in the new world." Are we in the new world?

These are the types of questions people born during this time frame may contemplate forever. However, Bartholomew will help you make not only the best and most rational decisions, he will also give you peace of mind, honesty, and the ability to communicate and experience the purity of life on this Earth when you light your candles to him. For those of you not born during this time frame, yet wish to light a candle to Bartholomew, you most certainly will benefit from his assistance. Light your candle between 4:00 P.M. and 6:00 P.M. on the following days.

Bartholomew / Nathanael
September 23rd through October 22nd

2001
May 31st 4:39 AM through June 2nd 8:54 AM
June 27th 10:10 AM through June 29th 2:27 PM
July 24th 5:07 PM through July 26th 8:15 PM
August 21st 2:18 AM through August 23rd 3:48 AM
September 17th 12:59 PM through September 19th 1:24 PM
October 14th 11:25 PM through October 17th 0:01 AM
November 11th 7:52 AM through November 13th 9:43 AM
December 8th 11:56 PM through December 10th 5:06 PM

2002
January 4th 7:23 PM through January 6th 10:38 PM
February 1st 2:44 AM through February 3rd 4:33 AM
February 28th 12:46 PM through March 2nd 12:50 PM
February 28th 12:46 PM through March 2nd 12:50 PM
March 28th 0:04 AM through March 29th 11:20 PM
April 24th 10:21 AM through April 26th 10:13 AM
May 21st 6:18 PM through May 23rd 7:36 PM
June 18th 0:10 AM through June 20th 2:40 AM
July 15th 5:38 AM through July 17th 8:11 AM
August 11th 12:37 PM through August 13th 1:59 PM
September 7th 9:56 PM through September 9th 9:46 PM
October 5th 8:50 AM through October 7th 7:55 AM
November 1st 7:27 PM through November 3rd 7:08 PM
November 29th 3:53 AM through December 1st 5:13 AM
December 26th 9:52 AM through December 28th 12:39 PM

2003

January 22nd 3:22 PM through January 24th 6:07 PM
February 18th 10:47 PM through February 21st 0:07 AM
March 18th 8:42 AM through March 20th 8:35 AM
April 14th 7:41 PM through April 16th 7:14 PM
May 12th 5:41 AM through May 14th 6:21 AM
June 8th 1:29 PM through June 10th 3:37 PM
July 5th 7:19 PM through July 7th 10:42 PM
August 2nd 0:47 AM through August 4th 4:11 AM
August 29th 7:40 AM through August 31st 9:58 AM
September 25th 4:48 PM through September 27th 5:50 PM
October 23rd 3:26 AM through October 25th 4:07 AM
November 19th 1:42 PM through November 21st 3:22 PM
December 16th 9:46 PM through December 19th 1:17 AM

2004

January 13th 3:37 AM through January 15th 8:31 AM
February 9th 9:12 AM through February 11th 1:56 PM
March 7th 4:30 PM through March 9th 8:01 PM
April 4th 1:51 AM through April 6th 4:22 AM
May 1st 12:02 PM through May 3rd 2:37 PM
June 25th 4:49 AM through June 27th 10:11 AM
July 22nd 10:38 AM through July 24th 5:06 PM
August 18th 4:09 PM through August 20th 10:35 PM
September 14th 10:53 PM through September 17th 4:23 AM
October 12th 7:31 AM through October 14th 12:08 PM
November 8th 5:22 PM through November 10th 10:03 PM
December 6th 2:46 AM through December 8th 8:42 AM

2005

January 2nd 10:19 AM through January 4th 5:58 PM
January 29th 4:12 PM through February 1st 0:49 AM
February 25th 9:58 PM through February 28th 6:18 AM
March25th 4:49 AM through March 27th 12:27 PM
April 21st 1:26 PM through April 23rd 8:23 PM
May 18th 10:29 PM through May 21st 5:46 AM
June 15th 6:58 AM through June 17th 3:22 PM
July 12th 2:08 PM through July 14th 11:49 PM
August 8th 8:08 PM through August 11th 6:32 AM
September 5th 1:51 Am through September 7th 12:09 PM

244

October 2nd 8:32 AM through October 4th 6:02 PM
November 26th 0:57 AM through November 28th 10:31 AM
December 23rd 9:26 AM through December 25th 8:02 PM

2006
January 19th 4:49 PM through January 22nd 4:26 AM
February 15th 11:08 PM through February 18th 11:10 AM
March 15th 5:12 AM through March 17th 4:56 PM
April 11th 11:46 AM through April 13th 11:06 PM
May 8th 7:09 PM through May 11th 6:23 AM
June 5th 3:08 AM through June 7th 2:39 PM
July 2nd 11:05 AM through July 4th 11:11 PM
August 26th 1:01 AM through August 28th 1:54 PM
September 22nd 7:06 through September 24th 7:53 PM
October 19th 1:19 PM through October 22nd 1:53 AM
November 15th 8:14 PM through November 18th 8:44 AM
December 13th 4:00 AM through December 15th 4:41 PM

2007
January 9th 12:15 PM through January 12th 1:06 AM
February 5th 8:15 PM through February 8th 9:08 AM
March 5th 3:25 AM through March 7th 4:14 PM
April 1st 9:43 AM through April 3rd 10:33 PM
April 28th 3:44 PM through May 1st 4:40 AM
May 25th 10:16 PM through May 28th 11:09 AM
June 22nd 5:43 AM through June 24th 6:25 PM
July 19th 1:53 PM through July 22nd 2:17 AM
August 15th 10:04 PM through August 18th 10:12 AM
September 12th 5:31 AM through September 14th 5:36 PM
October 9th 11:57 AM through October 12th 0:12 AM
November 5th 5:47 PM through November 8th 6:16 AM
December 3rd 0:01 AM through December 5th 12:29 PM

2008
December 30th 2007 7:37 AM through January 1st 7:30 PM
January 26th 4:35 PM through January 29th 2:33 AM
February 23rd 1:44 AM through February 25th 12:04 PM
March 21st 9:45 AM through March 23rd 8:04 PM
April 17th 4:10 PM through April 20th 2:58 AM
May 14th9:46 PM through May 17th 8:58 AM

245

June 11th 3:55 AM through June 13th 2:51 PM
July 8th 11:31 AM through July 10th 9:34 PM
August 4th 2:59 PM through August 7th 5:25 AM
September 1st 5:44 AM through September 3rd 2:00 PM
September 28th 2:05 PM through September 30th 10:25 PM
October 25th 8:47 PM through October 28th 5:46 AM
November 22nd 2:20 AM through November 24th 11:53 AM
December 19th 8:23 AM through December 21st 5:34 PM

2009
January 15th 4:30 PM through January 18th 0:19 AM
February 12th 2:32 AM through February 14th 8:49 AM
March 11th 12:46 PM through March 13th 6:21 PM
April 7th 9:22 PM through April 10th 3:21 AM
May 5th 3:51 AM through May 7th 10:46 AM
June 1st 9:17 AM through June 3rd 4:42 PM
June 28th 3:24 PM through June 30th 10:17 PM
July 25th 11:25 PM through July 28th 4:55 AM
August 22nd 9:12 AM through August 24th 1:15 PM
September 18th 7:26 PM through September 20th 10:50 PM
October 16th 4:29 AM through October 18th 8:21 AM
November 12th 11:22 AM through November 14th 4:22 PM
December 9th 4:48 PM through December 11th 10:30 PM
2010
January 5th 10:57 PM through January 8th 3:58 AM
February 2nd 7:14 AM through February 4th 10:53 AM
March 1st 6:30 PM through March 3rd 8:09 PM
March 29th 5:20 AM through March 31st 6:39 AM
April 25th 2:15 PM through April 27th 4:27 PM
May 22nd 8:49 PM through May 25th 0:15 AM
June 19th 2:12 AM through June 21st 6:12 AM
July 16th 8:23 AM through July 18th 11:40 AM
August 12th 4:42 PM through August 14th 6:23 PM
September 9th 3:00 AM through September 11th 3:18 AM
October 6th 1:50 PM through October 8th 1:50 PM
November 2nd 11:18 PM through November 5th 0:13 AM
December 27th 11:37 AM through December 29th 2:47 PM

Thomas, one of the twelve apostles, loved his Master. He had a passion for life and gave his all to the ministry of Christ.

Thomas had an undying loyalty to Jesus. In the eleventh chapter of the Book of John, Jesus spoke of the illness of his friend, Lazarus, saying that he must go to him. Lazarus, however, was in Judea. Since Jesus spoke of Lazarus as being asleep, the apostles - knowing that the Jews in Judea were seeking Jesus to stone him - asked Jesus why he did not wait for Lazarus to simply awaken from his sleep. At this point, Jesus told his disciples that Lazarus was dead and he must go to awaken him. Thomas, the loyal apostle, said to his fellow apostles, "Let us also go, that we may die with him." Displaying his undying love for his Master, Thomas - along with the other apostles - went with Christ to see where Lazarus's sisters had lain his body; thus witnessing, four days after Lazarus had died, their Master wake him out of his death.

Thomas was loved by Christ and all of the apostles. He could settle any dispute that arose because he had the ability to see all things from all points of view. Thomas was always concerned with what was true.

As with everyone who has a birthday between October 23rd and November 21st, doubt oftentimes slips into their personality. It is not so much that these people are pessimistic, they just find that trust comes harder for them than for other people when they are not living God's Will.

Thomas displayed his doubt in St. John 20: 24-30. When the other disciples told Thomas of Jesus's appearance before them after his crucifixion, Thomas doubted the resurrection, saying, "Unless I see in his hands the print of the nails, and put my finger into the place of the nailes, and put my hand into his side, I will not believe." After eight days, Jesus's disciples were once again gathered inside and Thomas was with them. Jesus came - the doors were closed - and stood in their midst, and said, "Peace be to you!" Then, he said to Thomas, "Bring here your fingers, and see my hands; and bring here your hand, and put it into my side; and not be unbelieving, but believing." Thomas answered, "My Lord and my God!" Jesus then said, "Because you have seen me, Thomas, you have believed."

247

People born during this October 23rd to November 21st time frame are blessed. They not only have the ability to evaluate every situation, but the ability to see things from perhaps God's point of view, thus helping everyone. Thomas might have doubted that Christ had resurrected, but when he was in the presence of Jesus, there were no questions in Thomas's mind that Jesus was indeed the Christ.

People born during this time frame possess the ability to look far beneath the surface to find the truth in everything. They are sensitive not only to their own needs, but also to the needs of everyone. Their sensitive nature takes them beyond the realms of the norm - at times, they possess the insight of a holy man. Light your candle to Thomas between the hours of 2:00 P.M. and 4:00 P.M. on the following days.

Thomas Didymus
October 23rd through November 21st

2001
June 2nd 8:55 AM through June 4th 2:56 PM
June 29th 2:29 PM through July 1st 9:11 PM
July 26th 8:16 PM through July 29th 2:42 AM
August 23rd 3:49 AM through August 25th 8:57 AM
September 19th 1:26 PM through September 21st 5:00 PM
October 17th 0:02 AM through October 19th 2:45 AM
November 13th 9:44 AM through November 15th 12:49 PM
December 10th 5:08 PM through December 12th 9:28 PM

2002
January 6th 10:40 PM through January 9th 3:55 AM
February 3rd 4:36 AM through February 5th 9:19 AM
March 2nd 12:51 PM through March 4th 3:53 PM
March 29th 11:21 PM through April 1st 0:46 AM
April 26th 10:14 AM through April 28th 11:10 AM
May 23rd 7:37 PM through May 25th 9:18 PM
June 20th 2:41 AM through June 22nd 5:40 AM
July 17th 8:12 AM through July 19th 12:00 PM
August 13th 2:00 PM through August 15th 5:23 PM
September 9th 9:47 PM through September 11th 11:42 PM
October 7th 7:57 AM through October 11th 11:43 AM
November 3rd 7:09 PM through November 5th 6:59 PM

248

December 1st 5:14 AM through December 3rd 5:56 AM
December 28th 12:40 PM through December 30th 2:59 PM

2003
January 24th 6:08 PM through January 26th 9:23 PM
February 21st 0:08 AM through February 23rd 2:44 AM
March 20th 8:37 AM through March 22nd 9:31 AM
April 16th 7:15 PM through April 18th 6:49 PM
May 14th 6:13 AM through May 16th 5:40 AM
June 10th 3:38 PM through June 12th 4:10 PM
July 7th 10:43 PM through July 10th 0:46 AM
August 4th 4:12 AM through August 6th 7:09 AM
August 31st 9:59 AM through September 2nd 12:29 PM
September 27th 5:51 PM through September 29th 6:55 PM
October 25th 4:08 AM through October 27th 3:53 AM
November 21st 3:23 PM through November 23rd 3:01 PM
December 19th 1:20 AM through December 21st 2:14 AM

2004
January 15th 8:32 AM through January 17th 11:16 AM
February 11th 1:58 PM through February 13th 5:33 PM
March 9th 8:02 PM through March 11th 10:55 PM
April 6th 4:23 AM through April 8th 5:48 AM
May 3rd 2:38 PM through May 5th 3:06 PM
May 31st 1:07 AM through June 2nd 1:50 AM
June 27th 10:12 AM through June 29th 12:14 PM
July 24th 5:07 PM through July 26th 8:46 PM
August 20th 10:36 PM through August 23 3:07 AM
September 17th 4:24 AM September 19th 8:28 AM
October 12:09 PM through October 16th 2:56 PM
November 10th 10:04 PM through November 12th 11:55 PM
December 8th 8:43 AM through December 10th 10:53 AM

2005
January 4th 5:59 PM through January 6th 9:42 PM
February 1st 0:05 AM through February 3rd 6:19 AM
February 28th 6:20 AM through March 2nd 12:27 PM
March 27th 12:28 PM through March 29th 5:55 PM
April 23rd 8:25 PM through April 26th 0:44 AM

May 21st 5:48 AM through May 23rd 9:36 AM
June 17th 3:23 PM through June 19th 7:43 PM
July 14th 11:50 PM through July 17th 5:33 AM
August 11th 6:34 AM through August 13th 1:45 PM
September 7th 12:10 PM through September 9th 8:00 PM
October 4th 6:03 PM through October 7th 1:26 AM
November 1st 1:28 AM through November 3rd 7:53 AM
December 25th 8:03 PM through December 28th 2:41 AM

2006
January 22nd 4:28 AM through January 24th 12:36 PM
February 18th 11:11 AM through February 20th 8:36 PM
March 17th 4:58 PM through March 20th 2:41 AM
April 13th 11:08 PM through April 16th 8:17 AM
May 11th 6:24 AM through May 13th 2:55 PM
June 7th 2:40 PM through June 9th 11:03 PM
July 4th 11:13 PM through July 7th 8:12 AM
August 1st 7:07 AM through August 3rd 5:12 PM
August 28th 1:55 PM through August 31st 0:57 AM
September 24th 7:54 PM through September 27th 7:14 AM
October 22nd 1:54 AM through October 24th 12:51 PM
November 18th 8:46 AM through November 20th 7:14 PM
December 15th 4:42 PM through December 18th 3:09 AM

2007
January 12th 1:07 AM through January 14th 12:10 PM
February 8th 9:10 AM through February 10th 9:00 PM
March 7th 4:16 PM through March 10th 4:35 AM
April 3rd 10:35 PM through April 6th 120:54 AM
May 1st 4:41 AM through May 6th 3:19 AM
May 28th 11:11 AM through May 30th 11:04 PM
June 24th 6:26 PM through June 27th 6:22 AM
July 22nd 2:18 AM through July 24th 2:28 PM
August 18th 10:13 AM through August 20th 10:43 PM
September 14th 5:37 PM through September 17th 6:19 AM
October 12th 0:13 AM through October 14th 12:56 PM
November 8th 6:19 AM through November 10th 6:57 PM
December 5th 12:30 PM through December 8th 1:09 AM

2008

January 1st 7:32 PM through January 4th 8:11 AM
January 29th 3:34 AM through January 31st 4:07 PM
February 25th 12:06 PM through February 28th 0:20 AM
March 23rd 8:96 PM through March 26th 8:09 AM
April 20th 3:00 AM through April 22nd 3:05 PM
March 17th 8:59 AM through May 19th 9:16 PM
June 13th 2:53 PM through June 16th 3:18 AM
July 10th 9:35 PM through July 13th 9:48 AM
August 7th 5:26 AM through August 9th 5:08 PM
September 3rd 2:02 PM through September 6th 1:09 AM
September 30th 10:26 PM through October 3rd 9:12 AM
October 28th 5:47 AM through October 30th 4:39 PM
November 24th 11:54 AM through November 26th 11:12 PM
December 21st 5:36 PM through December 24th 5:12 AM

2009

January 18th 0:20 AM through January 20th 11:28 AM
February 14th 8:50 AM through February 16th 5:51 PM
March 13th 6:22 PM through March 16th 3:20 AM
April 10th 3:24 AM through April 12th 11:59 AM
May 7th 10:48 AM through May 9th 7:48 PM
June 3rd 4:43 PM through June 6th 2:22 AM
June 30th 10:18 PM through July 3rd 8:10 AM
July 28th 4:56 AM through July 30th 2:09 PM
August 24th 1:16 PM through August 26th 9:15 PM
September 20th 10:52 PM through September 23rd 5:41 AM
October 18th 8:23 AM through October 20th 2:48 PM
November 14th 4:24 PM through November 16th 11:21 PM
December 11th 10:31 PM through December 14th 6:24 AM

2010

January 8th 3:59 AM through January 10th 12:08 PM
February 4th 10:54 AM through February 6th 6:02 PM
March 3rd 8:10 PM through March 6th 1:33 AM
March 31st 6:40 AM through April 2nd 10:50 AM
April 27th 4:28 PM through April 29th 8:34 PM
May 25th 0:16 AM through May 27th 5:13 AM
June 21st 6:13 AM through June 23rd 12:07 PM
July 18th 11:41 AM through July 20th 5:46 PM

251

August 14th 6:25PM through August 16th 11:31 PM
September 11th 3:20 AM through September 13th 6:49 AM
October 8th 1:51 PM through October 10th 4:06 PM
November 5th 0"14 AM November 7th 2:25 AM
December 2nd 8:42 AM through December 4th 11:56 AM
December 29th 2:48 PM through December 31st 7:18 PM

JAMES THE GREATER
NOVEMBER 22ND THROUGH DECEMBER 21ST

James - apostle to Jesus Christ, brother to John, the disciple - was strong and firm in his belief that Jesus was the Son of God. James was the first apostle to die after the church had been established in 44 A.D. After preaching the gospel in Samaria, Judea, and Spain, he was condemned to death by Herod.

James had the ability to speak to everyone in a childlike manner, so that all could benefit from the Word of God regardless of their ability to reason or understand the language of the teachers in the temples, or in the village centers. He was commanding, through his confidence and his speaking ability, and people came from miles around to hear all that he had to say. James had the confidence of his years and the naivete of a child speaking out whenever he could and wherever there was anyone around to listen to him preach.

James felt the lessons that he had received from Jesus were invaluable to him and proved this over and over as he continued to preach what he had learned. He was quick to understand the lessons of his Master. He loved and honored Jesus, and laid down his life for his truth.

James did not draw a lot of attention to himself through his ministry, but occasionally his tendency toward abruptness was displayed in his intentions when he felt the need to reiterate - with extreme accuracy - the teachings of Jesus Christ. At times, James allowed his anger and the ignorance of others to shade the knowledge he received from Christ. However, when the shading turned to clarity, his vision once again restored his faith in what he had learned. As James regained his strength in his belief system, which was that Jesus was the Son of God and, through Him, James would be with god in Heaven after this life, he continued to speak the words that Jesus had

252

taught him until the day of his death.

James possessed the same personality traits as those people born between November 22nd and December 21st. They are firm in their beliefs, right or wrong, and they will hold tight to what they believe. It is important to know the truth in this world. To release the anger that can destroy you, thus giving you the freedom to express yourself in this life in accordance with God's Will, obtain help from James the Greater, brother of John and apostle to Jesus. Light a candle the color best represented by your wish between the hours of 12:00 P.M. and 2:00 P.M. on the following days.

James the Greater
November 22nd through December 21st

2001
June 4th 2:57 PM through June 6th 11:21 PM
July 1st 9:12 PM through July 4th 6:19 AM
July 29th 2:44 AM through July 31st 12:14 PM
August 25th 8:58 AM through August 27th 6:00 PM
September 21st 5:01 PM through September 24th 0:45 AM
October 19th 2:46 AM through October 21st 9:09 AM
November 15th 12:51 PM through November 17th 6:37 PM
December 12th 9:29 PM through December 15th 3:45 AM

2002
January 9th 3:56 AM through January 11th 11:16 AM
February 5th 9:20 AM through February 7th 5:06 PM
March 4th 3:54 PM through March 6th 10:45 PM
April 1st 0:45 AM through April 3rd 5:56 AM
April 28th 11:12 AM through April 30th 3:01 PM
May 25th 9:19 PM through May 28th 0:52 AM
June 22nd 5:41 AM through June 24th 9:59 AM
July 19th 12:01 PM through July 21st 5:24 PM
August 15th 5:24 PM through August 17th 11:13 PM
September 11th 11:43 PM through September 14th 4:46 AM
October 9th 8:20 AM through October 11th 11:43 AM
November 5th 7:00 PM through November 7th 8:57 PM
December 3rd 5:57 AM through December 5th 7:36 AM

2003

December 30th 3:00 PM through January 1st 5:41 PM
January 26th 9:25 PM through January 29th 1:28 AM
February 23rd 2:45 AM through February 25th 7:09 AM
March 22nd 9:32 AM through March 24th 12:46 PM
April 18th 6:51 PM through April 20th 8:18 PM
May 16th 5:42 AM through May 18th 6:02 AM
June 12th 4:11 PM through June 14th 4:36 PM
July 10th 0:48 AM through July 12th 2:19 AM
August 6th 7:11 AM through August 8th 10:00 AM
September 2nd 12:31 PM through September 4th 3:49 PM
September 29th 6:56 PM through October 1st 9:20 PM
October 27th 3:54 AM through October 29th 4:34 AM
November 23rd 3:02 PM through November 25th 2:30 PM
December 21st 2:15 AM through December 23rd 1:54 AM

2004
January 17th 11:17 AM through January 19th 12:22 PM
February 13th 5:34 PM through February 15th 8:12 PM
March 11th 10:56 PM through March 14th 1:49 AM
April 8th 5:50 AM through April 10th 7:32 AM
May 5th 3:07 AM through May 7th 3:15 PM
June 2nd 1:51 AM through June 4th 1:11 AM
June 29th 12:15 PM through July 1st 11:59 AM
July 26th 8:47 PM through July 28th 9:55 PM
August 23rd 3:08 AM through August 25th 5:45 AM
September 19th 8:29 AM through September 21st 11:33 AM
October 16th 2:57 PM through October 18th 5:05 PM
November 12th 11:56 PM through November 15th 0:31 AM
December 10th 10:54 AM through December 12 10:40 AM

2005
January 6th 9:44 PM through January 8th 10:08 PM
February 3rd 6:21 AM through February 5th 8:30 AM
March 2nd 12:29 PM through March 4th 4:10 PM
March 29th 5:56 PM through March 31st 9:46 PM
April 26th 0:45 AM through April 28th 3:31 AM
May 23rd 9:37 AM through May 25th 11:09 AM
June 19th 7:44 PM through June 21st 8:50 PM
July 17th 5:34 AM through July 19th 7:24 AM

August 13th 1:47 PM through August 15th 5:11 PM
September 9th 8:02 PM through September 12th 0:55 AM
October 7th 1:27 AM through October 9th 6:42 PM
November 3rd 7:54 AM through November 5th 12:15 PM
November 30th 4:32 PM through December 2nd 7:40 PM
December 28th 2:43 AM through December 30th 5:43 AM

2006
January 1st 2:43 AM through January 3rd 6:41 AM
January 24th 12:37 PM through January 26th 4:30 PM
February 20th 8:37 PM through February 23rd 2:14 AM
March 20th 2:43 AM through March 22nd 9:34 AM
April 16th 8:19 AM through April 18th 3:11 PM
May 13th 2:56 PM through May 15th 8:57 PM
June 9th 11:04 PM through June 12th 4:17 AM
July 7th 8:13 AM through July 9th 1:23 PM
August 3rd 5:14 PM through August 5th 11:17PM
August 31st 0:59 AM through September 2nd 8:33 AM
September 27th 7:15 AM through September 29th 4:00 PM
October 24th 12:53 PM through October 26th 9:45 PM
November 20th 7:15 PM through November 23rd 3:24 AM
December 18th 3:10 AM through December 20th 10:37 AM

2007
January 14th 12:11 PM through January 16th 7:48 PM
February 10th 9:01 PM through February 13th 5:41 AM
March 10th 4:37 AM through March 12th 2:33 PM
April 6th 10:56 AM through April 8th 9:34 PM
May 3rd 4:47 PM through May 6th 3:19 AM
May 30th 11:06 PM through June 2nd 9:07 AM
June 27th 6:24 AM through June 29th 4:03 PM
July 24th 2:29 PM through July 27th 0:20 AM
August 20th 10:44 PM through August 23rd 9:18 AM
September 17th 6:20 AM through September 19th 5:50 PM
October 14th 12:58 PM through October 17th 1:02 AM
November 10th 6:58 PM through November 13th 6:59 AM
December 8th 1:11 AM through Secember 10th 12:49 PM

2008
January 4th 8:13 AM through January 6th 7:41 PM

January 31st 4:08 PM through February 3rd 3:51 AM
February 28th 0:22 AM through March 1st 12:32 PM
March 26th 8:11 AM through March 28th 8:41 PM
April 22nd 3:07 PM through April 25th 3:45 AM
May 19th 9:18 PM through May 22nd 9:53 AM
June 16th 3:19 AM through June 18th 3:49 PM
July 13th 9:50 AM through July 15th 10:19 PM
August 9th 5:10 PM through August 12th 5:41 AM
September 6th 1:10 AM through September 8th 1:44 PM
October 3rd 9:14 AM through October 5th 9:47 PM
October 30th 4:41 PM through November 2nd 5:11 AM
November 26th 11:14 PM through November 29th 11:45 AM
December 24th 5:13 AM through December 26th 5:55 PM

2009
January 20th 11:30 AM through January 23rd 0:16 AM
February 16th 6:53 PM through February 19th 7:24 AM
March 16th 3:21 AM through March 18th 3:18 PM
April 12th 12:00 AM through April 14th 11:26 PM
May 9th 7:49 PM through May 12th 7:08 AM
June 6th 2:24 AM through June 8th 1:57 PM
July 3rd 8:11 AM through July 5th 8:05 PM
July 30th 2:10 PM through August 2nd 2:06 AM
August 26th 9:16 PM through August 29th 8:43 AM
September 23rd 5:43 AM through September 25th 4:16 PM
October 20th 2:49 PM through October 23rd 0:38 AM
November 16th 11:22 PM through November 19th 8:59 PM
December 14th 6:25 AM through December 16th 4:31 PM

2010
January 10th 12:09 PM through January 12th 190:52 PM
February 6th 6:03 PM through February 9th 4:42 AM
March 6th 1:35 AM through March 8th 11:11 AM
April 2nd 10:51 AM through April 4th 7:05 PM
April 29th 8:35 PM through May 2nd 3:57 AM
May 27th 5:14 AM through May 29th 12:42 PM
June 32rd 12:09 PM through June 25th 8:18 PM
July 20th 5:47 PM through July 23rd 2:37 AM
August 16th 11:33 PM through August 19th 8:15 AM
September 13th 6:50 AM through September 15th 2:28 PM

October 10th 4:07 PM through October 12th 10:14 PM
November 7th 2:26 AM through November 9th 7:34 AM
December 4th 11:58 AM through December 6th 5:14 PM

MATTHEW, APOSTLE TO JESUS
DECEMBER 22ND THROUGH JANUARY 19TH

Matthew was the least likely person for Jesus to have chosen to be in his presence as one of his chosen twelve. Matthew was not a holy man when he met Jesus. He was a publican - that is, a tax collector - a Jew working for the Romans, collecting their taxes.

Matthew was a hard man to get to know, as his personality did not warrant close friends. In his early life, his personality drove him to succeed and to have material possessions. He continued to strive for acceptance among those he felt to be rich and powerful, Matthew lived his early life to please those he desired to be his friends.

Matthew would have been a social outcast among his own people, but he did not care. His love was for power and a position of honor. These things were more important to him than a social position among his own people. The importance which Matthew had been seeking was inevitably found in his position as tax collector.

Matthew projected the typical personality possessed by those people wanting to be on the winning team. Their alliance is placed in the hands of those with the most to offer at the time.

Like most people represented by this time frame, there was a change in Matthew's life. His change came on the day that Jesus, in the company of his disciples, went past Matthew's toll (or tax) table. Matthew 9:9 states that Jesus saw a man named Matthew sitting in the tax collector's place, and said to him, "Follow me," and he arose and followed him. After that point in his life, Matthew became a devoted follower and apostle to Jesus, and he went on to write the first gospel.

After the ascension of Jesus, Matthew preached to pagan nations and was martyred - possibly in Persia. Today, his body reposes in the Cathedral of Salerno, Italy.

257

As with Matthew, most people born between December 22nd and January 19th live their early childhood hoping to accomplish social acceptance and the material niceties that life has to offer. Their change in life will come as Matthew's change came to him; however, no one can make them accept it. It was Matthew's choice to follow Jesus, as Jesus only said, "Follow me" once.

There are many times in everyone's life when change is frightening, not knowing how the change will affect your life or whether or not there will be a point in which you can turn back. This, too, is your choice.

When life has offers and your choices are plentiful, light a candle to St. Matthew for clarity through our confusion. For clarity, light a white candle. For anything else, use the candle lighting dictionary guide to choose the candle color that will best represent the wish you desire. For all people following God's Path and making the right decisions, glory will be yours for generations to come.

The best time to light a candle to st. Matthew is between the hours of 10:00 A.M. and 12:00 P.M. For the best results, light your candles to St. Matthew on the following days.

Matthew Apostle to Jesus
December 22nd through January 19th

2001
June 6th 11:22 PM through June 9th 10:17 AM
July 4th 6:20 AM through June 6th 5:30 PM
July 31st 12:15 PM through August 2nd 11:50 PM
August 27th 6:01 PM through August 30th 5:45 AM
September 24th 0:47 AM through September 26th 12:02 PM
October 21st 9:10 AM through October 23rd 7:24 PM
November 17th 6:39 PM through November 20th 3:52 AM
December 15th 3:48 AM through December 17th 12:40 PM

2002
January 11th 11:17 AM through January 13th 8:39 PM
February 7th 5:07 PM through February 10th 3:13 AM
March 6th 10:47 PM through March 9th 8:53 AM
April 3rd 5:58 AM through April 5th 3:04 PM

258

April 30th 3:02 PM through May 2nd 10:41 PM
May 28th 0:53 AM through May 30th 7:33 AM
June 24th 10:00 AM through June 26th 10:00 AM
July 21st 5:25 PM through July 24th 0:37 AM
August 17th 11:14 PM through August 20th 7:14 AM
September 14th 4:47 AM through September 16th 12:52 PM
October 11th 11:44 AM through October 13th 6:49 PM
November 7th 8:58 PM through November 10th 2:24 AM
December 5th 7:38 AM through December 7th 11:52 AM

2003
January 1st 5:42 PM through January 3rd 9:54 PM
January 29th 1:29 AM through January 31st 6:42 AM
February 25th 7:10 AM through February 27th 1:22 PM
March 24th 12:47 PM through March 26th 6:49 PM
April 20th 8:19 PM through April 23rd 0:56 AM
May 18th 6:03 AM through May 20th 8:59 AM
June 14th 4:37 PM through June 16th 6:39 PM
July 12th 2:20 AM through July 14th 4:35 AM
August 8th 10:02 AM through August 10th 1:22 PM
September 4th 3:50 PM through September 6th 8:12 PM
October 1st 9:12 PM through October 4th 1:43 AM
October 29th 4:36 AM through October 31st 7:39 AM
November 25th 2:31 PM through November 27th 3:46 PM
December 23rd 1:55 AM through December 25th 2:11 AM

2004
January 19th 12:23 PM through January 21st 1:09 PM
February 15th 8:13 PM through February 17th 10:25 PM
March 14th 1:51 AM through March 16th 5:09 AM
April 10th 7:33 AM through April 12th 10:31 AM
May 7th 3:16 PM through May 9th 4:45 PM
June 4th 1:12 AM through June 6th 1:07 AM
July 1st 12:00 PM through July 3rd 11:20 AM
July 28th 9:57 PM through July 30th 9:52 PM
August 25th 5:46 AM through August 27th 7:07 AM
September 21st 11:35 AM through September 23rd 2:08 PM
October 18th 5:06 PM through October 20th 7:36 PM
November 15th 0:32 AM through November 17th 1:36 AM
December 12th 10:41 AM through December 16th 11:22 AM

2005

January 8th 10:10 PM through January 10th 9:05 PM
February 5th 8:31 AM through February 7th 8:25 AM
March 4th 4:11 PM through March 6th 5:47 PM
March 31st 9:47 PM through April 3rd 0:29 AM
April 28th 3:32 AM through April 30th 5:52 AM
May 25th 11:10 AM through May 27th 12:07 PM
June 21st 8:51 PM through June 23rd 8:34 PM
July 19th 7:26 AM through July 21st 6:54 AM
August 15th 5:12 PM through August 17th 5:37 PM
September 12th 0:56 AM through September 14th 3:00 AM
October 9th 6:43 AM through October 11th 10:04 AM
November 5th 12:17 PM through November 7th 3:29 PM
December 2nd 7:41 PM through December 4th 9:34 PM

2006

January 26th 4:31 PM through January 28th 5:08 PM
February 23rd 2:16 AM through February 25th 4:13 AM
March 22nd 9:35 AM through March 24th 1:20 PM
April 18th 3:12 PM through April 20th 7:54 PM
May 15th 8:58 PM through May 18th 1:17 AM
June 12th 4:18 AM through June 14th 7:31 AM
July 9th 1:24 PM through July 11th 3:45 PM
August 5th 11:49 PM through August 8th 1:46 AM
September 2nd 8:34 AM through September 4th 12:13 PM
September 29th 4:01 PM through October 1st 9:23 PM
October 26th 9:47 PM through October 29th 4:14 AM
November 23rd 3:25 AM through November 25th 9:39 AM
December 20th 10:38 AM through December 22nd 3:47 PM

2007

January 16th 7:49 PM through January 19th 0:13 AM
February 13th 5:42 AM through February 15th 10:33 AM
March 12th 2:35 PM through March 14th 8:51 PM
August 8th 9:35 PM through April 11th 5:21 AM
May 6th 3:21 AM through May 8th 11:46 AM
June 2nd 9:09 AM through June 4th 5:14 PM
June 29th 4:04 PM through July 1st 11:22 PM
July 27th 0:21 AM through July 29th 7:12 AM
August 23rd 9:20 AM through August 25th 4:33 PM

September 19th 5:51 PM through September 22nd 2:16 AM
October 17th 1:03 AM through October 19th 10:50 AM
November 13th 7:00 AM through November 15th 5:27 PM
December 10th 12:50 PM through December 12th 10:59 PM

2008
January 6th 7:42 PM through January 9th 5:12 AM
February 3rd 3:52 AM through February 5th 1:08 PM
March 1st 12:33 PM March 3rd 10:22 PM
March 28th 8:43 PM through March 31st 7:23 AM
April 25th 3:46 AM through April 27th 3:25 PM
May 22nd 9:55 AM through May 24th 9:49 PM
June 18th 3:51 PM through June 21st 3:32 AM
July 15th 10:20 PM through July 18th 9:38 PM
August 12th 5:42 AM through August 14th 4:55 PM
September 8th 1:45 PM through September 11th 1:18 AM
October 5th 9:48 PM through October 8th 10:02 AM
November 2nd 5:13 AM through November 4th 5:59 PM
November 29th 11:47 AM through December 2nd 0:42 AM
December 26th 5:56 PM through December 29th 6:40 AM

2009
January 23rd 0:17 AM through January 25th 12:54 PM
February 19th 7:25 AM through February 21st 8:04 PM
March 18th 3:19 PM through March 21st 4:04 AM
April 14th 11:27 PM through April 17th 12:17 PM
May 12th 7:09 AM through May 14th 7:59 PM
June 8th 1:59 PM through June 11th 2:50 AM
July 5th 8:07 PM through July 8th 9:02 AM
August 2nd 2:08 AM through August 4th 3:06 PM
August 29th 8:44 AM through August 31st 9:41 PM
September 25th 4:18 PM through September 28th 5:04 AM
October 23rd 0:39 AM through October 25th 1:06 PM
November 19th 9:00 AM through November 21st 9:08 PM
December 16th 4:32 PM through December 19th 4:37 AM

2010
January 12th 10:53 PM through January 15th 11:15 AM
February 9th 4:43 AM through February 11th 5:21 PM
March 8th 11:12 AM through March 10th 11:39 PM

April 4th 7:06 PM through April 7th 6:48 AM
May 2nd 3:59 AM through May 4th 2:48 PM
May 29th 12:43 PM through May 31st 11:04 PM
June 25th 8:20 PM through June 28th 6:50 AM
July 23rd 2:38 AM through July 25th 1:35 PM
August 19th 8:16 AM through August 21st 7:34 PM
September 15th 2:29 PM through September 18th 1:31 AM
October 12th 10:16 PM through October 15th 8:21 AM
November 9th 7:35 AM through November 11th 4:29 PM
December 6th 5:15 PM through December 9th 1:28 AM

JUDE - THADDAEUS
JANUARY 20TH THROUGH FEBRUARY 18TH

St. Jude - as he is referred to by many Catholics in the world - was the brother of James the Less. He was kind, generous, loving, gentle, and the most loved of all apostles.

St. Jude was sensitive to the needs and desires of others, and for Catholic parishioners today, he is the Patron Saint of Hopeless and Lost Causes. St. Jude has always been compassionate toward their troubles. It is said, that by saying a prayer as you light your candle to St. Jude, he will always come to your assistance. (This is typical of anyone born during the time frame from January 20th through February 18th. They, too, are strong in their conviction, in this life, to help those in need.) The prayer to St. Jude is as follows: **Saint Jude, pray for us, and all who invoke thy aid. Most Holy apostle, Saint Jude, faithful servant and friend to Jesus, the church honors and invokes thee universally with the most desperate and hopeless cases. Pray for me and bring speedy help, come to my assistance in this great need.** (Add the religious closing of your choice) **Amen.**

St. Jude is the author of the Epistle to the Eastern churches and it is said that he preached the gospel in Palestine. He was martyred in the first century.

In St. John 15: 17-20, Jesus said to his disciples, "These things I command you, that you may love one another. If the world hates you, know that it has hated me before you. If you were of the world, the world would love what

262

is its own. But because you are not of the world, but I have chosen you out of the world, therefore, the world hates you. Remember the words I have spoken to you." These words seemed to be directed at the personality of St. Jude. He had love in his life from all who knew him; however, as was mentioned in the words of Christ, these people loved him with their lips and not with their hearts.

There is nothing that the kind and generous heart of St. Jude cannot help you with. He will assist you in your time of need, as well as give you the insight to live your life to the fullest, fulfilling your heart's desires. It is not important to secondguess life. It is only important to accept it. The best time to light a candle to St. Jude is between the hours of 8:00 A.M. and 10:00 A.M. on the following days.

Jude Thaddaeus
January 20th through February 18th

2001
June 9th 10:18 AM through June 11th 10:51 PM
July 6th 5:31 PM through July 9th 6:03 AM
August 2nd 11:52 PM through August 5th 12:27 PM
September 26th 12:05 PM through September 29th 0:47 AM
October 23rd 7:25 PM through October 26th 7:52 AM
November 20th 3:54 AM through November 22nd 3:49 PM
December 17th 12:42 PM through December 20th 0:07 AM

2002
January 13th 8:40 PM through January 16th 7:58 AM
February 10th 3:14 AM through February 12th 2:51 PM
March 9th 8:55 AM through March 11th 8:54 PM
April 5th 3:06 PM through April 8th 2:54 AM
May 2nd 10:42 PM through May 5th 9:44 AM
May 30th 7:34 AM through June 1st 5:34 PM
June 26th 10:01 PM June 29th 1:58 AM
July 24th 0:39 AM through July 26th 10:02 AM
August 20th 7:15 AM through August 22nd 5:08 PM
September 16th 12:53 PM through September 18th 11:16 PM
October 13th 6:50 PM through October 16th 5:05 AM
November 10th 2:26 AM through November 12th 11:39 AM
December 7th 11:53 AM through December 9th 7:43 PM

2003

January 3rd 9:56 PM through January 6th 4:55 AM
January 31st 6:43 AM through February 2nd 1:53 PM
February 27th 1:23 PM through March 1th 9:24 PM
March 26th 6:50 PM through March 29th 3:23 AM
April 23rd 0:57 AM through April 25th 9:00 AM
May 20th 9:00 AM through May 22nd 3:39 PM
June 16th 6:40 PM through June 18th 11:55 PM
July 14th 4:37 AM through July 16th 9:11 AM
August 10th 1:23 PM through August 12th 6:17 PM
September 6th 8:15 PM through September 9th 2:05 AM
October 4th 1:44 AM through October 6th 8:17 AM
October 31st 7:40 AM through November 2nd 1:49 PM
November 27th 3:47 PM through November 29th 8:23 PM
December 25th 2:13 AM through December 27th 5:08 AM

2004

January 21st 1:10 PM through January 23rd 3:26 PM
February 17th 10:27 PM through February 20th 1:24 AM
March 16th 5:10 AM through March 18th 9:24 AM
April 12th 10:32 AM through April 14th 3:22 PM
May 9th 4:46 PM through May 11th 8:50 PM
June 6th 1:09 AM through June 8th 3:37 AM
July 3rd 11:21 AM through July 5th 12:24 PM
July 30th 9:53 PM through August 1st 10:33 PM
August 27th 7:08 AM through August 29th 8:32 AM
September 23rd 2:09 PM through September 25th 4:54 PM
October 20th 7:37 PM through October 22nd 11:12 PM
November 17th 1:39 AM through November 19th 4:36 AM
December 14th 10:09 AM through December 16th 11:22 AM

2005

January 10th 9:06 PM through January 12th 8:49 PM
February 7th 8:26 AM through February 9th 7:58 AM
March 6th 5:49 PM through March 8th 6:31 PM
April 3rd 0:30 AM through April 5th 2:43 AM
April 30th 5:53 AM through May 2nd 8:41 AM
May 27th 12:09 PM through May 29th 2:08 PM
June 23rd 8:36 PM through June 25th 9:01 PM
July 21st 6:55 AM through July 23rd 6:10 AM

August 17th 5:38 PM through August 19th 4:50 PM
September 14th 3:02 AM through September 16th 3:22 AM
October 11th 10:05 AM through October 13th 12:03 PM
November 7th 3:30 PM through November 9th 6:20 PM
December 4th 9:36 PM through December 6th 11:42 PM
January 28th 5:09 PM through January 30th 4:30 PM
February 25th 4:15 AM through February 27th 3:54 AM
March 24th 1:21 PM through March 26th 2:31 PM
April 20th 7:55 PM through April 22nd 10:42 PM
May 18th 1:19 AM through May 20th 4:37 AM
June 14th 7:32 AM through June 16th 10:04 AM
July 11th 3:46 PM through July 13th 4:58 PM
August 8th 1:47 AM through August 10th 2:09 AM
September 4th 12:15 PM through September 6th 12:55 PM
October 1st 9:24 PM through October 3rd 11:31 PM
October 29th 4:16 AM through October 31st 8:09 AM
November 25th 9:40 AM through November 27th 2:19 PM
December 22nd 3:48 PM through December 24th 7:41 PM

2007
January 19th 0:15 AM through January 21st 2:47 AM
February 15th 10:34 AM through February 17th 12:29 PM
March 14th 8:52 PM through March 16th 11:29 PM
April 11th 5:23 AM through April 13th 9:38 AM
May 8th 11:47 AM through May 10th 5:30 PM
June 4th 5:16 PM through June 6th 11:22nd PM
July 1st 11:24 PM through July 4th 4:51 AM
July 29th 7:13 AM through July 31st 11:39 AM
August 25th 4:35 PM through August 27th 8:33 PM
September 22nd 2:18 AM through September 24th 6:53 AM
October 19th 10:51 AM through October 21st 5:01 PM
November 15th 5:29 PM through November 18th 1:13 AM
December 12th 11:01 PM through December 15th 7:13 AM

2008
January 9th 5:13 AM through January 11th 12:43 PM
February 5th 1:09 PM through February 7th 7:44 PM
March 3rd 10:24 PM through March 6th 4:52 AM
March 31st 7:33 AM through April 2nd 2:54 PM
April 27th 3:27 PM through April 30th 0:09 AM

May 24th 9:51 PM through May 27th 7:36 AM
June 21st 3:33 AM through June 23rd 1:31 PM
July 18th 9:40 AM through July 20th 7:06 PM
August 14th 4:56 PM through August 17th 1:45 AM
September 11th 1:19 AM through September 13th 10:02 AM
October 8th 10:03 AM through October 10th 7:29 PM
November 4th 6:01 PM through November 7th 4:41 AM
December 2nd 0:44 AM through December 4th 12:22 PM
December 29th 6:42 AM through December 31st 6:26 PM

2009
January 25th 12:56 PM through January 28th 0:10 AM
February 21st 8:06 PM through February 24th 6:59 AM
March 21st 4:06 AM through March 23rd 3:07 PM
April 17th 12:19 PM through April 19th 11:54 PM
May 14th 8:01 PM through May 17th 8:16 AM
June 11th 2:52 AM through June 13th 3:31 PM
July 8th 9:03 AM through July 10th 9:41 PM
August 4th 3:08 PM through August 7th 3:32 AM
August 31st 9:43 PM through September 3rd 9:56 AM
September 28th 5:06 AM through September 30th 5:24 PM
October 25th 1:07 PM through October 28th 1:44 AM
November 21st 9:10 PM through November 24th 10:05 AM
December 19th 4:38 AM through December 21st 5:40 PM

2010
January 15th 11:16 AM through January 18th 0:14 AM
February 11th 5:24 PM through February 14th 6:20 AM
March 10th 11:41 PM through March 13th 12:40 PM
April 7th 6:51 AM through April 9th 7:45 PM
May 4th 2:50 PM through May 7th 3:23 AM
May 31st 11:06 PM through June 3rd 11:31 AM
June 28th 6:51 AM through June 30th 7:07 PM
July 25th 1:37 PM through July 28th 1:57 AM
August 21st 7:36 PM through August 24th 8:09 AM
September 18th 1:33 AM through September 20th 2:12 PM
October 15th 8:22 AM through October 17th 8:48 PM
November 11th 4:31 PM through November 14th 4:22 AM
December 9th 1:30 AM through December 11th 12:38 PM

JUDAS ISCARIOT
FEBRUARY 19TH THROUGH MARCH 20TH

For Judas, as for all those people born during the time frame from February 19th through March 29th, life was - and is - as stated in the nursery rhyme: "There was a little girl who had a little curl, right in the middle of her forehead. When she was good, she was very, very good, but when she was bad, she was horrid." This time frame, like the personality of Judas, is the epitome of this nursery rhyme - when times are good, they are very, very good, but when times are bad, they are horrid.

Jesus chose all of his apostles for a specific reason. Perhaps, until now, we might have questioned Jesus's intentions for picking Judas Iscariot. Was this intent that of Christ's, or that of divine guidance from His Father in Heaven? Judas was, indeed, one of the chosen twelve, as all of the apostles combined make up the personality of one whole human being.

There is mention in the Bible that Judas was the one who plotted to betray Jesus by going to the chief priest and asking him, "What will you give me to deliver Jesus to you?" Accepting thirty pieces of silver, Judas betrayed Jesus. This was an act that was atypical of Judas's innate personality. However, if he had not done this, it would have only been a matter of time before God's Divine Plan would have come to pass in some other form.

All living beings have a divine program. "Free will" is "when" and your "destiny" or "divine plan" is "God's Will." It is only a matter of time as to "when" God's Divine Plan will unfold in your life. As it was in Judas's life, so will be in your life. This is the reason that living a non-judgmental life is so important. All that you are is important to all that you will be, as Judas discovered.

Judas lived with Jesus and the other apostles. He preached the Word of God. However, Judas is now, and will always be through time and eternity, the apostle who betrayed Jesus - and for what reason, we will never know. Was it for the thirty pieces of silver? Perhaps Judas was the one, among the twelve, chosen by God to assist in the divine plan of mankind!

For all those born during this time frame who find it difficult to be understood, with an inability to understand the thoughts and motives of others, light a candle to Judas Iscariot between the hours of 6:00 A.M. and

267

8:00 A.M. All that God has to offer maybe obtained through His Divine Plan. To be all that you are capable of being, as well as understood, light your candle to Judas Iscariot for assistance on the following days.

Judas Iscariot
February 19th through March 20th

2001
June 11th 10:52 PM through June 14th 11:01 AM
July 9th 6:04 AM through July 11th 6:33 PM
August 5th 12:29 PM through August 8th 1:03 AM
September 29th 0:50 AM through October 1st 1:05 PM
October 26th 7:54 AM through October 28th 8:13 PM
November 22nd 3:51 PM through November 25th 4:19 AM
December 20th 0:08 AM through December 22nd 12:42 PM

2002
January 16th 7:59 AM through January 18th 8:33 PM
February 12th 2:52 PM through February 15th 3:22 AM
March 11th 8:57 PM through March 14th 9:23 AM
April 8th 2:56 AM through April 10th 3:38 PM
May 5th 9:45 AM through May 7th 10:19 PM
June 1st 5:36 PM through June 4th 5:48 AM
June 29th 1:59 AM through July 1st 1:46 PM
July 26th 10:03 AM through July 28th 9:36 PM
August 22nd 5:11 PM through August 25th 4:45 AM
September 18th 11:17 PM through September 21st 11:09 AM
October 16th 5:06 AM through October 18th 5:11 PM
November 12th 11:41 AM through November 14th 11:33 PM
December 9th 7:45 PM through December 12th 6:56 AM

2003
January 6th 4:56 AM through January 8th 3:13 PM
February 2nd 1:54 PM through February 4th 11:42 PM
March 1st 9:25 PM through March 4th 7:27 AM
April 25th 9:01 AM through April 27th 7:52 PM
May 22nd 3:40 PM through May 25th 1:56 AM
June 18th 11:56 PM through June 21st 9:03 AM
July 16th 9:13 AM through July 18th 5:16 PM
August 12th 6:18 PM through August 15th 1:58 AM

September 9th 2:07 AM through September 11th 10:06 AM
October 6th 8:19 AM through October 8th 5:06 PM
November 2nd 1:51 PM through November 4th 10:01 OM
November 21st 8:24 PM through December 2nd 4:54 AM
December 27th 5:10 AM through December 29th 12:06 PM

2004
January 23rd 3:28 PM through January 25th 9:03 PM
February 20th 1:26 AM through February 22nd 6:43 AM
March 18th 9:25 AM through March 20th 3:26 PM
April 14th 3:23 PM through April 16th 10:22 PM
May 11th 8:51 PM through May 14th 4:00 AM
June 8th 3:38 AM through June 10th 9:47 AM
July 5th 12:25 PM through July 7th 5:01 PM
August 1st 10:34 PM through August 4th 1:58 AM
August 29th 8:33 AM through August 31st 11:44 AM
September 25th 4:55 PM through September 27th 8:55 PM
October 22nd 11:13 PM through October 25th 4:23 AM
November 19th 4:37 AM through November 21st 10:09 AM
December 16th 11:23 AM through December 18th 3:50 PM

2005
January 12th 8:50 PM through January 14th 11:25 PM
February 9th 7:59 AM through February 11th 9:20 AM
March 8th 6:32 PM through March 10th 8:02 PM
April 5th 2:45 AM through April 7th 5:26 AM
May 2nd 8:42 AM through May 4th 12:33 Pm
May 29th 2:09 PM through May 31st 6:06 PM
June 25th 9:02 PM through June 27th 11:49 PM
July 23rd 6:11 AM through July 25th 7:21 AM
August 19th 4:52 PM through August 21st 5:00 PM
Jeptember 16th 3:24 AM through September 18th 3:41 AM
October 13th 12:05 PM through October 15th 1:37 PM
November 9th 6:23 PM through November 11th 9:20 PM
December 6th 11:44 PM through December 9th 3:00 AM

2006
January 3rd 6:43 AM through January 5th 8:42 AM
January 30th 4:31 PM through February 3rd 7:29 PM
February 27th 3:55 AM through March 1st 3:16 AM

March 26th 2:32 Pm through March 28th 2:29 PM
April 22nd 10:43 PM through April 25th 1:10 AM
May 20th 4:38 AM through May 22nd 7:22 AM
June 16th 10:05 AM through June 18th 12:52 PM
July 13th 4:59 PM through July 15th 6:37 PM
August 10th 2:10 AM through August 12th 2:20 AM
September 6th 12:56 PM through September 8th 12:21 PM
October 3rd 11:32 PM through October 5th 11:30 PM
October 31st 8:10 AM through November 2nd 9:45 AM
November 27th 2:20 PM through November 29th 5:28 PM
December 24th 7:43 PM through December 26th 11:02 PM

2007
January 21st 2:48 AM through January 23rd 4:51 AM
February 17th 12:30 PM through February 19th 1:04 PM
March 16th 11:30 PM through March 18th 11:40 PM
April 13th 9:39 AM through April 15th 10:45 AM
May 10th 5:31 PM through May 12th 8:17 PM
June 6th 11:24 PM through June 9th 3:24 AM
July 4th 4:52 AM through July 6th 8:56 AM
August 27th 8:34 PM through August 29th 10:23 PM
September 24th 6:55 AM through September 26th 8:21 AM
October 21st 5:02 PM through October 23rd 7:23 PM
November 18th 1:14 AM through November 20th 5:23 AM
December 15th 7:15 AM through December 17th 12:51 PM

2008
January 11th 12:44 PM through January 13th 6:22 PM
February 7th 7:46 PM through February 10th 0:15 AM
March 6th 4:53 AM through March 8th 8:21 AM
April 2nd 2:55 PM through April 4th 6:26 PM
May 27th 7:38 AM through May 29th 1:51 PM
June 23rd 1:32 PM through June 25th 8:48 PM
July 20th 7:08 PM through July 23rd 2:20 AM
August 17th 1:46 AM through August 19th 8:08 AM
September 13th 10:04 AM through September 15th 3:38 PM
October 10th 7:31 PM through October 13th 1:06 AM
November 7th 4:43 AM through November 9th 11:25AM
December 4th 12:23 PM through December 6 8:43 PM

2009

December 31st 2008 6:27 PM through January 3rd 3:48 AM
January 28th 0:12 AM through January 30th 9:24 AM
February 24th 7:00 AM through February 26th 3:22 PM
March 23rd 3:08 PM through March 25th 11:01 PM
April 19th 11:55 PM through April 22nd 8:08 AM
May 17th 8:17 AM through May 19th 5:28 PM
June 13th 3:32 PM through June 16th 1:50 AM
July 10th 9:43 PM through June 13th 8:32 AM
August 7th 3:34 AM through August 9th 2:22 PM
September 3rd 9:58 AM through September 5th 8:13 PM
September 30th 5:25 PM through October 3rd 3:18 AM
October 28th 1:45 AM through October 30th 11:54 AM
November 24th 10:07 AM through November 26th 9:09 PM
December 21st 5:42 PM through December 24th 5:38 AM

2010

January 18th 0:17 AM through January 20th 12:34 PM
February 14th 6:22 AM through February 16th 6:28 PM
March 13th 12:43 PM through March 16th 0:30 AM
April 9th 7:46 PM through April 12th 7:29 AM
May 7th 3:33 AM through May 9th 3:26 PM
June 3rd 11:33 AM through June 5th 11:47 PM
June 30th 7:08 PM through July 3rd 7:42 AM
July 28th 1:59 AM through July 30th 2:39 PM
August 24th 8:10 AM through August 26th 8:47 PM
September 20th 2:14 PM through September 23rd 2:45 AM
October 17th 8:50 PM through October 20th 9:20 AM
November 14th 4:23 AM through November 16th 4:56 PM
December 11th 12:39 PM through December 14th 1:12 AM

HOLIDAYS FOR LIGHTING CANDLES

The tradition of lighting candles has always produced a calming effect within one's psyche. Candles have been lit on religious holidays throughout the centuries. When using the information in the candle lighting dictionary in conjunction with religious and traditional holidays, you will find that your desires and wishes are easily obtainable.

Lighting a candle on a traditional holiday deals with the material aspects of life. An example of this might be: on the first day of Spring, being a traditional holiday, you may wish for a new car. In the candle lighting dictionary under "car," it says to light a yellow candle. Light your yellow candle on the first day of Spring, knowing that the "best" car for the "best" deal will be offered to you before the next season. Anyone can buy a car; however, experience has taught us that not all "deals" are what they appear to be, so lighting a candle on the first day of Spring for a new car will ensure success.

By lighting a candle on a religious holiday, you will have the assistance i your wish from the ones most high. Lighting a candle on a religious holiday will give you assistance on a religious, or spiritual level. If you light a candle on a religious holiday for spiritual guidance, there is a better chance of receiving it then, than if you light your candle for insight on Arbor Day.

When lighting candles, keep mundane issues or material wishes on a material level by using the traditional holidays or your ephemeral timing guide. If your wish is for religious guidance, or spiritual insight, light your candles to the apostles, religious saints and holy men, or on religious holidays.

Holidays, along with the Full and New Moon cycles, for those lighting candles on a quarterly cycle will find the ephemeral timing guide to suffice. It is said that if you are in need of a change, you can light a candle that will best represent the change that you are looking for at the time of the New Moon. (Use your candle lighting dictionary to choose the color that will best represent your change.)

When there is a need to end a situation, light your colored candle under the Full Moon. The ephemeral timing guide will also help you determine the proper time frame to light candles to incite change and end potentially-traumatizing dilemmas.

CANDLE LIGHTING TRIVIA

Did you know that people lighting red and green candles at Christmas time will bring to themselves anxiety, confusion and the fear of spending money, taking away from the spirit of gift giving? Yes, the prolonged lighting of red candles will incite anger and fear, while lighting green in conjunction with red instills a fear of and incites a need to spend money fast and furiously, with little thought as to how this money will replenish itself, or better yet, how you will replace it.

Did you know that blowing out multiple colored candles placed on a birthday cake will not bring you a wish? Yes, when you blow out a candle, it will stop the flow of energy, and when lighting a wide variety of colors at once, you are setting yourself up for major disappointments throughout the year.

Did you know when a lady of the evening lights a red candle for a prolonged period of time, the energy will not be for romance, but for anger and violence? Yes, red is a color of passion and sex; however, red used for over a few hours becomes uncontrollable, inviting violence to sneak in.

Did you know that lighting a red candle during a storm would bring the storm to you? Yes, particularly during electrical storms. Electrical energy is very strong, and will be attracted to the intensity of energy emanating from your red candle, thus bringing the storm to you. If you try this to see if it is true, expect a limb to fall on your house or lightning to affect your wiring.

QUESTIONS AND ANSWERS
ON FULL SPECTRUM COLOR

QUESTION: When lighting candles, how can you tell by the degree of the color what the candle will be good for?
ANSWER: Let's use red for the example. The deeper or darker the color, the more powerful the candle will be. If your red candle is a deep, rich, dark color, the degree of vibration that the candle will emanate will be much stronger than that of a candle with a slight red hue.

QUESTION: If the degree of vibration depends on the darkness of color, what is the difference between using a dark red candle for energy and lighting a light red candle for energy?
ANSWER: Red is a very powerful color because of its placement in the spectrum of color. Both candles will give you energy, but the darker color will perhaps give you more energy, than you can handle in one day.

QUESTION: If the color blue is for balance, what is the difference between dark blue and light blue?

ANSWER: Dark blue vibrates on the vibrational level that is equal to that of the ph balance of the human body, thus this balance is on an external or conscious level. The light blue color does not vibrate at this same rate, thus giving you subconscious balance, not conscious balance. Light blue would be a good color to light for meditation or for peaceful dreams.

QUESTION: When I light candles, I put them in the bathroom, so that the cats can't knock them over. Is there a special place that I really should put my candles?

ANSWER: Candles are lit to enhance your innate energy. They will not do anything that you, when centered, can't do for yourself. With this in mind, you don't need to light them in a special place.

QUESTION: I grew up in a Catholic family. We would always light candles when we went to Mass. When I light a candle to Saint Jude, is this the same?

ANSWER: Yes. When you light a candle giving thanks or paying reverence to a saint or apostle, this would be the only reason that you might want to place your candles in a special place, as lighting candles to pay respect is different from enhancing your own energy through the aid of the vibrational level of candles.

QUESTION: I brought a candle that was suppose to stay lit for five days and it went out in only two days. Is this common?

ANSWER: No. When your candle goes out quickly, there is a lack of this vibration within your psyche. You will need to continue to light the same color candle until it burns at a normal rate, according to the size of the wick and shape of the candle.

QUESTION: How can I tell how long a candle will stay lit?

ANSWER: When you buy a candle, the sales clerk could probably tell you, according to the candle, how long the candle should stay lit. It will be different for each size and shape candle.

QUESTION: Yesterday, I bought a candle that would not stay lit. Is there something wrong with me, or is it the candle?

ANSWER: The reason that you lit the candle still exists; thus, if that candle will not stay lit, light another. After the new candle burns at a normal rate,

274

you will probably be able to go back to your assumably defective candle and it will then stay lit. You answer the question as to where the problem is.

QUESTION: I really want a raise at work. The book says that if I light a green candle at the right time I can get my raise. My question is, if I do';t light the candle and I ask for a raise, won't I get one anyway?
ANSWER: You may get the raise; however, if you light your green candle, there won't be any strings attached to your new salary.

QUESTION: There is no reference to muted colored candles in the book. However, if peach is a combination of pink and orange, would we not have the benefit of both colors, if we lit the peach colored candle?
ANSWER: I said that the psychological studies on the muted colors were not conclusive. If you are referring to the vibrational energy of the color and not the psychological effects of the color, then yes, you would benefit from both colors by lighting a candle where the two colors have been combined.

QUESTION: When I use the timing guide, I get confused when lighting white candles. I don't want to release purity. Should I only light white candles during the bring time frame?
ANSWER: No. White is the only color that can be lit 365 days a year, because of its Godlike qualities and its purity in intent.

QUESTION: I have an obsessive personality. I can light candles for something everyday of my life. Is there anything wrong with this?
ANSWER: There may be if it continues to be true. However, if I were you, the first thing I would light a candle for would be to release my obsessions.

QUESTION: I really wanted to light a candle at the exact time for the new bring cycle - in hopes of obtaining better benefits at work. The problem was that I went on vacation and didn't get back until four days after the bring cycle began. When is the best time of the day to light candles for such things as better benefits, money, love, good health, losing weight and all of those things that everyone wants?
ANSWER: Great question. The different hours of each day vibrate at a different vibrational level. Use the dictionary section in this book to ascertain the specific color of candle to light to suit your particular need. Cross reference that color with the day of the week and the hour of the day corresponding with the color of your candle in order to obtain your wish. Example: Benefits (to obtain) the book says to light a green candle.

275

September 2nd 1992 is a bring time frame, it is also a Tuesday. The chart below states that on Tuesday, it will be most effective to light green candles at 5:00 A.M., 8:00 A.M., 3:00 P.M. and 10:00 P.M. Thus, by lighting green candles for obtaining benefit (i.e. money) during the bring cycle, and by lighting them during the hours specified, you will be enhancing your operative potential. This will enable your intent to be magnified - thus, achieved.

When lighting more than one candle, choose the time that corresponds with the first candle that you light. If your desire is to obtain money through creative endeavors, light your yellow and orange candle during the hour that represents money (green).

Sunday:

12:00 A.M. - **Purple**
1:00 A.M. - **Blue**
2:00 A.M. - **Red**
3:00 A.M. - **White**
4:00 A.M. - **Green**
5:00 A.M. - **Yellow**
6:00 A.M. - **White**
7:00 A.M. - **Green**
8:00 A.M. - **Yellow**
9:00 A.M. - **Gray**
10:00 A.M. - **Purple**
11:00 A.M. - **Blue**

12:00 P.M. - **Red**
1:00 P.M. - **White**
2:00 P.M. - **Green**
3:00 P.M. - **Yellow**
4:00 P.M. - **Gray**
5:00 P.M. - **Purple**
6:00 P.M. - **Blue**
7:00 P.M. - **Red**
8:00 P.M. - **White**
9:00 P.M. - **Green**
10:00 P.M. - **Yellow**
11:00 P.M. - **Gray**

Monday:

12:00 A.M. - **White**
1:00 A.M. - **Green**
2:00 A.M. - **Yellow**
3:00 A.M. - **Gray**
4:00 A.M. - **Purple**
5:00 A.M. - **Blue**
6:00 A.M. - **Gray**
7:00 A.M. - **Purple**
8:00 A.M. - **Blue**
9:00 A.M. - **Red**
10:00 A.M. - **White**

12:00 P.M. - **Yellow**
1:00 P.M. - **Gray**
2:00 P.M. - **Purple**
3:00 P.M. - **Blue**
4:00 P.M. - **Red**
5:00 P.M. - **White**
6:00 P.M. - **Green**
7:00 P.M. - **Yellow**
8:00 P.M. - **Gray**
9:00 P.M. - **Purple**
10:00 P.M. - **Blue**

11:00 A.M. - **Green**

Tuesday:
12:00 A.M. - **Gray**
 1:00 A.M. - **Purple**
 2:00 A.M. - **Blue**
 3:00 A.M. - **Red**
 4:00 A.M. - **White**
 5:00 A.M. - **Green**
 6:00 A.M. - **Red**
 7:00 A.M. - **White**
 8:00 A.M. - **Green**
 9:00 A.M. - **Yellow**
10:00 A.M. - **Gray**
11:00 A.M. - **Purple**

Wednesday:
12:00 A.M. - **Red**
 1:00 A.M. - **White**
 2:00 A.M. - **Green**
 3:00 A.M. - **Yellow**
 4:00 A.M. - **Gray**
 5:00 A.M. - **Purple**
 6:00 A.M. - **Yellow**
 7:00 A.M. - **Gray**
 8:00 A.M. - **Purple**
 9:00 A.M. - **Blue**
10:00 A.M. - **Red**
11:00 A.M. - **White**

Thursday:
12:00 A.M. - **Yellow**
 1:00 A.M. - **Gray**
 2:00 A.M. - **Purple**
 3:00 A.M. - **Blue**
 4:00 A.M. - **Red**
 5:00 A.M. - **White**
 6:00 A.M. - **Blue**
 7:00 A.M. - **Red**
 8:00 A.M. - **White**

11:00 P.M. - **Red**

12:00 P.M. - **Blue**
 1:00 P.M. - **Red**
 2:00 P.M. - **White**
 3:00 P.M. - **Green**
 4:00 P.M. - **Yellow**
 5:00 P.M. - **Gray**
 6:00 P.M. - **Purple**
 7:00 P.M. - **Blue**
 8:00 P.M. - **Red**
 9:00 P.M. - **White**
10:00 P.M. - **Green**
11:00 P.M. - **Yellow**

12:00 P.M. - **Green**
 1:00 P.M. - **Yellow**
 2:00 P.M. - **Gray**
 3:00 P.M. - **Purple**
 4:00 P.M. - **Blue**
 5:00 P.M. - **Red**
 6:00 P.M. - **White**
 7:00 P.M. - **Green**
 8:00 P.M. - **Yellow**
 9:00 P.M. - **Gray**
10:00 P.M. - **Purple**
11:00 P.M. - **Blue**

12:00 P.M. - **Purple**
 1:00 P.M. - **Blue**
 2:00 P.M. - **Red**
 3:00 P.M. - **White**
 4:00 P.M. - **Green**
 5:00 P.M. - **Yellow**
 6:00 P.M. - **Gray**
 7:00 P.M. - **Purple**
 8:00 P.M. - **Blue**

277

9:00 A.M. - **Green**
10:00 A.M. - **Yellow**
11:00 A.M. - **Gray**

Friday:

12:00 A.M. - **Blue**
1:00 A.M. - **Red**
2:00 A.M. - **White**
3:00 A.M. - **Green**
4:00 A.M. - **Yellow**
5:00 A.M. - **Gray**
6:00 A.M. - **Green**
7:00 A.M. - **Yellow**
8:00 A.M. - **Gray**
9:00 A.M. - **Purple**
10:00 A.M. - **Blue**
11:00 A.M. - **Red**

Saturday:

12:00 A.M. - **Green**
1:00 A.M. - **Yellow**
2:00 A.M. - **Gray**
3:00 A.M. - **Purple**
4:00 A.M. - **Blue**
5:00 A.M. - **Red**
6:00 A.M. - **Purple**
7:00 A.M. - **Blue**
8:00 A.M. - **Red**
9:00 A.M. - **White**
10:00 A.M. - **Green**
11:00 A.M. - **Yellow**

9:00 P.M. - **Red**
10:00 P.M. - **White**
11:00 P.M. - **Green**

12:00 P.M. - **White**
1:00 P.M. - **Blue**
2:00 P.M. - **Yellow**
3:00 P.M. - **Gray**
4:00 P.M. - **Purple**
5:00 P.M. - **Blue**
6:00 P.M. - **Red**
7:00 P.M. - **White**
8:00 P.M. - **Green**
9:00 P.M. - **Yellow**
10:00 P.M. - **Gray**
11:00 P.M. - **Purple**

12:00 P.M. - **Gray**
1:00 P.M. - **Purple**
2:00 P.M. - **Blue**
3:00 P.M. - **Red**
4:00 P.M. - **White**
5:00 P.M. - **Green**
6:00 P.M. - **Yellow**
7:00 P.M. - **Gray**
8:00 P.M. - **Purple**
9:00 P.M. - **Blue**
10:00 P.M. - **Red**
11:00 P.M. - **White**

QUESTION: Someone told me that Dr. James Young patented the process of obtaining paraffin from bituminous shales in 1850. Is this true? If so, what type of wax was used to make candles before 1850?

ANSWER: Yes. This is true. The answer to your second question is: As early as 3200 B.C., Egyptians used bees wax to light the pathways to buildings, monuments and tombs.

Records found dating back as early as 3000 B.C. revealed that in ancient

Crete, the Minoan civilization utilized candles for practical and ceremonial purposes. Their candles (made of bees wax) were used by only the most elite and the priests), where the common people used a crude product derived from the fat of sheep of cows. This "tallow," although inexpensive, often produced dense smoke and a distinct odor; similar to burning grease in a pan.

The only other practical alternative to bees wax was a sperm whale product called spermaceti. It was a medium priced substance that remained hard and brittle producing a steady light.

Other exotic materials came into use at various times and places. Among these were: *ozokerite* from Poland, *carnauba wax* from the cera tree in South America, Chinese wax (also called *ghedda* or insect wax) from China and the Pacific Islands, *montan wax*, coconut oil and palm kernel oil.

QUESTION: My boyfriend and I both light candles. I want to break up with him. I know that if I light candles to get rid of him, he will,at the same time light them to keep me. How will this work?
ANSWER: Both of your candles will work. Yours in the sense that your emotional attachment to him will be gone. You will no longer see him on every corner. His candles will also work; he will continue to see you wherever you are. He will still have you in his life, the only problem for him is that he will not be in your life.

QUESTION: Why would someone light a candle to James The Less just because they were born in June?
ANSWER: No one should light a candle to James The Less just because they were born in June. The reason that you would light the candle in the first place is that the world is full of counter-productive influences: i.e. judgment and dishonesty, confusion and dysfunction. The personality of James The Less is the epitome of the characteristic of those born in June. Thus, you would be lighting the candle to regain your own intrinsic sense of self worth and values. Once again, becoming centered within yourself.

QUESTION: I lit a green candle for money that continued to burn when the release cycle started. What should I do? Will the money go away< or should I snuff the candle out and start over when the bring cycle starts again?
ANSWER: No. If your candle is lit before the cycle is over, it will continue to work.

A Gentle Note From the Author:

Tina Ketch's Candle Lighting Encyclopedia is a psychological guide written
to enhance the stimulation of your psyche - to incite new and interesting
changes in your life. By applying the techniques outlined in this book, they
may aid in the healing of your life. However, this text should in no way or
fashion be used as a substitute for psychological or medical care and
treatment

For more information on the new releases by this same author, write to the
address below.
Tina Ketch is also available for classes and workshops.

Tina Ketch
P.O. Box 1172
Snellville, GA   30087